Ameena Meer is a writer and journalist and a former copywriter for Calvin Klein. *Bombay Talkie* is her first novel. She lives in New York.

Praise for *Bombay Talkie*

'Vivid, funny, graceful' Patrick McGrath

'Feisty, sexy, moving, as if Merchant Ivory swallowed *The Face*' *New Statesman & Society*

'Part cultural tour, part coming-of-age story, *Bombay Talkie* vibrates with the jarring, cheerful vitality of the souk' *Mademoiselle*

'An honest, provocative study of an increasingly rootless generation . . . Meer mimics accents and dialects, patterns of speech and use of idiom with fluency. *Bombay Talkie* is convincing, but also disturbing.' *Times Literary Supplement*

'*Bombay Talkie* heralds a new kid on the literary block, one who is not afraid to ask questions and does not shirk her responsibility in aiming the answers, with empathy and affection, right between your eyes.' *Asian Times*

Bombay
TALKIE

a novel by

AMEENA MEER

Library of Congress Catalog Card Number: 98–86459

A catalogue record for this book is available from
the British Library on request

First published in 1994 by Serpent's Tail,
4 Blackstock Mews, London N4

First published in this edition in 1998

Website: www.serpentstail.com

Printed in Great Britain by Mackays of Chatham, plc

10 9 8 7 6 5 4 3 2 1

dedicated to Ashraf Meer

thank you
to my family, who've financed my incredible phone bills, my sheaves of paper and books and computer hardware, which were part of this novel. Obviously, to my mother and father, for absolutely everything. My brother, Ashraf, for unstinting love and support, no matter what the disaster. My daughter, Sasha Iman Douglas, for kicking me in the ribs until I finished. Shezad and Rachel Abedi and Naveed Siddiqui for the apartment and the holiday that made this novel begin. Peter Gargagliano for free psychotherapy and cooking and xeroxing and messengering. Vivek and Gita Sahni for inspiration and love and free quotes. Christopher Bowen, Kevin Diller, and Eric Levenberg for introducing me to California girls. Henri Dommel for his ordeal and mine. Zia Jaffrey for sorting out my scrapes. My aunt, Bashan Rafique, for her faith and hospitality. Betsy Sussler for her patience and liberty with the red felt-tip pen. Hilton Als, Lawrence Chua, Adam Fuss, and Ram Rahman for not forgetting I was a writer. Patrick McGrath for his gentle advice. Caz Phillips for more free advice. Salman Rushdie for helping me make the jump. Ira Silverberg for his great gossip and encouragement. Marie Brown for her warmth and help. Andrew Douglas for expanding my range of emotions. James Nares for helping me feel like myself again. Darryl Turner for always being a friend. Neil Kraft for giving me the chance to do something completely different. Hanif Kureishi for being brave and taking the first step.

Down from the gardens of Asia descending radiating,
Adam and Eve appear, then their myriad progeny after them,
Wandering, yearning, curious, with restless explorations,
With questionings, baffled, formless, feverish, with
never-happy hearts,
With that sad incessant refrain, *Wherefore unsatisfied soul?* and
Whither O mocking life?

Ah who shall soothe these feverish children?
Who justify these restless explorations?

—Walt Whitman, "Passage to India"

"Though destitute of virtue, or seeking pleasure elsewhere, or completely devoid of good qualities, a husband must constantly be worshipped as a god by the faithful wife."

—Manu, *The Sacred Laws*, Hindu Scripture, 100 B.C.

Some names and their meanings

Adam—Adam
Alia—Close to Heaven, highly regarded
Amna—Peace
Bibi—Lady, wife
Imran— Family of Man
Jamal—Handsome, beautiful
Meera—Hindu saint and mystic
Muzzafer—Traveler
Rani—Queen
Sabah—Morning
Sanjay—Inner Light
Yasmine—Jasmine
Zenab—Mother of the Poor

Bombay
TALKIE

Sabah

The End

EVEN THROUGH the crowd in the temple, Sabah sees the boy lying on the red carpet. His face is deathly pale, so white it looks like his eyebrows and eyelashes were drawn with black Magic Marker. Blood drips scarlet like strawberry juice from the corners of his mouth and the sweat pouring down his face makes it glow like a moon. His body is contorted, one side curling into itself. She knows him. He belongs to her. Somehow, she knows he's part of her, like the skin that stretches across her jugular vein.

Her heart is pounding. She has to get to him. The adreneline buzzes in her ears. She runs straight into the Indian families chatting and milling around the room, forcing her way through lines of people doing the Hanuman puja, throwing boxes of burfi out of people's hands, knocking down toddlers with bottles clenched in their teeth.

Three or four men stand over the boy: A small bald man in an orange dhoti and a T-shirt rocks back and forth on his feet as he recites prayers in Sanskrit, the effort crinkling the red mark on his forehead. The sing-song rhythm of his voice is broken by a series of explosions outside, which make the building tremble. Another man waves a platter of lighted candles and kicks the boy with his stocking foot a few times, to make sure he's still alive until the prayers are over. The boy's body contracts like a weevil. He curls deeper into the fetal position, mumbling something unintelligible.

"What's wrong with him?" Sabah demands. "Why don't you do something? Call a doctor! Call an ambulance!" Another loud sputtering explosion punctuates her words.

The priest looks at her, a beatific smile on his face, his brow now smooth as a child's. "He has come here to go to God," he says calmly. "He is fulfilling his dharram."

"That's ridiculous! He's sick, you idiot! Do something!" Sabah squats beside the boy. He smells of vomit and rotting fruit. She touches his forehead, the skin is scalding wet. One arm and one leg are twisted into a distorted shape. A belt of blood is spreading around his middle. "Call an ambulance!" she screams. She rips an airline towelette out of its package and gently wipes his forehead and lips.

"Madam," says the man who kicked him, "you leave him. He is crazy. A crazy American. He takes drugs or drinking or something—for the July Fourth."

Miss America

SABAH IS walking down the street in San Francisco in a miniskirt and guys are yelling out of trucks, making kissing noises or honking. "You look so sweet, baby, so sweet."

She watches her reflection in the shop windows as she passes them. Office equipment store: she can see her face, straight nose (a little wide, but cute and kittenish), shiny brown hair framing the smooth honey-colored skin in not-unflattering waves. She smiles and adjusts her sunglasses. Restaurant furniture: she can see her torso, the jacket looks OK. Pizza parlor: she can only see below the waist because of the counter. She pulls her skirt down, half an inch closer to her knees, and smiles, she knows she has strong legs. Five feet, four inches, of which half are legs, good proportions, she thinks. She's lucky. "Don't pull it down, baby. It looks great." She has to get a mirror. How can a girl live without a full-length mirror?

The dress is a caramel brown, almost the same color as her skin, and she loves the effect. From a distance, it looks as if she's wearing nothing underneath the jacket. It's exciting. Not quite walking down the street in the nude, nothing obviously improper, but—not a business suit, anyway.

She's irritated by all the men yelling at her. It's not for you, she thinks. You think I give a damn whether or not you like it? One of these days, a scorching summer day, when all the men on the street are walking around half-naked, jeans slipping down their waists so she can see the tops of their fat behinds, sweat dripping down their pimply backs, one of these days, she's going to start screaming, screaming insults and obscenities, until even their rough faces turn red with embarrassment. That hot wave of anger, the rage will make her brave enough to do it.

Not today, today it's not worth the effort. She's late for her American Drama class, as usual. On a good day, the shouting doesn't bother her too much, sometimes it even makes her feel good, beautiful, sexy. On a bad day, she wants to wear a burkha. Or carry a machine gun.

One freezing-cold day last winter, she walked out of the door and a guy started hassling her, "Nice legs, woman. Real nice. Come back here and—"

"And what?" Sabah spun around. "What do you want? OK. OK. Drop your pants. Drop 'em now because I

5

don't have much time." All the men outside the building got quiet. The guy talking behind her, she wasn't even sure which one of them it was, didn't say a word. They stared at her.

"It wasn't me," said one of them. They all crowded together.

"It was him," said another one, wiping his eyes on a dirty sleeve. "Sorry."

"Hey, don't pay him no mind, lady."

"Yeah, he don't mean no harm." They all started laughing, and jostling each other.

That was the bravest she'd ever managed to be. She was puffed up with the pride of it all day. She started to tell her mother, on the telephone, but midsentence, she swallowed her words. She knew the response would be sharp, "If you go around looking cheap and accenting your body, you're just inviting all sorts of disgusting behavior."

She could almost hear her mother saying, "Don't you want to get married and live a normal life? I hear Rani's so happy." Rani was her mother's best friend's daughter, once Sabah's best friend, now living in India in nuptial bliss. Sabah's mother promised to send Sabah the wedding pictures.

"Sun treatin' you good today? Mm, like that dress. I like that dress."

Sabah readjusts her bag. She listens to the person behind her and something sounds strange. The footsteps are hard and uneven. Ignore it, she thinks.

"What's wrong? I asked you a question, lady. Don't want to answer me?"

Sabah walks a little faster, but not so fast that he thinks she's running. Calm, stay cool, she tells herself. She can hear his breath between his words and it sounds hoarse and quick.

"Look like you need to learn some manners. Look like I'm going to have to teach you some manners."

Sabah concentrates on her back. Her back is straight and strong. He is talking to her back. She tries to keep walking smoothly, nonchalantly. Even though every nerve in her body feels focused on his breath, his footsteps, she can distract herself. Nothing's happening, she reminds herself. I'm strong. She tries to make every step speak of strength and confidence.

"I'm going to have to take you home and tie you to the bed."

She's panicking now, a wild, nervous clawing in her stomach. She swallows. Down, she tells herself, stay down. She's got it under control. She wonders if she should go into a shop. Her heart is beating like a rabbit's.

"I'll tie you up and then spank your little ass, your tight little ass. You'd like that, wouldn't you?"

There is a crowd around some street musicians. Sabah ducks into the crowd. She stands there for a second, hiding behind a long-haired neohippie with a rainbow backpack, breathing hard. The muscles in her neck twitch. Her eyes dart around the crowd, trying to pick out the body that belonged to the voice. She sees a thick shoulder, a wiry arm in an old T-shirt, the side of an acne-scarred face between a group of students. A bus is pulling up across the street. She'll be later than if she walks, the way buses move in traffic. The scarred face turns toward her. She runs across the street and jumps onto the bus. She gets off in two stops, still trembling. Her breakfast is climbing up her throat. She tries to think about the play they're doing today.

She passes a group of Indians or Pakistanis at the corner. They leer at her and elbow each other as she walks by. Farther down the road, there's a group of their women, in salwar kameezes, their heads covered with scarves. Sabah cringes as they turn to look at her. She's embarrassed. They stare with a mixture of disapproval and discomfort. She knows them too well. She feels like the paper doll who's had the wrong outfit put over her body. The face peeking out is the same as the young Pakistani girl. Sabah can almost hear the mother as she walks by, pulling her daughter close and threatening, "If I ever see you dressed like that—"

7

What the hell is wrong with her? She can never get it out of her head. Why should she be ashamed of wearing a dress? Why should she feel different from any other American girl?

She walks into the cafe to get an iced cappuccino before class. The Bengali waiters all crowd up to the counter to look at her, their eyes caressing her long hair like their fingers itch to, dancing instead across the counter toward the paper cups. "Are you Italian?" a waiter asks.

"No, Indian," she says.

"That is what I thought," he smiles. "I am from Bangladesh."

Two Asian men watch her as she crosses the street. "Did you see that girl?" one says in Hindi.

"Hey," shouts the other, "Miss America!"

WHEN SABAH HAD only five days left in California, she thought, What the hell. This is my last chance to do what I want. It wasn't the first time she'd dropped acid anyway. But she might never again. "Time to put away childish things," she said to herself as she put the blotter on her tongue, the paper getting soft. She closed her eyes and imagined the printed face of Mickey Mouse disintegrating.

"The moon is like this other world," said Alan, staring out of the window at the sky.

"Yeah," agreed Mike. "Look at the mist. Just think if we could walk up those moonbeams right up into the moon."

Sabah lay down on the dorm-room bed, on the frayed brown comforter that Alan's mother must have bought for him at the shopping mall before he went away to college. Her back relaxed. The muscles on each side of her spine pressed into the mattress.

She rolled her tongue across the roof of her mouth. It sang. It floated like a ribbon of silk. It rang—like fingers running down piano keys. Her tongue was playing music on the roof of her mouth, an undulating ribbon of music. She did it again and again, just to hear the music in her head. She smiled to herself and looked around the room to see if anyone else could hear it. Of course, they couldn't. It was just for her.

The feeling was erotic. Her tongue was a little bird, flying in her mouth, playing music like a cartoon, flitting around her lips. She sat up, rolling forward the way her tongue was moving.

Her hand brushed against her thigh. It was electric. She touched her thigh again and little sparks flew out of her fingertips, tingling her skin under her jeans. The rough cloth was as tight as the skin above the muscles in her leg. She traced the muscles with her fingernails. She drew little circles on her leg. She tightened the muscles in her thighs and let the thick seams rub against them. The sensation was so erotic, so sexual, she was embarrassed. She looked at the guys. Rob was staring out the window. Mike was looking through a kaleidoscope. Alan was drawing pictures with crayons.

"Hey, Sabah, are you peaking?"

"Mmm," she said. She was afraid to speak. She tested her voice, "Yes." That came out OK. "I think so. This is pretty strong."

Everyone in the room burst into giggles. "Sabah, you can get off on anything."

"You're so lucky you're Indian, I mean, you're already so spiritual and everything," said Mike.

"Hey," said Alan. "How long does this last?"

"Three or four hours," said Rob. "And then a couple of hours of being tired and happy, like you just ran a marathon."

"I can see this beautiful pattern on the wall," said Sabah. There were interlocking figures on the white walls—like an Escher drawing made out of Indian miniature paintings—each one fitting into the other. They looked like Indonesian shadow puppets, with long noses and bony arms, all moving and gesturing, and blending into each other in an intricate design. Who thought of this? thought Sabah. The pattern took up the whole wall, everywhere she looked. There was another pattern on the floor, this time they were little elephants.

She felt a hand on her cheek. It was Rob. He leaned forward and kissed her. His tongue felt like an intrusion in her mouth, confusing her thoughts. It was taking up too much space. He pushed forward and his body seemed too hard, he was swallowing her. His tongue was poking into her brain, moving the ideas around. She wanted him to stop, but she didn't stop him. She sat there, with her mouth open, smelling his skin, feeling his hand grabbing her stomach under her T-shirt. And moving toward her breast. She felt the goose bumps rising on her skin. She squeezed her stomach muscles. He pushed her bra up.

She opened her eyes and looked at Alan and Mike. They were playing with marbles, rolling them around the carpet. The rest of the room was obscured by Rob's face.

"I'm going to control this marble with the power of my mind. My marble is going to hit your marble."

"No way, man. You lose. Your willpower is dead."

Sabah tried to look at Rob's face. She could see one closed eye. His eyelashes were quivering against his skin. He smelled like plasticine. She loathed him.

Then, all of a sudden, his tongue felt delicious. It swam toward her tongue. Their tongues did a dance, a slow duet, rolling around each other like eels in a sweet, clear lagoon. Sabah closed her eyes and felt the base of his wriggling tongue with her lips. She swallowed, as if she was gulping from a spring of fresh water.

The ring of the telephone ripped through the room like a chainsaw.

Sabah pulled herself away, her lips popping like a cap coming off a vacuum bottle. She untangled her fingers from Rob's. "I'll get it," she said. She picked up the receiver. And wanted to drop it instantly. Maybe she shouldn't have picked it up. She was horror-struck. Her heart was beating so hard it felt like it would take off and burst out of her chest, dripping blood and entrails as it flew across the room. "Hello."

"Hello, Sabah?"

"Yes."

"Sabah behta?" Sabah froze. Her heart stopped. "Sabah? You sound strange."

"Hey Sabah, who is it?"

Sabah spoke slowly, trying to make each word come out perfectly. "Hi, Dad. How are you?"

Two Little Indians

"IT WAS A BEAUTIFUL wicker pony cart and we had a little white pony to pull it," said Muzzafer. They were walking down a quiet New England road. "My mother had it made for us. She used to hate our walking in the sun. First, the cart went to the girls' school to pick up my sister, and then it came to pick us up. The ghorawallah used to lead it along." He kicked a pebble along a bit as he walked, bouncing it back and forth between his two feet, as if he were playing soccer. He stopped to move Sabah out of the way as a car drove through a puddle, splashing the sidewalk. Muzzafer liked the slow walks with his daughter after dinner.

"What was his name?" asked Sabah. She was eleven years old and she wore her jeans with a lime green kurta her mother brought back from India. She looked up at her father's face, he seemed bright and gigantic as he stepped under the street light. "The pony, I mean."

"Oh, I don't remember," said Muzzafer. "People don't think of animals the same way in India. We were so spoiled."

11

"Did you ever ride him?" asked Sabah, as they walked away from the lamp and his face melted and almost disappeared in the last grainy rays of daylight. It was impossible to imagine her big, gentle father as a spoiled boy.

"No, he was really badly trained. Finally, one day, he gave the cart a good kick and broke it. And the ghorawallah used to beat the poor thing so much. It must have been sold or given away or something." Muzzafer and Sabah walked through the darkness, the evening mist settling on their faces. "We had fun with it, though."

"If I were you, I would have ridden the pony. Maybe he was just scared of people, because he was beaten so much. Maybe he just needed someone to be nice to him and ride him." Sabah looked back up at her father. She'd just climbed a grade in pony club and she thought she was something of an authority. She had a sulky tone to her voice. Sometimes, she wished her father was just a normal American. She wanted him to talk about his childhood on the farm in Illinois. Like the fathers in the books she read in school.

"Maybe," he said. "But we were much younger than you are."

"Anyway," said Sabah, "if that's the way Indians think of animals, I will never marry an Indian."

"Don't say that, Sabah." Muzzafer sounded hurt. "It would be nice if you married one of us," his voice faded off into the screech of a bus pulling up across the road.

The bus pulled away and, for a few seconds, the only noise was the squeak of their rubber soles on the pavement and the hiss of the tires as the cars passed. "When I started school, I brought a picture of my sister, Amna. And then one of the other boys, I think this big Sikh boy, took the picture from me and said, 'Oh, your sister's so beautiful, I'm in love with her.' Everyone thought Amna was beautiful because of her blue eyes. And he started kissing the picture. And all the boys started making kissing noises. I got so angry that I grabbed the picture and tore it up."

The stars shone through the clouds like fireworks stopped in motion, just about to burst into sunflowers.

"Why?" asked Sabah. Those Indian boys sounded stupid to her. No boy in her class would admit to kissing a girl.

"Because I thought it was an insult to my sister that some boy was kissing her. That was considered an insult then."

"I wouldn't have been insulted."

"No, I shouldn't have been either. We were all so young. And that boy became a very good friend of mine later," Muzzafer looked down at his running shoes. They were size eleven, big white nylon shoes with pink and green fluorescent stripes. They looked large and foreign. It was almost too much of a shock that a tiny boy in India could become a huge man in America. He was surprised by the size of his feet, as if the change had happened in the past few minutes rather than in forty years.

"Don't you miss them now? Don't you miss your brother and sister?"

13

"Of course I do, but as soon as we're together everyone starts finding each other's problems. And Jimmy and I are very different. When you've chosen one kind of life, it becomes harder to understand someone else's choice."

"You think if I went back there, I could find some of your old stuff? They would be antiques."

"Who knows? You might find lots of things. But most of them would probably be broken. Things don't have the same value there," Muzzafer reached for Sabah's hand and squeezed it.

"Mom says we might go to India next winter with Meera and Rani," Sabah said, pulling her hand away and wiped her face with the sleeve of her kurta.

"We might. Do you want an ice-cream cone?" The empty parking lot of the shopping center stretched out in front of them, a black plain. Here and there the reflections of stars twinkled in the puddles. The pink neon lights of the ice-cream parlor seemed to melt into the humid sky.

"OK," smiled Sabah, taking her father's hand again. "But Yasmine will be jealous."

"HURRY UP, SABAH! Yasmine's sitting in the car already!" Muzzafer shouted from the doorway. A fall breeze lifted and dropped strands of his tawny brown hair, making it fall over his creased forehead.

"Please. Please don't make me go. I have a fever."

"Sabah..." Muzzafer warned, his mouth a straight line of exasperation, each end digging into his round cheeks. He pushed the hair back off his face.

"I feel so sick," moaned Sabah, kicking up the fringe on the Oriental carpet as she walked down the hall. "I hate Sundays. Two measly days of weekend. And I can't find my *Life of the Prophet*. I know I left it in the kitchen." Her own hair was almost as short as her father's, and, with the same square shoulders and straight hips, she was always mistaken for the son he didn't have. Her sister, Yasmine, on the other hand, was all girl.

Muzzafer leaned on the doorknob and slapped the pane of glass with his other hand. "You're going to be late again. I don't know why you can't get organized the night before."

"Rani doesn't have to go to Sunday school. Ever," Sabah whined. Rani was Sabah's best friend these days. Even though Rani's mother and Sabah's mother were friends and they both were always saying how happy they were that their daughters got along so well, Sabah still liked Rani. She wished she'd spent the night at Rani's house last night.

"That's because she's Hindu and she goes to India all the time. We're Muslim, so we have to go to Sunday school," said Yasmine, as she pushed the car door open for Sabah. "Anyway, if you love Rani so much, why don't you marry her?"

"I wish I could get divorced from *you*," Sabah slid into the back seat next to Yasmine. "Did you do your homework?" she whispered. She turned around and started rummaging around the back of the car for a pen.

Yasmine smiled, her lips as pink as the ribbons in her hair. She patted the neat pile of books in her lap. "Yes," she nodded. "Why? Didn't you?"

"You suck."

"Don't be rude," growled Muzzafer.

Sabah climbed between the seats into the front. She flopped into the passenger side. She turned on the radio to the Top 40 station and opened the Quran in her lap. "Dad, do you know the Sura Al-Quraish? Can you say it to me?" As her father recited the prayer, Sabah scribbled a phonetic translation into the thick book, blue ballpoint alongside the Arabic. "Wait, just say that line again..."

"Sabah, you won't learn how to read Arabic if you do that. How are you going to understand your religion if you can only read it in translation?"

"I will, I will, but I have to be able to say this today. OK, listen to this, *bismillah el-rahman, el-raheem, lee illah fil Quraish*..." The car turned the last corner and the blue and white minarets of the Islamic center appeared through the leaves of the oak trees on the suburban street. Muzzafer looked over at her, "Did your mother see what you were wearing when you left?"

"Jeans are not un-Islamic. And I'm taking Rani riding afterward."

"You should try and look a little nice when you go out, Sabah," he opened the car door. "You're thirteen now. A lady."

"Don't remind me."

"Mr. Khan said Sabah looked like a boy last class, remember?"

"All the girls in school dress like this!" she retorted, as she slammed the car door. Teenage girls wear jeans. Didn't

15

he watch TV or read magazines? she thought. This is the real, modern world.

The two of them ran through the gates, up into the courtyard, the sunlight turning the jets of water in the fountain into rainbow streaks before they splashed into the marble basin at the bottom. Sabah felt an ache of longing for the swimming pool. She stepped reluctantly into the bookshop, Yasmine following a step behind her, poking her with the edge of her book like a prison guard. Through the glare of the bulb on the glass cases, Sabah caught a glimpse of the brass platters embossed with Arabic script amid the velvet tablecloths. Above the entrance to the stairwell was a 3-D picture of the Kaaba at Mecca. It shook a little as they passed, the Kaaba changing sizes and colors, the crowds of worshipers throbbing and swaying around the black box. Sabah reminded herself to ask her father to buy her one when he came to pick them up. She and Yasmine ran up the stairs, the heels of Sabah's riding boots clumping loudly against the marble. Just as they reached the door, Sabah grabbed Yasmine's arm. "Wait," she whispered. She craned her neck to look through the tiny window. "He's gone," she said.

"No, Sabah," whined Yasmine. "We can't. Not again. And *I* did my homework."

There was another loud clattering on the stairs. They both gasped. Mona grinned. "Scared ya, huh?" The strap of her Indian book bag was slung diagonally across her chest like an army officer's rifle. "Come on," she commanded, "down the back stairs."

They crept past the room dividers that made the classroom. The voices of the children vibrated in the corridor, "*Alif, Ba, Tha...*" They could hear the click of Mr. Khan's pointer on the blackboard as he moved through the alphabet.

"Sabah," whispered Yasmine, "they're only on the alphabet. We're not that late." Sabah pinched her arm. "Ow! I'm staying," Yasmine pouted and stamped off toward the entrance.

"Baby," hissed Sabah. She and Mona slipped into the stairwell.

At the dark bottom of the back stairs, Mona creaked the door open. They leapt out into the garden. Mona collapsed against the wall. "Phew! Made it!" she gasped, like a secret agent in a spy movie.

Sabah jumped from one sunny patch of grass to another until she got to the oak tree. She climbed up to a wide branch and waved to Mona, "Come up!"

Mona grabbed the branch and pulled herself beside Sabah. "You won't believe it," she told Sabah. "My brother went on the school trip to Busch Gardens amusement park and when he came back, he was drunk. They had to carry him off the bus. He threw up all night."

"He was drunk? What did he drink?" Sabah was incredulous. She didn't know anyone who got drunk. Her mother and father never drank alcohol. Muslims never drank alcohol.

17

"I don't know. Beer, I guess," Mona shrugged, nonchalantly.

"Beer..." repeated Sabah, trying to control her amazement, to be as cool as Mona. "He drank beer." It still seemed inconceivable to her. He'd crossed that chasm that separated them from everyone else. It was awful. We don't do things like that, she thought.

Mona opened her bag and took out a wrinkled plastic bag containing two smashed cigarettes among the sandwich crumbs. "My father wasn't even really pissed off or anything. He has a girlfriend, too. My brother Asim does too." She put a cigarette in her mouth and lit it, "I'm having a nic fit."

Sabah nodded knowingly. She swallowed her revulsion. She stopped herself from imagining Mona's lanky brother, his dark limbs hanging off the bench of a schoolbus seat. The faint black mustache beaded with drunken sweat. She could be cool.

"Wanna drag?" Mona handed Sabah the cigarette. "I saw my brother and his girlfriend making out in the car. It was sick."

"Mr. Khan says kissing is OK in Islam," said Sabah, being still cooler than Mona, even though it sounded sick to her, too. What if he was both drunk and making out? she thought. She passed the cigarette back, her nose wrinkling involuntarily from the smell of the smoke. She hoped it wouldn't stay in her hair. She didn't think her horse would like it. "I am definitely going to kiss. I mean, a little. He said as long as you know where to stop."

"That's just because his daughter's probably pregnant. Nabila goes on dates and everything. A girl in my class got pregnant last year," Mona shook her head. "Anyway, the rules are always different for girls. If I had a boyfriend my father would murder me."

"Yeah," said Sabah, trying to scrape the taste of the cigarette off her tongue with her teeth. "What kind of cookies are they getting at break? Were you here last week? Everyone had to spit out the Oreos because they found out they had lard." She and Mona looked up at the classroom windows. "I'm starving."

"I'd give you a cigarette, but I only have one left," Mona apologized. "Do you want to go back? We can say we just got here. They're already on the life of the Prophet. I like the part when the spider builds the web over the cave so it looks like he wasn't there."

"I know. I never kill spiders." They climbed down the tree, bark and moss getting stuck in under Sabah's fingernails, smearing the front of her T-shirt. "Can I share your *Life of the Prophet* with you?"

Two Little Indian Boys

UNTIL HE WAS twenty-one, Muzzafer idolized Jimmy. His older brother got the exciting drama-filled life, while Muzzafer's seemed dull and predictable. Jimmy had won everyone over first, as all his teachers in school often reminded him, and more flamboyantly. Jimmy's boyish escapades were indulged—though he was almost thrown out of school for seducing the headmaster's daughter (and any number of servant girls)—and his facile tongue and good looks easily charmed his teachers as well. Muzzafer quietly worked in his brother's shadow, shining only in the unglamorous subject of math. Teenaged Muzzafer's reputation with women was timid and respectful (his tough sister Amna had a hand in whipping him into shape) rather than seductive, and in any case, all the girls wanted were details about Jimmy. Muzzafer was still starry-eyed when Jimmy went off to study in England, and his opinion of his brother was only slightly lowered when Jimmy dropped out to become an actor.

Later, after getting his M.B.A. in America, Muzzafer acquiesced to his mother's idea of an arranged marriage, and somehow won the wedding lottery. Muzzafer's wife, Bibi, was beautiful and elegant beyond his wildest dreams; what made her less of a prize was her creative, artistic edge—she'd been studying art history and wanted to paint—which seemed to point to a certain laxity of morals. But for Muzzafer, his new bride's most dazzling attribute—and what had cost her many suitors—was the same quality he loved in Americans: her lack of pretense. His wife and his new countrymen were often straightforward to the point of bluntness, their directness cracking and melting away the shiny layer of politeness like the rock salt New Englanders scattered on iced roads. Muzzafer brought Bibi back to Boston, where the winter's sharp wind and the soles of his boots snapping against the

19

frozen sidewalks made him feel fierce and hardy, unlike any-thing he'd ever known. The harsh weather, the struggle to find a dingy apartment, a bottom-level job that the ayah's son wouldn't have taken, making it on his own, rather than his family's, reputation gave Muzzafer a sense of himself. He and his wife were the new pioneers.

Muzzafer hadn't wanted to come back to Bombay again. The last trip was for Jimmy's filmi charade of a wed-ding, where Muzzafer found himself bogged down again in the swamp of family obligations, choked by his brother's col-orful reputation and swatting at social niceties. Muzzafer had hopped onto the flight back to America, already buttoning up his winter coat, never once looking back at his mother and father sniffling and waving from behind the customs booth. All his worst fears had been confirmed.

This time again, Muzzafer weakened, at his older brother's insistence. "Don't be an idiot, yaar! The next gener-ation of Noor Al-Hussains is about to begin!" Jimmy shouted over the phone, and Muzzafer, watching Bibi lead their little daughter off to bed, knew fraternal duty left him no other choice. At the moment, one plane ticket was all they could afford. Muzzafer left, three days later, making sure his return flight was impossible to postpone.

He sat with Jimmy, thumbing through newspapers and old copies of *India Today*, in the fathers' waiting room, unlike he had at his own daughter's birth. That time, he'd been so nervous that he'd had to escape the oppressive atmos-phere, the horrible gray light like a television screen without a picture, the sharp smell of medicine and disinfectant, the sick green walls with battered brown plastic corners. Muz-zafer could imagine the jerk in the pain-wracked body of a patient in labor as her stretcher hit the corner before being whisked through the swinging doors.

He'd driven to a roadside restaurant chain, where the piped-in music and soft orange carpeted floor had relaxed him. He sank into the velour banquette. A smiling waitress gave him a menu card illustrated with bright photographs of the food they served. All-American apple pie à la mode had a tiny flag stuck into the scoop of vanilla ice cream. He ordered that, in honor of his new American baby.

It was funny, but he only realized, maybe a year or two later, that he'd saved the little flag. He'd wiped it with his napkin and put it in the breast pocket of his blazer. Two years later, he'd been looking for a business card and the toothpick flag had fallen out on the closet floor. For a second, he had no idea where it had come from, and he started to throw it away. But, as it left his fingers and hit the bottom of the wastepaper basket, he realized how long he'd had it. So he fished out and dropped it into his sock drawer. One day, he'd give it to Sabah.

Muzzafer tried to drag Jimmy out of the hospital. But he knew his powers of influence were watery compared with Jimmy's will. "You could be here for the whole night," he warned his older brother. "Let's go and have dinner. We could get some kebabs."

"Are you crazy?" said Jimmy. He was certain he was going to have a son, that his wife was going to produce the next heir to the family. Muzzafer felt that same teenaged frustration in the face of his brother's irrational confidence, a confidence that seemed to be a sort of manifest destiny, resulting in exactly the absurd situation Jimmy had been sure of achieving. Feeling stupidly adolescent and envious, Muzzafer stormed out into the humid air. He raced the Ambassador down the deserted roads, breathing the salty Bombay smells of sea and frying onions, looking at the latest billboards and hoardings: third-rate imitations of American advertisements, in Muzzafer's mind. But he returned an hour later, bringing Jimmy a warm, greasy paper bag of bread and kebabs.

There was still no sign of any new life. Even Muzzafer felt pressured enough to smoke a few cigarettes with his brother. He was suddenly aware of what a rite of passage this

21

was for both of them. The burden of age and responsibility weighed heavily on his chest. Muzzafer felt breathless and tired.

Jimmy, on the other hand, was still fresh and bouncing with adrenaline and anticipation. When the nurse marched through the door, a blanketed package in her arms, Jimmy leapt to his feet like an athlete. "Adam!" he proclaimed, grabbing the baby from the disapproving nurse so that he could whisper a few lines from the Quran in his ear. Of course, it was a boy. The baby was everything Jimmy knew he would be. Muzzafer tried to distract the nurse, to give Jimmy a few moments alone with his son, but all he could think about was his own home. He could see his wife, as she would be now, reading aloud to their daughter, just bathed and ready for bed, sitting together on the blue sofa. The image soothed him and made him weak with yearning to be there.

22

SOMETIMES, AS BIBI walked home carrying the baby Sabah because the stroller was full of groceries and her back ached from being pregnant, she would feel the people around her cringe. They would walk a little faster as they passed, pull their coats tighter around themselves. She often didn't see them. In the struggle with the child and the shopping, her hair would come out of the braid and hang down around her eyes, like blinders on a horse. She only felt the brush of air as they passed.

When she and Muzzafer came to Boston, Bibi found it almost unbearable. It was more than missing her parents' airy, flower-filled house, her socialite friends, or her father's smoky study. It wasn't the long hours spent utterly alone, speaking to no one except the cashier at the supermarket. She'd been saved from desolate evenings waiting for Muzzafer to return by a friend, another young Indian woman called Meera, who had recently come abroad with her husband, an American painter.

The worst was not the dark, dirty apartment, not the walls stained black with mildew or the long climb up the concrete stairs. It was the smell. All around her was that smell, stronger than car exhaust or garbage or urine. The smell of white skin. Pink and damp like a newborn kitten or a hairless baby bird. The smell of their sweat seemed artificial and sick, even through all their perfumes and deodorants. She wondered why she'd never noticed in India or during her art classes in Europe. Sometimes, on a crowded bus in the winter, the steam escaping from the folds of damp wool and nylon, the smell was suffocating and Bibi thought she wouldn't live until the next stop. Now, fourteen years later, with most of her family settled in America, she suddenly realized that she'd stopped noticing it.

Born Again

"SABAH, DO YOU want to come in?"

"You should. All the women should do this."

Sabah didn't. Anyway, she was fifteen and everyone who met her thought she was a boy. She gripped her sister's arm and felt her organs shrink inside her, pulling away from her ribs so that she felt hollow, cold and hollow. She wished she could shrink inside this room the same way. She nodded her head yes. She tried to say something, but her voice wasn't coming out. She thought of the white-faced Mr. Goldstein, shaking her hand, pressing her palm in his cool, waxy one. "Anything we can do here at the Golden for you, please don't hesitate to ask. Please give that message to your mother," his pale eyelids flickered and his mouth twitched as he spoke.

"Oh, Sabah," wailed her sister, and the two of them, holding each other so tightly they could barely breathe, walked into the embalming room like Siamese twins. The room was white and scientific, long counters running around the sides like a school chemistry classroom. Their grandmother was lying on a metal table, her body half-covered with a white bedsheet. One of her aunts was lighting incense.

"Sabah, Yasmine," wept Bibi. "Come here, you should see this. You should help."

"Here, come here," sobbed another aunt. "Come, don't be afraid."

Sabah squeezed Yasmine's arm harder, feeling her fingernails digging into the flesh, trying to keep herself from screaming. They were walking in slow motion toward the body as if huge magnets were trying to pull them back, dragging them backward into the plush darkness of the funeral parlor.

There was a splash, someone was filling the sink with warm water. Steam rose above the sink. "Does the table have wheels?"

"No, I think we'll have to move her. Oh, God. Oh, God."

"Here, I'll lift this side. Oh, look at her poor legs. Oh, her poor, poor legs—"

"She was in bed for such a long time, my darling mother," her aunt kissed her grandmother's cheek.

The women lifted the table and then pulled her grandmother's body closer to the stainless steel sink. Sabah was surprised at how heavy the body was, how unwieldy. She thought people's bodies became light when they died. Her grandmother's skin looked like pale pink tissue, crumpled rose petals. They were washing her body now, with warm water, with scented soap and still her skin was so cold, her flesh was ice cold and limp. Sabah and Yasmine started crying as well as they helped wrap the body in white cloths, the tears flooding their eyes, pouring in sheets down their faces so they could barely see.

"Look at her, look at her skin. She's still so beautiful."

"You know, in Boston General, they never believed she was Indian. The hospital people kept saying, 'Mrs. Siddiqui, don't you have some English blood?'"

Sabah's mother cradled her grandmother's head in her arms, caressing her hair. Sabah looked up and saw the faces of the five women, red and smooth from crying. Each face tilted slightly toward her grandmother. For a minute, it looked as if the light were coming from her grandmother's body, illuminating the ivory faces, their heads covered with scarves, like a pietà, as their fingers smoothed the white fabric around the body.

"Oh, Sabah and Yasmine, will you do this for me when I die?"

In the funeral parlor, her grandmother was wrapped up to her neck in white cloth, only her face, like a plastic doll, showing through the cloth. She looked as if she were made of wax, like a pale pink candle. Sabah and Yasmine stood around; they tried to sit and recite prayers but they couldn't. All the folding chairs around the casket were full. People came in, one after another, and sat quietly with their thusbees, their lips moving as they pushed the beads through their fingers.

Her mother's youngest brother came late, wearing his motorcycle jacket, his helmet under his arm. His jeans were stained with car grease. "Why didn't anybody tell me?" he cried. "Why didn't anybody tell me she died? No one called me." He had just gotten off work at the garage and was on his way to his job as a bouncer at a bar. His name used to be Rafique, but now everyone called him Rocky. He threw himself down on a chair and cried into his huge scarred hands. Then he stood up and grabbed Sabah by the arm. "Come on," he said. They walked out of the funeral home.

They walked down the sidewalk in the darkness. "Want a cigarette?" he asked.

"No thanks, Rocky, I don't smoke."

"Good. Good. When did she die?"

"This morning, I think. Where were you?"

"I spent the night at a friend's house. I tried to call. I did once, but the line was busy and I had to get out. There's just too much going on in that house. I had to get out. You know, I had this dream. Umma came to me in a dream. When Abba died, everyone dreamed about him. Everyone but me. I kept praying. I kept saying my prayers and praying at night and I never dreamed about him. And then Darrell, this guy I work with, told me about Christianity, about born-again Christians."

"Oh."

"So I thought, why don't I try it? Because I'd been praying and praying and nothing ever happened. I decided that Allahmia wasn't working for me. And I prayed to Jesus Christ. And that night I dreamed about Abba. Do you understand that?"

"I guess." Sabah tried to understand. Jesus Christ. She'd grown up with Jesus Christ, every American grew up with Jesus Christ. She liked Christmas and Easter, but Jesus Christ was them, was everyone else, all those Americans, not us. We're Muslims. She thought about her grandmother pretending to read aloud from the Quran, when the stroke had made her eyesight so faint that she recited the prayers from memory, like songs.

"Last night I dreamed about Umma. She was calling me. She was telling me to come home. And I didn't pay attention. I just couldn't come back to the house." They stopped and watched a car drive past. For a few seconds the street was illuminated by the headlights, the rows of brick houses with red doors and neat gardens. Sabah kicked a pile of raked leaves off the sidewalk. "How have you been?" Rocky asked her. "I haven't seen you in a long time."

"OK, the usual. Fighting with my parents. Trying to get through high school," she felt the goose bumps rising on her arms. A shiver rippled through her. She wondered why almost every emotion she felt seemed to make all the hairs on her arms and legs stand on end.

"Do you have a boyfriend?"

"No."

"No, huh? If I was a girl, I'd screw like a mick." ·

Sabah nodded. She wondered what a mick was. She was pleased that he was honest with her, but she felt awkward and alone. Rocky was a cardboard cutout now. A stiff, dry Christian. That's the way she thought of Christians. Clear and cool. Not like the complicated mixture of fiery tempers and overwhelming affection that the Muslims seemed to be. He's not one of us anymore, she thought. He was three squares of pavement away, and each one had stretched and become a hundred-mile desert. He was almost out of sight. They started walking back.

"Yeah, well, take care of yourself. I worry about you, you know," he shrugged his shoulders in his leather jacket. For a second, she saw her crazy uncle there again, the one who taught her how to catch a baseball, the one who bought her ice cream when she couldn't take any more of her grand-mother's Indian food. The seven years between them shrank and narrowed.

The light from the funeral home shone down in a wide circle on the pavement. He stepped into it. His motor-cycle was there, black and glistening. "I have to go."

"OK," said Sabah. "Bye. Khudafiz. You can still say that. It just means 'God be with you.'"

"I know," Rocky said. His motorcycle roared away as the rest of the family was walking out into the parking lot.

AS BIBI WATCHED Sabah getting dressed for her first day of high school, she thought about her baby girl. When Sabah was in kindergarten, she brought home an invitation for Parents' Day. Muzzafer was working, so Bibi went alone. She felt so sorry for Sabah in that room full of children with cold, empty eyes. Their eyes and their parents' eyes

seemed like the flat blue beads her grandmother sewed on the
dolls she made from bits of old saris. Tiny, tiny blue eyes that
disappeared in a single blink of the papery eyelids.

They started singing a song about birds in the morning and Sabah in her purple-blue dress with her honey skin
was singing along with them as if she couldn't see how she
looked like a wash of color—blue dress, brown skin, red
cheeks—like the first bougainvillea flowers of the monsoon
after a Deccan summer. That afternoon, when she and Sabah
came home, Bibi started painting. Her first painting in the
United States was of her American daughter. Sabah, pig-
tailed, looked wide-eyed over the pages of Mother Goose.

HER UNCLE TONY was calling her. "Sabah, dinner! Your mother wants you to come downstairs." Sabah
ignored him. His Indian accent battered his words, so they
came out harsh and broken as though they'd been through a
meat grinder. She listened through the bathroom door,
knowing that he'd go and explain to her mother that she
needed some time alone, being a teenager and all that. Tony,
or Tarun, his real name, was obsessed with the concept of the
American teenager. He watched all the American pop movies.
None of that managed to improve his English, he just added
slang words at the wrong times. For one of India's best-
known scientists, sent to America to get awards and scholar-
ships, his English was barely comprehensible in the lectures
and seminars he gave. His round wife, wearing a gray cardigan over her brown sari, followed him quietly around the
world and sat in the back of the conference rooms and lecture
halls, rapt and unmoving in her folding chair.

"Sabah!" he shouted again. Her mother must have
sent him back. She hated the way he always seemed to be following her, asking her about school, about what she wanted
to be when she grew up. He always wanted to know what she
was doing.

"I'm coming," she answered. "I'm getting dressed!" She opened the door slightly and saw him walking back down the stairs. She slammed it loudly, knowing he'd look up at it, and wonder. "I have no privacy whatsoever!" she grumbled through the door. She knew he heard that, too; she heard the embarrassment in his footsteps.

When she finally walked into the the living room, he was the first to say, "Sabah, you look beautiful. Come and eat." He handed her a plate and led her over to the buffet. Sabah's mother glared at her for causing a scene.

"Sabah, Tony uncle offered to drive you to the party," said Bibi. "Isn't that nice of him?" She looked at Sabah, expectantly.

"Yes, it's really nice. Thanks. Thank you."

As quickly as she could fake eating, Sabah ran to the door, past the rest of the guests, before her mother changed her mind. It was the first dance she'd been allowed to go to. Here she was, already sixteen, and she'd never even been to a school dance.

Sabah got into the car, her boots crunching through the snow on the driveway, breathless with adrenaline. All that time in the bathroom, she'd been getting ready, showering and shaving her legs, putting on cream and deodorant and perfume, brushing her teeth. She'd known what she was going to wear for two days, it was a pair of white trousers and a white waistcoat that she wore with a black silk shirt; she felt like John Travolta.

"You look beautiful, Sabah," said Tony, turning the key in the ignition. The engine idled and warmed up. He smiled at her and patted the steering wheel with his gloves, "All the boys will fall flat when they see you."

"Thanks," Sabah hoped they would. She was glad she hadn't eaten dinner. She was so excited she felt like she'd swallowed hundreds of multicolored helium balloons.

Tony turned to back out of the driveway, his right hand brushing across Sabah's coat as he swung his arm around

29

the seat of the car. "Do you have lots of boyfriends, Sabah?"

"No," said Sabah. She had none. She'd never even kissed a boy before. She hoped she would tonight.

"I hope you know which way we're going," he said as he drove the car out onto the main road. "I can't believe you don't have a boyfriend. Is that true?"

"Yes," Sabah could feel the balloons bobbling and bouncing inside her. There was a boy in her math class. He hadn't said very much to her yet. Perhaps he'd see her all dressed up and fall in love, like in a story.

"I thought American girls had much more freedom than Indian girls." Tony stopped at an intersection and stroked Sabah's fingers. His suede driving glove felt soft, like a baby rabbit. There were little holes on the fingers, and thick black hairs sprouted out of his brown skin. "But you're lucky because you're both. As beautiful as an Indian girl and as free as an American one." He looked into her eyes and then turned the corner. "Now where?"

"Two more traffic lights and then left again."

"Are you sure?" he asked. His glove moved up under Sabah's chin. He slowed down as they approached the next traffic light. Sabah prayed for it to stay green. It changed to red. He stopped the car and turned toward her. He kissed her, his tongue moving around her mouth, and held her head in his hands, the way they did in movies. Sabah relaxed and let him unbutton her coat while he kissed her. She watched him, tried to decide if she thought he was handsome or not. She thought he could be, in an Indian movie-star way.

He stopped kissing her and drove the car into an empty parking lot. He parked the car.

Sabah felt all the balloons exploding in her stomach as Tony slid her back on the seat, kissing her, unbuttoning her shirt and unzipping her trousers. "You're so beautiful, Sabah," he said. Nobody had ever said that to her before. No boy, anyway. "You're really beautiful. Boys your age wouldn't appreciate you."

His mouth on her breasts, on her stomach, felt good, so good, but good and disgusting at the same time, like gorging herself on ice cream. She tried to figure out where the feeling was coming from, what part of her body, but the whole thing felt great. Except that it was bad. This is bad, remembered Sabah. She felt a wave of guilt wash over her like nausea, leaving her gasping. She thought of her mother saying, "Muslim girls don't do things like that..." while Tony fumbled with his own trousers and fell on top of her, saying, "Sabah, Sabah." For a second, Sabah felt the ice-cream feeling in her whole body and then it was gone.

She felt embarrassed and sick. His hips were still moving, and he was panting and grunting and shuddering. He was sweating, too, and Sabah wondered if her shirt was going to be stained and crushed by the time she got to the dance. She stared at the little dots on the roof of the car until they seemed to float forward off the white vinyl. She wanted to reach out her hand to touch them, to make them go back, but she was scared to move. He gasped and threw his body against her more violently. Her bladder ached.

Finally, he stopped. "Sorry, baby," he said, kissing her. "I'm guilty. Next time, I'll be better." If she didn't get to a toilet soon, she was going to throw up.

As soon as they drove up to the school, Sabah jumped out of the car and ran inside. "Don't worry about me," she shouted to Tony as she slammed the car door. "I'll get a ride home with Andrea's parents." She was satisfied by the look of panic that passed over his face. In the bathroom, she washed her face and combed her hair. She put on more lipstick and kajal. She wished she could get rid of that smell that surrounded her. She wanted to peel off her skin like plastic wrap to a fresh layer underneath. She rubbed her cheeks and arms with the rough paper towels until they ached. She found a can of air freshener in the back of the bathroom, with the extra rolls of toilet paper. It was called Alpine Mist. She sprayed it all over herself. She liked the way it stung and burned her skin.

31

She walked into the gym, stepping over streamers that had fallen off of the decorations on the ceiling. "Sabah," someone called to her. "We've been waiting for you." A group of girls from her class were standing near the coat rack. They seemed very young, just babies.

"Hey, Sabah," said another girl, "wait 'til you see all the cute boys here." Sabah hung up her coat, stuffing the gloves and scarf in the sleeve so it looked like she was leaving an arm there. "Ooo, you smell weird. Like a Christmas tree."

BIBI'S LIFE CHANGED when Muzzafer was promoted to vice president. They bought their big modern house in Lexington, fresh and new and rising out of the mud of the development like a seedling. They put Oriental rugs in the living room, and Bibi made a rudimentary painting studio in the sewing room. And there was a huge sweeping staircase that ended dramatically at the linoleum in the front hall. One evening, several years from now, the real estate agent had told them, Sabah would descend, transformed into a southern belle, in a long ruffled dress, to meet the young man and her parents waiting breathlessly below, for her senior prom; and that would make the staircase and the immense foyer all worthwhile.

Even now, after two decades of living in America, Bibi loved the festivity of suburban supermarkets. The automatic doors swinging open and the music playing in time to the wheel of her shopping cart, the fruits piled in beautiful neon stacks, boxes of new products, shiny and shrink-wrapped with carnival-colored labels: NEW, IMPROVED! WHITER! MORE NUTRITIOUS! STRONGER! FRESH SCENT! Each one was a work of art in itself. On Sundays, while Muzzafer read the business section and the girls fought over the cartoons, she often cut out coupons for new products. She always tried something if there was a coupon for it. And Sabah and Yasmine were always happy to eat the latest toaster tarts or honey crunch cereal. On days when she was depressed, frustrated with being a mother, and too distracted to paint, she opened the kitchen cupboards and looked at all the multicolored boxes on the shelves.

"Muzzafer, how else will she survive?" Bibi said to her husband as he hung up the phone. Jimmy had called and insisted there was no need for Sabah, or most girls, to go to university. Jimmy mentioned a young man he'd just met who was in a position to support a new bride in style, a fair-skinned boy who was looking for someone modern, but not too Westernized. He could be at their house for tea in ten days. Muzzafer sat up in his armchair, looking half at the news on the television and half at his wife's angry face. "Don't worry," he said. "My daughters are going."

Sabah, the teenager, had already climbed out of her bedroom window onto the roof. She sat there for a while, the damp air crinkling her hair, as she looked at the stars, before climbing down onto the porch. Once on the lawn, she stopped and lifted a flagstone from the path. She took out a package of rolling papers and a roach clip. Then she was off and running for a date with a construction worker her parents would never meet.

The van pulled up on the corner, two suburban houses away. Sabah jumped up into the passenger seat. "Hey, kid," he grinned, giving her a kiss. He shook a little sandwich bag at her, and she smiled and dropped the papers on the dashboard. For a second, her mother's voice warned, "Good Muslim girls..." in her head, like a fist around her heart, and she felt like screaming, "Stop!" and jumping out of the door. Instead, she stared at the patterned ceiling of the van, looked at the little pine-tree air freshener dangling from the rearview mirror. The blood started pumping through her veins again.

33

"Still not ready to introduce me to the 'rents, huh?" he said. "I can't believe your folks don't speak English. I mean, this is America, right?"

Sabah snapped the cardboard tree off the mirror, "I hate the smell of this thing. It's sick." She threw it out the window.

"Oh, man! I just got that at the car wash!"

SABAH'S PHONE rang exactly fifteen minutes after the door on the rental car slammed shut. "Can I come back?"

"You don't even wait 'til they get to Route 1. Yes, the coast is clear," said Sabah. She slumped back on the sofa and leaned over and turned the stereo on with her other hand. Handel's *Water Music* was her favorite record on sunny days.

"I can't believe you're doing this to me," said Rob.

Sabah's parents were the only ones at the graduation ceremony who looked cool and fresh. Her mother's embroidered cotton salwar kameez stayed crisp, as the other mothers in fitted dresses with elastic waistbands melted in their chairs. Muzzafer was spotless in his bush suit. The day was so hot, most of the students received their diplomas in their bathing suits, slathering themselves with suntan oil between speeches.

Afterward, the parents milled around the college grounds, becoming increasingly swollen and sunburned. Sabah's parents, on the other hand, knew hot weather well enough to retreat to the café for the rest of the afternoon. While Sabah squirmed in her chair, they discussed her future. They were heading back to the East Coast. California made Bibi nervous. Her strict North Indian upbringing made her suspicious of this place where everything seemed too easy, too relaxed, too free. It was certainly not a good place for an unmarried young girl on her own. How was she ever going to meet a boy of her own class out here? And now that she'd finished her B.A., it was time for her to start thinking about marriage. Bibi added that if she didn't get married soon, all the good boys would be gone. All Sabah could think about was that she wished they hadn't come. Their presence threw dark clouds on what would otherwise have been a few happy days of great weather—and the overcast seemed to stretch out endlessly across her future. She wished they were like the Californian parents, friendly and drunk, their red faces wet and cheerful with alcohol. Instead, her mother and father were gloomily sober.

Bibi took a letter out of her handbag, battered from a long trip crushed beside lipstick tubes and receipts and pencils, the blue INDIA postage stamps curling up at the edges. It was from Sabah's old friend, Rani. Bibi had already torn open the thin blue envelope, perhaps used the corner to write down an address or a telephone number. Sabah played with the envelope as she tried to explain herself, turned it over and ran her fingertips over the torn edge, poked her nails underneath, looking at the letter, the transparent gray paper with the blue ballpoint marks seeming fragile and exposed. "Rani is having bad time lately," said Bibi. "Please write back to her."

Sabah sighed. Quietly though, not loud enough for her mother to hear her. Twenty years in this country hadn't made them Americans. Indian daughters, from the beginning of time, were perfectly obedient. So far, she knew she'd been a failure. She was surprised that she was able to convince her parents to go back without her. Her excuse was that she still had to get things organized here. Ship her stuff off somewhere. Where? Say good-bye. Maybe in India she'd be able to straighten it all out, she'd thought. Maybe she'd be able to find a happy medium between what her parents wanted her to do (the good Indian girl) and what she wanted to do (the bad American girl). Maybe she'd figure out what it was she really wanted to be.

Now, sprawled across the sofa in a beam of sunshine, Sabah took a deep breath. She pulled off her T-shirt and let the sun warm the expanse of her stomach and breasts. She rolled over, hooked her legs over the headrest and let her head hang off the seat. Slowly, she turned her head and stared out the open windows at the hummingbirds buzzing around the thick fuschia bushes. For some reason, they never got confused and flew in the windows. She lifted her hips and pulled the envelope out of the back pocket of her jeans. She unfolded the letter on her stomach, enjoying the crackly feel of the aerogramme paper on her skin. "Dear Sabah, I'm beginning to think you're the only person who'll understand what's happening to me. I know we're both in such different worlds now, but—"

Rob crashed inside, his heavy shoes making the floor-boards tremble. He dropped his bicycle against the bookcase, threw his backpack across the room onto the sofa. The cat yowled.

"Hey!" Sabah jumped up, grabbing her T-shirt. She squirmed into it as she followed him out of the living room.

"Right. You know this is my apartment, too. In fact, I pay more rent than you do..." He flipped a lock of long curly hair out of his face.

Sabah noticed that his hair was longer than hers now. "Oh, Christ," she groaned, "I don't need to hear it from you too, my parents just left." She had to admit she was happy to see him. He seemed so natural, so normal.

"Sabah, you're twenty-one, almost twenty-two. That is the age of majority. You are an adult."

"Rob, I don't expect you to understand this. How could you? You and every other Californian are in your own little worlds—"

"Shut up! I've had it with your self-righteous Third Worlder trip—nothing's better anywhere else. Now where'd you put all my stuff?"

"The toolshed in the backyard," said Sabah, looking at her flat bare feet that always appeared so Asian, like they should be poking out of the mud of a rice paddy. "I'm sorry."

"Oh my God," Rob crashed out to the garden in his usual fashion, knocking over the empty glasses on the kitchen table on his way. "My stereo! My synthesizer!" Sabah hurried along behind him.

"The deal is," she gasped under the weight of a box of records, "if I go to India for three weeks, help my friend Rani sort out her life, find a suitable husband, and absorb some culture, I'm free for the next few years."

"Great," Rob's guitar banged into the wall, the strings reverberating from inside the case. "Then what?" His blue eyes were red and his lips were quivering. He looked like a small boy who'd lost his teddy bear.

Strange, thought Sabah, how a six-foot-tall guy can look like a little boy. How, despite his lumbering arms and legs, he could look weak and hurt, look like he needed to be held and protected.

"I love you, Sabah. Sometimes, I don't think you know what that means," the box slipped from his hands and he turned around and faced the wall, sobbing into the fold of his arm.

Sabah wanted to shrink him down, fold him in her lap, and stroke his hair. She wanted to give him back his toy. "Oh, baby," she said. She waited and then she pulled his other arm, turning him around as he clumsily wiped his eyes. She kissed his cheek but stepped back when he tried to kiss her again. She leaned against the door frame, watching him, now shirtless, pick his boxes up. Was she heartless? She watched the muscles in his back twist and ripple as he moved, and was disgusted with herself for the desire she felt rising. "I don't know," she said. Why can't she just lie? "I'm just not ready to take risks for anybody yet. Who knows? But I'll make a bet— you'll forget me before I forget you. Five bucks. I swear."

Rob opened the closet door and started rehanging all his clothes. "You even took my name off the mailbox. I mean, that really made me feel homeless. I ride my bike past the house and my name's not even there." He put his alarm clock

37

back on the bedside table. "Who did you say lived here, anyway?"

"Another girl. Who had already gone home for the summer. You think Maria would want these sundresses? There's no chance I can wear anything like this for the next few months."

"Good luck," Rob shook his head. "Some greasy guy's going to put his hand down your shirt and you'll be on the next plane in half an hour. You *and* that Rani girl." He reached out and grabbed the waistband of Sabah's jeans. He pulled her toward him and unbuttoned her fly with one hand while the other pushed her hair back, lifted her face to his.

"Watch it," Sabah gave him a whack with a cushion. "Those are my people you're talking about. Five bucks says some blonde beach bunny'll put her hand down those baggy old boxer shorts first. Five smackers!"

Adam

You May Be a Lover but You Ain't No Dancer

CRACK. THE TAPE RECORDER turned on and the girls started moving. Jimmy, Bombay's best-known (lip-synching) singer and movie villain, roared with laughter. His daughter Alia called, "Come on!" Her face flushed, her eyes and teeth glittering like diamonds, "Come and dance with us!" And, just as quickly, she turned her back and returned to the dance, the music seeming to fill every empty space in the living room with heat and light. They'd left their shoes piled in a heap on the gray wall-to-wall carpet. The girls were dancing in a circle, glossy black hair flying out behind them as their clothes, prints and silks and brocades, swirled into tilting multicolored stripes, ribbons of gold weaving through—like the canopy on a carousel.

"Wait!" shouted Adam. "Wait, I've got to do my dance!"

Jimmy said, "Come on, Adam, you're the star to-night!" And his friends raised their glasses and laughed with him: "To Adam's last night in India! To your son's new job!" And all the crystal chandeliers seemed to be tinkling like fairy laughter along with them.

Adam was racing up the stairs to get his cassette, yelling down at his sister, "Alia, introduce me! Introduce me!"

He ran into the center of the room. "Alia!" he urged. "Now!"

Alia blushed and reluctantly changed the tape on the tape recorder. "This is Michael Jackson," she mumbled. Adam glared at her, but then the music started and he was transformed. He swooped around the room, his arms swimming like fishes. He moved his lips to the words and batted his eyelashes coquettishly like a Hindi film star. He grabbed his mother and spun her giggling across the carpet. He threw himself onto the sofa, jumped up and kissed one of his aunts.

Alia stood in the doorway, her face pink. Everyone was laughing, her aunts, her uncles, all her friends. "Well done, Adam!" He gyrated his hips, the sequins on Alia's tight trousers glittering as they caught the light. He put his gloved hand to his lips and blew a kiss. Alia looked at her friends. They were all laughing. They were all watching Adam and laughing and laughing and Alia knew that she would hear the story whispered a hundred times in school next week.

"You silly boy," giggled Zenab, as Adam finished by throwing himself at her feet. "What a joker you are. What a clever little son I have. Everyone will love you in Paris! They won't let you come back to your mother."

"Of course I'll come back to you, Umma," panted Adam, kissing her. "I promise."

THE SERVANT MET the postman at the gate. "Bhai, there must be something here from Paris today, Memsaha'ab is driving the whole house crazy. If there's no letter here from her son, she will fire us all again."

"A letter," said the postman, handing him a wrinkled aerogramme. "God is on your side this morning."

Jimmy, or Syed Jamal Noor Al-Hussain offstage, read Adam's letter aloud at lunch, punctuating his phrases by laughing and slapping the table: "I tried to do some washing yesterday and all my shirts have become purple. It is very embarrassing in the bank." Jimmy laughed so hard, he started coughing, and the bearer had to run to him, the tray of water glasses clinking and splashing, to thump him on the back. "I have to work very hard, sometimes I don't come home until eight o'clock at night. So far, I don't have much pocket money, so on my birthday, I will go to see a film." Thank God, thought Jimmy. Adam will finally become a man. He'd have to do it the hard way, for once, just like his father did. That was the only way he'd ever have any self-respect. He imagined Adam in six months, in a French suit, smoking a cigarette, drinking black coffee and showing his father the sights of Paris—and the women. He'd never really learn about women in India. Sure, there was an abundance of young girls here, if you wanted just anything, but if you wanted a woman who knew something, knew a little about— well, if Adam was going to learn about life—and about women, as Jimmy knew from experience—he had to be some place where he could have some fun and not have to live down the results, and Europe was the best place.

Zenab cried. It was all she could do to keep her kajal from smudging and the tears from making thin streaks through her rouge. She sat in her bedroom after lunch, sinking back into the quilted headboard. She felt like a tiny child sitting on the huge bed alone. She read and reread his letter, until the paper was soft and illegible.

43

Zenab found she missed him most at night. He used to draw her curtains and then slide across the green satin bedspread. He took two or three of the big embroidered cushions and tucked them behind his back. As Zenab said, "Adam, really, you'll spoil them." He'd tell her what he'd done that day, giggling about his teachers and describing breathlessly the escapades of the other boys. He was so good at telling stories that Zenab felt like another schoolboy herself. It was so exciting. As a girl, she'd always daydreamed about what the boys did all day, while she suffered through the long monotone lectures in the girls school. She'd sat for hours in her stiff wooden chair, imagining their pranks and games and rude jokes. Zenab drifted off to sleep with the sound of raucous laughter and clattering shoes in her ears, the smell of ink and smoke and chocolate around her, as sharp as if she was there herself. Her last memory was always of Adam's soft goodnight kiss before he crept away.

When Jimmy finally came home at night, stumbling through the dark room and tripping over the heavy teak furniture, the perfume of his latest heroine still in his hair, he would sigh, "What a dinner, what *ghazab-ka-khana*..." Zenab wondered whether Adam was eating well in France. French food was not very healthy. She lay awake for hours worrying that Adam was living on a diet of hamburgers.

Or if, when Jimmy crept into bed at midnight, the weight of his body making Zenab roll across the mattress toward him, he said, "Ah! Clean sheets and the smell of the rath-ki-rani flowers from the garden..." Zenab's dreams were plagued by visions of Adam tossing and turning on dirty sheets, being bitten by bedbugs. The French were not very clean.

Sometimes Jimmy had had a long night of card playing, gambling a little, and drinking; discreetly, of course, and only if there was imported scotch, not that Indian whiskey or those bhang and alcohol combinations that poisoned and blinded scores of factory workers. After the game, he would wake her up and say, "I'm getting better at cards all the time, but then, so are my friends, so the fun of the game is never lost." Zenab reminded herself that a bank training program was the best thing for Adam, and playing cards wasn't really a vice. She thought of Adam's sweet good-bye kiss and then couldn't stop the tears from rolling down her cheeks until she fell asleep.

Jimmy often awoke from the shock of her wet pillow, now cold and saturated, touching his ear or his cheek.

ALIA'S TEACHERS SENT a note home saying how hardworking she was. "A very diligent student, always brings all her essays on time, always early to class. What she lacks in writing skill, she makes up for with her illustrated pages." She was the school's field-hockey champion, running through the muddy fields in her white salwar kameez, dupatta flying behind her and never once getting caught as she pushed aside the other girls and whacked the ball into the goal, off the goalkeeper's ankles.

While the other girls giggled and read fashion magazines, Alia ignored them and tried desperately to keep her eyes trained on the columns and columns of tiny words, to keep her hand from sketching pictures in the margins, coughing in the dark, dusty library. She'd heard what people murmured about singers' daughters, even though no one dared say it to her face. She'd heard the comments the other parents made when they visited the hostel and found out that Jimmy's daughter went to school there. She'd even heard the teachers talking among themselves in the common room. Once, when her mother redecorated the house, there was a huge photo spread in a society magazine. Someone tore out the picture of Alia's apricot-and-gold bedroom and hung it like an imported box of chocolates in the back of the classroom. Alia pretended not to notice. She did, though. That's why doing well in school was so important. She was going to be something— not a wife—maybe a famous artist, she was going to leave

45

here. She didn't tell anyone. But she knew she could do any-thing Adam could, that any boy could. She knew she could. And nothing was going to upset that. All her hard work and frustration were focused on that goal like the crack of the hockey stick hitting the ball.

Graduating third in her class only increased her frus-tration. How was it possible that she could work so much harder than Amna and Jyoti, and they could write their papers and slog only the week before exams and then do better than she did?

Jimmy was proud of his daughter. She would make a good wife for a professional man. She worked hard. She had some brains, but not too much, she wasn't *too* quick. Really, she was the perfect mix for a young girl. And what a perfect hobby, painting, all the better, it would keep her at home. Finding her a husband would be easy. She made that lazy son of his seem hopeless. Adam was a terrible student. He stayed home from school at the slightest sniffle or the beginning of a sore throat. He was always being excused from games. "My leg is paining me, sir." And the other boys laughed and said, "Leave him, sir, nobody will take him on their team, anyway." His academic work was even worse. Whenever his teachers called home, Adam slunk quietly into his mother's arms. "Umma, they're unfair to me. I work, I try to work hard on my studies, and my teachers just don't like me."

His pale blue eyes became pink and he sank into the folds of chiffon. His mother, with her baby chick nestling under her feathers, felt her ancient maternal instinct rising like Durga's anger in her throat. Then there was nothing Jimmy could do. Even the ayah saying, "Memsaha'ab, baba is very naughty in school, he—"

"Enough," Zenab would reply, pushing the old woman aside. "Nobody is going to be unfair to Adam." It was true that Adam was not popular in school. He seemed to be the scapegoat for all the other boys. He was small, fair haired and frail, and lacking in both wit and physical ability. His father's fame only made him less popular. His teachers found him irritating and usually ignored the other boys teasing or bullying him.

But in his own home, Adam was the main attraction. Alia idolized him. Zenab found his jokes hilarious. Jimmy saw raw talent in Adam's play acting. "So, young fellow, going to be a big star, just like your father?" said Jimmy and Zenab's friends when they patted him on the head, and the women bent their rouged cheeks to his lips and said, "Give auntie a kiss like Papa does."

Jimmy walked into the bedroom on the seventh night, while Zenab sat red-eyed in front of her big carved mirror, brushing her hair a thousand times before she went to sleep. "What do you think these two pieces of paper are in your husband's hands?" he winked at Zenab, as she smiled. "What? What are they? Guess. No, no, you must guess," he insisted as his wife grabbed for them and he hid them playfully behind his back. "What are these two lovely surprises for my lovely wife?"

47

Zenab was laughing like the ingenue starlet she'd been twenty-five years ago. "Come on," she laughed. "Give!"

"Oh, laughing now, are you?" he said. "Why are you laughing and not crying and shouting at your poor husband? But since you ask so nicely—here!" A stained aerogramme, PAR AVION, the unmistakable French postmark, and a plastic Air India folder: he held them up like a winning hand of cards. "Another letter from your naughty son and..." he paused for dramatic impact, "three round-trip tickets to Paris!"

"What? Oh give them to me! Give!" She snatched them away and immediately opened the letter from her son. She looked up from the ballpoint scrawl. "Oh, how nice. He has a friend now. He sounds much happier." She smiled at her husband, "And now we'll be able to meet his friend."

"We go to see quite a lot of films together," wrote Adam. "Marc is teaching me to speak French. I'm learning twice as fast as I was with my tutor. I think I'll be fluent by the end of my time here. It is much easier to learn French if one sees the city at the same time. Like *voiture* is car, and Marc has a Peugeot that his father bought him when he finished school. We see most of Paris in Marc's *voiture*. I've also bought some nice clothes with Marc's help. He has very good taste, I think." Adam ended his letter with *"Au revoir."*

"Thank God, Adam has finally found a friend his own age," said Jimmy. "You see," he told his wife. "That is why I had to get Adam out of this house full of women." Then he thought, a house full of women, that's a good name for a song. I must tell the songwriter to write one to go with it. He'd been needing a new hit.

Twenty-four Years Earlier

HOOFBEATS CLACKED ACROSS the driveway. Horns honked. "The horse! The horse!" someone shrieked. "Oh, he's so beautiful!" Jimmy recognized the voice of one of his female cousins.

He was sitting on a plastic lawn chair in the garden in a silk shirt and trousers and a thick brocade coat. "Give me the most expensive one you have," his mother had said as she threw the bolt of fabric across the sheet, sending the sock-footed assistants scrambling after it. "My film-star son is getting married. Finally." She harrumphed and looked at the equally self-righteous salesman (himself, he had a wife cooking his dinner, and four children at home), his legs crossed on the bedsheeted floor.

"Well, if Mallika Begum's oldest son is getting married, what else but the best? And every performer wants to look his best when he's in the public eye," he acquiesced, a chubby finger pushing a strand of oiled hair from his forehead. "All the stars in Bombay buy only from Ali Kamali's. Didn't you read that article about my shop in *Stardust*?"

So now Jimmy is wearing the heaviest silk brocade from his neck to his knees. Forty-six degrees centigrade. Even the fans and air coolers blowing full blast don't make a difference. Jimmy can't breathe. They've hung the sehra over his face. The ropes of jasmine flowers are unbearably sweet and thick. Sweat is dripping from his face and getting stuck at the tight collar. The shirt is soaked and Jimmy can feel the rings of sweat forming on the coat around his neck and under his arms.

Now and then there is a scream of delight as one of his female relatives walks in and sees him. "Oh look, look! Just see what a darling he's looking. No, no, not one more luddoo before the party. I cannot." The second sentence is addressed to one of the twenty servants stumbling through the crowds of guests with silver trays full of sweets piled in sticky mountains.

A manicured hand squeezes his cheeks. Fingers stuff yet another buttery sweet into his mouth. He chews. Swallows. Water, he thinks. He has to have a drink. If he doesn't, his mouth will cleave shut. His tongue is congealing into a sugary mass.

"What? A horse? Who said we were using a horse?"

"A horse? In this weather?"

"A horse? That's mad, the boy can't even ride!"

"He doesn't ride himself, there's the horsewallah with him."

Jimmy's mother's voice ended the discussion. "My son is going to the wedding in an air-conditioned car!"

Jimmy is ceremoniously helped to his feet by too many people. He almost falls. "Ha!" shouts his brother Muzzafer, "Drunk already!" Somehow he manages to make it down the stairs and into the car.

"No need for sunglasses this time, my boy," his father thumps him gruffly on the back.

The car pulls out of the driveway amid cries and horns.

In the reception hall, Jimmy is sitting on the platform for two hours, the jasmine beginning to turn brown and wilted on his face. "Where is she? Where is she?" murmur the guests. He can hear his mother and sister moving frantically through the crowds, their polite conversation tense and shrill. Someone falls down into the chair next to him. "So, heard the news, I guess," Muzzafer pats him on the shoulder. "Don't worry about it, old man."

"What are you telling him, Muzzafer?" his sister Amna approaches and asks. "Jamal, Farida is saying that she's changed her mind. No one knows where she's gone."

And above all the din, his mother's voice saying, "Syed Jamal Noor Al-Hussain, the recording-star genius, with hundreds of hit songs and ten gold records, educated in India and in Europe, and the oldest son of the Noor Al-Hussain family. This handsome boy is looking for a wife. A good and homely girl to love him and take care of him, to become the wife of . . . a *star!*"

Zenab stood up. All through the chaos of the wedding, she'd been trembling in her chair. Listening to Jimmy's mother, she'd broken out in a cold sweat. Her own mother, sitting beside her, usually attentive to her daughter's every whim, had been distracted by the excitement. The bride had run away! What a delicious scandal! It would be conversation for months. Zenab, on the other hand, was overcome by the sensation that her moment had arrived. She knows it's time. She stands up. "I will," she pronounces clearly and definitively to the "ahs" of the crowd.

Zenab had been in love with Jimmy since she was twelve. His record "Love Is a Flame in My Heart" was the first one she ever bought, after saving her pocket money for weeks. She'd had to bribe her brother to go to the record store and buy it for her. And then bribe him again not to tell her parents. She and all her friends had cut out his pictures and glued them inside their desks at school. He had been her inspiration all through her singing lessons. And what luck, when she'd been an extra in the film he was in and been asked to sing part of a song with him because his partner was not well. Zenab had been paralyzed for a few seconds; it was just too wonderful. She'd felt the blood rushing to her face and she'd started to feel breathless and faint, spots of color dancing in front of her eyes. Somehow she'd managed to sing along as he lip-synched, and even a year later, she sang along with the record of the film at least once a day—"How can you hide your eyes from me, my darling? They are all my light. Without them, I am blinded, alone in the darkness." Zenab can never separate Jimmy from the voice or the lyrics, even though, in tiny print on a corner of the album cover, the real singer and writer are credited.

As Jimmy's mother puts the embroidered dupatta over her head and kisses her cheeks, her sister hisses, "What are you doing, Zenab?" And her mother thinks, Now I'm the gossip, but she cheers herself up realizing she has the inside scoop on the story. It's fortunate Zenab is wearing her new pink gharara. It's the most beautiful piece of clothing she owns. Her grandmother had embroidered gold flowers on the skirts and the gossamer kurta. The heavy satin drapes her limbs like an altar cloth, and she glides across the room like a fairy princess, her mother and sister trotting nervously along behind her.

There is a chaotic hour in the ladies' room, with ten attendants painting her hands and feet with a quick liquid dye, no time for real henna or complicated cake-decorating patterns. Someone braids jasmine into her hair. Someone else puts lacquer on her finger and toenails. Jimmy's sister and cousin-sisters wander in and out of the room saying, "She's quite pretty, isn't she?" Blue velvet boxes are opened in front of her, the glittering jewelry lifted and hung on her forehead, around her neck, on her ears, around her ankles.

Flashbulbs explode as she walks out. The guests cheer. Jimmy's mother is right, she is marrying a star. And now, she too is a star.

51

Jimmy sneaks a look through the ropes of jasmine over his face. "Who is it?" he whispered to his brother in the hour the girl had been in the dressing room. "Who is it?"

"How should I know?" said Muzzafer. "I've never seen her before in my life."

One of his cousins came up, "Not bad, yaar, she's better looking than the first one."

"Who is she?" Jimmy demanded.

"Someone said her name is Zenab Memon, an actress or something."

"No wonder she does such dramatic things. Better watch out, Jamal-Jim. Next thing you know she'll be breaking plates on your head. These filmi girls are very independent."

"But she saved your skin, old man."

"Shut up, that's my wife you're talking about."

And Zenab climbs the stairs, looking down, transformed from an outspoken young actress to a shy bride, surrounded by six young women singing and holding a cloth above her head, her father walking slowly beside them, holding up the Quran.

Zenab, Zenab, thought Jimmy. Where have I heard the name before? Had she acted in something he'd sung in? He couldn't remember.

Now they were sitting together on the platform, as they should have been all along, as Zenab knew they should have been. When she was twelve, an old man who smelled of betel nut had held her pale hand in his brown wrinkled one. "You will marry the first man you love," he had told her. "A man with a mustache. A very famous man. And it is through your own strength that you will marry him. Yes, you are a very lucky woman." Of course, she had nothing to do with the fact that Jimmy's fiancée had run away with a French diplomat. But there she is, sitting beside the man intended for her by fate. Jimmy is her kismet.

An Evening in Paris

JIMMY, ZENAB AND ALIA fluttering behind him, checks into the hotel. It's 2 P.M. Not such a bad place, for Paris. A little dark. The curtains are all drawn, even in the middle of the afternoon. The man at the desk wears a grayish suit with a mottled sweater underneath and has tiny eyes that jump from Jimmy's hands—pale, brown-haired fingers—to the fat tortoise-shell pen with a twenty-four-carat gold clip, Mont Blanc, no less—he'd bought it on his first trip to Paris when he was seventeen—to the watch, also gold, of course, a heavy metal strap that was not at all loose on his wrist. The smell of Jimmy's aftershave—he always bought more from duty free—is wearing thin under the cigarette smoke and sweat-infested polyester.

You can't live without polyester in the Third World. It never wrinkles, practically never stains, it can be smashed against a rock and scrubbed with powerful chemicals in an already-polluted river and still be a magenta-and-turquoise flowered tunic like his wife wore or a white shirt like his own.

"Come on," he turns to his wife and daughter. A bell-boy picks up their bags.

"Room, sir?" he asks. The three of them squeeze into the tiny cage of a lift. There's a mirror in the back and Jimmy straightens his hair and shuffles his papers, pretending he's not looking at how they all look together.

"A good-looking family," thinks Jimmy. His wife, in diffuse light, still has the sweet features of an Asian starlet. His daughter is lucky, she's inherited her father's fair skin. Unfortunately, she has her mother's tendency toward acne. In the heat, or in moments of tension, her face is mottled with red sores and scabs. Jimmy hopes her skin will stay clear until they get to London. Someone had mentioned a boy, working for the bank there, who was getting ready to settle down and start a family.

Today, Alia's wearing the T-shirt she'd bought especially for the trip. It's bright purple and says C'EST MOI. The French Alia managed to learn in school is so heavily accented with Hindi that she has not yet been able to get anyone to understand her. But she is sure everyone will love her T-shirt.

She'd been excited about wearing it for weeks. She'd sat up at night, drawing pictures of Adam and herself, wearing her T-shirt, in France. When Aurangzeb dragged their suitcases up from the garage and emptied out the mothballs, the T-shirt was the first thing Alia packed. And unpacked. And packed again. She refused to let the ayah do any of her packing, but she gave into her mother's and the ayah's insistence that she take the requisite number of salwar kameezes. A girl couldn't walk around too often in trousers or English clothes, like a boy could, it made people think she was cheap.

Moments before they were leaving, in the chaos of Aurangzeb and Akbar getting all the bags and filled-to-bursting suitcases out the door and into the back of the Ambassador, and the cars of cousins and Jimmy's parents and Zenab's sister and her husband and three children all pulling into the driveway at once and everyone tumbling out of the doors, Alia disappeared. She ran up to her room, bumping her suitcase up the stairs behind her. "Wait! Wait!" she shouted through the door at the servants. She unpacked her T-shirt again.

And the servants shouted down, "Baby is changing, saha'ab! She's coming, saha'ab, just coming!"

Of course, they were late for their flight. And with Zenab's sister's children all trying to carry suitcases, one was left in the entrance way, and Jimmy had to send a servant back to get it just as they were checking in. Zenab started worrying, "Oh no, my gold shoes were in that bag. If that bag is lost, two of my johras are wasted. I won't be able to wear the blue one at all and—no, darling, don't worry, it's not your fault. Jimmy's just sent someone to get it. Oh, I hope we don't miss our flight."

Jimmy's mother wanted perfume, of course: "But don't spend too much. Just buy it from the duty free, then you can buy a bigger bottle." And Zenab's sister was busy writing down the brand name of the blender she wanted from the John Lewis department store on Oxford Street. She'd seen it in a catalog already, so she knew the price and everything. Her daughter wanted the new Jane Fonda exercise video. "But baby, you don't do the old one, it's been sitting there for ages," said Zenab's sister. Her husband wanted a bottle of whiskey, Johnny Walker Black Label. "Please write all this down, Alia," said Zenab. "You write much faster than I do."

"Now telephone the moment you get there," said Jimmy's mother. "You have the name of the hotel, don't you?" She started whispering prayers over Alia's head, blowing into her hair and then kissing her. "Don't you want some chocolates to eat on the plane?"

"Did you find the suitcase?"

One of the airport officials followed Jimmy's career. "Oh, Mr. Jimmy saha'ab, how are you? And this is your beautiful wife? And your daughter, how lovely she is. And your mother, how do you do, Madam?"

"Colonel Gupta, this is my father and my wife's sister and her husband—"

Colonel Gupta took off his hat and shook hands or bowed to everyone. "How lovely to meet them all. My son really enjoyed *Taxiwallah*—it was so nice of you to send complimentary tickets for him." Jimmy demurred but the official went on, rubbing his hands together as if he were washing them. "A little late, saha'ab, but no problem. No problem, you are first-class. We'll just make some more space for your things."

"There is one advantage to this idiotic career you've chosen." Jimmy's father slapped him on the back again. "Don't give your autograph to too many pretty ladies." He winked at Zenab.

They managed to avoid customs and the search. Their overweight luggage was taken free of charge. "You see," said Jimmy to his wife and daughter as the plane took off, "sometimes it's very lucky to be recognized."

Mind's Illusions

EVERYTHING LOOKS BETTER when Adam and Marc are walking along the street. Each bounce of his running shoes on the cobblestones makes Adam more buoyant, makes his father's angry voice more distant. They stop and lean against the wall overlooking the Seine. Adam looks down into the muddy water, bottles and old shoes swimming in little circles near the edge. Marc faces the street, and when Adam looks up at him the sun lights the edges of his hair so it glows around his fine face like a halo.

"Look, Adam," he says, "look at Notre Dame." Adam follows Marc's eyes to the sparkling stained-glass windows. A shaft of light stabs his eye and he blinks, looks away, back at the water. A *bateau mouche* floats by. Adam waves at the tourists.

At the base of the Eiffel Tower, they are surrounded. "Postcards? Postcards?" Vendors flip open accordions of Paris scenery. But Marc is pulling his arm, twining his long fingers through Adam's, dragging him into the entrance. Before Adam can protest, the lift is off and they're rising up and up above Paris and the cars and people around the tower look like a carnival of colors, the metal roofs of the cars gleaming like candies and the scarves flying out of the convertibles like little flags. Adam is giddy and breathless. His father's rumpled forehead, his mother's tear-filled eyes, the images slip out of his mind like droplets of water. His anxiety falls away, far, far below them. He's ready for anything.

Marc waves his hand majestically across the scene, "This, my friend, is Paris." He smiles, strokes Adam's cheek, "Next stop..."

IN THEIR HOTEL ROOM—gray carpeting, gray patterned wallpaper, brown bedcover—Jimmy tries to telephone his son. "What is Adam's number?" he asks his wife. The phone rings, or at least it sounds like it's ringing. "Is this the engaged sound or the ringing sound?" Zenab holds the phone to her ear.

"Look, how sweet!" Alia shouts from the bathroom. "Little baby bottles of shampoo! Little tiny soaps! They're so sweet and French looking!"

"Don't shout, darling, Abba is phoning Adam. Why don't you make a little drawing for us?"

"Where is he? Are we going to see him now?"

Jimmy listens: the phone clicks and some music starts, "I heard it through the grapevine. I'm just about to lose my mind. Honey, honey—honey, this is no grapevine, this is the source. Leave a message for Adam after the beep. *Veuillez laisser un message après le beep.*"

"When did you get this blasted machine?" says Jimmy into the receiver. "Why have you gone out when you knew we were coming? Your mother and your sister and I are here in the Hôtel Fouquet, room number 115. We're waiting for you, so call back quickly." He hangs up. "He's not there. Zenab, do you have Adam's number at the bank?" He lights another cigarette. Where is that boy? He even knew the flight number. He could excuse Adam for not coming to the airport, their flight having been delayed for two hours in Germany, but to not be home when they called—"I left a message on this silly telephone machine he has. God knows where he's getting the money to buy phone machines."

"Oh, why didn't you let me leave a message?" Alia complains. "I've always wanted to leave a message on a phone machine."

"I hope he's all right," says Zenab. "Poor thing, perhaps he was so worried about our flight being late, he's gone to the airport to look for us. I hope we didn't miss him in the airport."

"Let's just go to the bank and surprise him!" says Alia.

"Alia, why do you keep shouting like that? It's not nice. Here's the number—there, under the phoolwallah, can you read it? But perhaps we shouldn't disturb him while he's working."

Jimmy decides to call Adam anyway, but he only manages to reach the old school friend who gave Adam the job. They agree to meet for dinner. "All right, Kureishi bhai, we'll fix it up for dinner," says Jimmy. "Eight o'clock." He hangs up the phone and stares at the floor.

"What's wrong, janoo?" asks Zenab. She and Alia have already begun to unpack. One slippery salwar kameez after another is hung in a glistening row in the closet. Saris and matching blouses looking like trees ripe with fruit and flowers. "Give me your suits. Give me Abba's suits, Alia." Beside the array of colors and patterns, Jimmy's suits look stodgy and dull. "Shall we go and meet him?"

"No." Jimmy decides to change his shoes. Brown suede shoes that he bought in London. English shoes were always good. Dependable. Not like these blasted French. "He's not at work today. He's already begun his holiday. Perhaps he's gone out with Marc. Why are these shoes sticky? What is this?"

"Oh no," says Zenab. "The rasmalai must have leaked out. Don't worry, we'll just clean your shoes. Alia, go and wash Abba's shoes. Oh, I hope nothing else has leaked. Let me just look at your suits."

"Wash my shoes? They'll be ruined. What rasmalai? You brought sweets from India?"

"It's Adam's favorite. He's dying for it. And I brought him a little chicken curry, and some rotis. Because I knew I wouldn't be able to cook here. I really hope he's not in the airport waiting for us. Perhaps he brought Marc to the airport to meet us. I hope he's all right. He must be so excited about seeing us."

"Zenab, for God's sake, let the boy go without something for once. We've come all this way to see him and he doesn't even manage to come to the airport. Next thing you know, you'll be sending him the dhobi and boiling his water—"

"Is Adam coming with Kureishi bhai?"

"Kureishi's going to try to reach him. We'll leave a message here at the hotel, telling him where we've gone."

59

A Beginning

AS SOON AS ZENAB told him she was pregnant, barely eight weeks gone, Jimmy knew he would have his son. All through those seven months, as Zenab puffed and sobbed on a wave of hormones, Jimmy plied her with food appropriate for a growing boy. First of all, meat, heavy and strongly spiced, seemed like the most important food for a very young cricket player. Jimmy made certain his son would be unbeatable in the field. Then gallons of creamy buffalo milk every morning and afternoon, and buttery omelets and fresh parathas, fresh fruit juice, all making the nausea bubble through Zenab's stretching body as they satisfied Jimmy's paternal urges.

Fortunately, Jimmy was out most days and evenings and Zenab could safely gasp and wretch in her bathroom and push the untouched tray across the bedspread, back to the waiting servant. The smell alone was enough to pitch her stomach into a hurricane. Zenab's first pregnancy, then, served to make the rest of the household as well fed and glistening as it made her pale and hollow cheeked, on her own diet of toast and fruit.

When the final month arrived, Jimmy telephoned all his relatives to make sure they would be present for the birth of his heir. He even insisted that his brother Muzzafer come home from America. Jimmy never paid too much attention to his younger brother. The boy Muzzafer, scrawny in Jimmy's hand-me-down shirts and shorts, had always seemed too earnest, too disapproving of Jimmy's pranks and whimsical behavior. Though it was obvious that both Muzzafer and their sister Amna worshiped him, they never seemed convinced by his explanations. "Have some fun, you bloody fool!" Jimmy used to encourage the young Muzzafer as they walked home from school. But every time Jimmy managed to convince his male sibling to commit some minor naughtiness, Amna got him back under control.

As for Amna, she was as strong willed as her older brother. Probably the first girl in St. Francis's to discover Gloria Steinem, she was determined to mold Muzzafer into an Indian feminist man. Fortunately, when Jimmy's child was due to be born, Amna was at home, in the midst of her Ph.D. thesis on Indian women and the veil, and Jimmy didn't have to cajole her to Bombay from anywhere else. However, Jimmy did not manage to get his sister to leave her desk for the event.

"Jimmy-bhai, women have babies all the time. Almost any woman can have one. In the village, the babies fall out in fields while their mothers are working," said Amna, bleary eyed from studying, gripping another cup of thick tea. "I wish Zenab luck, but this is India. I don't think a new baby is anything to get excited about—and if you're so sure it's a boy, there's even less reason." She shut her bedroom door behind her as she disappeared into her books and papers for the rest of the night.

Now, as Jimmy smoked cigarettes in the waiting room of the hospital, accompanied by Muzzafer, he could sense his brother's irritation. As they got older, Jimmy found it increasingly difficult to ignore his brother's unspoken judgment. He tried to rely on his old powers of self-indulgence to block Muzzafer out.

"Please to wait here, sir," the nurse had said to them, leading them into the pale green room with flickering lights. Muzzafer paced. Jimmy dropped himself into a plastic orange Eames Chair that instantly cracked and collapsed, leaving him in a pile on the dirty floor. Cockroaches scuttled out from under his trousers. "God, when was the last time they cleaned this floor?" said Jimmy. "It's horrible."

"Let's eat supper," said Muzzafer. "Who knows how long this will take. How about a few kebabs and a Coke or something?"

"Are you crazy?" said Jimmy. "My son is about to be born. I have to go in and say the kalma in his ear. What if I'm not there? Then?"

"For God's sake, her mother is in there with her. They don't want men around during these things. I was eating apple pie with ice cream at Howard Johnson's when Sabah was born—and look at her."

"She's a girl," said Jimmy, "and she's American. You could read the prayer a little late. For my son. Never."

"What makes you so sure you're going to have a son?" Muzzafer stormed out. But he returned an hour later, as Jimmy was on to his third pack of cigarettes. "I've brought you some nan-kebab. Eat. You're going to be awake very late." They sat in the flickering light, eating the kebabs and smoking. In the green pallor of the room, their faces looked old. They contemplated old age. "When I'm old and have no one to support me because my daughter has squandered all my money and married an American good-for-nothing, will you support me?"

"Why not?" said Jimmy. "Why shouldn't I support you?" He licked his fingers and bit into another kebab. "If only you had waited three years. If Sabah was a little younger, I could have married my son to her. How could you have been so rude as to have children before your older brother?"

Just then the door opened and the nurse walked in, carrying a silent reddish shape, wrapped in blankets. She almost fainted from the rush of cigarette smoke and the smell of sleep and spices and cold food trapped for hours in the windowless room. "Here he is, Mr. Jimmy, sir. Your son," she gasped. As Jimmy lifted the child's ear to his lips, she asked, "You are the singer, sir? And your wife, she was an actress? You were in *Disco Diwali*?"

Jimmy interrupted his prayer. "Yes, yes," he said, pretending to be annoyed. "Please don't disturb me. Can't you see I am saying the kalma?"

"Here," said Muzzafer, "I'll explain whatever you want to know about Jimmy. We're practically brothers. In fact, we are brothers. Let me tell you what Jimmy was like as a child. Shall I sign his autograph for you?"

Jimmy looked at his son. "See what a famous father you have? What a lucky little boy you are, Adam. How lucky you are..." This boy was going to grow up into a hero. Jimmy knew that. He looked a little weak right now, but birth was an exhausting process. There was no question about it. This was Adam. His son.

Paris by Night

SOMEHOW, IN THE middle of dinner, Alia starts speaking French. Not the short, accented syllables she'd fumbled with before, but flowing sentences of beautiful French, with the proper pauses and useless flourishes and swirling phrases. Her wide lips become soft and round as they move into petulant French phonemes.

Even in the candle-lit restaurant, it's obvious that Kureishi and his wife are embarrassed. His wife's pale Pakistani complexion has become an erotic red. Zenab thinks it's inspired by the restaurant. It really is so French, the big wooden beams in the ceiling and the table cloths and the red flowers and all those waiters in sweet little farmer suits. In fact, she barely noticed when Alia started speaking French because everyone else was speaking in French, too. "Well," says Kureishi, who'd thought he was impressing everyone by ordering and vaguely translating the menu, with help from his wife who was taking a class in the morning at the Sorbonne, "why didn't you tell us you were speaking French so well? You could have saved your uncle and auntie from having to explain the menu to you." He glares at Alia and slaps Jimmy on the back so hard his jaw snaps shut because he'd been watching his daughter, open mouthed. "So, so, Mr. Jimmy Al-Hussain, what a surprise your children are. It seems even you don't know what they're going to come up with."

"Oh ho," says Jimmy, straightening his shoulders, "of course we all knew Alia could speak French. She's been studying it for years. She even did her O Levels in French. She's just a little shy. Now, she'll have no problem. Very good, Alia. Well done."

"It's too bad your son is not a little more shy," sniffs Farkhunda. She gives Zenab a cold look. "He is also learning to speak French very quickly."

"Oh, perhaps he learns more quickly than we thought," Zenab smiles and pats her husband's shoulder. "You see, darling, what a clever son we have. I knew his teachers were too hard on him. As soon as we see him, we must ask him to speak French for us."

As for Alia, she doesn't know where the French had come from. It is as though all the sounds she'd heard during the day had become part of her brain without her realizing it. And then the sounds just play back out of her mouth. She's like a record player that had been going at 45 and was switched to $33\frac{1}{3}$. The words make sense now. She would have been shocked herself if it hadn't felt so natural. She thinks she's speaking French like Adam, as if she's using his mouth. "What time did Adam say he would come?" Alia asks.

"Listen," says Kureishi, "about Adam—well, about this holiday he's on. You know, Jimmy, it's more than a holiday. Well, we told him we couldn't have him working for us any longer unless he buckles up."

"What? He's not working? Well, he damn well will," Jimmy's eyebrows knitted together. He thinks he'll get drunk again. He starts gulping his whiskey and soda.

"He can only work if he comes to work, and he rarely does that," says Kureishi. "It's not that he's not a bright boy, but he needs a little guidance. And his friends, well, Marc...he's not...I wouldn't let my son meet boys like that." Kureishi looks nervously at his wife, and then at Alia.

"Why?" asks Zenab. "He seemed very nice in Adam's letters. He was taking him to meet his family and to have dinner here and there."

"Listen, old chap," says Kureishi, "I don't know how I can tell you this—" He looks around the restaurant.

"What nice people come to this restaurant," says Zenab to Farkhunda. "Look at that older couple there, they are so distinguished. It was a very good choice."

"Yes," says Farkhunda icily. "We come here often with our daughters."

"Oh, you should have brought your daughters, Alia would have loved to meet them. Wouldn't you have, Alia? Look, Alia, look at that girl. Now she's a well-dressed French girl. How beautiful she's looking. Don't you think so?"

"If Alia is anything like her brother, she would have been bored by our daughters. They're very simple girls, very unsophisticated," says Farkhunda proudly.

"Look," says Kureishi. "I don't know where Adam is, or if he's coming. But..." He looks at Alia again and then he whispers in Jimmy's ear.

"What!" shouts Jimmy, his face distorting into a twisted red mask of a Kathakali dancer. His eyes bulge out of the sockets. "How dare you say such a thing about my son!" He stands up suddenly, his plate crashing to the floor, gravy and steak splashing Kureishi's suit, pomme frites in Zenab's lap. "Do you know who you are speaking to?" he shouts at Kureishi. Kureishi squirms in his chair. Except for Jimmy, the restaurant is almost silent. The rest of the diners look away politely and continue their conversation in hushed, hesitant voices so as not to miss any of the excitement. Jimmy is in character now. "Why should my son work for you and your stupid bank? I'll buy him ten banks if he wants them. Your little bank! I could crush your little bank with two words! There is no one in India or Pakistan who doesn't know who I am, from the rickshaw wallahs to the Hindujas! You write, you telephone your head office and just see what they do—you won't be able to get a job in any bank on the subcontinent. And I don't need to drink your whiskey." Dramatically, Jimmy picks up the whiskey glass, as if he were magnified twenty times on a crackly movie screen in Lahore. Jimmy holds the glass up to the light and swirls the remaining liquid. Kureishi knows the camera would cut in close now—he's watched Jimmy's knuckles a thousand times on video in *Revenge*—the fingers trembling with passion, each wrinkle, each hair magnified a hundred times—the way he's watching them now. "Keep your stinking French sherab!" Jimmy throws the drink

65

in Kureishi's face, and his wife gasps, "Kureishi!" and rushes a napkin to his face as Jimmy, his wife and daughter marching after him, leaves the restaurant.

Out in the street, Jimmy's head spins. He collapses laughing against a wall. "Ho! Ha! Did you see Kureishi's face! He won't dare speak like that to me again, will he?" He stands up and then collapses again. "Zenab, call a taxi. I'm not feeling well."

As though on command, a taxi pulls up in front of them. Zenab stares at it. She's never directed a taxi herself before. She puts her hand on the door and it swings open. There is a shuffle as a good-looking young man smelling of cologne and cigarettes jumps out. He winks at Alia and holds the door of the taxi open for them.

Zenab freezes for a second; the boy looks so much like Adam, the same flop of brown hair across his forehead, his big gray overcoat like the one Zenab bought him in London last year. Alia stops to stare as well, her "Adam!" caught in her throat. The taxi driver has to get out and push the two paralyzed women aside to help Jimmy into the taxi.

The driver gives the door of the taxi a push. He gets back inside and clicks his own door shut. The sounds of the street disappear. All Zenab can hear is Jimmy's snore as he slumps sideways across Alia's shoulder.

JIMMY CAN BARELY open his eyes. The sun is slicing through the curtains in brilliant streaks. Each ray stabs his eyeballs. His head aches so much he fantasizes about chopping it off. "Darling? Janoo?" Zenab's voice sends shock waves through his brain. "He's still sleeping, Alia. We'll quietly, quietly go out. We'll just leave a note for him. I know, let's go and buy some perfume downstairs." The door bangs shut like a mallet on his head. He squints. His vision blurs, then clears. It's noon. Jimmy stumbles toward the refrigerator. He grabs the first thing he touches, a can of orange drink, and presses it to his face. He takes out the ice-cube tray. It's encrusted with frost, so he presses it whole against his eyes. He drops the orange drink and heads to the toilet. Eventually, he makes it back to bed, dropping his thick body on the mattress and letting the ice melt and drip down into his ears. Oh, God. He might as well go deaf too. I heard it through the grapevine. Grapevine. Perhaps Adam and his friend have gone to London. The thought reassures Jimmy. London is a saner place than Paris, certainly. Adam could be in London now. Jimmy rolls over to the phone and calls the travel agent. Tomorrow they'll go to London. If Adam is there, he must be staying with his aunt. Maybe he'll even meet that boy for Alia. Jimmy tries to remember his name. He'll have to ask his sister Amna to find out a bit more about him. At least that would be one problem solved. Jimmy makes reservations for the afternoon flight. Then he falls into a half coma.

67

Bumbai

MID-JANUARY DURING Jimmy's second year at the university, his parents received a telegram: SYED JAMAL NOOR AL-HUSSAIN YOUR SON DIED STOP PLEASE SEND MONEY STOP FOR FUNERAL STOP CONDOLENCES HAROON STOP. It was a winter day, the air dry and scratchy with the smoke of brushfires, and the telegram was a week late. It arrived crumpled and stained from the red betel-nut juice and the dusty fingers of the postman. His mother cried briefly, but she was a stolid woman, known more for her actions than her emotions. She comforted herself with the thought of her younger son, Muzzafer, hardworking and still bright with potential, in school in India. She put on a starched white cotton sari and sent all the servants into the kitchen to start preparing her famous pakoras and samosas and sweets for all the consoling friends and relatives who were beginning to descend like wasps on candy. The curtains were all drawn, and then the chiks pulled down on the veranda so that only tiny trickles of sunlight seeped into the drawing room. Jimmy's father booked a ticket on the next steamer to England.

"Jamal died? How?" Jimmy's uncle Ishtiaque was incredulous. "But—here, here, bring those pakoras here, I've just come back from England, I can't think when I last had good food—listen, I've just seen Jamal, he's perfectly well, nothing wrong with the boy—just a little chutney, this is lovely, did you make it yourself?"

Jimmy's mother sat forward in her chair, her eyes narrowing and her sari crumpling around her waist like writing paper. "What do you mean? He was well?"

"Chai, Uncle?" Jimmy's sister Amna poised the teapot above Ishtiaque's cup.

"But we've just got a second telegram saying he died of pneumonia," said Jimmy's father. "Perhaps he got it suddenly. Anyway, Haroon is Jimmy's best friend. He would never want to hurt him or his parents."

Ishtiaque poured milk and heaps of sugar into his tea and stirred it enthusiastically. "Well, sir," he said, "I think you'd better stop sending Haroon any more money. I'll be back in London in a fortnight, and I'll find out what's become of the boy. Just one more samosa—that's it. Perfect, Amna, thank you. What a lovely girl you've grown up into, if only I had a son for you..."

Jimmy's sister Amna glared and almost grabbed the serving dish from his fingers. Her bullheadedness had already gained her a reputation for being unmanageable, if not unmarriageable.

Despite Ishtiaque's reassurance, Jimmy's father wired money to London. Enough for a funeral, in a good hall. They were so far away from Bombay here on the family's land. He was worried that if anything else happened he wouldn't hear about it for weeks. He knew Jimmy's English friends were of a certain class. He had to be sure his son looked good on his last appearance. He telegrammed Haroon to send him a list of expenses.

At the end of the month of mourning, when the curtains were pulled open again and the whole house emptied of guests, they received a telegram from Ishtiaque. JAMAL ALIVE AND WELL STOP HAVE BOXED EARS STOP STOP ALL FURTHER PAYMENT STOP.

In London, Jimmy had been running a little low on funds. He'd been living beyond his means—dinner out, and theater, does get expensive, and one needs the suits to go with it and, of course, one must invite one's friends from time to time—and he'd spent more than the whole year's generous allowance by half-term. He'd even had to let his servant work in an Indian restaurant a few days a week. He didn't dare tell his parents, but he knew that they would never refuse to pay for their eldest son's funeral.

However, in their glee over the new flow of cash, Haroon and Jimmy had been careless. They were found smoking cigars in all the best restaurants in London. They'd both improved their wardrobes drastically. Suddenly they had gained a reputation as two wealthy young men who'd just come into their inheritance. Jimmy did nothing to dispel the rumors. In fact, they pleased him. He even let hints spread that he was a dethroned Mughal prince who had a secret cache of Kashmiri sapphires in his mattress. That had been especially useful in seducing young women.

Ishtiaque walked into the fashionable restaurant and found his nephew and Haroon digging into huge beef Wellingtons. White napkins as big as children's sheets were tucked under their chins, and two pretty English girls sat on either side of them, finishing off plates of oysters.

Ishtiaque demanded an extra chair from the waiter and joined them, telling jokes loudly and slapping the girls on the thighs. He gave into their nervous insistence—"Please,

please, really, you must, we haven't seen you in ages"—that they buy him dinner as well. It was during coffee that he told them that he had just returned from India himself. He smiled charmingly at Jimmy's escort and she returned his smile. Jimmy choked and coughed and turned white. Haroon, on the other hand, continued the game. He asked politely about everyone. Ishtiaque related the anecdotes of his voyage, whispering amusing asides to Jimmy's friend, who laughed and occasionally blushed and put her hand to her mouth. Eventually he reached the subject of Jimmy's parents. His mother was blinded by sorrow, he told them, and his father was selling off all of Jimmy's inheritance and giving it to the poor to ensure Jimmy's ascent to heaven. Jimmy's face drained. Ishtiaque called the waiter and ordered two dozen long-stemmed red roses and a bottle of the best champagne. He then boxed his nephew's ears soundly and ostentatiously. He left them, now red faced and silent—the champagne, the roses, and the girls on his arms—with the tab on their bill. Ishtiaque always enjoyed the best of everything.

Down and Out in Paris and London

THE GLASS DOOR swings gracefully closed behind them. Zenab glides across the carpet, but Alia is transfixed. She can't move. She's less intimidated by the glass and chrome and mirrors than by the faces. Everywhere, the faces are staring at her, laughing, pouting, winking. Faces with blue eyes and black hair, blond hair and green eyes, brown hair and yellow eyes. The faces offer their high cheekbones and pointed noses, swanlike necks and creamy skin like boons to the homely masses. Some orifices are isolated from their heads: sultry eyes peering out from under eyeshadowed lids, furrows of mascaraed eyelashes, lipsticked mouths. A salesgirl walks toward her, and Alia suddenly feels as if she's just seen herself in a circus mirror. She is sweaty, pockmarked, and ugly. Hideously ugly. And the salesgirl is suntanned and perfectly coiffed. She's so thin, Alia can see her hip bones creasing the front of her skirt as she walks. Every feature is painted, perfumed, and enhanced. Alia wants to run. "This is your mother?" she asks, tiny gold earrings bobbing up and down on her ears.

"Alia, come here, behti. Look at this lovely pink lipstick," says Zenab. "You must try it. It would be perfect for you. Such a young color."

Alia looks at the face above the display. It looks nothing like her. The thin aquiline nose, the sea blue eyes. She could never look like that. "You try it, Ummi," she mumbles, hoping her mother hears her and the salesgirls don't.

"No, darling, this is for a very young girl. Oh, look at this reddish one. It's so beautiful. Now, this one I like."

This is a joke, thinks Alia. This is a joke and she will never be as beautiful as these perfect faces, so she should just leave here quickly. The face stares back at her with a half smile, as if she shares Alia's thoughts. "Just try," she would say to Alia. "Just try to look like me."

"Madame, please," says one of the salesgirls. "Let me suggest something for you and your daughter. Somethings exactly that you need. Here," she says to Alia. "Mademoiselle, you sit on this chair. I will make you very beautiful."

JIMMY REGAINS consciousness to the sound of French voices and the smell of perfume and creams, profuse and overwhelming. He thinks he's in a brothel, he's twenty-two again. He closes his eyes tighter to savor the moment. He opens his eyes and his wife and daughter are sitting in front of the television, applying nail polish to their toes. "Alia?" he says.

A voice says, "Yes, Abba?" and she lifts her head, but the girl who is speaking is unrecognizable. Her pouty lips are outlined and glossed with pink and her face is a solid shade of beige, except for a slight pink stripe across her cheeks. Her eyes look like freshly caught rainbow trout, green and blue and iridescent. She blinks slowly. "Yes?"

Oh my God. Another nightmare. Jimmy squeezes his eyes shut. "Darling," coos Zenab. "Would you like some tea?" Jimmy opens his eyes to an even more hideous sight: Zenab is equally transformed. This is a scene from some bad European film. "Yes. Bring some tea," he croaks.

Jimmy decides they'll spend their last evening in the hotel room, watching television and having room service. "Isn't this exciting, Alia?" says Zenab. "We're having room service, just like in a video." Alia and Zenab watch one movie after another while Jimmy goes even more rapidly through packs of cigarettes. The smoke seeps into the walls, the sheets, the wall-to-wall carpeting. Eventually, they all fall into an exhausted sleep in a haze of perfume and cigarette smoke.

THE PHONE RINGS at 3 A.M.

"*Adam!*" screams Alia into the phone. "Where are you? Oh. Oh. Yes, I'm fine. We had room service last night. How are you? No, nothing really. The weather's beautiful here, how is it in London?"

"*London!*" Jimmy grabs the receiver from his daughter. "Where the hell are you? What do you mean by leaving for London when we've come all this way to see you? You expect your poor mother to defend you all the time? Of course I'm angry!"

Zenab takes the phone. "Hello, Adam, my darling. I'm so happy you called! I've been missing you—we've all been missing you so much. We'll be with you in London tomorrow." She can't help glancing at Adam's photograph, which is lying on the bedside table. She'd had the photographs developed after he left, and she'd been waiting to show them to him. He was laughing in the picture, dancing in his Michael Jackson outfit, his last night in India. "Yes, your father's very angry, behta. Why didn't you stay a little longer? We waited for you in the restaurant. Please rest, you get very tired when you travel. Of course we'll meet you anywhere you want. All right. Ten-thirty. Yes, I've written the address. The taxi will know? Khudafiz, behta."

"Ten o'clock! Are you mad?" shouts Jimmy into the receiver, but Adam has already hung up.

Café de Paris

ZENAB'S DUPATTA slams in the taxi door as they get out, and she briefly risks the same end as Isadora Duncan, until she and Alia, shrieking, stop the taxi from pulling away from the curb. Jimmy doesn't notice. He's looking at the Café de Paris, at the hordes of young people pushing their way up to the ropes. They're horrible looking. Black, black everywhere, black coats and black trousers and dyed black hair. And the girls. Girls wearing nothing but their underwear, black bras and black net stockings. Jimmy can understand what Adam sees in this place, but he should have known better than to call his mother and sister here. Jimmy forces through the crowd with a grace learned in Third World mobs. He's used to this, these are like the crowds at his own concerts, although, he hates to say it, his audiences are better dressed than these English. "Come on, Alia. Stay with your mother. I'm looking for my son, his name is Adam," he tells the doorman, a black man, who is also wearing black. Jimmy looks at him closely, the boy is wearing false eyelashes and lipstick. He steps back a little and Alia moves forward. This is the closest she's ever been to a black man. She'd been told that black people all carry knives and rob people. He's handsome, though, and she can't see his knife.

"Oh, you're Adam's dad, are you? He's been waiting for you." He unhooks the velvet rope and lets them in, ignoring the screams of the women waiting behind them. "Hi," he smiles at Alia, and winks, "have fun." Alia sniffs hard as she passes to see if he smells different. She'd also heard that black people smell different. He smells like aftershave lotion and hair gel. Alia likes him. She wishes she could stay outside.

Zenab pulls Alia inside. She's sure that if Adam had known what kind of a place this was he would never have called them here. "Don't worry," she tells Alia. "We'll leave as soon as we find Adam. Don't stare at that man, he could be dangerous," she warns, in Hindi.

Inside, Jimmy feels like he's on a film set. The question is, Which one? All around him are people in costumes and makeup. Girls in their underwear, girls dressed like boys, boys with no hair. He sees some Indians or Pakistanis; they probably recognize him. How embarrassing. Instead, they stare at him blankly. He's just another old man to them. He turns back to look for Alia and Zenab and finds his face inches away from that of a blind man, must be blind, his round black sunglasses would make it impossible to see anything. "Hey, good-looking," says the blind man. "What are you looking for tonight?"

A rainbowed face pushes itself close, "Are you an agent? I'm the dancer tonight." The boy blinks his long false eyelashes, blue and purple and red and orange and yellow eyeshadow crinkling and unfurling like flags behind his eyelids.

Alia pulls her mother's arm. "Oh, this is fun, Umma." She pulls her into the darkness. She can't believe her luck. "Come on, Ummiji, please. Let's go and dance. I'd love to dance. I've always wanted to go to a disco." The two of them

mingle with the crowd, their flowered salwar kameezes melting into all the Indian-print psychedelia and flower-power
dresses.

"Zenab, Alia!" Jimmy calls after them, but he is
surrounded.

"Ted here's not so good, you've got to see my mate
Linda. She's the best dancer in the club. She even does top-
less, y'know? I mean, she can make the two tassels swing in
different directions at the same time. That takes practice,
don't it?"

The faces and bodies press against him. He is pushed
into a corner and then down, onto a sofa. "Sit down. Sit, gov,
relax. Can I get you a drink?"

"He's an agent? Listen, gov, here's my card. You only
looking for dancers?" There are people sitting all over the
sofa, squeezing in beside him and sitting on the arms. There
is even a boy—he's not sure anymore which ones are boys and
which ones are girls—perched like a parrot on the rounded
back of the sofa. A few of the faces look Indian, too, but
they're strange, like masks, like hijras, and their voices are the
same as the rest of the people around him.

Just then, a smart young man with a cool pink face
and a gray suit, his tie a clean red slash across his shirt, cuts
through Jimmy's admirers. "*Excusez-moi, Monsieur,*" he says,
"I am very sorry, *très désolé*, you are Adam's father?"

"Yes, yes, but—one minute." Jimmy has found one of
the rosy English beauties he loves. "My dear, you have a very
lovely face. You might be just the type I am looking for in my
next film. Why don't you give me some place where I can
reach you? Your phone number?"

"I'm really a singer, but I do some acting as well."

"Bloody hell, Phoebe, I found him first. What the
fuck do you mean stealing my break?" the rainbow-eyed boy
shouts. "You don't want her. She can't dance, can't sing, can't
act to save her life—"

75

"*Monsieur*, I am so happy to meet you," the cool young man says. "I am so sorry we are late."

"In fact the only thing she is good for—"

"Please, *Monsieur*," says the young man. "Come with me."

Jimmy stands up. "Don't worry, I'll be back in a few minutes," he tells his English rose. He pushes aside the rest. "Excuse me, I'm sorry. You're just not right for the part. Pretty girl, so English, eh?" Jimmy puts his arm around the young man's shoulder. "So what are you two doing in London? French girls not enough for you?"

"Marc Cosnard de Closets, *Monsieur*. I am very pleased to meet you," he shakes Jimmy's hand firmly.

"Well, well, very pleased to meet you," says Jimmy. He's impressed. Marc is polite, well dressed, nothing like the rest of the garbage in this place. And what a strong handshake, a handshake that gives you confidence. Jimmy can't believe what Kureishi said. No poofter handshake that. "So what have you boys been doing, eh?" he chuckles. "When you're young, you don't think before you do things like this, do you? Now where is that son of mine?"

"He has just joined your wife and daughter inside. I think perhaps they are dancing." Marc leads Jimmy down the long, round passageway. They walk in a circle looking down at the dance floor, which seems like a pit of writhing bodies, a torture scene from the inferno. Jimmy stares for a minute at the horrifying sight. His dinner lurches in his stomach. He can't make out anything recognizable.

Marc is descending into the pit, and Jimmy feels the sweat rising like steam above the gyrating crowd as he follows his son's friend down the stairs. They sit at a table on a little platform, beneath a huge gold clump of cherubim and swirls and flourishes that hangs from the staircase.

"Perhaps you know already that the Café de Paris was bombed in World War II?" asks Marc. "This was a very popular place for jazz musicians at one time."

"No, I didn't know that, that's very interesting. Where do you think Adam is?"

"There," Marc points at the dance floor. Jimmy follows his finger, but it seems to end at a dark trembling mass.

But then, as his eyes get used to the light, he sees Adam, followed by Alia, climbing the long staircase out of the pit. "Oh, there you are," says a voice. Zenab plops into the chair next to him. "You must come and dance. It's so lovely. We've been having such a lovely time. Adam and Alia just went up to look for you. I decided to come back and speak to Marc—isn't he sweet?—and here you are. Janoo, let's have something to drink, I'm dying of thirst." She's smelling of alcohol. Her face is swollen and wet and her kurta is sticking to her in a very unbecoming way. That's why women shouldn't drink, thinks Jimmy. A few glasses of champagne and they lose their heads. She's put on weight recently as well. He sees Adam's head over the edge of the balcony. He's joined by Alia. Somehow, there's a light shining on their faces; they seem to be spotlighted. Jimmy watches them wave at him like a slow-motion scene from a film. They wave and he swallows his drink and waves back, his arm moving across his vision like a windshield wiper, all the worry and frustration of the past few days clearing away in a smooth arc. He raises a glass of champagne that has miraculously appeared on their table. Suddenly, he feels a pain like a huge stone has been thrown at his chest, he's thrown backward, he feels like he's flying backward in space. He hits the ground hard, choking with the force. He's being crushed under the stone, he can't catch his breath, he's pressed against the ground under the weight of the stone, he tries to catch his breath. Zenab is screaming. Alia is screaming. Jimmy tries to breathe and he gasps and he can't see anything.

JIMMY TRIES TO open his eyes, but he's blinded. He can't see anything but black. He hears voices, Alia, Zenab, Adam. "I'm blind," he croaks. They can't seem to hear him. They keep speaking.

"Now, it's not bad, really. I like Paris. But at first, I really missed you, Umma. I thought I'd never come back. And I'm not very good at banking, you know."

"Of course I know that, darling, but your Abba wants you to do business. It's a very stable job."

"But Abba didn't do business," says Alia. "His father also wanted him to do business, that's why he sent Abba to England. That's what Dada-abba told me. He said—"

Jimmy's whole body aches. He thinks about his father. He thinks about the anger in his father's face when he told him he was going to be an actor. Jimmy was terrified. He thought his father would kill him, literally. His father had just come back from his morning constitutional walk and was standing in the doorway with his huge brass-knobbed cane, a slight breeze brushing past him into the room. Jimmy thought he was going to be clubbed to death. Jimmy could remember every spot on the kurta pajama his father was wearing that day, every crease, every wrinkle in the homespun fabric. He could even remember the sounds coming from the kitchen in the courtyard, the rhythmic chopping of onions, the sounds of sticks being broken and shoved into the stove. At the time, the snapping wood had made him think of his own bones.

"Alia, this is not something a young girl can understand. It is very serious for a young man. He has to have a good job so that he can support his family. Adam, if you had just gotten better marks in school, you could have done your university in England. Your Abba would have been so proud of you if you had gone to the same university as he did."

Jimmy's voice had quavered while he spoke, the pitch rising so high it broke and he had to cough to get his words back. And in spite of the fear, Jimmy had known he couldn't go back to university in England. Now, as the scene replayed in his mind, for the first time in years, Jimmy felt the same fear, tense and overwhelming, gripping his body. He wanted to shout. This time, the accompanying physical pain was a hundred times worse.

"I could still do a course in design in New York. You know, a lot of Americans change jobs and go back to university."

"Adam, boys don't study design. How will you get a job? Anyway, that's not the kind of work boys from good families do."

"But, Umma, can't I just go to New York and have a look at some of the art schools there?"

"My poor darling. You're very artistic, but it's not practical. I would love you to do anything you want, but in the end, if you do what your Abba wants you to do, you'll be happier."

79

"But Umma, I've already got a ticket to New York. I've paid for it myself and everything."

"I also want to go to New York," Alia chimes in.

"Shh, be quiet, behti. Adam, your father is not well. How can you leave him and go to New York?"

Jimmy feels his body seize again. He sees his father's face in front of him and he contracts, he tries to crouch. His mother's voice follows every movement, climbing and sinking, like harsh music to a dance. He can hear it, "After all your education... after all your education... after all your education," like the needle stuck on a record. He sees his father's cane rising, the grain of the polished wood sweeping past his eyes, but he can't move. He feels as if there are ropes around his neck and arms, but his fingers are too stiff to seek them out. He tries to open his eyes, to wake up, but he can't. "I'm blind," rasps Jimmy.

"Oh, he's awake. I think he's saying something."

"No, behti, he's just talking in his sleep."

There is a click of heels on the floor. Jimmy is shaking. His whole body is vibrating as if a jackhammer were smashing through his sternum. A brisk British voice. "I'm sorry, visiting hours are over. Really, Mrs. Al-Hussain, there's no need for you to stay."

Jimmy hears Zenab protest. Oh, God, don't go, he thinks. Only Zenab can save him, he wants to hear her voice, feel her soft, comforting body.

"His heart attack was very minor, really, Mrs. Al-Hussain. There's no need for you to make such a fuss."

Then the room quiets. His family exits. Jimmy hears the footsteps and voices receding. He sees the cane, the brown wood, rising again. He jolts, feels the crash of pain and the white light smash through his brain like lightning. He falls into the darkness.

IT IS A BODY, a deep yellowy brown like the color of dirty teeth. Alia can't pull herself away from it. "Come on, Alia, we're never going to make it to the Egyptians! Hurry up! It's almost closing time," shouts Adam as he disappears around a display case.

"Shh," says a red-cheeked English woman. "This is a museum." The sign says it's a mummified, dried body. Alia can imagine it, lying in the hot sand in the desert, she can almost feel the dry, windless air and the gritty sand on her face. She'd been to the desert before, one winter. The body is almost the same color as sand, and she can see its yellow bones like tent poles poking out under a sagging canvas. There are some paintings on pieces of wood, faces of beautiful women, with kajal around their eyes and turquoise in their hair. They're faces Alia recognizes, they look Indian to her, their brown eyes look like her mother's eyes. This body could be one of these faces, she thinks. She wants to show them to

Adam, but he's already gone. She puts her hands on the glass and tries to imagine what the body would feel like.

JIMMY FEELS fingers on his face. Suddenly, there's light on his eyelids, pink and yellow light streams into his brain. He blinks. He opens his eyes. "And how are you feeling today, Mr. Al-Hussain?"

"Huh, oh," Jimmy chokes a little. "Ah, I'm fine. No," he struggles with his facial muscles. He manages what he thinks is a smile. "No, I'm not fine. But I'm feeling better. You can call me Jimmy," he says stoically, like the injured soldier he'd played in the Hindi version of *A Farewell to Arms.*

"Of course you are. You gave us all such a shock," the nurse bustles around him, tucking in the sheets and picking up things. Jimmy is a little disappointed. The nurse he had in the film was much prettier. He's not impressed with this nurse's plump cheeks and fat fingers. "Your wife should be here any minute."

"My wife?" says Jimmy, and he remembers Zenab. "And my son?" Shouldn't a man's son be at his bedside when he is not well?

The nurse looks disapproving. "He might come as well, but I have asked Mrs. Al-Hussain to be very careful these next few days. You're still very weak, and we don't want to tire you out. Actually, we'd prefer it if she came alone. But, of course, the choice is yours."

Zenab bursts into the room, pale and red eyed. "Oh, my poor jan," she sweeps down onto the bed, and Jimmy expects a trail of organ music. It's a perfect melodrama and he loves it, it all makes sense. "Oh, God," says Zenab. "I was so worried." She sits beside him on the bed and throws her arms around his shoulders. "What if I had gone back to Bombay without you?"

81

It occurs to Jimmy what his wife's life would be like if he died. A woman without a husband in India loses all her status, all her respect. Jimmy thinks of the beautiful young Zenab who'd climbed the dais to be with him. He feels very protective of his wife. He squeezes her hand, with the little strength he has. "Don't worry, my darling," he says to Zenab. "I'm not ready to leave you yet. But when can I get out of this awful place?"

On Our Way Back Home

"UNCLE, WILL YOU have another glass of milk?"

"Milk? Milk?" Jimmy tosses the glass off the tray. "Why do you keep bringing me milk? I hate milk!" The milk soaks into the design of the Oriental carpet. The servant girl scurries out of the room, banging the door shut behind her.

"Sorry, Uncle, sorry," she mumbles from behind the door. And then Jimmy can hear her shouting, as she clatters down the stairs, "Amnaji, he's not drinking. He's breaking the glasses. It's not my fault!"

He's getting claustrophobic. There are thick curtains over the windows and thick carpets on the floor. The heavily embroidered bedspread is suffocating him. He's lying in his sister's canopied bed. The whole room has been dedicated to his recovery, but his sister's salwar kameezes and saris are still hanging around the room in heaps, on chairs, on the dressing table, on the posts of the canopy, some of the clothing is even on top of the canopy, making dark, lumpy shapes hanging above him that scare him when he wakes at night. Amna was never very tidy, even as a young girl. She always felt she had more important things to do than cleaning up after herself. "That's the only reason the men get to do everything in India. Women would control the country, and much better than men do, if they weren't so busy cleaning and shopping and taking care of everyone," she said. So here she was, in London, making her career and not tidying her house. The servant obviously had the same priorities.

"Bhaijan," says Amna, striding into the room. Since coming to London, Amna had exchanged the delicate steps of Asian women for the American stride, long steps full of confidence. Amna is the only woman Jimmy knows who can stride in the constriction of a well-wrapped sari. Zenab glides in behind her. "Bhaijan, what's this I hear about your not drinking your milk?" Amna's big, strange blue eyes flashed. Jimmy had always harbored a secret suspicion about the origin of those self-possessed, European-looking eyes.

"Yes, janoo, you must drink it," Zenab agrees, looking unhappily at her pale husband.

"What do you mean 'drink my milk'? Since when have I become an infant to be fed milk to? Of course I'm not drinking my milk. I hate the stuff. Especially this horrible skimmed milk you keep giving me. If I have to have milk, why can't I have gulab jamun or rasmalai?" After a good sleep, Jimmy feels strength and bad temper bubbling up inside him.

"Now you're really behaving like a baby. Of course you can't have sweets. You'll just become sick. You're supposed to be recovering, you fool," Amna retorts. "If you won't drink the milk, have some boiled vegetables or something."

"Boiled vegetables? I'd rather have died and gone to hell. And how dare you call me a fool!"

"Thobah, God forbid, Jamal, how can you say things like that?" says Zenab. "You must eat something. Look, you're becoming so thin. It's not nice." Jimmy really is looking gray and weak, she wishes she could make him a little chicken curry, but Amna's strict instructions make her a little nervous as well.

"This is England, Bhaijan, everybody eats boiled vegetables. Stop feeling so sorry for yourself," says Amna, definitively.

83

"If I have to eat English food, I want a beef Wellington," he growls.

"Come on, janoo, Adam and Alia are coming back from their holiday in four days. Do you want them to get worried about their father? That's really unfair, Jamal."

"Why shouldn't I shake them up a little? It might do them some good," Jimmy murmurs. He feels himself fading a bit now. He sinks back into the pillows and closes his eyes.

ALIA AND ADAM make their way across the stone beach. The round stones look like eggs, thinks Adam, like hundreds and hundreds of sea turtle eggs about to hatch. They sit on some pylons and watch the sea. Beneath them, an English couple frolics in the water. Their bodies are white and corpulent, like fleshy white fruit. Adam watches the woman's breasts, like marshmallows, bob on the surface of the water. What fruit is white? He thinks of Marc's pale pink body, dotted with tiny freckles. He thinks of lying in bed with Marc, curled behind him, his brown skin against Marc's freckled one. He licks Marc's freckles, licks his shoulders like scoops of ice cream that don't melt. Marc's skin always tasted washed and clean, as if he'd just stepped out of a lake. To Adam, Marc looked like a water boy, a nymph, his long legs and long waist, as if he might be kneeling on a water lily. When he needed a haircut, he looked like a beautiful girl from the back. His round buttocks could have been carved from pink marble.

Alia climbs down and sits on the beach. She picks up stones and throws them into the water. She misses, they bounce off other rocks. It's a new game. Alia throws the pebble, and it must ricochet off as many rocks as possible before it hits the sea.

"Want to go in?" Adam asks Alia.

"It looks cold."

"It probably is."

They move slowly toward the water, tripping a bit on the stones. Alia puts her foot in the water and screams. "Ah! Oh! This is disgusting!" The mud is sticky and cloying, and seaweed swirls around her ankles.

"Come on, you baby!" Adam grabs her arm and pulls her into the water up to her chin, flailing and screaming.

"Seaweed! Ugh, seaweed!" she shrieks.

Adam splashes her. "Remember that time we went to the beach in Bombay? The last time before I left?"

"Yes, and we had a picnic with Pinky and her brother. And all those junglee boys kept coming over to our side." Alia does a sort of a breaststroke.

"And the camel wallah, remember him? He got really bugged because I wanted to ride my camel myself, without him holding on to me. And then the camel started running away."

"That's right. How did you get him to stop?" Alia laughs.

"I don't know. He just stopped himself." Adam swims a little ways ahead. "There are some people in Paris who have never even seen camels."

"Or vultures," says Alia.

Adam starts swimming farther out to sea. His head and arms become bobbing shapes above the waves. Alia looks at the water around her. It is brown, like the water in a nallah or a gutter. She makes little ripples with her fingers. "Adam! Don't go too far!" A wave leaps up and catches her in the face. Alia swallows a gulp of salty water. It stinks like old fish. She coughs and gags. "Adam!" she screams, panicked by the water. Adam is either ignoring her or is too far away to hear. He continues to swim, his head becoming smaller and smaller in relation to the sailboats on the horizon.

"Adam!" Alia starts swimming back. Adam's head is now half the size of the boat. "Come back! Remember what Ummi said!" His head is a quarter of the boat. He keeps swimming.

85

At the shore, Alia runs through the slimy mud back to the stones, half backward, trying to see her brother. "Adam!"

The white couple cavorting in the water stop to stare at her. "Adam!" she shouts and waves at the tiny head. They wave back, smiling. Adam's head disappears.

Alia trudges back through the stones. She climbs a pylon. The tide is coming in, and the sea looks blacker and more dangerous. Alia watches for Adam's head. She wonders what she would do if he drowned. What would Abba do without his son? "A son makes a man's life complete," he used to say. "Now, my work is done." He would kiss Adam, or as he got older, pat him roughly on the back. Alia steps off the pylon back onto the stones. She finds her shoes in the shadows and puts them on. And Umma. When she took out her jewelry and laid it out on the shawl to show her friends, she would hold up the best pieces, the biggest, the most intricate work, and say, "This sita-rami is for Adam's wife. Of course, Alia will also have a necklace, but this one is for my son."

The vegetable wallah used to say, as the cook squeezed and thumped the produce, "Having a daughter is like having one son less. If one has one son and one daughter—that is a very good marrow, just picked this morning—one may as well have no children at all. The marrow is only five rupees."

"Five rupees, why don't you just rob people on the street," protested the cook.

"I have five daughters to marry, you can't give me one rupee for each one's dowry?" answered the vegetable wallah, rocking back and forth, his cracked brown hands gripping the handle of his cart.

"What does this have to do with your daughters? I'll take it for two rupees and even then you'll make a profit. And that's only because you've been coming to the house for so many years."

"Two rupees? My daughters will be married in rags, already they're eating me out of my house. At least four rupees. Look at these peppers, the chili is practically bursting out of them," he smiled widely, his teeth like a broken black fence around his pink tongue. Alia blushed with anger and regret for her sex.

"Two rupees, here, take it. Aren't you ashamed of yourself to be charging such prices in front of Bibiji's daughter?"

"She's a very nice girl—lots of chili in her, too—but girls only make problems. And the spicy ones are the worst. They can't help it," he would laugh and spit a stream of red betel juice over his shoulder.

Alia thinks about playing in her brother's room late at night while the ayah breathed heavily on the bedroom floor, under a mountain of blankets. She and Adam pretended they were knights going to magicland to fight for the good queen and the bad queen was the big carved mirror beside Adam's bed. The first test of valor was jumping back and forth over the ayah's body. Sometimes they took the cat with them as well, if he wasn't too vicious. His bony body was their secret infallible weapon, he could be thrown spitting and yowling at the enemy.

When she was twelve, Adam got *The Godfather* for her and marked all the pages with sex in them, so she didn't have to read the whole thing. She fell in love with all the boys in his class. Sometimes, he even told her what they'd said about her. Other times, he blushed and told her to shut up and stop asking. Then she knew they'd said something interesting.

Sometimes she and Adam were so close she could hear what he was thinking or feeling, before he spoke. Often, when she made a drawing, she felt like all she could sketch were Adam's ideas. Other times—lately—she felt she'd become deaf.

He used to like to come with her to the tailors when she had her salwar kameezes made. "No, put a bow there. Not too big," he'd tell the tailor. "Try this cloth."

87

The tailor would squirm, readjusting the cellophane tape on the bridge of his glasses. "But saha'ab, this is gents' fabric. This is not for ladies."

Adam would look at the completed suit and say, "Wait till they see this at your next tea party." But Alia's clothes usually saw nothing more than the library and the field hockey court. Poor Adam, his masterpieces usually came home in the evening smeared with dust and ink or spattered with mud. Oh, poor Adam, thinks Alia. What a terrible sister I am. She runs toward the village. Her legs feel like lead, they're incredibly heavy and slow, like she's running underwater. Run! she thinks. She's almost at the top of the hill now, her head spinning and her lungs throbbing. "Help!" she tries to scream, but she's too breathless. "Help!" Alia sits down on a rock fence, panting. There is no one in sight. Oh, God. She closes her eyes and starts saying prayers.

88

"What are you doing, leaving all my things down by the water?" Adam is standing above her, dripping wet, his clothes hung over his shoulder. "Somebody could have stolen my watch. I can't leave you alone for one minute." Alia stands up, tears still running down her cheeks. "Let's go and eat something," he says. "I'm starving. I met this boy farther down the beach. He's going to meet us at the pub."

After lunch, on the way to the station, Alia's bag keeps bumping against her leg as she walks. She can already feel a bruise forming. She wonders if she'll get a scar on her leg. "Bhai," she whines to Adam, "I can't carry this. You take my bag and I'll take that one."

"Come on, Alia, don't be such a baby," Adam takes her bag and hands her the smaller one. "You know, Alia, in England, girls take care of themselves. They're not always complaining about things."

"I am not complaining all the time. Why are you being so mean to me?"

"Oh, shut up, we'll miss our train." Adam thinks of Marc again. He compares him to the English boy. He imagines himself back on the beach, in a sunburned stupor, in a daze. He thinks of that long hour of lying on the rocks, the setting sun still hot on their backs and the soles of their feet, the algae cool and slippery against their stomachs. He thinks of the English boy's soft lips.

"You're just mad that Marc went to New York without you. Anyway, you'll never go to New York. Abba won't let you." Alia is practically dragging Adam's bag against the pavement. She hopes the bottom will be torn. Serves him right for being so unkind.

Adam imagines Marc in New York, like Kojak, wandering around the streets in his gray jacket. He had friends in New York, though. He probably wasn't alone, dreaming of Adam. He'd probably made friends with a long-lashed Puerto Rican boy in tight jeans, like the ones everyone had told him about in France.

"What do you mean I won't go? Of course I will if I want to." Adam stalks into the train station. "Anyway, you're a girl. How would you know what I can do? Two please," he tells the ticket seller. "First class to Victoria Station."

"First class?" Alia jabs Adam. "Why are you buying first class?" The clerk looks questioningly at Adam.

"Shut up, Alia—how much? Yes, first class, please— because if we take second class who knows who you'll have to sit next to." Adam blushes. The clerk stares at him. "Thank you. What time is the next train?"

"Don't blame me. You just want to spend all of Abba's money." They walk out onto the platform.

"Alia, do you want everyone to think you're a cheap Paki? Look, I don't want to talk to you anymore if you're going to be so rude to me. I'm your older brother, remember?" The train pulls into the station with a rush of air.

"I don't care. All you talk about is Marc, anyway. Why should I care if I never hear about him again. Where is our compartment?"

"Just follow me and don't get lost," Adam says, stepping onto the train.

"Oh, it's so beautiful," says Alia, as Adam slides open the door to their compartment. They sit on the green velveteen seats. Alia switches the reading light on and off. She puts her fashion magazines down on the little table. "Adam bhai, let me sit on that side for a minute and you sit on this side. Do you think you get a better view if you're facing the same way you're going? What lovely windows. And look at these little curtains." She bounces on her seat a bit, trying to get the train to start moving. A middle-aged businessman enters their compartment.

"Alia, sit still," says Adam, carefully. The businessman sits beside him.

"Shall we buy a drink?" asks Alia. "I'm sure you can buy drinks on this train. Let's get a Coke."

Adam is leafing through *Le Monde*. "Perhaps in a little while, Alia," he says, with a slight French accent.

"Oh, you're reading in French. That's really good. I can speak French now, too."

Adam looks at the businessman out of the corner of his eye. The businessman doesn't lift his eyes from his newspaper. "Of course," says Adam. "How could I live in Paris and not read the newspaper?" He sits up straighter in his seat and turns the pages.

The businessman is like a wax figure at Madame Tussaud's, thinks Alia. "How long is the trip to London?"

"Listen, will you be quiet if I buy you a Coke?"

"And some chocolates."

"D'accord," says Adam.

In the corridor, he pinches Alia. "What's the matter with you? That man will think you're a shopowner's daughter. A bhajiwallah or something."

"Why would he think that? I ironed my salwar this morning."

"Because the English think all Indians and Pakistanis are cheap and dirty, like the shopkeepers."

"We are not! They're much dirtier than we are."

"Of course they're dirty. Haven't you seen the way the Asians live? Europeans are much cleaner than that."

"What do you mean 'they'? You're also an Indian."

"I'm practically French now. I've been away for a long time, you know. How can I be expected to think of myself as an Asian? Which kind of chocolates do you want?"

The cool, gray London air envelops them as they reach the outskirts of the city. Alia flips through her fashion magazines. In this light, the photographs look luminescent. They are like candy, beautiful and delicious. Alia wants to climb into them. Adam is talking to the businessman. He has also turned out to be a banker. Alia looks up from time to time, but mostly she imagines herself as one of the models. As she looks at each picture, her face molds itself into those expressions.

Alia's eyes start to feel red and dry. Her eyelids clap shut every time they go over a bump. Adam is deep in conversation with the businessman.

"Alia, wake up. We have two more stops," says Adam. Alia opens her eyes and the last of the green landscape has metamorphosed into a gray geometry.

"We're in London." Alia looks around sleepily. The businessman is gone. She and Adam are alone in the car. "I want some tea," she whines.

"Listen, Alia. Jonathan just told me that I can go straight to the airport from Victoria Station."

"Jonathan?"

"Marc and I bought tickets before you came to London. I've already got my things here, all packed. I can go straight to the airport and catch a flight tonight."

"To New York? Abba won't let you," she warns.

"Of course to New York, where else? I could stay with Marc's friends. And Abba doesn't *have* to let me."

"But what will you do there? Shouldn't you telephone first?"

"Marc must have organized things already. He must be waiting for me. Maybe you should telephone to say I'm coming. I'll buy you a phonecard in Victoria Station."

"But what will you tell Umma and Abba? How can I go home by myself?"

"You can do it, Alia. Come on, you're in England now, you can take care of yourself here, like English girls do. Just think of a story to tell Abba so that he won't come to the airport and drag me back. Come on, Alia, I've helped you out before. I've got to go. I have to, really, before it's too late." Perhaps Marc had already fallen in love with someone else, a street kid with a baseball hat and bicycle shorts. Perhaps Marc is sitting in a restaurant right now telling another boy the same things he'd said to Adam. Perhaps it's too late already.

"How can I do that? How can I? Don't you think they'll ask? As soon as the door shuts, they'll say, 'Where's Adam?' And then?" Alia is jittery with fear again.

"Say I've gone to meet a friend. That's not really a lie, is it? Say I've gone to meet a friend and I'll be back soon."

"Which friend? I don't know any of your friends." Her arms and legs feel paralyzed.

"Make one up. Don't you have any imagination at all?"

"Victoria Station," crackle the loud speakers through the train. Passengers in the neighboring compartments start heaving their suitcases down from the overhead racks. "Victoria Station, London."

Down from the
Gardens of Asia

SABAH'S NECK ached. Somewhere over Japan, she realized she had made a terrible mistake. Why the hell was she going to India? She must have gotten too carried away reading *Kim*. Beside her, a tiny, wrinkled woman in an equally wrinkled white salwar kameez was snoring and beginning to lean on her shoulder. She smelled of ithar perfume and mustard oil. Sabah realized the woman had oil in her hair, and she worried about the stain it was probably going to make on her shirt. The movie was an American teen romance, love among the lockers. Sabah was suddenly overcome with nostalgia for her American youth. I'm an American, she thought. American, not Indian. She felt no relationship at all to the immigrants packed into economy class with her, all wearing Indian clothes and smelling of sweat and spices. Four hours to Delhi. Her parents thought she should get to know the rest of her family; her mother insisted she be on the lookout for a husband. Her mother thought Rani might set a good example.

Sabah looked at the men around her, mostly workers on their way home with crates of video machines and tape recorders. There were a couple of displaced young men in pseudopunk haircuts and studded leather jackets. A Sikh with a denim turban and matching Levi's jacket was playing with his food tray and on his sixth pack of Marlboros. It's too late, she thought, this is not the adventure I wanted. All she wanted was to go back to California.

ONE WEEK, five thousand miles, and light years later, walking down the long air-conditioned hall of the Taj Hotel, Sabah stepped into the gift shop. It was so hot outside even the swimming pool wasn't appealing. A layer of tiny drowned insects and suntan oil covered the surface. Fleshy foreign tourists lay in plastic chairs, their skin red and blistered. Sanjay was late for their lunch date. Sabah wasn't surprised; even in San Francisco, he was always on Indian time. She just wondered how late. She was getting tired of waiting for everyone in India. Rani still hadn't managed to return her phone calls.

"Hello, Madam, can I help you?" the Kashmiri rose to his feet, his gray-blue eyes like thunderclouds on his pale face.

"How much is the silk kurta?" She wasn't supposed to be looking at things for Rob, she reminded herself. Anyway, she'd won her bet with him; he had even mailed her five dollars and written what he thought was a poetic description of his new girlfriend—without mentioning her name—in his last letter. But she couldn't help thinking how the silk would shimmer across his suntanned chest.

"That is a gent's kurta, Madam. We also have ladies'."

"I know it's for men, but how much is it?"

The Kashmiri was already shuffling through heaps of silk kurtas, throwing one after another aside. "Madam, you know, this is not a very good one. Let me show you top quality, only six hundred rupees."

"No, that's OK. I'll take that one." Sabah dropped some money on the table, probably too much, and grabbed the shirt. She walked toward the door.

"You are English, Madam? That is a very nice shirt you are wearing. Very nice. It is English?" The Kashmiri came over and slid his fingers through the buttons on her T-shirt, he stroked the skin across her sternum. His fingers twitched over her breast like lizards' tails. "Very nice cloth. You can't find this kind of shirt in India." He smiled at Sabah.

Sabah jumped. What a shock. She wasn't even sure if she'd imagined the whole thing. Had he really wanted to feel the shirt? "It's made in India," she said, half falling backward. "You can get them everywhere, on Janpath—my *friend* is waiting for me. Bye." Sabah stumbled out into the hall, trying to look composed.

The Kashmiri's gray eyes followed her, "Come back soon. Nice Angrezi girl..."

She met Sanjay outside, as he was getting out of his car. Somehow, even Sanjay, his usual old self, wasn't reassuring. "Wait," she told him, trying to get into the passenger seat. "Let's go somewhere else."

The valet, a huge man topped with a massive gold-trimmed turban, stood impatiently by the door. "Parking, sir?" he asked.

"What are you talking about? I've just come," said Sanjay, half in and half out of the Ambassador. "This was your idea to come to the Taj."

"It's terrible," said Sabah sheepishly. "I made a mistake. You were right. Let's leave." She's losing her edge.

"Oh, come on," said Sanjay. "Don't be silly. We might as well eat while we're here." He stands up with his foot on the running board and grins at Sabah. In his loose linen suits and his round glasses, he looked like a character from the forties. As if he'd had just stepped out of the frame of a yellowing black-and-white snapshot, an awkward smile on his face. The only thing typically Indian about him was the color of his skin.

A second valet rushed to Sabah's door. "Actually, the coffee shop's not so bad. It's just so boring now. And I know the menu by heart. And *everyone's* there."

IT TAKES SABAH ages to get over her jet lag. She almost falls face down into her plate at dinner, like a character in a sitcom, while her aunt and uncle's faces blur and their voices hum around her head like background music. Then, at four or five in the morning, she finds herself wide awake. Her eyes refuse to submit to another second of dreamtime, while outside it's still dark, still night. The light from the street lamps is white and sparkling, not yet turned to the dull yellow of daylight. The bells and cries of the junkmen, calling for old bottles and plastic bags, are rough and cracking, fresh from sleep. Night birds, vultures, and bats, are squawking and fluttering through the air. In the alley between the houses, cats yowl and fight.

After the endless morning that had bound her in anticipation, constantly alert for the tiniest sign that the household might be stirring, Sabah resolved to put her time to good use. Since then, she's been getting up and dressing, then slipping out to the Taj Hotel swimming pool. The chowkidars, barely awake themselves, rub their eyes and call a car for her.

The taxi rattles down the road, the seats puffing out clouds of incense each time she bounces on the cushions. The driver's chosen deity on the dashboard is slightly suntanned from the smoke of the morning's puja, stained with orange marigold flowers. It's cool and damp in the morning. Even wearing jeans and a cardigan, she shivers. The untrustworthy dawn seems to promise to stay the long hot day ahead.

At the hotel, Sabah puts on her best neocolonial atti-
tude and stalks like a European past the guards. Despite her
initial nervousness, they don't even check her room number,
they just say, "Good morning, Madam," and hand her a fresh
blue-and-white striped towel.

At this time of day, the pool is deserted. The water,
having just been skimmed of bugs and floating debris, is
motionless and greenish blue like plastic. Sabah dives in,
breaking the cellophane surface first with her fingers, then
her forehead. The water rushes past her ears, hits her rib cage
with a shock. By the time it reaches her feet, she no longer
feels anything but the ache and stretch of her muscles as they
begin to fill with blood and sugar.

She has to swim laps diagonally because the pool is
short and shaped to look like a pond. At each end, she grips
the rim to reorient herself. She tries to keep from touching
the inside of the pool because the tiles are coated with a green
slime. Once she used the wall to push off and her legs slipped
sideways, leaving her shuddering and out of control like car
tires in mud. But she recovered and forced herself to swim the
usual half mile, or what she thought to be that distance.

She likes the rhythmic sound of each arm as it lifts
out of the water and then scoops back in. She likes the feeling
of her legs pumping up and down and her shoulder blades
spinning like machinery. She is deafened by her own body.
The thoughts that wash through her brain are limited to her
own reflections: her last few hours with Rob, the taste of an
ice-cream cone when she was ten or eleven, a painting her
mother did of an Indian girl reading in the patterned shadow
of a carved screen, Sanjay, Rani, and her husband. Nothing
else intrudes.

When Sabah gets out of the pool, her skin is hot and
prickly with chlorine and chemicals. The water dripping
down her forehead is warm and salty as it reaches her lips. She
wipes her face and wrings out her hair. Then she wraps the

99

towel around herself, conscious of the hungry eyes of the guards. They congratulate her as she walks to the changing room. "Well done, Madam," they smile. "How many times today?" She's thankful for the darkness and silence of the marble room, still dazed from her underwater reveries and not yet ready to enter reality.

No one's ever awake when she returns to the house. Sabah releases the door so that it eases noiselessly back into its frame. She takes off her shoes and pads silently back to her room. Inside, she pulls off her T-shirt and drops it on the floor. She lets her jeans fall around her ankles and steps out of them, first letting her feet glide over the cloth, enjoying the warmth and texture on the soles of her feet before they touch the cold stone floor again. Naked, she gets into bed, the sheets cool and soothing against her swollen skin. They billow and then relax around her body. She falls asleep while her wet hair soaks through the cover of the pillow. There are two hours until breakfast.

"LET'S SIT DOWN, everyone." Tiny flashes of light spark off the crystal and china. "Sabah, you're here, next to Sanjay. I hope he's interesting enough." Mahinder pulls Sabah's chair out for her with one hand, and with the other he tosses his shock of movie-star hair off his face. The top three buttons of his shirt are open, revealing several gold necklaces cushioned in a nest of curly black hair. The boys stand around, twirling the ice cubes in their scotch, looking on amusedly at his orchestrations. But, for Sabah, the real center of attention is Rani. Sabah keeps staring at her, she can't believe how beautiful she is. Rani's only slightly taller than Sabah, but she seems about a foot higher, almost architectural, all lean, graceful lines. Her long neck rises out of the plane of her shoulders like a Corinthian column, topped by a froth of black ringlets of hair pinned up at the nape. In the drape of her sari, she looks more like a gleaming coffee-colored Athena than a buxom upsara.

"He's so good-looking," Rani laughs, her eyes a flash of clear white and brown, and Sabah can't help smiling herself, pleased that Rani's explosive laugh hasn't been transformed into a demure, Indian wifely one. "You can't expect him to be interesting, too, that's not fair."

Sabah shivers as she sits down. It's her first real Indian dinner party. As Sanjay steered the car through the chaotic nighttime traffic, Rani whispered that Sabah's success tonight would be a guarantee of a fabulous future social life. Sabah's unruly brown hair is pinned up too—with Rani's frantic last-minute assistance—and she can feel a blast of cold air on the back of her neck. "Aren't you freezing?" she asks Sanjay.

He passes her the butter plate. The pats of butter are hard and crumbly. "Of course not, I love it. We're lucky to be here. It's forty-three degrees—that's about a hundred farenheit—outside. You should absorb all the cold air you can." He leans over and helps himself to most of the butter on the plate, his neck straining against his stiff collar. His starched shirt looks exactly like the napkins.

"Nice shirt," says Sabah.

"Isn't it fab?" says Sanjay. "It's by that new designer. He had them made up from tablecloths. And they're selling like that," he snaps his fingers. "I can't tell you."

"Listen, Mahinder, it's really cold, can I have a shawl?" asks Rani. She's wrapped the end of her sari around her shoulders. She smiles conspiratorially at Sabah. Sabah imagines running her fingers along the lines of Rani's perfect collarbone. "And can you get one for Sabah, too? She's very politely freezing. She doesn't dare to ask for one." Sabah can almost feel her awkward American fingers scraping across Rani's smooth skin. She winks at her.

Sanjay helps Sabah put the shawl on. She hasn't got the knack of all these huge pieces of cloth yet. She's relieved.

101

She should have known she could count on Rani. A plate of yellow soup appears in front of her. "What kind of soup is this?" she whispers to Sanjay.

"Mulligatawny—that's Angrezi for dal soup," Sanjay laughs. "What kind of bakwass is this? If you're going to give us dal, give it to us properly. Not all full of water. Give this to that little Frenchie, who can't tell the difference. Thank God he's gone back to work for that bank in Paris."

"Speaking of which," laughs another boy, "did you hear about Marc's midnight drives?"

"What? What?" says Rani, bouncing in her chair. "Tell us!"

"Don't be silly!" interrupts Mahinder, a pained look on his face. "Anyway, it's so mean to talk about him once he's gone."

"This servant—a little boy, really—was saying that the French saha'ab paid them to go for rides in his car at night—"

"God, what a scandal!" laughs Rani. "And then?"

"Rani, how can you ask? Anyway, it was all so vague," says Sanjay. "Servants love to make up all kinds of stories. Someone told them that if you have a 'de' in your name, you're some sort of royalty, so now they can't bear not deifying on him..."

"How much does he pay them?" giggles Rani, her soup spoon slipping into her bowl with a little splash. "That's how we'll know what they actually have to do."

"That's completely useless evidence, the little prince paid five hundred rupees to take a scooter rickshaw to the airport."

"So what does that make him? The Rajah of cupboards and wardrobes? Listen, did you hear he's got a *'petit Indien'* in Paris now? Some film star's son..."

"Who?"

"Oh, really, you all," says Mahinder. "You're horrid. None of you have any manners. Sabah, I hope you're going to be a good influence on them." His upper-class Indian accent sounds like a thin coat of paint over rusted metal, it keeps flaking away and his harsh, mangled English breaking through.

"Don't look at me," says Sabah. "I'm really badly brought up." Mahinder's voice makes her squirm. She looks back at Rani, an elbow denting the smooth tablecloth and the hand stretched open to Sanjay.

"Everyone knows Americans have no manners," says Sanjay. "How rude of you to expect her to have any, Mahinder. Anyway, all scientists know that social rules are Darwinian ones. And I'm starving, so I may be the first to go." He opens his silver cigarette case and hands it around. "Anyone?" He drops one on Rani's palm. Mahinder jumps to Rani's side to light it. Sanjay lights his own.

"I don't know what's wrong with you all," complains Mahinder, his hair flopping back into his face. "I try to do an elegant dinner party, for once, with just Indians, and you're all being so badly behaved. Well, I'm not going to let you spoil it. Here, do you want some wine?" When Mahinder says wine, the *W*s become *V*s.

Cheers go up from the table. "Wine? Where did you get wine?" asks Sanjay. "I've been trying to get some for weeks." The bottle is poured generously into all the glasses.

"Someone told me that they're making an Indian wine now that's supposed to be as good as a European wine," says Rani. "They've imported the grapevines and everything. They're in some place that has the same climate as some part of France, except that our growing season is much longer."

"It's not polite to get so technical while people are eating," says one of the boys. "Where can you get this stuff?"

"Nowhere, of course," says Sanjay. "It's for export only, just like everything else we make in this country."

"Next thing you know we'll be getting rid of the girls, too," says Mahinder, smiling at Sabah. "How sad. All our

103

beautiful Indian girls will leave, and we'll have to make do with boys," he winks.

"The girls?" says Rani. "The girls are going to be stuck here. The boys have been leaving for years. Why do you think Sabah's father works in America? The only chance for the girls in this country is for them to get out. Sabah, for God's sake, don't you ever marry an Indian!"

"Rani's had quite a bad time," Mahinder leans toward Sabah, murmuring, his warm breath brushing her ear. "Don't take it too seriously."

"Rani, face it. Nothing is better anywhere else," nods Sanjay. He grins, "Let me tell you about this party I went to in London last week…"

The Land of Kings

SABAH WATCHES the heat ripple over the rows of cars parked in front of the rosebushes. It's only slightly cooler where she's sitting, in the shade of the red stone overhang at the entrance. She imagines the hotel as a palace again, herself as a graceful Rajasthani princess, swathed in diaphanous layers, peeking out through the stone latticework at the arriving guests. There's the clop of hoofbeats as turbaned men throw themselves off stamping horses, laughing and slapping each other on the back while the horses are led away, swords glistening at the noblemen's waists. And then the jeweled fingers pushing aside the embroidered curtains of palanquins. Women stepping carefully out, a hand draped for stability over the arm of a servant, slippered feet touching down on the red stone, eyes lowered beneath the transparent dupattas. Sabah had read that the Rajput princes kept their women in purdah.

No wonder, she thinks. Even Rajasthani rickshaw drivers have sculpted features, sharp Aryan noses and carved cheek bones, mustaches curving up like smiles on their golden faces. And when they laugh, she can see their straight white teeth. Muscles ripple through the brown skin on their arms and legs. Sabah can imagine a princess's revulsion at the soft touch of a pasty white prince, damp between his rolls of fat.

Sabah's plopped herself and their bags down on the red carpeted stairs. She coughs and swallows, trying to clear the dusty desert air from her lungs.

A group of tourists in baggy Indian-print clothes troop past, staring at her—half expecting her to beg for change, she thinks. She just another sneaky, starving Indian— cameras bobbing on the tourists' sweat-soaked stomachs as they board their dee-lux video coach. A loud caterwaul comes from the garden and they all start jumping off the bus, snapping off their camera cases with their pink fingers, pointing and shouting. In the middle of the lawn, a male peacock jumps onto the edge of the fountain and fans open his tail feathers for a crowd of hens. The females ignore him and peck around in the grass. The tourists whoop. A stunning Rajasthani man, case in point, wearing unfortunate trousers that stretch skintight around his bottom, flairing into wide bells over his platform shoes, steps slowly out of the bus. Modern Indian fashion.

105

"Please, please, ladies and gents," advises the guide, "do not shout. You will frighten them. These were once the pets of the Maharaj of Jaipur. Like some people have parrots, the Maharaj of Jaipur liked peacock. The new Maharaj of Jaipur, his grandson, is still living in this city with his family," he adds, proudly.

The tourists nod and sigh appreciatively, dreaming of the Maharajah and his Mahareeni watching their peacocks from the balcony, while the tour guide checks out Sabah. Then he hurries his flock back on their air-conditioned bus. They drag their heavy legs up the stairs and pull their floppy hats off their wet foreheads.

Sabah looks down at the white salwar pants she put on at dawn today instead of her jeans, before she got the train, third-class-unreserved, from Delhi. They're now covered with tea stains and gray with train soot, every crease smeared black as if drawn on with charcoal. It's eleven o'clock, and the cool morning breezes have long since been replaced by the mounting midday heat. After fighting her way through a ferocious crowd to the front of the ladies queue in the bus station, only to watch the last tickets be handed over to someone who bribed the ticket seller, she's beginning to think it was a bad idea to take a day trip to Jaipur at the last minute. At least now she knows why Rani started laughing when they suggested she come along.

106

"Sabah, just see how you're looking!" Sanjay laughs as he walks through the brass doors, the doormen holding them open reluctantly.

Sabah cracks her sunburned face into a smile, "Look at yourself!" He is as filthy as she is, but he'd been smart enough to wear gray from the start. Anyway, she already knows what her face looks like. When she'd washed a bit in the hotel bathroom, she'd left a soot imprint of her hands and face on the white towel. It looked like the shroud of Turin.

"You'll never guess who I met in the hotel. One of your aunt's friends—the foreign minister's wife, Maya. She's going to give us a ride back to Delhi in her van!"

"Good job. I'm starving. I wonder if we'll miss dinner."

"They're going over to the city palace first, do you want to go with them? Otherwise, they'll come back and get us afterward."

"No," says Sabah. "Let's have ice cream at the coffee shop. I'm not into old guns and swords and hunting knives anyway." The thought of heaving her backpack down the hot, airless hallways of the museum is not appealing.

"Ice cream? Why not?" says Sanjay. The soot agrees with him. Rather than looking bedraggled and bad tempered from sitting for seven hours cramped together on a wooden bench, he looks like an archaeologist on a dig. That forties-screen-idol look again. He hoists both bags onto his shoulders. "But we've got to be back out here at eleven sharp, because they're late already."

After an hour of playing with the hotel matchbook, opening and closing their menus, and shaking the sand out of their socks and shoes, they give up waiting for their ice cream to arrive. "I'm so hungry," says Sabah, sitting on the stairs again, "my stomach's growling. You know, I didn't have dinner last night either."

"Well, we'd better stay here because they'll leave if they have to wait."

The van finally pulls into the entrance way an hour and a half later. The driver holds the door open for them. "Madam is waiting for you at the city palace," he tells Sanjay.

They climb inside, Sabah whispering to Sanjay, "Can we ask him to stop for bananas or something? For one second?"

"Don't be stupid, Sabah, they're in a rush."

The van drives through the gates of the city palace and stops at the far edge of the courtyard. A bearer in a white-and-gold uniform pushes aside a curtain in the wall and opens the door of the van. "Please," he gestures, bowing slightly.

"Oh, my God," says Sanjay.

"What?" asks Sabah. "What does he want?"

"He wants us to go into the palace."

"No way," says Sabah. "There's no way I'm going to meet the Maharajah of Jaipur in a bunyaan. I'll go buy some bananas."

"That would be rude. Come on," Sanjay jumps out of the van. He looks back at Sabah, "I can't go in without you." Sabah gets out hesitantly, and the two of them follow the servant up the wide ramp to the royal quarters.

"I can't believe I'm doing this. How embarrassing."

"Do you know why they made these entrance ways like this? For the elephants to climb up. So the princesses wouldn't have to go outside to get on."

They walk into a cavernous room, crystal chandeliers alternating with ceiling fans hanging from the arched ceilings. A covered balcony runs the length of one side of the room, overlooking the river. The Maharajah and his wife sit on brocade sofas, sipping iced drinks, while Sabah's aunt's friend, Maya, is chatting with them and a group of Englishmen in white linen suits. "Playing the Raj to the hilt," whispers Sanjay.

"This could be a bowling alley," answers Sabah. "You could play four games of basketball at the same time."

"The game is to guess who's sleeping with whom," Sanjay whispers back. "I already know two of the Maharajah's mistresses—Air India stewardesses—first-class."

"You're just in time for lunch," says Maya, winking at them.

"Yes, come, come," encourages the Maharani, standing up and floating across the Oriental carpets toward the endless table. She stops to touch the hand of one of the blond Englishmen, who leaps athletically to his feet. "Come." The Maharajah follows them and takes his seat at the head.

"No, really, we can't," protests Sabah. "I mean, we just show up at meal time. And how can we sit down at the table, covered with dirt?" Her mouth is watering and she wonders whether they can all hear the loud rumble of her stomach.

"We ate at the hotel," agrees Sanjay, looking longingly at the plates heaped with glistening fruit and sweets running the length of the white tablecloth.

"Of course not, don't be silly," says Maya, not commenting on their appearance. "You must eat. We've been waiting for you. Do you want to wash up a little?" She points to a bearer standing at the far end of the table, a silver pitcher in one hand, a folded towel over his arm.

Sabah walks toward him. He stands beside a large silver basin, its sieve top covered with a layer of pink rose petals. Sabah holds out her hands and the bearer pours the scented water over them into the rose petals. He hands her the towel. "Wow," says Sabah. "How cool."

"Sabah, your American upbringing is showing," says Sanjay, washing his own hands the same way, but Sabah's already marveling at all the little metal dishes around each platter. "That's a thali," he explains. "You put the dal in one katchori, the subzi in another. Rani would be totally shocked that you don't—"

"If they're royalty," whispers Sabah to Sanjay as they sit down, "why do they eat on tin plates?"

"They're not tin, you idiot. They're sterling silver."

"Sabah," calls her aunt's friend from a distant region of the table, "this is Gitangeli Jaipur."

A plump eighteen-year-old girl pulls out the chair beside Sabah and Sanjay. She sits down and opens the napkin on her lap. "Hi," Sabah says to her, "I'm Sabah and this is Sanjay."

"Hello," she says, looking sullenly at their blackened clothes.

"I don't—we don't always look like this, really. I swear," apologizes Sabah, unfolding her napkin on her lap and dropping it to the floor. She bends down to pick it up and knocks her spoon and knife down as well. Sabah kneels under the table, looking for her silverware. A row of legs away, she sees a thin leg poke out from under a sari. The toes, like claws, climb up a trousered leg on the other side. A manicured white hand appears to receive it. Sabah jumps up, banging her head on the edge of the table. As she emerges from under the tablecloth, she finds her head inches away

109

from a gleaming silver platter, red liquid dripping danger-ously toward her face. "What's that?" The bearer steps back and stands beside her chair with a plate, of potato curry. Sabah ladles it on to her plate and another bearer appears in his place with tandoori chicken. "It's just that we traveled all day on the train and—oh, wait, can I have some more of that rice—God, and I'm starving. This is really good . . ."

"Have some more," says the princess, stretching lan-guidly in her chair. "I just can't eat anything in this heat."

"Sabah, for God's sake," says Sanjay.

"OK," says Sabah, "can I have some of the eggplant? Are you in school?"

"Aubergine. Stop it now," Sanjay hisses.

"I was in boarding school, but I just finished my A levels. So I've come home," she says apathetically. "Are you American or Indian?"

"Totally American," says Sanjay.

"Well—everyone asks that, it's sort of confusing—I'm Indian, but I'm from America. I was born there. Yes, please," Sabah puts her glass down so the bearer can fill it with more lime and soda. "What are you doing home? I mean, what is there to do in Jaipur?"

"Nothing," says the princess, looking at her Swatch.

"What do you do all day?" asks Sanjay.

"I've been learning painting."

"Sorry?" Sanjay's wide brown eyes get even wider.

"A teacher's been coming to teach me miniature painting."

"Every day?" asks Sabah.

"No, one or two days a week. Will you have some sweets?" She passes a cut-glass tray of chocolates to Sabah. "The rest of the time I sit at home. I don't have very many friends near here. I suppose one could go riding . . ."

"Chocolates! I thought you couldn't get any in India," Sabah takes one off the tray and bites into it. "Is this caramel?

Oh, I don't want caramel. Sanjay, will you eat this? I really want one with nuts." She picks up two or three more.

"You can take them with you," smiles the princess. "My father brings them from abroad. Here, do you want some of these jelly-gum things? They're supposed to be very nice. And try the marzipan."

"Thanks," says Sabah. "Listen, why don't you come with us? You could have a great time in Delhi. If you're not doing anything here..."

"I've never been to Delhi alone before..." The princess hesitates, winding a lock of her hair around her finger.

"Don't worry," Sanjay assures her. "It's very civilized. And there are amazing parties. Come along, it'll be good fun."

"I'll have to ask my mother," the princess says, gloomily. She drops her hair and splashes the water in her fingerbowl.

"Come on, kids," says Maya. "We're having coffee over here." She drifts back to her previous seat, walking arm-in-arm with the Maharajah, the two of them murmuring to each other in low voices. She stops, halfway across the room, remembering them, "Sabah, do you want to have your palm read? Balraj is excellent."

"Yes, come," says the princess. "He's very good. And then I'll show you the rest of the place. Do you want to see it?"

"I'd love to," says Sanjay.

A small South Indian man with horn-rimmed glasses sits reading on a sofa on the far side of the room. As Sabah walks toward him, he quickly closes his book and stands at attention, folding his glasses and putting them in his breast pocket. "Hello, hello," he says. "Please sit down. You would like to have your hand read?" He looks at Sanjay and Gitangeli, standing there expectantly. "It will take some time, you know."

"Leave it, Sabah," says Sanjay. "Let's see the house."

"I've always wanted to have my palm read. You guys

go and see it. I'll come when I'm finished," says Sabah, settling down on the sofa and hoping her hand is not so dirty as to make it illegible.

"A lot of intelligence, here, see," says Balraj, holding her hand and following the line with his finger. "Very creative. You are an artist. And here is marriage, here," he squeezes her hand and turns it sideways. "You will have two, three sons, and you will get married."

"My mother will be thrilled," sighs Sabah.

"Twice."

"She'll die."

"Or maybe three times. It is not clear."

"She'll kill me."

"There are many men in your life. Someone who loves you...a foreigner. You don't trust him."

Sabah sees Rob sitting at the kitchen table, the cat drinking out of the cup of coffee in his hand, while he watches her pack, looking sad and lost. She concentrates on Balraj's smooth forehead, the thin strands of black hair on his shiny scalp.

"There is another one who loves you, but you don't see it. He is a friend. An Indian. Neither of these will you marry."

"Who?" asks Sabah, but she knows the answer to that one, too.

Balraj studies her hand and his face becomes serious. "And there is a girl, a beautiful queen—" He looks up at Sabah's face and then back at her hand. "Rani ..."

"Rani?"

"I see a very big tragedy here."

"What? What tragedy?"

"Terrible. Something very difficult. Be careful. Be very careful of your friends..."

"What do you mean?" Sabah pales. "What about Rani? Tell me!"

Balraj lets go of her hand. "No, it is not clear." He moves over slightly and picks up his book. He resumes reading.

"What is that?"

"This? It is Dickens. *Bleak House*. I prefer to read only the classics. I read English honors at university."

"*Bleak House*? What about my hand?" Sabah can hear laughter and bits of conversation drifting over from the other seating area. She looks over to see the Englishman's eyes locked with the Maharani's.

"I cannot read anymore." He goes back to his book.

"Look, if something terrible is about to happen and you know about it, it's unfair of you not to tell me..."

"Sabah, do you want some coffee?" asks Gitangeli. "If you're staying for a little while, we could watch some videos. I just got the new *Top of the Pops* from a friend in London."

"Sabah, you will not believe it. This place is too fab. There are Lalique Crystal chairs. And the paintings downstairs, two impressionists...," raves Sanjay.

"He won't tell me the rest of my fortune."

"Sabah, you know a palm reader can really only tell you honestly about your past. For your future, he can tell you what might happen, but it's up to you to make it happen, or to change it," says Gitangeli. "Sometimes, even talking about something isn't good because then you might make it happen rather than avoid it." Balraj nods in agreement without raising his head.

"I just want to know. All right, forget it. He's just a palm reader. Let's go ask your mother if you can come with us."

"Sabah," whispers Sanjay, as he hands her a cup of coffee. "You should see her room, she has every single fashion magazine from Europe, the latest ones. And a CD player and a massive television. And they have a free telephone line. You can call long distance to any place in the world. I just called all my friends in London. And just look at the bathroom..."

113

"I wonder if there are any more sweets on the table," says Sabah, looking off toward the table. She looks back at the Maharani. The Maharani of Jaipur is posed perfectly for a portrait of a queen: her silk sari draped gracefully around her shoulders, one elbow resting on the arm of her Louis XIV chair, her face, as it turns toward Sabah, calm and radiant. "Auntie," says Sabah hesitantly, "can Gitangeli come with us to Delhi? I'm sure she'd have a really nice time. We have lots of extra space."

The Maharani's gaze sweeps quickly over Sabah's disheveled clothes. "No, I'm sorry," she says as she turns back to her Englishman. Gitangeli looks away. "Gitangeli has to stay here."

"It would be no problem, really. She can stay with me at my aunt's house."

The Maharani continues flirting and ignores her. The Maharajah stands up and slaps his leg loudly with his riding crop. "Cheerio!" he says. "Have a lovely time." He puts on his riding cap and strides out of the room, his boots clacking against the floor.

"Forget it, Sabah," murmurs Sanjay. "She's not allowed to go anywhere. She can't leave the palace, poor thing."

As they leave, the Maharani and two of the Englishmen follow them down the ramp to their van. Gitangeli, with a sulky look on her face, has disappeared. The Maharani kisses Maya goodbye, the translucent green beads dangling from her ears and around her neck sparkle in the light, like wet leaves. One of the Englishmen stumbles on a loose stone, and the other one says, "Be careful, dear. I *told* you to wear your glasses today. All this sand is terrible for your contact lenses," and helps him up.

"Must you always nag me," complains the other, pulling himself free and brushing off his trousers.

"Even I figured out that one," Sanjay says, under his breath. Sabah climbs into the van, and he hands her a napkin full of sweets. "Gitangeli packed this up for you, so you wouldn't starve on the journey." He gets into the front seat beside the driver and puts a rap music tape in the deck. "Gitangeli gave me this, too. The latest one."

"Poor girl. What a drag to be stuck in there," Sabah rolls up her window as the air conditioning starts to take effect. "For a Maharani, she doesn't have very good taste—except in men—those glass beads. They look like pieces of an Italian chandelier."

"You twit, those are emeralds! Rani's really going to be sorry she couldn't come. Poor thing, all alone with her in-laws!"

Delhi

"ARRANGED MARRIAGES are so much more intelligent," says Sanjay, turning on the cassette player. "Sabah, can you give me the tape that's in the glove box?" He clicks the tape into the machine and rolls down the window. "How stupid you Americans are, going around marrying the first person you fall in love with." He pushes his straw hat back with the tip of his finger. "The love wears off, and then you're poor, you detest the person, and you've got nothing in common with him."

Sabah slides her feet out of her chappals and puts them up on the dashboard. "All right, an arranged marriage is logical; love is absurd. But what about bride burnings, you know, dowry deaths? What about monogamy?"

"Don't be silly. With people like us—once you're married—after a decent time, you do what you want. Look at your aunt and uncle," Sanjay says.

"Look at what?"

Sanjay steps on the accelerator as the traffic light changes to red. He waves at the policeman standing in the middle of the traffic circle. "Did you know Mahinder's father is the new chief of the Delhi police?"

"I've only kissed one Indian in my life."

115

"Sabah, look, there are some people you sleep with and some people you marry. They're two separate things."

"You're right, people get lust and love confused." She imagines Rob's face, flushed with excitement, his eyes closing, his wet mouth dropping open. Despite the heat, she shivers, swallows, feels those goose bumps again.

"Do you have any money?" Sanjay slows down at the corner and puts some change in the palms of the children crowding up to the window. They dance around and point at Sabah, giggling and holding out their hands. A little girl pokes her head in Sabah's window. *"No papa no mama no mangiano bambino,"* she laughs.

"That was Italian?" Sabah marvels. The little girl's naughty face is streaked with dirt. Her hair is orangy brown from malnutrition. Sabah scrabbles around for some sweets in her bag. She drops them in the little wrinkled hands.

"Don't touch them, Sabah! They're full of germs," Sanjay warns. "There are a lot of Italian diplomats in this neighborhood. At the Taj Mahal these days, all the little urchins speak Japanese." He lights a cigarette, steering the car with one hand and gesturing with his cigarette in the other. "I know this one woman, she told her husband she was having an affair. Just outright told him. Very cool woman. She said, I don't want a divorce, this is a perfectly good marriage. She said, why should my children have a broken home? I love you, but I want to sleep with someone else. I mean, everyone has affairs. It's only the middle class that has bride burnings and dowry deaths or gets all moral. Those people in the villages are all happily doing *everything*. And people like us don't worry about hell or being reborn as an insect. Anyway, you don't have to worry about finding a husband. That's your parents' job. All you have to do is be discreet. That's where Rani's not doing it properly."

"Not properly? She's perfect."

"You know, flirting around and going out alone all over the place and shouting up and down about her husband everywhere."

"What's wrong with going out alone? I go out alone." A hot gust of air burns Sabah's feet. She jumps, "Ow! Turn off the heat, for God's sake! It's boiling outside."

"This is an Ambassador, Sabah, not a foreign A.C. gaddi. That's the cooling vent for the engine. If you turn it off, smoke starts coming out of the hood."

"SABAH, YOU haven't said hello to Sanjay." Sabah turns around and there's Sanjay, sitting on the sofa, wearing the same sunglasses he wore last summer in San Francisco. They are round and black, very black, she can't see his eyes at all. He smiles. His teeth are a white crescent moon on his brown face. Sabah is sitting on the sofa across from him, and they're talking about something that only they know about, a secret. Sabah looks at Sanjay's eyes, but all she sees is his skin. His skin. His face suddenly becomes huge, and his skin, it is no longer skin anymore, it is a mass of sores, of round, bleeding holes, there is barely any skin between them. "Sanjay's caught an awful disease," someone's whispering in her ear. "He's being very brave about it, though, isn't he?" Sabah moves away from the voice and closer to Sanjay. He's her best friend, she loves him, how can she listen to people talk about him? But she's looking at his face, at his neck, at his hands. She's repulsed. She's supposed to kiss him good-bye and she can't. He puts his arm around her shoulder, they are walking now. "Listen, you have to help Rani. I'm all right." Sabah can feel his breath on her cheek as he speaks. She can feel the heat radiating from the feverish sores. She's afraid she will get blood on her face. He's looking at her, waiting for her reaction. She is horrified. She wants to pull away. How can you do

117

this to him? she thinks. She feels sick. "Rani must have told you," he says, "I'm gay. But Rani needs your help..." Of course she knew, she always knew. He stares at her and she smiles, she wants to reassure him. She looks across the garden. They are standing in a garden. It looks like the president's rose garden, manicured bushes and little fountains and this hum, this loud hum. There are insects hovering above the bushes in gray buzzing clouds. She looks at her hands and they are swarming all over them, they are all around her, biting her. She can feel them biting her through her clothes, her jeans. Her hands are red with blood. Her face is burning. The insects dive again and again, tearing off chunks of flesh. Her shirt and jeans are streaked with strawberry stains. And Sanjay is grabbing her, trying to keep the bugs away from her, he's saying, "Come on, come on, we've got to get you out of here." Sabah screams and hears her scream turn into a low moan.

118

She listens to the moan fade into the loud hum of the air conditioner. The room is dark, except for the stripes of light coming through the curtains. Her face and hair are soaked with sweat. The air is hot and still. The Russian air conditioner obviously stopped doing its job hours ago.

Someone is knocking at the door. "Bibi? Sabah bibi? You have a guest."

Oh, Christ. She forgot. She jumps out of bed and picks her jeans and T-shirt off the floor. She washes her face and brushes her teeth in two minutes. Whoops, too late for the boiled water. She looks at the bottle beside the sink. There's some gray stuff floating at the bottom. She picks it up and shakes it, to make sure they're not swimming in there. She studies the bottle.

"Sabah bibi, saha'ab is saying please hurry," the servant opens the door slightly and smiles conspiratorially at Sabah. He nods his head, "Very good, saha'ab. Very nice. Come, come."

"Yes, thank you. I'll be there in two minutes, I promise." She puts on kajal. Some rouge, some concealer for the dark circles under her eyes. OK. She looks—

"Awful. Sabah, what have you done? You obviously don't want to have a career in modeling. What did you do all night?" Sanjay looks over at her and then, back at the road, quickly, as a scooter rickshaw swerves into his lane. He sniffs, "You smell of chlorine."

"I did have a late night, but not that late. I guess I should have put teabags on my eyes." She looks at herself in the rear-view mirror. "What is this job I'm not going to get, anyway?"

"You should have gotten up earlier and drunk the tea, your face is still swollen. It's that Indian designer I told you about, he needs photographs for his next collection. I thought you'd be great in photographs. Plus it might be good publicity for your parents' husband search. We'll print your age and specifics underneath." He winks at her and takes a sharp left. Sabah is thrown against the door. "These Marutis really handle well, don't they? I think they're made for Indian driving."

"Yeah," says Sabah. "I'm glad I didn't have breakfast. And I am not photogenic. Not at all. And my air conditioner broke down last night."

"I hope he wasn't planning on shooting you today," Sanjay looks at her again. "Oh it's horrible when your air conditioner breaks down. You poor thing. Maybe I can get you some teabags at the hotel. Oh, by the way, Rani's in this shoot too."

Sabah's first memory of Rani was when both of them were three or four years old, sitting in the kitchen eating hot dogs. Someone's mother, it must have been Rani's, had cut the hot dogs up into little cylinders and left them with forks and a bottle of ketchup. "Mummy, Mummy, I'm almost finished," she was shouting.

119

Sabah was trying to eat hers faster, she definitely didn't want Rani to finish first.

"Now we have to clean our plates," said Rani. She took the bottle of ketchup and poured it on her empty plate. Then she picked up her fork and spread the ketchup all over the plate, making swirly designs as if she were finger painting. Of course, Sabah had to do the same thing. She thought it was beautiful. She wondered why they didn't get to do this at home. She put her fingers in the ketchup and made elaborate patterns. "We have to do this because my father does," said Rani. "Want to see where he works?"

Sabah followed Rani out of the kitchen into a huge room with windows all around and sunlight pouring in like yellow paint. And there was real paint. Paint in pots, in tubes, in little globs on pieces of wood, towels streaked with color. There were boards and papers covered with paint. In the middle of the room was a high table cluttered with bottles and jars of paintbrushes. "Come here," said Rani. She dragged a paint-covered chair over to the table. She climbed the chair onto the table, smearing red and blue paint on her knees. "Here," she opened a can and handed Sabah a tiny cookie with a flower drawn on it in icing sugar. "These are for my father to give to me when I come to visit him while he works."

"Oh," said Sabah. "My father gives me paperclips. Lots of paperclips." She noticed that there was paint on the cookie and on Rani's hands.

Just then the door opened, and Rani's mother and Sabah's mother walked in. "What have you two been doing?" said Bibi. But she wasn't really paying attention.

"This happens every day," said Meera. "Look at yourself, Rani. Just think if your grandmother saw you now." She laughed, and then she continued talking to Sabah's mother.

Of course, that wasn't the first time she'd met Rani. She'd known her for years, since she was born, there were photographs to prove it. Sabah's mother, Bibi, and Rani's mother, Meera, with two babies at the beach. Bibi and Meera with their toddlers in the park. Rani's father had met her mother when he was making a series of paintings in India. She'd caused a scandal by eloping with him to America, leaving behind the man chosen for her by her parents. When Sabah's father moved to Boston, Sabah's mother's first friend was Meera.

Sabah was a month short of fifteen the night Meera rang the doorbell at 2 A.M. Her mother let her in. Meera was crying. She was holding shopping bags stuffed with clothes, and her hair, usually in a long braid down her back, was open and disheveled. Rani wasn't there, she'd been sent to boarding school in India. "Sabah, please go to sleep," said Bibi. Since Sabah just stood there, staring at Meera, her mother said, "Could you put the kettle on first?" From her bedroom, Sabah could hear them talking. She couldn't make out the words, just the low, worried voices and then, when her mother put on a Lata Mangeshkar record, Meera's sobbing, loudly this time, like a child who's been told she can't have something.

In the morning, she'd crept down to the room. It was littered with teacups and cigarettes. She ate a few of the cookies on the tea tray. They'd lost their crunch during the night, they tasted like sponges. She looked at the records they'd listened to. There was an orange on the table, with fingernail marks in little patterns around the peel. Sabah knew her mother had done that. Her mother did things like that while she was talking. She dripped wax from the candle into little shapes, she drew pictures on her napkin, she made patterns in the salt dish. Sabah would go down the next morning after a dinner party to find what her mother had made the night before.

She crept back up the stairs and creaked open the door of the guest room. The blanket rose and fell with the breath of a sleeping shape. She opened the door of her parents' room. It was dark. Her father was tying his tie. He put his finger to his lips and then pointed at her mother. She

121

was sleeping too. Muzzafer picked up his shoes and walked out with Sabah. "She was up very late," he said. "Don't wake her up."

Whatever the tragedy was, Sabah felt pleasantly excited, in anticipation of the drama about to happen. How lucky that Meera came here. "Why is Rani's mother here? What happened? Did someone die?"

"No, I'm not really sure. You'll have to ask your mother for the whole story, but I think she's having some problems with her husband. Don't you have to go to school? Yasmine has already gone."

"No, I'm taking a mental health day. I'll do some work, though. Don't worry," Sabah reassured her father. She couldn't bear the thought of slamming lockers and blaring radios, the cheerful drone of her suburban junior high school, while the story unfolded at home.

Sabah found out, through bits and pieces of over-heard conversation, as she made cups and cups of tea, that Meera's husband was having an affair with another painter, a young American woman. Meera stayed with them for a month. She went out with Bibi from time to time, but most of the time, she sat in the living room listening to Indian records with a box of tissues beside her, or she talked on the phone. "I can't believe it," she kept saying on the phone. "Does this mean that everything he said to me so far meant nothing? That I gave up my friends and my parents and everything for nothing? Yes, I know. And to top it all off, she's blonde."

At the end of the month, Meera and Sabah and Bibi went back to her house. Meera's husband wasn't there. They walked around collecting Meera's things and packing them into suitcases. "Sabah," said Bibi. "You go upstairs and pack Rani's things. You'll know what she thinks is important." Sabah turned on Rani's radio and looked in her closet. She hadn't seen her much in the past two years. She wondered what Rani liked to wear. She decided that even if Rani was very grown-up, all stuffed animals on the bed were probably essential. She packed those first. Then the pictures and messages on the bulletin board. She looked at the pictures of Rani with her friends at boarding school. Sabah thought about boarding school. Rani had told her it was nothing like the boarding-school stories in the Enid Blyton books. Sabah was envious of Rani's freedom anyway.

Something crashed downstairs. Sabah heard screaming.

"What's going on? Are you guys OK?" she shouted as she ran down the stairs. The screaming and thuds were coming from the room off the kitchen. Meera stood in the middle of the room throwing jars of paint against the walls, each bottle smashed and the paint dripped down the wall like the blood from a firing squad. "You bastard!" she screamed. "Haramzada! My parents were right about you!" She smashed one jar after another, she squeezed the paint from the tubes and smeared them on the windows. She splashed jugs of liquid paint on his canvas and papers. When she ran out of paint, she descended on the brushes, cracking the handles like sticks of kindling. "Haramzada! Son of a pig!"

Finally, she stopped, exhausted. She started crying, wailing, louder than Sabah had ever heard a grown-up cry. She cried so hard she slipped on the paint and collapsed on the floor. Bibi walked over and picked her up. She hugged Meera, both of them getting covered in paint and crying.

They stayed like that for a long time. It seemed endless to Sabah. She stood in the doorway watching them, squirming uncomfortably. She didn't expect her mother's friends to act like that. Perhaps Meera would be embarrassed that she was there. "It's all right, Sabah," Bibi said soothingly. "Can you help Meera put her things in the car?"

Meera went back to India after that, and Sabah hadn't seen her again. She'd heard about her, and sometimes Meera used to telephone Bibi, though usually they wrote to each other. Bibi had even got an invitation to Rani's wedding, but it was about the same time as Sabah's college graduation, so they couldn't make it to both. Sabah saw the pictures Meera sent of Rani. She was wearing tons of jewelry and makeup and her head was covered with a red embroidered dupatta so that Sabah barely recognized the girl she'd known. Her friends at college thought the pictures looked like *National Geographic.*

All this time in India and she still hadn't met Rani's husband. Someone said he was away somewhere—London? In the photographs he'd been quite good-looking, one of the best-looking Indian men she'd ever seen. In fact, she wondered where Rani found him. "Hey, Sanjay?" says Sabah. "What the hell is going on with Rani's husband?"

"Oh, God," says Sanjay, his neck craned as he looks in the rearview mirror, "you mean you don't know about it? I thought you were her best friend. Oh, damn, how close am I to that car?"

"Why don't you let the valet park it?"

"Because then it'll definitely get smashed. And I'll have to give him two rupees for doing it. You know, Rani's marriage was arranged, and everyone thought—well, it was really difficult because her father's American and her parents are divorced and—you know what people say about Meera."

"No, I have no idea. But it can't have been that hard, because he's really handsome. I've seen pictures of him." Sabah climbs out of the car.

"It was more or less an arranged marriage, I mean, she met him and all that, several times before. Is your door locked? She really liked him and he was impressed by her—her modeling career was really taking off. She'd just done the Bombay Dyeing adverts—"

"Hi!" Rani walks toward them across the parking lot. "Sabah," says Rani. "I'm so glad you're here, too. I was starting to have some doubts about this."

124

"Oh no you don't," says Sanjay. "You're just being snobs because the designer's not from Bombay or Delhi. Come on, you two." Sanjay herds them into the hotel lobby. "We can all go see the Russian exhibit at the Museum of Modern Art after this."

"I have a better idea. You take us to the Mirage tonight," says Sabah. "I'm sure my aunt won't mind if Sanjay takes me. I'm dying to see the place."

"Rani's there every night, anyway," laughs Sanjay.

"Once in a while," protests Rani. She winks at Sabah, "but it's *the* place to be."

"A true disco baby speaking," smiles Sanjay.

"My grandmother would murder me if I went as often as you do, Sanjay," laughs Rani.

"Don't lie, Rani," says Sanjay. "Sabah might believe that you don't sneak out of the back door as soon as your grandmother goes to sleep."

"You know," says Sabah, "I have an uncle who used to be a bouncer in a club. His name is Rocky. He has tattoos and he wears a spiked dog collar around his neck. I swear."

"What? You have an uncle called Rocky?"

THE BLARING MUSIC seems to get absorbed by the white marble. Sabah can only hear the bassline through the heavy wooden doors. THE MIRAGE is spelled above the door in brass letters. "Is there anything that doesn't happen in a hotel here?" asks Sabah.

"No," says Sanjay. "Look at all those Marwaris in their bush suits," he giggles, as a group of lacquered and perfumed disco-goers passes, all khaki and red lipstick and lamé salwar kameezes. "Just look at that shiny thing, how cheap!"

"That'll be one hundred and eighty rupees," says the young man. He's standing in front of a sort of wooden pulpit, like a priest, his brown suit buttoned and his shirt ironed, his head bent over the heavy guest-list book.

"Are you kidding?" says Sabah. "Sixty rupees each to get in here? What a rip-off. No way. I'll wait outside. My bouncer uncle would kill me if he knew I paid to get into a club."

"Come on, Sabah," Sanjay says. "It's not so much money. That's less than six dollars. How many places can you go in New York for five dollars and fifty cents? I'll pay for you, OK?"

They pass the doorman and walk in. As her eyes adjust to the light, Sabah makes out the dark shapes of bodies, in clusters around the bar and tables, barely visible in the colored light. Sabah looks down and realizes that the light is coming from the dance floor. *Saturday Night Fever.* The floor is made of flashing colored lights. And the music is the latest in disco-pop. Everywhere are young men with their shirts unbuttoned and gold chains sparkling on their chests. Sabah stands by the bar watching the young men dancing discreetly with the girls in salwar kameezes. Everyone's doing a polite two-step. Here and there in the crowd, she sees a trendy Occidental type—a group of foreigners, their hair and skin conspicuously pale and their clothes graphic—probably fashion mongers, sent to supervise clothing designs in factories, or hip Japanese kids. Sanjay emerges again. She walks toward him, watching him lean down to a woman's upturned head, her Louise Brooks hair cut falling off her angular jawline as she tilts her head, so he can kiss the other side. She's wearing a clean black dress and ropes of pearls are draped around her neck.

"Who is that cool woman?" Sabah murmurs as Sanjay comes back to her.

"You idiot," Sanjay laughs and elbows her. "That's Rani. She just had her hair cut. Doesn't she look fab?" Sanjay takes Sabah's hand and leads her over to the table. "Rani, may I present our latest young American? This is Sabah. She's just come to India, and she's still in culture shock."

"I haven't shocked you, have I?" laughs Rani. "God, I hope I haven't been transformed that much since this afternoon."

"Rani, the girl didn't recognize you!"

"I didn't think I was looking that bad," Rani kisses Sabah. "Here, let me introduce you to everyone. This is Pierre, from the French Embassy, and this is Brian, an American, one of your countrymen. Watch out, he's got a weakness for beautiful Indians. And you probably couldn't make out Mahinder, our budding Amar Bose, who's skulking in the shadows as usual."

Mahinder kisses Sabah as well. "It was just because Rani was looking like a Behanji for the shoot. She thinks the photographer will be nicer to her if she reminds him of his sister. By the way, you look really beautiful, Sabah."

Pierre smiles, *"Bonsoir.* Good evening." Sabah can make out a sharp nose, white shirt, gray jacket, red striped tie.

"Wait," says Brian, "did she say you were an American?"

127

"Don't ask her," says Rani. "It's a long story, but she's as American as you are. Maybe more. Sanjay, you explain to Brian what it's all about. Sabah, you sit here. I feel like you've been ignoring me since you got here."

"Me? Ignoring you?" Sabah sits down on the chair next to Rani. "Sanjay, can you get me a drink, too? Mineral water, lime, no ice."

"Mineral water! Don't be silly. Get this girl a real drink. Come on, what do you want? I'm having this delicious fruit-and-rum thing. Do you want one?"

"No, really. Thanks. I'll have the water. I don't drink."

"Really?" Pierre is incredulous. "Not even a little wine?"

"That's his national beverage, you know," says Sanjay. "Don't insult it."

"She's a Californian," says Brian, winking at her. "You probably lift weights and don't eat red meat either."

"Sabah, have some wine at least," says Sanjay. "You didn't drink any of the wine at Mahinder's place? You're mad. Listen, Brian, you missed the most fab dinner at Mahinder's the other night. That's what you two get for having diplomatic schedules."

"Even with a nice dinner, you have no wine?" asks Pierre. "Impossible."

"Leave her alone, you guys. Don't you know that France has the highest rate of alcoholism in the world? Sabah, it's really good that you don't drink," says Rani.

"But you smoke, of course," says Pierre, offering her a cigarette.

"Take it, Sabah," says Sanjay. "Pierre gets the best cigarettes from his commissary. Pierre, please buy me a case of Marlboro Lights—everyone in my family smokes those."

"No thanks," says Sabah.

"Of course not," says Brian, "smoking is completely out of fashion in California. Californians are so healthy, they make everyone else sick." He smiles, "But look at Sabah; they've got the best bodies in America." He sings in falsetto, "I wish they all could be California..."

"You have no vices, do you?" says Rani.

"Listen to this song," says Sanjay. "I love this song. I have to dance to it. Come on, Sabah. Let's dance."

Sabah has always hated the song. It's too cute and American. But all of a sudden, it reminds her of college dance parties. It makes her feel at home. She taps her feet under the table. "Yeah, OK. Come on, Rani, you dance too."

"If one of these lazy men dances with me."

"Rani," says Sanjay, "we're all going to be fighting to dance with you."

"Listen," pleads Mahinder in Hindi. "Don't leave me alone with these two firungis."

Sabah can feel the music playing back her last year in college. She hasn't danced in weeks. Her muscles are coiled in spirals. She wonders whether she'll explode as soon as she starts moving.

Sanjay is dancing, rocking back and forth and waving his arms. The rest of the group is also moving across the dance floor. Pierre and Rani are doing a fifties rock and roll, she and Brian are doing an American shuffle, and Mahinder has already caught the eye of a young boy farther down the dance floor. Sabah swings a little and watches Mahinder zigzag through the crowd to the boy. Mahinder is speaking to him, he puts his arm around the boy's shoulders. The doors of the disco swing open, letting in a flood of light from the lobby. Mahinder and the boy turn into silhouettes as they walk out. Sabah closes her eyes and feels the music move into her, the bass thumping like her pulse. As she warms up, she gets more animated. She starts laughing, she can't stop laughing, she's happy and giddy, and her hair's in her face and mouth and her limbs fly around her as though the music comes from a snake charmer's flute. Some guy doing a slow thing behind her keeps banging into her as she writhes, so she bounces a few steps away. Three beats later, he's behind her again, sliding a hand over her polyestered bottom. Sabah turns and giggles hysterically into the shocked face of an Indian airline steward, still in uniform. The steward rushes off the floor. She dances through about five songs in a row. One by one the others sit down, sweaty and breathless, ordering rounds of drinks. Sabah keeps dancing.

After a few songs, Rani gets up and joins her, but she's drunk now. Her movements are wild and suggestive. Sanjay is dancing again as well, and Rani kisses him firmly on the lips. Then she throws her arms around Pierre, pushes his hair back, and whispers into his ears, his face becoming more and more pink as she speaks.

Mahinder walks back in across the dance floor.

"Rani, leave the poor boy alone," says Sanjay, pulling her back.

129

Rani straightens up. "Don't you dare tell me what to do. Who are you to talk? Pierre doesn't mind, anyway, does he?" She smiles at him.

"No, no," says Pierre, blushing further. He looks at Mahinder. "Of course not."

"Sabah," says Rani, "let's get out of here. I'll give you a ride home." Her eyes are bloodshot. "I've had it with all of these babies."

"Don't be stupid, Rani," says Sanjay. "Sabah's aunt will kill me if I don't bring her home. And you shouldn't be driving either."

"Really, Rani, remember the last time you wrecked the car?"

"You think I care? I don't care if I wreck ten of his cars. That idiot. He'll bloody well buy me another one."

"Rani," Sanjay puts a hand on her arm. "Calm down. These three firungis—including Sabah—are going to be completely frightened. Just sit still for a little while."

"What do you mean? Sabah's the only one here who knows me. She's the only one of all of you who I can talk to. She doesn't give in to all this bullshit." Rani is crying now, her mascara dripping and her lipstick smeared about her mouth like blood. "Sabah, you don't know what it's like, do you? You're lucky because you don't know what we have to go through here."

"It's OK, Rani," says Sabah.

Rani sits next to Sabah and buries her face in Sabah's T-shirt. She is hot and Sabah can smell the sweat and alcohol steaming off her hot skin. "We thought it would be better here," she weeps. Her tears soak into the T-shirt. "Mummy and I thought it would be better."

"Don't worry, Rani," says Sabah. "It'll be all right." She pats Rani on the back. She's not so sure. She doesn't even know why Rani's crying. Sabah's never been good with people who are crying. She feels voyeuristic. She strokes Rani's hair, awkwardly. She looks up and notices that Pierre's hand is in Mahinder's lap. They are looking into each other's eyes. Mahinder already has his driving gloves on. He slips a gloved hand under Pierre's jaw.

"Come on, Rani," says Brian. "I'll take you home. Sanjay, you follow me in Rani's car." The boys carefully help Rani up and out of the hotel. She starts to totter at the door and Brian picks her up, his muscles flexing against the sleeves of his T-shirt, his face tensing. Pierre carries her handbag and Sanjay picks up her shoes as she kicks them off in the parking lot. Sabah's amazed at how gently they move her, how carefully they help her into the car. Even Pierre seems to treat Rani like a small child. Sabah and Sanjay get into Rani's car. Pierre follows Mahinder to his white Toyota.

"Hey," says Sabah, "a Toyota. How did Mahinder get an imported car?"

"Nice car, Mahinder," shouts Sanjay out of Rani's window. "Who bought it for you?" He turns the ignition key and grins at Sabah. "You can get anything, even in India, if you have the money."

"Mahinder! What did you have to do to get that car?" Rani screams from Brian's car. "How much self-respect did you—" Brian rolls up her window.

"Friend's Colony!" Brian shouts at Sanjay.

"Right!" Sanjay yells back. He zooms out onto the highway. "Oh, God," he says to Sabah. "I can't believe it. Her husband would die if he knew, he would just die. Anyway, why should she tell you all her personal problems in the disco? How rude."

"So what's going on with her husband? You only give me two words at a time."

"Oh, it's such hangamma. In the beginning, no one thought she'd get married at all because of her father and she's an Anglo-Indian and all that. Anyway, no one in Hemant's family said anything about a dowry. And then his grandfather started making a fuss and saying they wanted some huge sum of money. It was just absurd. And Rani—how could she ask her mother to come up with the money? Her mother had already bought all this jewelry and all. Just imagine, Rani's mother didn't get any jewelry from her husband because she married an American. And she didn't have much herself, because her parents hadn't given her anything when she got married. So she had to go and buy it all herself. And well, people say all sorts of things about Meera."

"What? What do they say?"

"She's all over the place. The woman's having affairs with God knows who—"

"Oh, that's just Delhi gossip. There's always ten times more talked about than there is happening."

"I've seen her myself at parties, Sabah. It's embarrassing."

"I can't believe it. She was never like that in Boston," Sabah wonders if her mother knows all of this.

"Well, now she's a Delhi socialite."

"Forget Meera, what about Rani?"

"Hemant told Rani she had to quit her modeling and come to London. She wouldn't, so he went off alone and left her with that witch of a mother-in-law who keeps demanding money. And, in the meantime, Rani's on every billboard, and out every night, making herself look worse and worse. I mean, it's not whether she actually *does* anything—"

"Which she doesn't."

"It's her firecracker image that people talk about. Like, she smokes and dances in public, without her husband."

"That's ridiculous."

"Sabah, your image is really important if you're a girl. If she just behaved like a wife outside . . ." He grins, "As for you, you've got to stop batting your eyelashes at Brian. Did you see the way he was looking at you? He's falling in love."

"I never batted a single eyelash!"

It's four in the morning when they finally pull up at Sabah's aunt's house. Sanjay's car idles outside as Sabah tries to sneak into the darkened compound. She walks gingerly, but her high heels still clack sharply against the driveway, sending waves of vibrations through the concrete. The gate screeches open, waking the chowkidar who'd been asleep in his chair, his head leaning back against the house, his mouth open and a tiny trickle of drool sliding down his chin and dripping onto his khaki uniform. "Hello, hello," he says, blinking and jumping from his chair. "Namaste, baby." He looks at his watch and shakes his head. "Very late," he warns her. "Everybody sleeping." He runs down the path to ring the doorbell for her.

"No," warns Sabah, picturing her aunt's lips pressed together with restraint, over the lacy neck of her nightie. Sabah watched those same lips curled back over the sharp teeth this evening, trying to keep her attention on yet another lecture on the fragile reputations of Indian girls. "Don't," says Sabah, trying to explain to the chowkidar in rough Hindi and gestures that she's going to climb in the window.

The chowkidar smiles. "Oh," he nods, knowingly. "Memsaha'ab." He contemplates the situation for a few seconds. Then he says, "No problem," and disappears behind the house.

Sabah walks around the house in the other direction, stepping in the flowerbeds, turning the doorknobs and pushing the windows. Every one is tightly locked. Her aunt must have had a security panic and checked every possible entrance before she went to bed. Sanjay seems to think she's safely inside, because she hears his car drive away.

The chowkidar reappears with the cook. He's barefoot and wearing his pajamas, an old undershirt and a faded lungi wrapped around his waist. "Oh-oh, Bibi," the cook says. He helps her out of the bushes. "Come."

Sabah follows the two men to the servants' entrance

133

at the back of the house. She sees a light, hears children talking and a baby crying in the servants' quarters. She realizes she's woken his whole family two hours before they've got to get up for the long day. Her ears are reddening with embarrassment, she can feel her face getting hot. He unlocks the door for her and holds it open. He puts his finger to his lips, "Quiet, quiet, Bibi."

"Sorry. Sorry for waking you up. I'm really sorry."

The cook smiles and winks at her, "No problem. Good night." Sabah walks into the darkness, feeling the wall for the light switch. "It's very late, baby. You don't tell Memsaha'ab, OK?"

Sabah clicks on the light. "Thanks. Thanks a lot," she murmurs gratefully.

134   SABAH'S EYES CAN'T leave the flame. She follows the path of the oil lamp, the brass becoming duller and the flame brighter in the fading daylight. Rani is murmuring softly as she moves the lamp around the altar. She puts the lamp down and picks up the tiny vase of ghee. She empties it over the lingam, the lumpy liquid dribbling and splattering, each yellow clump of butter melting into oil as it slides down the hot stone and collects in a little pool in the lotus flower. Rani pours the milk next, and it washes down over the shiny stone and floats on the surface of the pool of ghee. Sabah puts the bowl of marigolds down on the black stone. "Here," says Rani, "have some prasad." Sabah takes a beige rectangle off the plate. She nibbles it. It tastes like marzipan. "That's almond burfi."

"It's good," says Sabah. "Now what?"

"That's it. That was the puja. Now we clean up. It's funny. I haven't done it in years, well, not like that, anyway."

"It's like magic, isn't it?"

"My grandmother used to tell me that Shiva was the god of young girls. That if you pleased him, he would give you anything you wanted. I only realized that a lingam was a penis when it was too late—when I got what I wanted."

"The metaphor is sort of obvious," Sabah smiles. She gets up. Rani picks up a marigold flower and crushes it, the orange staining her long fingers. "Maybe we all worship men in reality... they always get to be the gods. What I can't figure out is how you fit this into your life, I mean your American life. It seems surreal."

"I sometimes wonder why I put up with all this bullshit."

"It depends whether or not you consider it bullshit, I guess. But you're too stubborn and too smart to let anyone make you do what you don't want to, Rani."

"I wish I was. People talk me into things. Sabah, sometimes I wonder about going back to America, about my father. But then, how could I leave my mother? She has a bad enough time, she really needs me here. She wrote to me every two days from Kashmir. And she telephoned on the days she didn't write letters. Really, Sabah, she's very attached to me. She could barely manage to leave me in Delhi for the summer. She tells me everything about her life. Even some things I shouldn't know. All her little adventures that she makes me promise I'll never have. She says she'll kill me if I live my life like she does. Who would she have? And she's done so much for me since she left Daddy. And my grandmother, she has an idea of the kind of person she wants me to be—and where would I go?" Rani picks up the milk and ghee vessels. "I'm really sorry about last night. I shouldn't keep blabbing to you, like a complete idiot."

"No," Sabah leans over and picks up the silver plate of sweets. "You want me to carry anything else? Do you leave the flowers?"

"My grandmother must be waiting for us to have tea with her, and my mother's probably back from her shopping. Come, let's see what she's bought," Rani smiles. "I asked her to pick up my sari blouses at the tailor. I hope she remembered. I just bought this beautiful sari, you'll die when you see it. If the blouse is here I'll wear it tonight to the dinner party. You'll also wear a sari, OK?"

"I don't know, I still haven't figured out how to tie it on. I have to make the ayah do it."

"You just come over here a little early and I'll tie it for you. Then we'll go together. But you should really learn to wear a sari properly. What if you end up living here? Anyway, even if you don't, you are an Indian, you should know something about your culture."

"Well, if my sari tying is amateur, at least it won't kill anyone, Rani," laughs Sabah. "I'll drive your car home, OK?"

"Don't be silly. I'm a great driver." Rani looks at her mother, who is trying push the door open, loaded down with brown paper packages. "Don't say anything, Mummy," she warns her mother. "Everyone knows mothers don't like their children's driving."

"Rani, for God's sake, call the servant to help me with all this. And both of you just standing there like little frogs with your eyes open. Come and take something. Really, you young people," says Meera. She kisses Sabah. "Hello, darling, have you had any word from your mother? Rani, please have the tea put on, I'm ravenous. Oh, and I brought your blouses— —what a hassle that tailor is, you mustn't take anything to him again. He wanted to charge me twice what I normally pay because he said you wanted them quickly. Come inside, Sabah." Rani, Sabah, and the servant follow Meera, still talking and shouting instructions, into the house.

"Are you married, behti?" asks Rani's grandmother as she pours the tea. "Such a pretty girl you are."

"Sabah, you have to try these little cakes, they are so delicious," says Meera, passing a plate heaped with pineapple and whipped-cream-covered cakes. "Don't worry, Mummy, we'll get Sabah married off," she smiles at her mother.

"They are yum," agrees Rani, squashing three onto her plate. "I've already had two this morning."

Sabah looks at Rani's slim waist. She's pulled her sari back around her neck to make it easier to eat. Her smooth stomach is exposed. "Rani, if I want to have a body anywhere close to yours I have to stay away from pineapple cakes," says Sabah.

"Don't be silly," says Meera. "You're so thin, Sabah. You must eat. Rani, have you heard from Hemant?"

Rani's face loses its expression. "No," she says. She rearranges the folds on her sari.

Rani's grandmother looks up. "I thought you received a letter yesterday, behti. Didn't you?" She looks confused. "Yes, yes, the servant had a letter for you from abroad." 137

"No, Nani, that was from a school friend in America," says Rani reassuringly. "From Darleen. Remember her, Mummy? She sends you her love."

"Oh, yes, how sweet of her to write to you. Please write back to her. You must keep up with your friends, Rani, it's very important," Meera smiles at Sabah. "Otherwise people get wrapped up in their own lives and things get forgotten. I used to write to Bibi once a month when I left America. And that's how Sabah came to see us in India. Just think if we'd never had the chance to meet her."

Sabah smiles back. "I remember all your letters. And we still have all the pictures of you and Rani in the photo album."

"Speaking of photo albums," says Meera, "you must see Rani's wedding pictures. Have you seen them? You've only seen the ones I sent your mother, I think."

"Mmm," says Rani. "You'll see tons of people you recognize. Everyone was there—Sanjay, Mahinder, even Brian and Pierre. It was really fun. I'll just get them."

"Yes, you must show them, Rani," says Meera. "I'll leave you two alone to catch up. Poor Rani isn't going to have too much time to behave like a school girl now," she teases. "She's got an impatient husband waiting for her in London. And as for you, Sabah, it's about time you got married as well, isn't it? Don't worry, I'll introduce you to lots of nice boys while you're here. I've promised your mother I'll do that."

"Thanks," says Sabah.

"LUCKY YOU," says Rani, as Meera's heels click down the stairs.

"No, I'm serious," insists Sabah. "Maybe she'll come up with someone good. I have nothing against meeting single men."

"You idiot. Here's the album. There's a video, too, but I can't stand the sight of it right now. It's too real. You don't mind, do you? I'll show it to you another time."

"No, I don't mind. Anyway, I've got to get home sooner or later to get my sari for tonight. But if you don't want to see the pictures either, that's—"

"Stop being so formal, Sabah. I've known you for years so you might as well start behaving like one of the family. All right, this is Hemant at his parents' house. He's getting mehndi—you know, henna—on his hand as well. Just a little, though. And people are feeding him sweets. Oh, and these are the clothes my grandparents sent for his family. The cows. This whole procession is my friends—I wish you and Yasmine had been there—taking the things to Hemant's house. I wasn't there at this part. I was locked up at home, it was so boring. I was dying to go and hear what his parents said."

Sabah flips through one page after another. They do look like *National Geographic*. She's overwhelmed by the colors, the brocade clothing, the creamy brown skin and bright lipsticks, the glittering jewels. "This is amazing, Rani, it's really amazing."

"I know, just try to guess what it cost my mother. I felt terrible through the whole thing. I kept trying to telephone the food people to ask them to bring cheaper food, or the phoolwallah to ask for fewer flowers," Rani laughs. "Just think if they'd listened to me. Mummy would have killed me. Oh, and this is the night. Here's the religious ceremony—for my grandparents."

Sabah looks at a photograph of Rani, dressed in red silk from head to toe, gold flowers cascading down her dupatta. Her face is hidden by the cloth. She's walking, caught mid-step and slightly off balance, around an earthen pot, from which a tiny wisp of smoke is rising. The tall young man ahead of her is looking straight into the camera, his eyes clear and gray under his red turban. With his neat mustache, he looks like a miniature painting of an Indian prince, proud and self-possessed. Sabah stares at his face, trying to see the personality underneath. "God, is he handsome, Rani. You could have done worse." She looks at the Rani sitting next to her.

Rani pulls the picture out of Sabah's hand, "Don't spend too much time on them, you've got masses to look at before you go. And I've got some even better pictures of him right here—"

As Rani's fingers grasp the picture, Sabah looks at it again. The picture blurs as it moves and Rani becomes a scarlet flame burning out of the pot and haloing her husband like a medieval icon. "That's a really beautiful picture. Who took it?"

"I think it was his brother. He went absolutely camera mad at the wedding. Even the pundit got fed up with him. You know when we were walking around the fire and all? He

139

tried to make us do it a few extra times just to get a good shot. Here, look at this one—there's Sanjay dancing like a complete fool. And there he is laughing his head off—what a nut he was! He was totally drunk. Actually, everyone was totally drunk. Look, here's Sanjay dancing with Gitangeli. Doesn't he look handsome? You're not jealous, are you?"

"Oh, God, no. Sanjay is just a close friend."

"That's not what I've heard," Rani provokes. "I've heard a lot of gossip about you and Sanjay. Even Mahinder's beginning to talk." She smiles and looks toward the door, "Don't worry, I won't tell my mother about it, or she'll be chasing him all over the place."

"Just what I need. Are you sure she can't hear us?" Sabah rolls her eyes. "God, I really am gossip already."

"Well, people are talking about it," Rani says, "but it's OK because everyone knows you've got to marry a Muslim. Everyone knows these mixed marriages come to no good end. So Sanjay's off the list because he's Hindu. And Brian's an American and we all know what that means..."

"Basically, there are no Muslims handy. And nobody's stupid enough to put Mahinder on it—"

"God, no!" laughs Rani. "Even if he were a Muslim, you'd be safe there. Though his parents *are* desperate...just imagine! His sister would kill you. I mean, thank God for her he doesn't like girls."

"It's true, isn't it? He even chooses her clothes for her," Sabah giggles. "How horrible. I shouldn't be so catty. Especially now that I know people are talking about me, too. Oh, Christ, my mother will die. Hey, Rani, why aren't there any eligible Muslims around? Am I the only one?"

"They're all in Pakistan, I suppose. Or all the ones you'd want to know."

"Not all of them. I've got relatives in Bombay."

"That's true, there are a lot of Muslims in Bombay, in the film industry and the arts and all. But most of the upper-class Muslims left India during partition. And old wounds take a long time to heal, everyone still remembers all the Hindu-Muslim violence during the partition riots. Not to mention all the tension between India and Pakistan, all the little wars, Kashmir... Most of the Muslims who are still in this country are very poor and uneducated. There's a lot more crime in Muslim areas. So a lot of people think Muslims are cheats and thieves, uncivilized. Or that they all secretly support Pakistan and they're trying to overthrow the Indian government from the inside. A lot of people here, without really knowing the reasons, think about Muslims the way white Americans think of black people. So, as Mahinder says, of the PLUs—"

"The what?"

"People Like Us, as opposed to the LCs, the Lower Classes. There just aren't very many Muslims. Anyway, you're lucky you're not from a working-class Muslim family in old Delhi. Because then you'd really have it bad. Girls get very little education, they're married at about fourteen, they've often got three kids by the time they're eighteen or nineteen. And their husbands have an even harder time finding work because of all the prejudice against them—oh, you'll have to talk to some political type about it, I'm too superficial for this," Rani grins, but then she becomes serious, "Sometimes I really think Indians are bullshit. Half the problems here are caused by talk—for most women, the one thing that keeps them from doing anything is simple conversation, spoken words."

"You mean like, 'That's not allowed'?"

"No, I mean our reputations. For a woman in India, the most precious thing she has is her reputation. One piece of bad gossip and you're finished. Parents spend their whole lives protecting their daughters from being talked about, and in between they make up stories about other people's daughters so their own look better. At least if you have some money

141

you can buy your way out of it, but if you're poor, you've had it. Even if a family likes to have their daughters around, even if they can afford it for a little while, they marry them off as early as possible to save their reputations from being ruined."

"Oh, come on, you don't give a damn about your reputation, Rani," teases Sabah, trying to give the conversation a lighter tone. "What about the other night?"

"It's true, Sabah, you won't believe it. Some girls are married off at twelve, thirteen, just to make sure they won't do anything. As for my reputation, it's already gone, so I don't care, you can say whatever you want. The problem is that Hemant's parents do."

"I was kidding, Rani. I haven't heard anything bad about you." Sabah swallows uncomfortably, realizing she's lying. She tries to look earnest. "Anyway, I'd be glad to have an arranged marriage. I don't know how I'd ever keep anyone in love with me long enough to propose otherwise."

142

"Look, Sabah, whatever you have or haven't heard about me, I don't care, really. But can I just ask you one favor?"

"Sure."

"I know I don't know you that well. I mean, I haven't seen you or written to you in years, so—but, I still consider you a really close friend. All the years I was in boarding school, when I first moved back to India—we're both half American, aren't we?—I always thought that if anyone could understand me..."

Sabah nods. She wonders why people always seem to be confessing to her. Just yesterday Sanjay started telling her things about his family, his parents and his brothers. How he had to go into the family accounting business because he was the oldest son, his brothers could get out of it. How his mother really spoiled him because she always felt guilty that he'd had to leave his literature study at Cambridge and come back do his accounting exam. How his brothers got to do all the things he'd wanted to do, and how they flaunted their freedom, how envious he was of them. Sabah wished he hadn't told her. She'd felt uncomfortable all through the dinner with his family that night. His mother's voice had seemed cloyingly sweet, and she could barely stand to look at his brothers' faces when she asked one of them to pass her something.

"So if I say anything to you, will you believe me? Will you promise to believe me, even if no one else does?" Rani looks into Sabah's eyes.

"Of course," says Sabah. Rani looks so helpless. There's something about seeing an adult looking so weak that makes Sabah squirm. She feels like she should leave the room, or look away to allow Rani some privacy, some dignity.

"Even if everyone else is telling you it's not true, will you believe me?" Rani's eyes are brimming with tears, the tip of her nose is slightly pink.

Sabah puts her arm around Rani's shoulder. She feels like a schoolboy on his first date. "I believe you. I'll believe you. Of course I will," Sabah repeats it to herself. "Of course." She squeezes Rani's shoulders. "I promise."

"Hemant just wants to get rid of me. He's fed up with me, or, I don't know," Rani says, wiping her eyes. "And he's having affairs—and it's not just gossip, he's told me that himself."

"Leave the bastard, Rani. Just get out."

"This sounds pathetic, but I can't. I made a commitment, a promise, and I really want to make it work, somehow."

"If you do leave him, you can come back home with me," offers Sabah. "My mother would be thrilled to have you."

"Thanks," Rani smiles for a second. "But what about my mother? And Hemant's grandfather won't let me go without the dowry they wanted in the beginning, sixty-five thousand dollars."

"What? No way!"

143

"Well, it's inflated now, but they think Hemant's worth a lot more with his green card. Which he got with my American passport," Rani smiles again. She dabs her eyes. "Look, I'm sorry. I'm very weird lately. I'm very emotional. Things are"—she catches her breath—"pretty difficult right now."

"Rani!" Meera's voice carries up the stairs. "Aren't you going out tonight? You'd better hurry. Brian's coming to pick you up in twenty minutes, he just called to tell you."

"Oh, my God," says Sabah. "I don't even have my clothes or anything. What time is it?"

"Don't worry," laughs Rani. "If he says twenty minutes, he means an hour. At least. And you can wear one of my saris. What size shoes do you wear?"

"I CAN'T BELIEVE we have to climb these stairs in this heat," complains Sanjay. "I hope it's cooler up there."

"I know," agrees Rani. "These barsati-roof parties are not for summer."

"They're mad."

Sabah is sweating. In the heat, the music seems even louder, blaring down the winding staircase. Every few steps, there is a niche carved into the plaster wall, and the god or goddess is illuminated with candles in clay pots.

"Look at these moorthies," says Sanjay, stopping to catch his breath. "Aren't they fabulous? I don't know where her father got them. They're hundreds of years old."

The pop music seems discordant in the presence of the ancient statues. Sabah's not sure which one of them is more out of place. She wipes the sweat off her forehead, trying not to spoil the makeup that Rani so skillfully applied to her face. What the hell, she thinks. I'll look flushed no matter what. She's worried about Rani's heavy silk salwar kameez. She wishes she'd let Rani convince her to wear a sari after all, because then at least her stomach would be cool. She hopes she's not going to stain the clothes. The kurta is practically dripping with sweat.

Brian is galloping up the stairs ahead of them, they can hear his footsteps echoing down the stairwell. "Hurry up, y'all!" he shouts down.

"Oh, God, these Americans with their jogging shoes," Sanjay groans. "He'll probably have a heat stroke at the top."

Rani laughs, "And then he'll go back and tell everyone how dangerous India is for foreigners."

As she walks out of the staircase, Sabah's startled by the rush of cold air. The entire roof is covered with a white canvas tent and air conditioners, and fans are whirring and humming in every corner. Sanjay grabs her hand and pulls her into the crowd. A loud crack erupts behind her. Sabah jumps. "What was that?"

"Those are the mosquito lamps, you twit," says Sanjay. "I'm so glad they've started the food already, I'm starving."

"So am I," says Rani. A waiter tottering nervously with a tray of mixed drinks pushes her, and her lips are inches from Sabah's ear. "I haven't had anything to eat all day." The words reverberate through Sabah's head.

"What? Are you kidding?" says Sabah. "You had about thirty cream cakes for tea. Listen, don't you think we should say hello to the hostess before we get in line for food?" But Sanjay's squeezed into the food queue, kissing and greeting people as he moves ahead.

Before Sabah and Brian have made it up to the top of the queue, Sanjay's already made the rounds of the party. "Fabulous barsati, isn't it? Don't you want some prawns? They are freaky! By the way, I barely know anyone here." The smoke and the smell of roasting spices waft through the room. Between the guests, Sabah can see men in white Nehru jackets throwing marinated meats on the grills.

145

"Sanjay," says Brian, "you're supposed to know everyone in Delhi. If you don't know anyone here, I'm going to be a lost cause." He looks around vaguely, then smiles at Sabah, "I'll just have to bore this beautiful woman to death. You know what bureaucrats are like."

Sabah smiles back. He reminds her of Rob.

"You know loads of people, Brian. I just saw some of the embassy types over there," says Sanjay. "And look, there's Miriam. Miriam! Miriam!" Sanjay disappears into the throng.

Brian apologizes, "I'm getting to be socially inept. That's what comes of spending all day interviewing people who want American visas." His eyes twinkle. "I give them student visas and they stay forever and have kids who grow up like you," he looks at Sabah appraisingly. "Well, that's not such a bad trade-off. Look, I'm dying of thirst. Do you want me to get you a drink? It doesn't look like any of the bearers are coming in our direction." He looks across the room. A few white shoulders are visible, but none of them are near enough to see him waving his arm. "Don't tell me," he whispers conspiratorily. "Club soda, lime, no ice, but make it look like a gin and tonic. Right?"

Brian leans so close she can see every pore. She looks at his neck and imagines making love to him, his head thrown back and the veins pressing against his throat, a tight buttock vibrating in her hand, the movement in his hips rippling through to his chest. Sabah nods.

"Pretty good, eh? I used to be a bartender in New York. Now that I know what you drink, I'll never forget you." He gives her a Tom Sawyer look and walks toward the bar.

Sabah feels lost. Brian's loose, loping gait and earnest face make her homesick for California. She considers running after him but he's already disappeared. She looks for Rani and Sanjay, but they've been enveloped into the groups of people grabbing prawns and tandoori chicken. She can't find anyone familiar. The fluorescent lighting in the tent makes the faces around her look harsh and painted. She can't seem to piece together the exotic clothes. The puffed raw-silk sleeves, the décolletage and ice-cream-scoop breasts; gleaming red, orange, and green saris; black satin shirts and crushed-velvet skirts and trousers; they seem to be torn and glued onto the guests like an opulent collage. Flashes of light from the jewelry sting her eyes. All the rouged and powdered faces make her feel like she's at a costume party. "Sabah!" She feels a cool hand grip her wrist, she turns and sees white teeth and red lipstick. And then, Rani's face. "Sabah," says Rani, "I just told Mahinder that Jimmy is your uncle, and he's completely impressed. He's telling everyone—you'll be the star tonight!"

"Oh, God, why did you do that? Mahinder's All-India Radio. I don't want people to know I'm related to him."

"Don't be silly, when they find out your uncle's a famous singer, you'll get invited *everywhere*. So promise me you'll take me with you."

"Sabah." Another young woman walks up to them. "Mahinder just told me that Jimmy is your uncle. What fun! You must have a great time in Bombay."

"I've never even been to Bombay," says Sabah. "And I'm not proud of being related to a pseudo-ghazal singer. That's the kind of thing you're embarrassed about. I'd rather tell you about my uncle Rocky. He's a biker."

A whole group of people have joined them. "What are you talking about? Jimmy sells a lot of records. He's practically the next Talat Mahmood," says someone.

"He's not Talat Mahmood," disagrees someone else. "That's taking it a little far—"

"Just because people like us don't listen to him, that doesn't mean anything really," says the first girl.

"Well, if you have a working-class audience, you have a much bigger market. Jimmy's a real star, not an artsy type."

"What do you mean 'people like us'?"

"Listen, I think my grandmother has one of his records, shall I put it on?"

"Yes, that'd be good fun—one of those real old sixties classics."

Sabah escapes into the darkness of the dance floor—an empty storeroom with speakers in each corner. The pop music blasts, the voices distorted through the speakers. The bass line throbs through her body. She dances madly around the room and kicks off her high-heeled sandals to cool her feet on the cement floor. As she tosses her head, her hair pins fling to the floor, she hears a few clink as one song fades out and the next one begins. She dances on them, and they bruise the soles of her feet like sharp stones. Rani's kurta is drenched, the silk feels like polyethylene clinging to Sabah's body.

"Sabah," says Sanjay, his footsteps on the concrete, breaking through the beat. Sabah stops dancing. "What are you doing here all alone, your usual dance-floor aerobics?" He puts his arm around her shoulder. "Come on outside, you twit. Everyone was wondering where you'd gone. Do you want to go to the disco?"

"Who's going?"

"Rani, definitely, and Brian, of course, if you're going, which you are, and that woman—what's her name?— the one you were talking to before..."

Sabah blinks as they walk back into the party, she wipes her wet face on her sleeve, probably smearing the rouge into the eyeshadow. "Don't be so disgusting," says Sanjay. "Here, have a napkin. Let's get out of here. I've already spoken to everyone."

"Or anyone who's interesting or good-looking," says Rani. "The party's over."

"You're right," says Sanjay. "And the prawns have been finished for hours."

To Sabah, the party looks only slightly less crowded than when they came in. Everyone looks drunker and more relaxed, but only slightly less dazzling.

"I'll just say good-bye to Miriam."

"Oh, where is she?" says Sanjay. "I've been looking for her for hours. Everyone's been saying how pretty she's looking. What a fabulous dress!"

"Sabah, come over here," says Rani. She's moving across the terrace. "Come with me, I want to show you something." She looks back at Sabah to make sure she's following her.

Sabah watches Rani. She wonders whether she's drunk again. Rani seems to be walking steadily. "Excuse me," says Sabah, pushing her way through a group of people.

"You're Sabah, aren't you?" asks one of the young men. "The American girl." His aftershave is overpowering, even from a few feet away.

"Yes, you're Jimmy's niece," adds a girl. "Do you know—" Sabah can see Rani's long, straight back fading into a dark corner of the tent. She runs after her.

When she catches up, Rani is standing in an unlit corner of the terrace, where the canvas has been lifted to let out the smoke from the barbccuc. She's leaning down over the wall. "Look," Rani says, taking Sabah's hand.

Sabah looks down. In the light of a small fire, she sees a tiny boy wearing a shredded gray shirt and no trousers. He's sitting on the edge of a stagnant pool of water, splashing his hands in it. She hears a shout, some voices. A girl, no more than eight or nine, in a ghagra skirt, walks into the light. She scoops the baby up onto her hip and walks back. Sabah can make out some buildings, huts of mud and plastic bags and wobbly sticks.

"Miriam's parents' bedroom is right underneath us," says Rani. "When they had the house built, the jhuggi wasn't there."

A few ragged children have come out into the light from the party. They are dancing and shouting to the music.

"I'm sure there's some food left," says Sabah. "Should we wrap up some kebabs and throw them down to them?"

"How many?" says Rani. "Five? Ten? Twenty? And can you bring some more tomorrow? Because they don't keep well if you don't have a refrigerator."

One night in a beach town in California, not sure of a friend's address, Sabah got off at the wrong bus stop. She ended up at the beach flats, the squat rows of little tenement houses and motels that ran the length of the boardwalk. In the pools of light from the street lamps, Chicano laborers sat on the hoods of their cars, smoking cigarettes and drinking bottles of beer. The harsh fluorescent lights made heavy shadows under their eyes, made their thick mustaches look even more menacing against their reddish green skin. *"Que linda! Hey mamasita!"* A few of them threw tired phrases in her direction. A young woman walked out of one of the pastel buildings, the shards of peeling paint crunching under her heels. She had a baby on her hip, and she was leaning from his weight. As Sabah walked by, the woman stared at her. Each of Sabah's steps seemed like a long, slow-motion action mirrored in the woman's eyes. Sabah could still feel her stare, like a spotlight, several blocks later, when she was back in the suburban part of town, walking down the sidewalks in front of the neat lawns and split-level houses with birds-of-paradise growing in their hedges.

"Do you feel like Marie Antoinette?" laughs Rani.

"What are you two doing?" asks Sanjay. He is standing behind them, taking the last gulp of his drink. "Let's go. This party is finished."

"SABAH, DARLING, come downstairs."

Damn. Her chappal misses the step and they turn into skis. She's flailing and trying to grab the bannister and bang! She's down on her back, each marble step hitting her spine, until she crashes at the bottom. Oh, Christ. She'll never get used to these things.

Even as a kid, when they all piled into the station wagon smelling of plastic wrap and tuna fish; the four of them sitting for hours in the stagnant rows of station wagons; the windows rolled down and Sabah singing "A Hundred Bottles of Beer on the Wall" to her sister until her mother gave her cookies to keep her father from slapping them, and the last chorus hung around them in the humid air; she hated those rubber thongs.

The first thing she did, when the car finally pulled into the parking lot, was kick off the flip-flops and run screaming over the hot asphalt and across the burning sand into the sea.

Her mother would stop and sigh, "Oh, Sabah." She would rearrange all the picnic baskets and towels and swing her weight as she moved Yasmine to the other side. Slowly, she picked up the blue-and-white slippers. She shook the sand off them and dropped them into the bag.

Muzzafer would laugh and say, "Bibi, this girl is just like you were in Simla."

"This is my niece, Sabah," her aunt says as she walks into the room. There is a whisper of crêpe de chine as she gestures. "Come in and sit down. Do you want some tea?" Her aunt is pouring amber liquid into the cups. The steam swirls into genies above them. She peers into the pot. "Oh, Sabah, could you make some more tea?"

"Sure." Sabah gets up and walks into the kitchen. Why, in a house where the servants outnumber the family two-to-one, does her aunt ask her to make tea? Something about girls looking domestic and helpful. Sabah's not sure she even believes the teapot is empty.

As she walks into the kitchen, the servants jump up. They hide their bidis behind their backs, but curls of smoke waft out over their shoulders. "Ek pot tea," she says, in her pidgin Hindi, pretending not to notice that they were smoking.

151

The cook nudges the bearer, who laughs and says, "Tea, chai."

Sabah repeats, "Chai," and then adds, "please."

"Good. Very good," says the cook encouragingly. It's only taken three weeks in India for the servants to understand her. The bearer lights the stove under the massive aluminum pot with the end of his leaf cigarette. They've finally stopped discussing how strange it is that she looks so Indian but speaks Hindi like a firungi. Now, she's just an oddity to be pointed out to the workmen who come to repair the leaking bathtubs and toilets.

In any case, Sabah only asks for the most basic things. She's too embarrassed to ask them to do anything she can do herself. She keeps flashing back to junior-high American history classes. Abraham Lincoln's freeing the slaves had a strong impression on her adolescent consciousness. When she was fourteen, she'd had nightmares about being a slave shipped from Africa. She would writhe and kick in her bed, imagining herself packed with hundreds of others in a ship's hold: bitten by lice, forced to eat, sleep, and relieve herself in a space too small to stretch her legs, for months at a time. In the darkness, she would feel her mother stroking her face, "Sabah, Sabah, you're at home, jani. Slavery was horrible. But people are always unkind to each other. During partition, your grandparents saw so much, so much fighting and killing, among people they had known all their lives, Hindus and Muslims doing horrible things to each other. They had to live with those memories so that they could stay in India and help the poorer people who couldn't leave. Everyone suffers, Sabah. It's good that you feel it. Maybe some day, you'll do something about it, the way your grandparents tried to." Still, it took Sabah a year to separate herself from the smells and sensations that were so vivid in her dreams, to no longer burst into tears at the stories of abused women slaves.

The servants find it shocking that she insists on doing things for herself that are below her station (and perhaps threaten their jobs). "No, no, baby," they tell her when she tries to wash dishes. The cook grins as he takes the sponge and the soap away from her. "Don't worry," he says. "No problem," with that Indian nod, as he dives into the suds.

"Sabah, I want you to meet Auntie Sarla and Auntie Shireen. And this is Uncle Mahesh." Sabah thrusts out her hand to "Uncle" Mahesh, just as he presses his together into a namaste. Saved from another faux-pas. She struggles to pronounce the word "uncle" in reference to someone she's known for about ten seconds.

She sits on a cushion on the floor, feeling the bruises from her descent. The conversation—"Well, I don't know, it takes so much time and one has to be fond of things like that..."—on gardeners versus gardening oneself—"But I love being outside, digging around, it's a very good way to get exercise and so satisfying..." continues, and Sabah can't think of anything to say. This is just as well, because young women are meant to be seen and not heard. Or was it not speak until spoken to? "The point is," said her aunt as she buttered her toast this morning, "you're young and you're beautiful. You don't have to call attention yourself, you already do. After you have children and you're a little more tired, you'll have no choice but to speak up."

"Will you have a sandwich? Sabah, could you?"

Obediently, Sabah gets up and passes the tray of sandwiches to the three guests. While the servants continue smoking bidis and gossiping and squatting on the kitchen floor, no doubt. She repeats the action with the cakes.

"So Bunty has gone back to San Francisco." The teacups clink in their saucers. Sabah listens to the crunch of the cucumber sandwiches. Are they supposed to crunch? "We were so keen he would become a doctor like his grandfather."

"That's true, Bunty really should have studied medicine."

"Sabah, are you sure you've never met Bunty?"

Sabah shifts on her cushion and gets a sharp jab of

153

pain from her bruises. She does not remember ever in her life meeting someone named "Bunty." "I think we're probably in different circles." Wrong answer. Her aunt looks disapproving. "Actually, my college makes me very isolated—everything I do tends to be in the same neighborhood and—" That was feeble.

"Sabah, you really must show him around Boston when you go home. The poor fellow's feeling very homesick all the way in California. Oh, and your mother called, she wants you to call your uncle in the hospital," her aunt sipped her tea. "Such a lovely woman," she adds to her guests. "Very artistic, like her daughter. It's so sad about her brother, really..." Her aunt's voice drifts off as Sabah walks back into the kitchen.

Sabah's heart is throbbing as she dials. She hopes he's all right. "Hi, Rocky," she says, tentatively. She feels the familiar goose bumps and the sweat on her forehead.

"Sabah! All the way from In-ja!" answers the scratchy voice. "How are ya, Sabs?"

"How am I? How are *you?* What are they doing to you?"

"They're going to take out my hips. What a bitch, eh? My bones turned to dust from all the fucking cortisone they pumped into me."

"How horrible!"

"I'm in so much pain—my nerves are so tight that my brain's receiving TV signals. Every time I close my eyes, I see MTV. And if they give me one more shot of morphine, I'll be a human controlled dangerous substance."

"Oh, Rocky."

"Hey, listen, did you hear about my starring role in this movie about born-again bikers? This guy wrote a review that went, it's too bad I'm so ugly 'cause I should be an actor. I wasn't sure if I should thank him or slug him. My friend Darrell said he'd go kick his ass."

Sabah laughs, but she can see Rocky's hands, his wrists—they must be thin now—scabbed and peeling with eczema, like his back and neck, the scars in his hands filled with black grease that never disappeared, even after scrubbing them with Ajax. "What a drag…" She wonders what the nurses make of his dog collar and wild black hair.

"I'm so skinny, my nose is bigger than my head."

"I guess you can't ride your Harley, either."

"Are you kidding? I have no legs! Ever heard of a biker with no legs? Listen, what do you call a man with no arms and no legs you hang on the wall?"

"What?" Sabah can see him: his dry lips stuck to his teeth, his skin cracked like an Ethiopian landscape, his eyes watery from pain and medication. The tattoos must be shrunken and chalky.

"Art! You should know that, Miss Artsy-fartsy. The best thing about being half dead is that I hear a lot of jokes. What do you call a man with no arms and no legs in a pile of leaves?"

155

"What?"

"Russell! What do you call a man with no arms and no legs lying on the floor? Matt. What do you call a man with no arms and no legs you throw into a swimming pool? Bob. Want to hear a dirty one?"

"Sure."

"Nah, I don't want to corrupt my little niece. You know, my whole life, everyone's been telling me what a bad influence I was on you."

"No you weren't. You're my hero. I spent my whole life wishing I was as cool as you."

"Thank God you turned out the way you did, despite me. You're great, you graduated from college and everything."

"Big deal. Tell me."

"No, I have to wait 'til you're married. Are you getting married yet?"

"No."

"Good. Whatever you do, don't marry an Indian. As soon as they get married, they blow up like balloons. Then they waddle around whining and complaining. Or maybe that's just the women."

"Thanks a lot."

"Don't do it. I'm serious. You'll regret it."

"That's what I figure. But that's all everyone talks about in India. My friend Rani is having the worst time. And her husband's not even here. I'm really worried about her. She actually thinks that he wants to get rid of her."

"Tell her to split. That's what my wife did. I get home from work and there's a delivery guy with a king-sized mattress. So I get him to bring it upstairs and the bed's gone. And then I notice that *all* the furniture's gone. Not to mention the kids. I mean, they weren't *my* kids anyway."

"Rocky, I can't believe it." Sabah wishes she were there. She wishes she could give him a hug. "Well, don't forget that you're my role model. You are. So you better get out of there."

"Squeaky Fromme is a better role model than I am. Or John Hinckley, Jr. I'll be out of here as fast as I can, that I swear. The only thing worse than the complete humiliation of a hospital . . ."

"Sabah," her aunt's voice summons from the living room. "Auntie Shireen and Uncle Mahesh are leaving now."

"Rocky, I have to go. Take care of yourself, OK? I love you. Say a prayer for my friend Rani, if you guys do that. She can use all the help she can get."

"All right. What do you call a man with no arms and no legs and a hard-on?"

"What?"

"What terrible, sick jokes. Don't tell your mother I told you these. I love you, too."

"What is it?"

"Bye! Write to me! Bye!" The phone clicks off.

"Wait!" Sabah shakes the receiver and fiddles with wires but there's not even a dial tone. The whole machine's gone dead. "Damn these bullshit phones! Goddamn it!" She bangs the phone down on the counter. The cook looks alarmed. She stomps out, letting the kitchen door slam shut behind her.

In the hall, Sabah mumbles something about looking forward to meeting Bunny in New York when she returns.

"Sabah," says her aunt while they hear the gate clanging shut and the car driving away through the dust, "their son's pet name is *Bunty*, and he's a very nice boy. He's quite a successful young stockbroker."

The midafternoon sun has become very bright and Sabah's aunt is silhouetted against the windows. Sabah squeezes her eyes shut and she can see her aunt in negative. All the reds turned green, all the greens turned orange, like a roll of color film. The sun is giving her a headache.

157

"I've been wanting to speak to you about the people you've been spending time with here—God, these things are so uncomfortable," her aunt says, unhooking the clip-on earrings she wore for tea. "If you spend too much time with a fast crowd—as Auntie Shireen was saying—Rani doesn't have a good reputation in Delhi, you know. Your mother doesn't understand because she's an artist. And of course, people will talk more about you because you've just come from America," her aunt stands up and pats Sabah's cheek.

"Mmm," says Sabah. All she can think about is calling Rocky back. She wishes she could help him. Fix his body. She wishes she could help Rani. Fix her brain. Maybe Rocky is the only person who'd really be able to help her.

"I'm going for my rest, Sabah," her aunt says as she walks toward the stairs. "If anyone calls, please be a darling and take a message." Halfway up, her footsteps stop. Sabah imagines her turning around, a whisper of silk and flesh. "Sabah? When you go out tonight, please remember, this is not America, and you're an Indian girl."

"TEN RUPEES! Ten rupees! Ten! Ten!" the salesman is throwing the clothes up in the air as he makes his pitch, tossing them like salad. They fall in a heap on the plastic sheet in front of him. "Come here, ten rupees! Good clothes, ten rupees! New clothes, ten rupees! A shirt for baby, ten rupees!" He's laughing as he yells, competing with all the other salesmen on the street for the best rap.

"Sabah, look at this shirt," says Rani. She holds up a white cotton shirt. "It's really nice." She examines it more closely. "Or maybe I'm just hung over from last night."

"Hey, do you have any idea what you would pay, just for the label on that shirt in America?" Sabah forgets the heat and starts scrabbling through the piles of clothes. "I'm sorry for complaining before, Rani. I thought this was just a tourist rip-off." She looks up, but Rani has already moved on to the next salesman and the next pile of surplus clothing. She squints back at Sabah and then puts her hand on her forehead to shade her eyes from the sun. "Hey!" says Sabah. "Aren't you buying that white shirt?"

"No, I'm looking for something really good," Rani shouts back. She's already four stalls ahead of Sabah, digging through piles of sundresses.

Sabah skips the next stalls because she thinks if Rani didn't find anything worthwhile in them, she probably won't either. She's already holding a plastic sack crammed full of cotton shirts. "Rani, how do they get this stuff?"

Rani smiles. "The good old Indian business sense. An exporter comes to India, orders his factory to make a thousand shirts. They make five hundred extra and sell them for more on the street than they do to the wholesaler. Or, like most Indian businesses, they are so disorganized they don't get the order ready in time for the season, then the buyer won't accept them, and they're stuck with fifteen hundred cotton sundresses to sell to Russian diplomats."

"Why Russians?"

"Because they're the ones who really shop here. This market has a reputation for having good prices because everyone knows Russians don't spend much money, but they're dying to buy things to take back to Russia. Of course, if you ask an exporter, he'll say all of the stuff here are garments that didn't pass inspection. Rejects and samples. Some of them are, but most are just sneaky Indian businessmen who want to make a few extra bucks."

"Oh, Rani, look at that jacket." Sabah points toward a black baseball jacket that makes her think of tough Italian boys in Brooklyn. "My friend Rob, in San Francisco, would kill for that jacket. With a white T-shirt? What do you think?"

"Don't give him more than fifty rupees."

"But what if it's more? Come on." They walk slowly, through the shimmering heat toward the jacket, which is hanging on a pole, high above the shop.

"How much is that?" says Rani, in Hindi.

"For you, Madam," answers the shopowner in English, "it is only two hundred rupees. It is very good fashion. Very new style. You are from which country?" He smiles and leans back, dust crumbling from the creases in his tight polyester pants. He wipes his forehead with a piece of cloth. "French? *Parlez-vous français?*"

"From this country, you fool. So don't think you can charge me tourist prices. We'll take the jacket for thirty rupees," Rani says, continuing in Hindi.

"Thirty rupees? No. Serious prices, Madam. This is not joking. All right, one-fifty. OK?" He calls over one of his assistants who hurries over to take the jacket down.

159

Rani fingers the material. "Look at this stitching, Sabah. This is junk. It'll tear the first time it's washed. And the zipper's not very good."

Sabah looks at the jacket. "Rani, everything here will fall apart. That's understood," she whispers. "I think it looks good."

"This is rubbish," says Rani. "We'll take it for forty rupees. Pack it up."

"No, Madam. Forty rupees is too cheap. I make no money. In France, this thing is very expensive. Very, very expensive. Big fashion. Here I give you cheap price, because you are so beautiful. You give me seventy rupees, OK? Seventy rupees because you talk just like Indian girls. And because you are both very beautiful." He winks at Sabah.

"How dare you be so rude to my friend?" says Rani. "Why should we buy anything from you? Come on, Sabah. Let's go. There are hundreds of jackets here." She starts to walk away, Sabah following her reluctantly. "I can't believe it," she says to Sabah. "Did you see how he winked at you? What does he think you are?"

"Madam, madam!" the shopowner is shouting after them. "Madam! No problem! You see this jacket, very good quality. No problem!"

"Rani, that wasn't so bad," says Sabah, trying to calm her down. "So he winked at me, so what? Rob would love that jacket."

"Forget it, Sabah. You're not going to buy anything from him. He was so disgusting. And did you notice that he refused to speak Hindi to me? They all treat me like a foreigner. Let's have a cold drink." They walk to the tea stall, their sandals kicking up clouds of dust in their wake.

The thick, green-glass bottles sweat in their hands. Sabah wipes a gray trickle of dust and water on her salwar. "Christ, it is hot. I wish I'd bought some better sunglasses before I left."

"It's left you with more money to spend here, though," smiles Rani. "Look at how much you've got."

"I know," says Sabah. "I don't know how I ended up buying all this junk." She surveys the three plastic bags, each one practically splitting from the number of clothes smashed inside. "That's why I don't buy things right away. Otherwise I end up with so much—and I don't wear half of it."

Sabah looks at her bags sadly. "What have I done? It won't even all fit into my suitcase."

"I told you this was a very dangerous shopping area."

"I thought you were just talking about lecherous shopwallahs." A blind beggar walks toward them on stiff twiglike legs, one bony hand on the shoulder of the gnarled woman leading him. She beats an oil can with the heel of her hand. The change they've collected jangles in it like a cymbal. "Allah theygah!" he sings, his voice deep and resonant as an opera baritone's. The woman bangs her can. "Allah theygah!" She bangs again, rocking rhythmically back and forth. "Allah theygah!" The shoppers and salesmen clear a path for them on the busy road. She stops in front of a group of women with shopping bags and holds out the can. The blind man is silent. The women drop a few coins into the can.

The beggars resume their song. They stop in front of the chai stall. The woman holds out her can to the people standing around drinking tea and soft drinks. The owner, sprawled across a bench, wipes the sweat from his face with a washrag. Then he pushes himself slowly to his feet and walks toward them, waving his fat arms and shouting, "Go! Chalo! Go away!" as though they are crows.

Rani drops her soda bottle and stands up. She rushes over to the chaiwallah. "Stop it. Leave them," she orders. She puts some change in their can and then gives a few rupees to the chaiwallah. "Give them tea. Go on," she prods the reluctant man. The woman looks at Rani. She gives her can a shake and the blind man booms out, "Allah theygah!"

161

"You think there's a point?" she says, as she sits back down beside Sabah.

"Of course," Sabah watches them sip their tea, slowly and gracefully, as if the woman's hair isn't knotted and orange from malnutrition. Sabah puts down her empty bottle and opens her purse. She pulls out a few wrinkled bills. It looks like play money to her anyway. She goes over and drops them in the can, now sitting silently on a plank of wood. "I don't think I have enough money to buy the jacket anyway," she says.

"You idiot," Rani grins. "I'll give you the money. But, I'm telling you, you're going to lose the whole game. You'll never get a good price in this market again." Rani gets up. "OK, I don't have any honor left, but if you want to risk yours too, it's your choice. Let's go."

Sabah looks down the road at her jacket. The shopowner can see them coming. He is smiling and waving. Sabah can hear the blind man's voice in her ear, "Allah they-gah!" They're Muslims. God will give. She wonders whether God has anything to do with it.

"Look at him, Sabah, how irritating. He knows he's won. Sanjay's picking us up in—oh no, in about five minutes. Listen, we've got to hurry. Just give him the sixty or seventy rupees now and let's get out of here."

"IT'S ALL THE same to me. Which one do you want to go to?" They are standing in yet another vast marble lobby of a five-star hotel, trying to decide on a restaurant. Sabah looks at the raised waiting area, there are maroon carpets on the floor, red velvet chairs and red-and-gold tiffany lamps growing like mutated flowers out of the clumps of ferns. In the middle is a white marble fountain, water gushing out into a moat around the elevators. "This is too weird. It looks like a bordello."

Sanjay is giggling. "You are mad, Sabah. Absolutely mad."

As soon as they sit down in the coffee shop, Sanjay wants to see everything they bought. "Let Sabah go first," says Rani. "My shopping was very boring. Sabah had to do the buying for both of us."

"Look at this beautiful jacket! Where did you find it?" Sanjay has already put the jacket on, and is sliding the zipper up and down enthusiastically. "They should have bigger mirrors here." He's looking at himself in the mirror behind another table. "It's great, it's really cool."

"That jacket's the prize of the day," says Rani. "We really fought for it. What are you having?"

Sabah laughs, "Cold coffee—Rani apparently gave up her family honor for it. I only had to pay in self-respect. Cold coffee with ice cream. Don't forget the ice cream."

"Don't worry, Sabah. You still have a little self-respect left. More than enough for an Indian girl," says Rani. "Sanjay, the waiter's been standing beside you for about half an hour. Please tell him what you're having—and in any case, my family honor is now my in-laws' family honor. And as far as they're concerned..."

"Just a fresh lime soda, sweet."

"Oh, forget it, Rani. Your honor is intact."

"Rani," says Sanjay. "You've got to stop saying things about Hemant's family, you know. It looks bad."

"I don't care, at least I'm honest about it. Everyone thinks I'm a cheap Anglo-Indian. And who knows what my husband thinks."

"Rani, Hemant's family are completely gammars, they are the most backward conjoos, stingy people—everybody knows that. Whatever people say about them, that's another thing. But, really, if you keep talking like that, people are going to think—"

"Well, Hemant must be better than they are," adds Sabah.

163

"In any case, you're lucky you don't have to live with them. You can go off to London and you're far away from all this gossip and family gup."

"Look, Hemant doesn't want me to come to London. Oh, yes, he writes to me, telling me to come, but that's only so that he can make my life so unhappy there that I'll leave him. You know, his mother writes to him and calls him about twenty times a day to tell him that I was seen here with so-and-so, there with so-and-so, and that I never come to see them, and that there are six girls, prettier than I am, from good families, just waiting for our marriage to break up."

"Don't be silly, Rani."

"I'm not being silly. It's true. Sabah believes me. Don't you?" Rani looks into Sabah's eyes.

"Of course."

"Rani, Sabah hasn't grown up here. How can she understand this. Mothers-in-law are supposed to be horrible. It's their place in society—just watch a Hindi film," Sanjay tries to joke. "Just give her some time. Go over to her house from time to time and cook or something. Or make some mitthais for her to serve to her guests. Then she'll be OK."

"Sanjay," laughs Rani, "You know I can't cook to save my life. If you grow up on boarding-school food, your taste gets ruined. But I do visit that miserable woman."

"You do?"

Sanjay elbows Sabah, "Of course, she visits her. She's got to visit her. Actually, you should really be staying there, shouldn't you, Rani?"

"I know. Thank God for the modern world. I get to stay in my mother's house. Their place is such a mess, I can't tell you."

"Sabah, you've got to see their house. They've got so much money, and they live like they've just come from the village. I'm serious."

"It's this huge house in Maharani Bagh, and the paint is peeling and there are big water stains on the walls."

"And none of the bathrooms work, you've got to use baltis for everything."

"You're kidding," says Sabah. "You have to use buckets in the bathroom?"

"Not only that, but they spend so much when they go abroad. They buy everything. Two hundred pounds at the chemist, four hundred pounds buying a little makeup, seven hundred pounds for a few things for the kitchen. It gets me very depressed when I'm in London with them."

"That's horrible, Rani," says Sanjay, aghast. "They don't buy anything for you?"

"Never," says Rani. "My mother-in-law says, 'aren't you buying anything, behti? I thought modeling was very well paid.' But what's really funny is what they do with all these things when they take them home."

The waiter puts their drinks on the table. "Thanks," Rani says, pouring milk and sugar in her tea. "They take it home and they use a few things, a few little things. And the rest they stuff into the cupboards and the drawers—unopened—seriously. They don't even remember what they have. And then they go on using Indian things."

"They must be saving it all for their daughter's dowry."

"Unbelievable," says Sabah. She sips the cold coffee through a straw. She'd been told not to use straws, they were often washed and reused. No ice—unless it was made with water boiled for at least twenty minutes. No straws. She enjoys them both, so she forgets. Her stomach feels pleasantly cool and full. The coffee shop is calm, air conditioned and insulated from the sounds from the street.

"Sabah, how would you like to meet her? Let's go drop in on my mother-in-law."

"You are insane, Rani," says Sanjay. "All of us just land up at your mother-in-law's house?"

"Why not? She keeps saying, behti, come over. Bring your friends—she'll die if I actually do it."

165

"Can we do that, Rani?" Sabah's curiosity is piqued. "No offense, but the woman sounds like a witch."

"Yes, we must. It'll be a cultural experience for you, Sabah. You can write it in your diary or whatever. Yes, yes, yes. We have to go."

"Rani, don't be silly. We are *not* going," says Sanjay firmly. He takes the basket of bread sticks from the waiter and thumps it on the table definitively.

SABAH SITS ON the edge of the sofa. Not that it's any dirtier than the tea stall where they were this afternoon, but they walked in the house through the kitchen. The floor was sticky under her sandals. On the counter was a wide chopping block, with a large slab of meat, still wrapped in burlap, on it. Flies buzzed and swarmed over the dried blood. "Will you have a cold drink, Sabah?" the mother-in-law had asked. "Rani, just check to see what we have."

Rani opened the refrigerator. In between the pots of uneaten leftovers, the shelves were caked with rust and spilled food. The walls were black with mildew. Several bottles of cola and soda were piled on top of each other on the bottom shelf. Rani took three bottles out and put them on the counter. She opened a cupboard, the handle greasy with finger marks. She took out four glasses. "What will you have to drink, Ma-ji?"

"Whatever you give me, behti," she walked slowly into the living room, leaving Rani to bring the drinks. Sabah looked back at Rani, but she was pouring the drinks in glasses and boiling water for tea, almost simultaneously. Sabah and Sanjay followed the mother-in-law.

"So," says Rani's mother-in-law, moving her chair a little, "you are a Muslim?" Her eyebrows seem permanently fixed into a scowl above her gray eyes. She's wearing a faded cotton sari that was once a dark green or black. Rani gives her a cup of tea, carefully measuring two spoons of sugar and a splash of milk. Her mother-in-law holds the teacup in her lap, stirring it slowly. "Rani, this tea is very dark. Don't you know that dark tea is bad for your skin? I thought models had to worry about things like that." She puts the teacup back in the tray. Sabah notices how tightly her sari is tied, as if she is ready for combat. Rani picks up the entire tea tray and walks back into the kitchen. Sabah can hear water running as she refills the kettle. "Rani, don't throw away that tea. Tea is becoming so expensive now, you know."

"Yes," says Sabah. She looks over at Sanjay. He is squirming in his chair. He pretends to sip his drink. There are photographs all over the walls. Photographs of Hemant, Rani's husband, and his sister and brother, from their early childhood to Hemant's wedding, are framed in a variety of ways. Over a mantelpiece is a large painting of the three children and their mother. The three of them look sternly down at Sanjay and Sabah, like a painting of some British ancestor, except that the mother is wearing a sari.

"And you are also modeling?" asks Rani's mother-in-law.

"Well," says Sabah. "Not—"

"Sabah did the last shoot with me, Ma-ji," says Rani, walking in with a new tray of tea. She makes her mother-in-law a second cup.

"Yes, quite a lot of Muslim girls are modeling these days, I hear. There are quite a lot of actresses as well, aren't there? But I suppose there have always been a lot of Muslim actresses."

"That's because they're so pretty, Ma-ji," says Rani. "You know, Sabah comes from America. But we're trying to convince her to stay in India." She passes a small plate of biscuits around.

167

"No thanks," says Sabah.

"Oh, you knew Rani from that time only?" asks Rani's mother-in-law, her eyes getting rounder and her thin, dry lips stretching around her teeth. "You knew her when they were living in America?"

"Yes, I've known Rani since I was born. Her parents were friends of my parents. I think my father still meets her father sometimes. I think his paintings are doing very well in America now," Sabah hesitates.

"Well, now Rani is trying to be an Indian girl. She's got to forget all about that if she's living here. Don't you, Rani? You know, in India, girls are very lucky. After you're married, no one expects you to work outside as well as having children and taking care of the house and your family and all. I feel so sorry for these American women, running here, running there. They don't even have time to look after themselves." She reaches for a third biscuit. When her face is still, the ends of her mouth point down, like a fish's, thinks Sabah. "Sanjay, you were at Hemant's wedding, weren't you? Yes, yes. How is your mother?" Sabah notices that none of Hemant's wedding pictures include Rani. In all of them, Hemant is alone, in a raw-silk utchkan, garlands of jasmine and roses around his neck. Sabah thinks he looks like he's joining a religious cult.

"Yes, Auntie," says Sanjay. "She's fine. Actually, we can't stay for too long, because I've promised my mother I'll drive her to my father's sister's house."

"Rani, I'm so glad you've come. I just remembered that Hemant telephoned this morning. He couldn't get through to your house. He wanted to tell you he's coming to India on Friday, and he wants you to be packed and ready to go back to London with him," Rani's mother-in-law says, with a self-satisfied smile. She drops her empty cup on the tea tray.

Rani's face is drawn. "He's coming Friday? How can he come Friday? He hasn't even had time to write to me. How could he get a ticket and all so quickly?"

"I know, behti. Every time Hemant writes to me he tells me how hard he has to work. But his company is sending him to Bombay and he's rearranged his flight so that he'll come to Delhi and then you both can go to Bombay together."

"My uncle lives in Bombay," says Sabah. "Maybe you could visit him when you're there. I hear Bombay's a really exciting city. Much more interesting than Delhi, anyway. It's like the difference between New York and Washington, that's what everyone says. You'll probably have a great time." Sabah is babbling and she can't seem to make herself shut up. She swallows her next sentence.

Sanjay stands up. "Auntie, I think we'd better go. My mother will be really angry if I'm too late. Thanks so much for the cold drinks and all. Come on, you two." Sabah picks up their glasses and takes them into the kitchen.

"Leave them, leave them," says Rani's mother-in-law. "Rani behti, are you leaving too? We have to get the house ready for Hemant. You two can stay in the downstairs bedroom. I hope we can get someone to come and fix the toilet there, I've been ringing the man for three days now."

"Sorry, Ma-ji. I can't stay just now. My grandmother is expecting me to help her make dinner." Rani picks up the tea things. She takes them to the kitchen and starts washing them quickly.

"Here," says Sabah, "let me help. I'll put them away." She's disgusted at the thought of putting the clean glasses and plates back into the greasy cupboard, but she does anyway.

"Rani," whispers Sanjay, as they leave the house. "Don't they have any servants?"

"Not while I'm in the house," laughs Rani. She opens the car door. "Let's all three of us sit in front, OK? I'll feel too lonely if I have to be without either of you. I have three days left of fun before the guillotine."

"Don't be so gloomy," says Sabah, getting in beside her. "I'm sure it won't be that bad. Maybe we can all come down to Bombay."

169

"Yes, we'll all get to meet Jimmy. I'll send an autographed picture to Ma-ji. She'll die. She thinks actors and actresses are morally bankrupt. Almost as bad as models—they make prostitutes look like they're earning an honest living."

"HEMANT WAS the first person I ever slept with."

"No way," says Sabah, picking up her cup of tea. "I thought you were the first of India's liberated women."

"That was after I got married. When things started going bad. When Hemant—" Rani looks up at the servant, who is hovering around the teapot. "Go and bring some cakes," she dismisses her. Rani is running around the room picking up pieces of clothing and throwing them into her suitcases or back on the floor. "Anyway, if I was liberated, you think I'd be a fashion model? People in America think fashion models are dumb, but glamorous and beautiful. People in India just think they're dumb. And cheap. When someone told my grandfather there were posters of me all over Bombay—he didn't talk to me for a month. And Hemant left town."

"Too bad you're not in New York. You'd get into all the clubs. No, no. I like that one," says Sabah. Rani is holding up dresses, one after the other for Sabah's approval.

Rani stops and lets the dresses slip into a pile. "Hemant had the most beautiful skin, it was like café au lait, it was so smooth and soft and brown. And his mouth. His mouth was like—I don't know—I'd never even really kissed anyone like that. Here I was, in my wedding clothes, waiting for him to come back upstairs—he'd gone down to get something, drinks or something. I sat on the bed, but then I felt stupid, it seemed too obvious. So then I got up and went to sit on the sofa. And just as I sat down, I realized I'd spoiled the flower petals that were arranged on the bed, so I went back quickly to try and put them right. And still he didn't come. I sat on the sofa and spread the lainga—— the skirt—out in front of me, like those stupid wedding photos you see. And then I put my dupatta over my head and tried to look shy. And I really was shy. I was terrified. I looked up at my face in the mirror just as I heard him opening the door, and I looked like, God, like, a murderer had just broken in or something."

"It sounds like something out of a romance novel. When I think of how I lost my virginity: wedged between the door and the steering wheel of my parents' station wagon," laughs Sabah. "It was so American, I guess."

"And what you don't realize is how much it hurts. Or it did for me, anyway. We were kissing and all, and I was really enjoying it. I was dying to actually make love. And then when he put his penis inside me, I started yelling because it hurt so much! I was saying, 'Stop it, stop, that's enough, I hate this. Stop.'"

"What did he do?"

"Poor guy, here he is in the throes of ecstasy and I'm screaming my head off for him to stop and saying I hate him and all," laughs Rani. "Poor thing! And you know, when you get married, for days before, they rub your body with sandalwood paste, so my skin felt like mul-mul, you know, like a scarf. But when I think of that night, I think of the pain and that smell, the overpowering smell of sandalwood. God, it still gives me a headache. I can't stand the smell of sandalwood."

"He must have been crushed. Men have no egos in bed."

"No, he just kept talking to me, very gently, saying, 'It's supposed to hurt. Don't worry. It's supposed to. Just relax, if you relax you'll enjoy it.' I didn't, of course, I was just crying and crying."

"That's terrible, Rani."

"It sounds a lot worse when I describe it, but when I think back, he was so sweet, really. He was a completely different person. I wish I could get him back like that."

171

SABAH SQUEEZES Rani's hand. It's cold, despite the heat and humidity. "Can you see anyone?" she asks.

"No, they must still be in customs." Rani stares down the corridor, the flickering lights making her face look even more drained than it is. Sabah is not sure whether her lips are really trembling or whether it's the effect of the light. Rani looks at Sabah. "Thanks for coming with me."

"No problem, I don't have to work tomorrow. I just wonder if it's me Hemant wants to meet as soon as he gets off the plane. I feel sort of weird about this, Rani."

"No, don't be silly. Why should he mind? He'll be so tired from his trip he won't be able to talk to me *and* the whole rest of his family who are waiting to ambush him. He'll be glad I have someone else to talk to. Do you want another coffee?"

"Sure. My mother says they arrive and leave at an uncivilized hour in India so that they'll always arrive at a civilized time in the West."

"Who knows?" They step around the sleeping bodies on the floor, the brown and gray blankets rising slightly with each breath. Families mill around the lobby in little groups, the young men running back and forth to look through the sliding doors for relatives coming back from Europe. They stare at Sabah and Rani. The girls step from foot to foot, uncomfortable in their high-heeled shoes. They wind their oiled braids around their fingers. The mothers look up from the babies they are feeding or soothing, the whites of their eyes yellow with exhaustion.

"Two coffees," says Sabah, holding up her hand.

"You've got to make an effort to speak Hindi, you lazy girl. That's the only way you're going to get any better." Rani takes the plastic cups of frothy liquid from the counter. "I love the airport coffee, it's so sweet and milky, it tastes like coffee ice cream. When I was a kid, I used to love going to the airport to meet people just because of the coffee. And the train station for the tea in those mud pots—have you ever had that?—it smells of smoke."

"Baksheesh, baby, baksheesh." Sabah looks down at a thin hand, brown skin framing the lined white palm. She follows the arm up to the face of the woman, half covered by her sari. She shudders. The woman has huge brown Bambi eyes and thick curly eyelashes. But her eyes are the only recognizable feature on her face. Her nose is gone and she has no lips, her mouth is a gaping hole. Sabah looks back at the hand and realizes that the tips of the fingers are gone. Sabah puts a five-rupee note in the woman's hand, her own fingers aching in sympathy.

"Five rupees? Sabah, are you crazy? Come on, let's go back to the front."

Sabah follows Rani, conscious of the heavy earrings stretching her earlobes and the shine of the gold thread in her sari. "Rani, I wish we'd changed before we came. It's weird to be walking around the airport so dressed up."

"But this is the way I should meet my husband, isn't it? All dressed up like a new bride. And I wanted him to see you for the first time in a sari. Don't worry, you're looking lovely."

"Where is your father-in-law?"

"What?" Rani looks anxiously at the doors. "I think they're coming out now."

"Where's your father-in-law?"

"Oh. Oh, my father-in-law, he must have gone back to the car to see how Ma-ji was. Look, here's the first one. Oh, God." Rani pushes her way up to the front, through all the waiting people who've begun to move toward the exit door. "Come on, Sabah. Come up here. Then we'll see him before he sees us. Look, you can see the customs counter from here. Don't worry, as soon as Hemant steps out of the door, he'll be surrounded. His cousins and aunts have come as well. They're probably all sitting in their air-conditioned cars."

"Don't make fun of them. They're the smart ones and we're idiots, sweating here. I wouldn't mind sitting in an air—"

Rani grips Sabah's arm, "There he is. Look, they've stopped him at customs."

Sabah looks up as the steel doors slam shut. "I didn't see anything," she says, moving closer to the doors. A guard eyes her suspiciously.

"Look, look," Rani jostles the guard in an effort to wave to Hemant. "He's good-looking, Sabah, you're right. It's so stupid, it's really stupid. But I guess that's what love is." She looks at Sabah and then she smiles and turns away, blushing, her cheeks and the tip of her nose scarlet. "I still feel silly when I see him."

The guard steps in front of them. "Sorry, Madam. Not allowed." He looks at Rani's face and his own softens.

"Bhaisaha'ab," Rani addresses the guard sweetly, "my husband is coming. I haven't seen him in a year. Please. We're just married." She looks virtuous and forlorn.

The guard steps back.

Sabah and Rani walk through the doors. Sabah recognizes the young man from the photographs, in a blue suit this time, looking down at his open suitcases. A customs officer is rifling through them, tossing expensive ties and ironed shirts all over the sticky counter. "Electronics, saha'ab?" the customs officer is demanding.

"How dare you?" says Rani. "Do you know who this man is? He's working in England to help the reputation of this disgusting country and look at how you treat him." She is rapidly folding clothes and putting them back in the cases. "How will India ever become anything if you go around treating your representatives like this? Don't you care what other people think of you? No wonder the English think we're so rude." She snaps the clasps shut and pulls the suitcases off the counter.

"Sorry, Madam," says the customs officer apologetically. "What is your good name, Saha'ab?" He stamps the passport.

Rani snatches it away. "Thank God. Electronics! What rubbish! You think he smuggles them in his clothing like a common thief—"

Hemant takes the suitcases from Rani's hands. He looks at Sabah. He seems completely overwhelmed. His eyes are red and there's dried toothpaste in the corner of his mouth. He grips Rani's arm and pulls her around, "Come, let's go."

Rani turns and looks at Hemant. As their eyes meet, she blushes again. She looks down at the floor. "Yes," she says. She follows Hemant out to the lobby. The guards salute him as he passes.

Sabah walks a few steps behind them, feeling like a voyeur again. Rani's hand is on Hemant's arm, but he's ignoring it.

175

"My God, Rani," Hemant is saying. "Don't you have any self-respect?" As they step out the doors, they are enveloped by a mob of coolies all grabbing Hemant's suitcases and throwing them onto trolleys or hoisting them up onto the cloths on their heads.

"Hemant! Hemant!" His mother is hugging him, and his father is slapping him on the back. Rani steps out of the throng and puts her arm around Sabah. Sabah takes her hand again. It feels hot and swollen.

SABAH IS STANDING on a long green lawn. She's wearing a pink dress and holding out her arms. She can feel the sun warming the inside of her arms, the soft skin on the inside of her elbow is slightly wet. Behind her is a marigold bed; only a half step backward and her white sneakers would sink into the black soil, the wet earth sticking to them and soaking through the canvas. But she doesn't; she is posed and smiling on the lawn. The sun is shining down, glinting off her hair, and she knows that if she touched the top of her head, it would be hot to her hand. She feels comfortable. Warm and happy and honey brown technicolor.

"How old were you there?" asks Rani.

"Five, I guess," says Sabah. "Typical suburban American child. I'm probably looking across the street at the neighbor's house, because their two sons were my best friends, Donny and Ronny. They came to my birthday parties in tiny little suits and ties with their hair wet and combed back. There's this picture of us all playing croquet somewhere."

"What a darling you were. Do you remember you and me and Yasmine used to spit watermelon seeds into your mother's flowers? We'd sit on the steps and eat it because your mother didn't let us come inside."

176

The phone on Sabah's bedside table rings loudly. She picks it up and hands the phone to Rani. "It's for you. Hemant."

Rani's face tenses, her forehead wrinkling. She bites her trembling lower lip. "Hello," she says, hesitantly. "I just wanted to spend a little time with my friends before I go— are you coming home soon? Oh. Yes, you're right, I—" She puts the receiver down. "He hung up," she says. "I knew I shouldn't have left my mother-in-law's today. God, I'm such an idiot."

"No you're not, Rani," says Sanjay. "Don't you start believing his rubbish either. Who does he think he is?"

"My husband."

Sanjay looks away.

"Rani, do you remember when one of the watermelon seeds sprouted?" says Sabah, breaking the silence. "Remember?"

"Yes," Rani smiles. "We were so excited, the three of us." She picks up the photograph and looks at it again. "Sabah, I'm going to miss you so much in London. You have to promise to visit me. Promise! Let's see what else you have in your suitcase."

"Of course, you idiot. Here, this a picture of my friends from college in California," Sabah holds out the pictures, trying not to look at them, already feeling the creeping ache in her stomach when she thinks of Rob.

"Rani, don't get all weepy and sentimental yet. Otherwise, you'll have to repeat the whole performance in Bombay. Why else do you think we're coming? Watch out, Sabah, you're going to spill your drink," warns Sanjay, taking the photos from her.

Sabah spins and grabs the glass of water just as it slips off the edge of the table, pushed by all the books and clothes. "What reflexes!" she shouts, a little too loudly, trying to get the tightness out of her face. "I'm great under pressure!"

"You're a nut," smiles Sanjay, handing the photographs to Rani but still watching Sabah.

"Wow, who's that handsome tall boy? A boyfriend?"

"It's a long story. His name is Rob. He's a musician."

"Don't you dare fall in love with any musicians," says Sanjay. "They are penniless. You'll die. Anyway, he looks exactly like Brian. Typical American. How boring."

"That's just because you want Sabah for yourself, Sanjay. I love that old picture."

"I take it everywhere. It makes me feel like a little kid."

"It's so American. It makes me homesick."

"What was so funny was that in this typical American house with its little square lawn, my mother was growing coriander and mint with the flowers. To make chutney. Because in those days, you couldn't buy it fresh anywhere." Sabah thought about being five, imagined herself sitting on the edge of the flowerbed, her bottom half-buried in the warm earth, her scrawny legs sticking out akimbo, as she picked off leaves of mint and coriander. She crushed the leaves, rolling them between her hands, until the green juice tinted her palms. Then she'd suck in the sharp scents, lick the fresh mint and the soapy coriander off from the heel of her hand to her fingers, partly for the taste and partly because she enjoyed the tickle of her tongue. When Ronny or Donny came over, she'd quickly wipe her hands on her dress and explain that they were magical flowers that only bloomed at night.

"Not right in front of the house?"

"Yes, of course she did, Sanjay. All the Indians used to do that. My mother was lucky because she didn't have to cook Indian food every night for my father. He was perfectly happy eating any rubbish."

"I used to love the food at your house, Rani. Hot dogs and jello and macaroni and cheese. Yasmine and I were so envious of you."

178

"Were you? I envied you for having Yasmine. I always wanted a sister," Rani smiles.

"Rani, you'd better call Hemant back as well. Perhaps your mother-in-law has plans for you two. It's your last night in his house and all."

"My mother-in-law has lots of plans for me, Sanjay, and she tells them all to Hemant. Fortunately, they're both too lazy to carry any of them out," she laughs. "No, you're right. I'll be a good wife and go to her house tonight. Anyway, Hemant has to have dinner with a client, so I'll practice my cooking skills on his parents. But don't worry, we still have five days to lie beside the Taj Hotel swimming pool and gossip. I absolutely must get a suntan before I go to London."

"*Bonsoir*, good evening, salaam," says Pierre. He bows slightly as he opens the door. Sabah stares. Pierre blushes and frowns, his pink face burning red, drowning out

the freckles. He's wearing a white churidar and hat and a little embroidered waistcoat.

"Oh, my God," giggles Sanjay. "Listen, Pierre, I hope
you don't mind I brought Sabah along. I didn't really—"

"No, no, please," says Pierre, his voice strained. "It's
just that—I wasn't expecting anyone extra. Perhaps, you'll
find this quite boring." He looks embarrassed.

"Don't worry, Americans are very sophisticated,"
laughs Sanjay.

"But, of course," says Pierre, regaining his composure.
"It's just an evening of Indian music. A small performance.
Please," he gestures them inside.

The living-room floor is covered with white sheets,
and the guests are all seated there, leaning uncomfortably
against long cushions, or standing awkwardly sock-footed in
their bush suits, holding drinks. On one side of the room, a
tabla and a harmonium are arranged, surrounded with huge
cushions and low tables with pitchers full of water. Sabah
inhales, the smell is amazing, cool and sweet. Ropes of jasmine and roses are strung along the walls like Christmas
lights. She looks around for a familiar face. Then she realizes
why Pierre was so shocked to see her. She's the only woman
here. Everyone else, including the serving boys dressed in
white with brocade turbans, is male.

"Sabah!" someone calls out. Sabah sees Mahinder, in
a dhoti, sitting cross-legged in front of a cushion. She hurries
over to him. "You mad girl," he laughs. "Pierre must have
freaked out. Actually, it's lucky Rani couldn't come. Doesn't
he look hep?"

"He is completely freaked out that Sabah's come,"
says Sanjay. "Why didn't you tell me what this was?"

"Because I thought it would be fun, an ethnic experience for our American. Look at the servants. Pierre thinks
he's back in the days of the Raj." He watches each new guest
enter with great amusement. "What fun!"

179

"Mahinder, is there going to be real music and all at this thing?"

"Yes, look, here are the musicians."

The men start sitting down around the floor. Occasionally, one of them glimpses Sabah and squirms uncomfortably. The music starts: the long, slow breaths of the harmonium and the singer's whining voice contrasting with the rhythm of the drummer's bouncing palms across the tablas.

Then the door to the kitchen opens and a slim girl dances into the room, her face covered with a red dupatta. She dances suggestively around the room, spinning, so that her ghagra rises up around her like a red-and-gold umbrella, the heavy bracelets visible around her ankles.

The men cheer. So that's what this is, thinks Sabah. She'd read about nautch girls, in *Kim*, she thinks. Another thin girl dances slowly into the room, this one in blue. They dance together, and then one of them dances over to a guest, lifts her dupatta, and bats her eyelashes.

Or his eyelashes. Sabah realizes that both of the dancers are completely flat-chested. The men are smiling at each other. One of them reaches over and grabs one of the boys around the waist and pulls him toward the floor. The boy jumps delicately out of his grasp, blowing him a kiss. Sabah looks into his face. He winks at her. He looks about ten or eleven, his face is completely hairless. Just like his body, she thinks. He's a baby. "They're boys," she whispers to Mahinder.

"Of course they are, you goose. What do you think this is?"

Sabah looks over at Pierre. He's lying back against a cushion, a hookah beside his elbow. He lifts the mouthpiece to his lips and inhales. He smiles and watches a businessman in a cream-colored suit pull a serving boy down into his lap.

"Oh, my God, look, over there, do you know who that is?" The smile drops off Sanjay's face. Sabah follows his wide-open eyes: the young man has a thin mustache. He looks familiar, Sabah's seen him before—

"I can't believe it. That's Hemant, isn't it?" says Mahinder, even he looks shocked.

"Come on, Sabah," Sanjay is pulling her up. "We've got to get you out of here." He turns away from the dancing boys.

"Sanjay, you're such a bore," says Mahinder, half teasing. "No, you're right, no real husband material here, Sabah." He looks at the little boy being caressed by Hemant.

"That's my ayah's son—the son of the woman who brought me up, Sabah. Let's go."

Sabah looks at the face of the boy as she walks out, trying to feel sorry for him, but his painted mouth is scornful, his eyes hard. Hemant is sticking twenty-rupee notes into the waist of his skirt. The boy laughs and yanks the man's silk tie, but he keeps looking at Sabah.

"I just taught him how to read last year."

The boy grins at her. She's not sure whether she should smile back, but she can't see anything behind his hard eyes. She can't see anything in his face except his eyes like black stones and the cheap red lipstick cracking as his lips tighten across his white teeth. All she can see is his taunting grin, which makes her feel like he just spat at her.

181

Gateway to India

"YOU'RE SURE this is the right address?" asks Sabah, peering out of the tinted windows of the car.

"This is the address you gave me," says Rani. She rolls the window down a little, the humid air from outside quickly overwhelming the air conditioner. The brass numbers on the gate are the same as on the piece of paper.

"What a house," sighs Sanjay. "What a house." The three of them stare at the huge marble house. There are several cars in the driveway, all of them white. An Alsatian dog appears in the arched doorways of the veranda. He gallops out of the shadows, barking and snarling across the lawn.

"I can't believe my uncle lives here," Sabah shakes her head. "No wonder he never came to visit us."

The chowkidar swings open the pedestrian gate, rubbing the sleep from his eyes. He nods at them, "Yes?"

"Is Al-Hussain saha'ab there?" asks Sanjay. "This is his niece from America. She's come to see him."

"Mr. Jimmy?" says the chowkidar. "No, Mr. Jimmy is in England. He's gone away for a long time," he says in Hindi. Sabah and Rani are already getting out of the car, unloading all the packages Sabah's mother had sent for her in-laws. The chowkidar doesn't look as if he trusts them. He leans back against the post and lights a bidi. He inhales deeply and looks at Sanjay through the feeble smoke, "These are Mr. Jimmy's relatives?"

"Yes," says Sanjay, taking control. "Now, please call us inside because it's very hot. And," he adds, "help Baby with her boxes."

"I'll call the ayah," says the chowkidar. "It's not my job to carry things." He starts to shut the gate, but Sanjay pushes it open and holds it as Sabah and Rani walk in. The three of them follow the chowkidar to the house, the dog trotting along beside them, sniffing and panting.

"Sabah bibi. How grown-up you are. How beautiful, why haven't you come to see us in all this time?" says the ayah in a flood of Hindi, hugging her and taking the packages and holding Sabah's chin in her rough hands, trying to look at her at the same time. "Hindi, yes?" she asks, her lips stained red with paan juice, her teeth black and corroded.

"She understands it," says Rani.

"Oh, my God," whistles Sanjay. "Look at this place." They're standing in a marble foyer that looks like a movie set. A huge staircase sweeps down from the balcony, wrapping around a fountain. Plants surround the fountain and reach leafy tendrils up to the balcony and down again to the splashing water. On the wall is a massive neoclassical painting of a ballerina, in an ornate frame.

"It looks like a hotel," marvels Sabah, "or a bordello. It's hard to tell the difference in this country." She smiles at the old ayah who is throwing her dupatta over her gray hair and pushing them toward the living room while shouting for the bearer to bring them mango milkshakes and cake. "I can't believe this."

"Let's ask if we can see the whole place," Rani whispers back.

The sitting room is even more ostentatious than the entrance, and the white carpets seem to have some sort of thick padding beneath them so that Sabah's feet sink with each step. She feels like she's walking through mud. Sanjay throws himself down in an armchair. Sabah looks at the milk-white sofa the ayah is gesturing her to sit on. She feels very grubby. She looks at Rani. "Rani, my jeans are going to leave black marks on the seat. I can't sit here," she says.

"You have to," smiles Rani. "Just sit on it the way you were sitting at my mother-in-law's."

The ayah kisses Sabah's head. "You look just like your mother when she got married," she takes Sabah's chin in her hand and peers into her face, "but you have a little of your father as well. I can see Muzzafer when he was such a little boy, even younger than you, running all around the house." She gets up to pass the milkshakes to everyone.

Sanjay is already up and checking out the contents of the bar. "Wow," he says to Sabah, "look at all this imported stuff. Scotch and all. I'd love to put a little rum in my milkshake, delicious. Too bad." He picks up his milkshake and goes back to the armchair.

"Everyone is gone," the ayah says sadly. "You won't get to meet our little Alia. She would love to have met you."

"When will they come back?" asks Rani, perched on the edge of the sofa. "We'll be here for several days."

183

"Oh, sorry, bibi," says the ayah. "They are not coming back for some time. Jimmy saha'ab is sick in London."

"Sick?" says Sabah. "In London? That's terrible. My father will be really worried. What does she mean? Ask her what's wrong with him."

The ayah presses her red fingers into her breast and makes a choking sound for Sabah, "Heart attack."

"Heart attack? Is he all right? Is he—"

"Now, no problem," nods the ayah. "He is fine."

"My God, I have to call my dad! Where is Jimmy uncle now?"

"No problem," smiles the ayah reassuringly. "He is with Amna."

"My aunt in London," Sabah explains. "My father's sister. I last saw her when I was ten."

"Sabah," says Rani, shocked, "don't you know any of your family? I hope you've told your grandmother you're here."

"My father never wanted to keep in touch with them," Sabah explains. "I called my grandmother yesterday. I left a message with the servant or something. She didn't call me back. But what am I going to say to her? I guess she called my dad about Jimmy's heart attack."

Sanjay sips his milkshake. "It's the age, I guess. All our fathers are getting to the age when they have heart attacks. God knows, the way Indians eat. All that oily food and sitting in a chair worrying about money the whole day. In any case, Sabah, you must call your grandparents again. No one ever gets phone messages here." He looks up, "Hey, look, a gold record."

"That's not all," says Sabah. Jimmy's awards and posters are everywhere, as well as framed pictures of himself shaking hands with various celebrities. In between, there are framed prints of impressionist paintings. "We won't ask who hired the interior decorator."

184

"What a beautiful house," says Rani. "Can we see the whole thing?"

The ayah is thrilled. "Of course, of course. It is a very beautiful house, isn't it? Zenab bibi has very good taste. She decorated it completely herself. Everything is from foreign. From England, I think. Come, come upstairs."

"I can't believe this," says Sanjay. The master bedroom is blinding, the thick silk curtains and the satin comforter engulfing the king-sized bed are parrot green. The carved wooden furniture is almost medieval. When the ayah leaves, he flops backward across the embroidered cushions on the bed and looks at the ceiling. "I feel like I'm in *Citizen Kane.*"

Rani sits down on the skirted chair in front of the dressing table and picks up a heavy silver hairbrush. "Just hold this, Sabah. You could murder someone with it," she says, picking up a lipstick and rolling the gleaming red stick out of the gold case. "And look at all this imported makeup. At least they're using it."

185

Sabah is already down the hall. "Look at the girl's— Alia's room. You won't believe this, Sanjay, come down here!" Sanjay jumps off the bed and runs down the hall.

"Oh, wow," he says. "How old is the girl?" The walls are covered with pink flowers, the carpets are salmon pink, the pictures on the wall are painted in tones of peach and apricot.

"Ugh," says Rani. "It would make me sick to my stomach to wake up here. But look at the lovely balcony she has. How romantic." She opens the glass doors and walks out onto the balcony. "Look at this big tree. Perfect for lovers to climb up. Oh, how horrible. It's full of vultures!" Rani shudders. "Especially in Bombay. You know, with the towers of silence and all."

"Oh, Rani, everyone tells you that vulture story, it's rubbish." Sanjay closes the glass doors as Rani walks back in.

"What vulture story?"

"You know the Parsis put their dead up on these huge towers and they get eaten by birds and all. And everyone in Bombay tells a story about this vulture flying over and dropping a hand or a foot or something on their balconies."

"Horrible," says Rani. "Don't talk about it. I hate dead things. I even hate thinking about them. When I see vultures, I feel like I'm going to die myself. Let's go back to the Taj."

Sanjay laughs, "Rani always thinks she's safe if she's in a five-star hotel."

The ayah comes into the room. "Sabah bibi, why are you going to a hotel? You must stay here. Zenab bibi will never forgive me if you don't stay. And your friends also. Look, there are so many rooms."

"I'm sorry," apologizes Rani. "We'd love to stay, but my husband is also here and he's staying in a hotel." She looks at Sabah, "I won't see Sabah again for a long time, so I want her to stay there, too—at least until I leave. And then she can come and stay here."

The ayah shakes her head, "Hotels are so expensive. And the food—it's not house food, you know, you could get sick." She leads them downstairs. "But I can see you are all stubborn, all young people, like my little Adam."

Sabah looks back at the house as the car drives away. She tries to imagine what it must be like to live there. She thinks about Zenab, lifting the heavy brush to her head. She imagines the adolescent Alia, waking up everyday in her pink room, with the vultures' beaks clicking against the window. "It must be so strange to live in a place like that," she says. "I mean, you don't feel like you're in India. Like my room, as a kid, was typical: a bunk bed and a toy box..." Sabah drifts off. Sanjay has gone to sleep in the front seat, lulled by the air conditioning.

Rani is looking distractedly out the other window and chewing her lip. "Sabah," she says. "I'm so scared. I can't tell you how scared I am."

"It'll be OK, Rani. Hemant's not so bad, he's just making some decisions, I think. And he's having a hard time dealing with your being a star. That's normal. It's an ego thing. He's jealous."

"He hates me."

"No, he doesn't. You'll work everything out. And if you don't, you can come live with me in America. I know lots of American guys." Sabah raises her eyebrows a few times to make her point.

"All right," Rani forces a weak smile. "We'll move to a sweet little apartment in San Francisco or New York, with flower boxes in the windows. We'll eat macaroni and cheese every night. And we'll be free and young and beautiful and have lots of handsome friends."

"Of course," Sabah says cheerfully. "We'll go to all the right parties. As soon as I get back I'll find an apartment big enough for the two of us, OK?" Rani's eyes are red and brimming with tears. "Don't worry, you're hardcore."

187

"Oh, God, I wish I was." Rani reaches for Sabah's hand, and Sabah realizes Rani's shaking, her whole body is vibrating. Sabah brushes the hair off Rani's face. Then she presses her lips to Rani's forehead until the trembling stops.

A Midsummer
Night's Dream

THE TAXI TURNS a corner and Alia can see Amna's brick house. She looks up at the tall windows to see whether her father is looking out, but all she can see is a reflection of the London sky, a thick cloudy gray, as if the house is only a cardboard façade, and she can see straight through it to the other side, like one of her father's movie sets. Adam has gone to visit his friend Shezad, she reminds herself. Adam has gone to visit his friend Shezad, she says again, softly, under her breath like a mantra. "Adam has gone ... Adam left some things at his friend Shezad's house that he has to pick up. Adam's coming back—" She can almost hear Adam's voice in her ear.

"That'll be nine pounds, forty pence, Miss," says the driver.

Alia looks at the house. The leaves are falling from the trees in wide circles. She takes a deep breath.

"You did want number forty-seven, didn't you?"

Her hand trembles when she touches the doorbell. She can feel the sweat, cold and sticky, under her arms, dripping like little insect feet down her neck. Her face hurts. She must look a mess. Her clothes are all wrinkled from sleeping on the train, and the cardigan still has bits of bramble in it. Her hair's coming untied, and her nose and cheeks and shoulders are all sunburned.

Her aunt Amna opens the door, "Alia! Darling! How lovely and healthy you're looking. I'm so envious! Come inside, come in. Here, don't bring all those bags yourself, I'll just call the servant. Where's Adam?"

Zenab comes running down the stairs, her georgette sari floating along with her like a pastel cloud. "Alia, my baby! You're back. How have you been, little one? Oh, you've got sunburned, and look at your clothes. And you've lost weight. Where is Adam?"

Alia looks at her mother's soft brown eyes, she can feel herself melting. "Umma," she says. Her throat tightens and then she knows her face has turned white. "Adam has gone to see his friend Shezad." Her eyes fill with tears.

"What's wrong, behti? What is it?" Zenab is alarmed. "Oh, you poor little thing, how could he make you come by yourself?" She hugs Alia, who is now sobbing into her sari. "Come on upstairs, darling. As soon as Adam comes home, Abba will speak to him."

"Well done, Alia," says Amna, her clear blue eyes boring straight into Alia's mind, so that Alia squirms in her chair, and then they disappear again beneath her thick eyelashes as she pours a cup of tea. "It's about time you learned to take care of yourself."

"What rubbish are you talking, Amna?" says Jimmy. "My daughter does not have to learn to take care of herself, I can tell you that all right. Why the hell should she get married at all if she can take care of herself? London is a dangerous city, Alia. You should thank God that you were so lucky."

He is sitting in a chair now and has the television on. But Alia notices that he looks frail. His skin is gray and sags on his frame. She feels sorry for him. This is the first time in her life that her father has shouted at her and she hasn't been frightened. His anger is a thin façade over his weak body.

"Yes, Alia. London is not Bombay. If you had telephoned, Amna pupee and I would have come to pick you up," agrees Zenab, curling a twist of auburn hair around her lacquered fingernail. "It's terrible that Adam sent you alone."

"What's wrong with the boy? He never manages to get anywhere," says Jimmy. "Who is this Shezad? Ring him up! Tell Adam his father wants him home immediately, no excuses!"

"Shezad's the one who just got married to that beautiful English girl," says Amna. "Zenab, do you remember I told you about that lovely wedding in that English mansion?" She laughs, "The poor old lord was probably rolling in his grave, watching all those Pakis turning his estate upside down. You should have come to London sooner, bhaijan. Don't worry, Shezad's a very nice boy. Have a cup of tea."

"A nice boy? What kind of nice boy goes off and marries some Angrez girl? What was wrong with him, he couldn't find a Pakistani good enough? Perhaps none of them would take him. Alia, go and get me some sugar." Jimmy feels exhausted. He leans back in his chair. What is it about his son that does this to him? He hasn't even been able to do much research into that boy for Alia. He looks at the television. A woman in a bikini is pouring ice cubes on her chest. They melt and slide down the smooth brown expanse of her stomach. The camera pulls back and she's lying on a beach: white sand, blue sky, bluer water, and palm trees. Jimmy closes his eyes and the woman's flat stomach becomes blistered with an ugly purple scar that twists and bubbles from her breasts to her bikini bottom.

"Do you want to sleep for a little while, janoo?" asks Zenab. "Adam will probably be back any time. Amna, do you have his phone number?"

"Oh, don't worry about him. He's probably enjoying himself. Bhaijan, you rest. Come downstairs, Alia, we'll show you all the things your mama's bought for you."

"Oh, yes, Alia. And tomorrow we'll all go to Harrod's. I want to buy some clothes for Adam before we go."

Every time her mother or her aunt mentions Adam's name, Alia's stomach turns over. His name seems to echo, over and over, through the room. How will she tell them he's gone? Perhaps she should say she didn't know. Perhaps she should say that he told her he was going to his friend's house. When Jimmy talks about Adam, Alia feels completely sick. It's not her fault, anyway, she thinks. She told him not to go. "Yes, of course, Umma. We'll go to the shops tomorrow." She thinks her mother will understand. Maybe she'll just tell Umma. Umma will fix it all. Yes, she'll tell Umma somehow, but not Abba. Not yet.

"Do you like this scarf, Alia? When I was buying one for myself, I also bought one for you. Aren't they lovely? I knew you'd like them. Which one do you want?" Zenab holds up the two scarves. They are both crisp and bright, Alia can still smell the department store on them, the perfume of the salesgirls, the glass cleaner and the wood spray and all the plastic bags.

"You choose, Umma."

"Your mother knew you'd love them," says Amna. "You could wear them as dupattas, they're so big." She stops and takes a sip of tea. "I don't know why you want to wear dupattas, though. They're such a bother. They're always getting caught in the door of the car or the computer printer or the escalator. Or I step on them. Zenab, I cannot tell you how many dupattas I've torn holes in with the heels of my shoes. But Abba—that's your grandfather, Alia—he would die if he knew I was roaming around London without a dupatta."

"Well, life is so much easier in India, isn't it? So much more relaxed," says Zenab, stroking Alia's hair. "We don't have to hurry the way you do, Amna. And dupattas add such softness—it's sad that one has to give those things up."

Alia looks out the window. The sky above the buildings has become a deep purple. The servant is moving from room to room, drawing the curtains and turning on the lights. She clicks on the light in the kitchen, and the room is bathed in warm light. "Alia, can you make some more tea?" There are pots of vegetables and rice bubbling on the stove. Alia stands in the steam while she turns on the kettle, letting the smell of spices soak into her skin. She inhales, swallowing up the scents. She longs to be back in her kitchen in Bombay, with the khansammah, the cook, rolling out the chapatis.

"Do you think we should wait for Adam for dinner?"

"No, don't be silly, he's out with some boys his own age. Let's eat." Amna looks at her watch. "Oh, God, it's nine o'clock already. I'm so sorry. You must be starving. I'm starving. I'm surprised we haven't heard a shout from bhaijan upstairs."

After dinner, Alia sits on the edge of the bed while her mother sorts out her clothes. "This salwar must be washed. What did you do to it, Alia? And these things. What are you going to wear tomorrow? We have to go to a lunch party, and then we'll go shopping. Or perhaps we'll have to shop the day after, all the shops close at six o'clock."

By the soft light of her bedside lamp after dinner, everything in Alia's room looks dreamlike. Alia watches her mother sitting on the floor, her dupatta wrapped four times around her neck like a scarf, her loose salwar and kurta opening out like a parachute around her and mixing with the heaps of clothes.

Zenab's attention wanders from the suitcases she's been organizing. Her brown eyes focus on her daughter. Alia looks like a little bird, perched on the edge of the bed. "Behti, you're looking so thin. Perhaps you're not eating enough iron. I'll buy some iron tablets tomorrow. Do you want a glass of milk?"

"Umma, I—Adam—" Alia mumbles.

"Oh, are you missing him, Alia? Don't worry, he'll come soon. I'm also missing him. Tomorrow, you tell the servant to buy you chocolate and all the things you need to make chocolate mousse. Just like Adam's recipe. Perhaps you should check downstairs. There might even be the things you need to make it right now."

"Ummi, Adam's not coming," Alia says, barely coherent.

"If he said he'll come, of course he'll come," Zenab gets up and kisses Alia. "Don't worry."

"He didn't say he'll come. He's gone to New York," Alia's eyes are swimming with tears again. I'm a baby, she thinks. I'm really a baby. Zenab's face looks like one of those smudgy paintings she saw in the museum. I promised Adam, she thinks. I promised him, and here I am crying again. I can't even wait one day. I promised I would take care of myself like an English girl, and here I am crying again and blurting everything out to Umma.

"Don't be silly, Alia," says Zenab. "How would he go without telling anyone?"

"He told you, Ummi. He told you he was going to New York. He told you he bought a ticket and everything," chokes Alia. "I told a lie. He never went to his friend's house. He went to the airport. Now he's gone. He's gone and he's lost and he's in New York—and it's my fault." Alia breathes a sigh of relief. She feels like she's torn off a very tight corset. She collapses in her mother's arms.

"Don't worry, Alia. Of course it's not your fault," Zenab squeezes Alia. She rocks her like a baby in her arms, and a flood of images sweep into Zenab's mind. She's holding

Jimmy as he's collapsing in the disco, suddenly the music is crashing and medics are swarming through the dancing bodies. Zenab can hear sirens and radios and then she's staring at Jimmy's face, shrunken and papery, the only thing not moving in her spinning vision. Then she's lying on her bed in Bombay, sick and pregnant with Alia, while Jimmy cavorts on the beach with one of his leading ladies. The humid Bombay air only makes her more nauseated. She hears the door creak open and soft, unsteady footsteps on the carpet. Then she sees baby Adam, in a little white kurta, pulling himself up to the bed. He steadies himself by holding her head and he kisses her face with his tiny pink mouth. Her baby boy.

The night before Adam left for Paris, the living room was crowded with relatives and friends who'd come to wish him goodbye. Everyone was eating and drinking and helping Adam pack last minute things. All the ladies wanted Parisian saris: "There's a lovely sari shop in Paris, one of the best in the world, you must go there, Adam. I can't remember the street name, but I'm sure you'll find it." And in the midst of it all, the stereo was playing and all the young girls were dancing around the room, fluttering with light like colored flames. Adam stood in the middle of the room, wanting to stay with the girls, wanting to play and dance. Zenab watched him. She saw Adam's face change, his sweet features become firm. It seemed that, as she watched him, the baby fat on his cheeks tautened and the faint brown hairs darkened on his upper lip. She realized as he walked across the room to join his father's friends that he had left her.

And then, somehow, he had looked across the room at her, had caught her eye, as she sipped her Coca-Cola. He stood, holding his first watery whiskey and soda, listening to one of his uncles tell him an anecdote. His uncle started laughing, and Adam turned, his other hand self-consciously touching his blazer, and he caught her eye. She could tell that he saw how sad she was. He smiled and disappeared upstairs. "OK, Alia!" he had yelled down the stairs, just the way he used to when he was a little boy. "OK, introduce me!"

He danced onto the floor, moving his lips along with the tape so that it looked like he was really singing it himself. And he wore a costume and everything—some shiny trousers of Alia's and Zenab's gloves and even some makeup. He sang and did a dance that would have impressed even Michael Jackson, he was so dramatic. And everyone was clapping and laughing and Jimmy was patting Adam on the back, it felt like the whole room was shaking with laughter and high spirits.

Zenab closes her eyes and tries to wish herself back there. She tries to force her whole being into that instant, those three minutes, to push her body back to where her mind is, where Adam is still slipping on the silk carpets and winking at her as he regains his balance.

She opens her eyes. "Alia," says Zenab. "Abba is still not well. He has to stay calm. You know how angry he becomes. So we'll wait a little while before we tell him. All right? In the meantime, perhaps we'll find out where Adam is." Zenab imagines Adam alone on the streets of New York. She sees thieves jumping out from behind gray buildings, thugs with dirty faces, and knives glinting on the subway. She's seen quite a lot of videos of New York City.

Alia sniffs. She feels weak with relief. "I might have his phone number. I think it's Marc's."

"Don't worry, we'll just telephone the silly boy and tell him to come back." Zenab stares at the pile of clothing on the ground. She strokes Alia's back. She pushes her hair out of her face. "Alia, let's get up. What is the time in New York?"

"I don't know. I think it's earlier there."

"You go and get the phone number. Come on. Let's go down to the kitchen so we don't wake your pupee and Abba."

her eyebrows, pulling them up, tightening her forehead. She looked at her mother, to see whether Zenab needed support.

But Zenab simply said, "Yes, Adam's become completely French. Who knows how we're going to feed him when he gets back to Bombay. I think I'm going to have to bring half of Harrod's food hall with me." The other women laughed as they spread their napkins on their laps and speculated whether their own spoiled sons, born and bred in England, would ever be able to live on the subcontinent.

Zenab was not joking when she said she had to bring half of Harrod's food hall with her to India. She was considering bringing the whole thing. She'd already bought so much prepared and canned food that she'd had to ship back the cases rather than include them in her luggage. Zenab had thrown herself into her shopping with a seriousness Alia had never seen before.

In the past four days, the only thing that had relaxed the long lines that creased Zenab's face from her nose to her mouth was buying things she thought Adam might need when he came back to India. "I suppose it will be some time before he's used to Indian milk again," she said to Alia. "It's so lucky they sell this long-life milk. Could you ship the carton to this address?" she asked the salesman. Or: "Adam will need a nice briefcase if he's going to work in Bombay, don't you think?" Alia would help her mother decide whether low-fat milk was better than whole, or whether a brown briefcase would go with more things than a black one. All the while, she kept seeing Adam sitting alone on the bus, a long bus with blue plastic seats, driving through the deserted streets of the city at night. In the flickering light of the bus, all the seats were empty except for his. Adam leaned against the window, barely able to make out the shuttered shops outside, staring at the dark shapes of people in apartments.

Zenab picks up the empty cups of chocolate and puts them in the sink.

In the morning, Alia and Zenab are back on Oxford Street, spraying men's cologne on their wrists. "Which one do you think he'll like?" asks Zenab. "We won't ship it, because he might want to use it right away when he comes back to London." Zenab smiles at Alia. For the first time in a week, she looks conspiratorially at Alia and says, "I think it's about time we did a little shopping for ourselves, don't you?"

Alia smiles back, but she doesn't feel as relaxed as her mother does. "Yes, Ummi," she says, so sobered by the thought of going home that even the piped-in music and bright lights of the store fail to distract her. "Perhaps I should buy some notebooks for school."

"Notebooks," laughs Zenab. "Don't be silly, let's buy some pretty things for you to wear in your hair." She takes Alia's hand and pulls her around the glittering costume jewelry counters. When Zenab stops to try on a pair of earrings that look like diamond pavé tiger's heads with emeralds in their teeth, Alia reaches for a pair of red-glass earrings that hang like crystalline droplets of blood about to drip onto her shoulders. "I like these."

"They're very sweet," says Zenab, "but if you're going to wear jewelry like that, you should wear real, don't you think? It's so sad to wear paste if it's not dramatic." They walk slowly toward the hair clips, stopping to sample a perfume or to handle a rope of false pearls. "Now you see," says Zenab, "we can get real pearls for the same price in Hong Kong."

Zenab picks up a velvet bow and arranges Alia's hair. Zenab loves the feel of Alia's hair, the wavy locks still soft and silky like a child's. She feels a wave of affection for her daughter. "Look at this, Alia," she holds up a mirror, "isn't this lovely?" She takes off the bow and tries a big gold clip on Alia. As the hair slips from her hands, Zenab has a feeling of looking back at herself as a child, her own mother braiding her brown hair. She remembers braiding her sister's hair sometimes when they were late for school, while her mother braided hers, the three of them standing in a line in front of the mirror. Zenab thinks of her grandmother putting her mother's hair in a thick plait shiny with coconut oil and smelling of jasmine. She can see them in a long line, her great-grandmother standing behind her grandmother, pulling the brown hair to make her daughter stand up straight, her great-great-grandmother behind her. A long line of women, braiding the hair of their daughters and sisters all the way back into eternity, to the beginning of time, to the beginning of women.

"Yes, it's beautiful, Ummiji," says Alia quietly.

A cash-register drawer slams shut, the metallic clank tossing Zenab's thoughts like loose change to the back of her mind. Zenab is suddenly thrown back into the department store, the smell of the cosmetics counters surrounding them.

"Would you like to see anything else, Madam?" asks the salesgirl.

"Shall we buy it?" Zenab asks Alia.

They leave the store just as it's closing, the salesman turning the key in the lock behind them. They stand in the fading sunlight, waiting for Amna to pick them up. "It's so lucky we've had such good weather," says Zenab.

A fruit seller is starting to pack his piles of melons and grapes back into their boxes. The evening sun reaches under the canopy on his trolley, lighting the peaches like blushing faces. Alia misses the open fruit market in Bombay, where she can smell the ripe fruit and straw even before she's carrying the heavy newsprint bundles in her arms.

A red double-decker bus pulls up in front of them. There are a lot of Indian faces mixed in with white English ones. Alia stares at them. There are some Indian girls in short skirts and jackets, just like English girls. They are laughing and telling jokes with harsh British accents. Alia feels sorry for them, having long gray English lives without any hope of the hot Bombay sun burning through the clouds. She wonders whether Adam ever worried that he was going to spend the rest of his life in Europe. Whether when he passed a supermarket in Paris or London, he longed for the shouts of fruitwallahs in Bombay, missed having dirty-faced children crowd around him asking for change or sweets, whether he thought perhaps he'd never hear the crank and rumble of a juice-pressing machine spitting out frothy glasses of sugar-cane juice again.

"YOU KNOW," Amna says pointedly at dinner, making Alia almost drop her plate, "I'm surprised Adam went off with Shezad and dropped his plan of going to New York. He and Marc were so keen on it."

Zenab looks up calmly from the small coffee table they are using as a buffet. "Adam and I are very close. He never does things unreasonably."

Jimmy holds out his hand to take his plate from Zenab. Since Jimmy's heart attack, they've begun having their meals in his bedroom, to keep him from climbing up and down the stairs too often. "Reasonable?" Jimmy's fed up with the bedroom, the house, the gray London weather, the women getting him things. "Headstrong is more like it. That boy is headstrong. At least his stubbornness will help him in the business world. That's the only thing that's going to save him."

"Adam has an artistic nature, really. He's very sensitive."

"Sensitive, my foot. He just wants to go out and have fun."

"Bhaijan, speaking of going out, did you have your walk today?"

"Of course, I walked all around these deserted suburbs of yours," Jimmy grumbles, but he feels a surge of energy go through him. His strength is returning slowly. He's itching to leave England.

"Thank God, Allahtherashukr," says Zenab. "You're sounding much better, janoo."

Kiss Kiss

RANI LEANS toward Sabah to give her a kiss goodnight, her lips shiny and enameled, moving in slow motion to Sabah's cheek, but then Rani turns her head and kisses Sabah dead on the mouth. Sabah's lips sink into hers, her teeth click against Rani's before they open, moving apart so that Rani's tongue can glide into her mouth. Her fingers are stroking the stretched tendons in her neck, caressing her eyes, her cheeks, her ears, the other hand massaging, teasing, a tingling breast.

Sabah reaches for Rani's calf, she grabs the rounded muscle, moves up her leg, digs her fingernails into the soft skin under her knee, a muscle tightens beneath her hand and she follows it to where it relaxes and disappears in the mass of her buttock.

Rani's breasts are pressed against hers, and Sabah gasps, reaches her fingers under the elastic of Rani's panties. Rani stretches her leg around Sabah's waist. She groans, and the rumble in her throat gets louder, turns into a shout...

"You bastard! Haramzada!"

Sabah hears a crash as something smashes against her wall. She opens her eyes. The room is black. She shakes her head, the dream is gone. For a second, she thinks the person screaming is Meera, shrieking at her husband again. She thinks she's thirteen and she's lying in her bedroom in Boston. She sucks in her breath. The green smell of mango skins fills her nostrils. She hears the low hum of the hotel air conditioner. She's in Bombay. The person screaming in the next room is Rani.

Sabah jumps out of bed. She clicks on the light and squints, blinded for a second by the glare on the glass of her watch. It's four-thirty. She's only been in bed for an hour. She splashes her face with water in the bathroom and throws on a dressing gown.

She can't find the key to her room in the aftermath of clothes and makeup strewn around the tables and chairs, from the last two days of parties. She gives up and leaves the door ajar, watching the hall for thieves as she knocks on Rani and Hemant's door.

"Who is it?" shouts Hemant. Sabah hears heavy footsteps, and then Hemant's scowling face is inches from hers, she can smell the whiskey and after-shave on his skin.

"What's going on? Are you all right?" Sabah can see Rani, her eyes swollen and red and her mouth twisted, poised to spit insults. She glares at Hemant's back. She's taken off her gold sari and she's wearing only her blouse and petticoat, she looks like a long brown cigarette in gold foil.

"Nothing's wrong," says Hemant, "except that this bitch of a woman doesn't think I'm good enough for her and her filmi friends." He's drunk as well, and his words are slurred and heavily accented with Hindi.

"Rani," Sabah tries to push Hemant out of the way, "do you want me to do anything?" She wants to grab Rani, hook an arm around her waist, throw Rani's thin body over her own square shoulders, and carry her away.

Rani tries to smile at Sabah, her lips twitching. "Don't worry, Sabah. I got myself into this—of my own free will—and I'm adult enough to know what to do. *I* don't need to ask my mother to make my decisions."

"What the hell do you know about making decisions?" Hemant yells, falling back against the wall with a thud. "What the hell do you know about anything in life except how to use your goddamn body to sell washing machines? The reason you don't listen to your mother is because she does it for free. You get *paid!*"

Sabah walks into the room, broken eyeshadow boxes and bottles of perfume cracking under her chappals. She steps on a lipstick and slips, smearing a red stripe into the carpet. The room reeks of alcohol. A smashed bottle of whiskey lies under the television, another bottle is overturned on the dressing table and the pool of liquid drips slowly to the ground. The carpet is littered with glittering pieces of broken glass. Sabah stops. She's scared to touch Rani.

"Don't you talk about my mother, you bastard!" Rani is screaming and shaking so hard, Sabah thinks about an article she once read about spontaneous combustion. "You fly to Paris to fuck French whores! You pay more for one blow job than I make for ten modeling jobs and you don't even send me one rupee to buy a stick of kajal! Not one rupee! And how much did that last one cost that you were boasting about? How much for the bubble bath? How much for the fucking champagne? How much so she would touch you? Or is it *he?* You know why? No self-respecting woman—or man—would touch you unless they were paid. You're right. I have no fucking self-respect."

"That's right, Rani. Tell Sabah about this. Tell the whole bloody hotel and all of Bombay what kind of marriage we have! Tell them I'm gay and you're a whore! Why not? You've already told everyone in Delhi." Hemant's eyes are bloodshot and the veins are throbbing in his temples. "Everyone in Delhi has to be watching you and talking about you all the time! You have everything you want. You're the middle-class Indian wet dream. Isn't that it? What you've always wanted? Everyone is looking at you! Every rickshaw driver and paanwallah falls asleep at night masturbating to your picture, Rani. They dream about grabbing my wife with their dirty black hands. My wife. Rani, queen of kutch-nahi.

207

It's because of you that I stay in London. You think I want to see my family embarrassed by a drunken dancing girl every night?"

"You and your fucking family honor. Where's your family honor when you're in Paris? Ask why I won't have a son! Because what kind of honor would this family have? Honor!" Rani spits at Hemant. "Here's your honor. Why don't you do what every other cheap Indian husband would do now and burn me. Why not? Don't worry, no one cares. Right, Sabah?"

Sabah steps forward. She walks toward her, tripping on the debris and broken glass on the floor. She falls down, her knees smacking the concrete beneath the carpeting. She catches herself with her hands and gets up. She slides along the wall, trying to stay as far away from Hemant as she can.

"Now that you're living abroad you can just send for another wife. Just like everyone else in your class," laughs Rani. "How much dowry you'll get! How many scooters and refrigerators! I can see your mother rubbing her hands together right now. And counting the pieces of jewelry she'll get back. Here. Look, here are some matches." Rani picks up the beige packet of hotel matches and throws them at Hemant. She picks up the bottle of whiskey and pours the remains over her head, "Here, I'm ready."

"Rani, I really should burn you." Hemant bends over and picks up the matches. He shakes his head and stalks toward her. "If I was a good Hindu I would burn you just to save you from your own life—look at the kind of life you lead! What kind of wife are you? What kind of wife are you!"

Sabah stands in front of the dressing table. She grips the edge of the table and feels a shard of glass cut into her palm. A slash of pain rips through her body like an electric shock. Her hands and legs sting with tension.

"Are you proud of yourself? Don't you know that a good wife should think of her husband as a god! Burning you would be a kindness! You think I'm going to save you? You should be touching my feet and asking me to forgive you. Did you touch my feet in the airport when everyone was watching you scream? Did you? You should touch my feet!" he bellows, standing in front of her, his breath blowing the hair on her forehead. "Do it! Now! Now! Now!"

Rani stares back into his eyes. She doesn't move.

"Did you hear me?" he screams, waving the package of matches for emphasis. "Touch my feet!"

Rani spits.

The glob of saliva hits Hemant on the lip. It sticks there for a second, shiny and bubbling.

Hemant lights the match.

There is a hiss and a crackle as the alcohol catches the flame, and then there are flames everywhere and Rani's sharp scream cutting through it all. Sabah runs forward to grab her, but the flames leap hissing up in front of her like snakes, and Hemant throws himself backward into her and she's crushed against the wall. She tries to push him back, he's so heavy, she can't move, her rib cage feels crushed, she can't breathe. Rani is screaming and screaming and screaming like an endless siren, and Sabah tries to push Hemant back, but he is collapsing on top of her and she's coughing and her hands are wet and slippery. She pushes Hemant toward the door and there's blood all over the door, there's blood all over her hands, there's blood drying and crackling with the heat on her face. She touches her legs and they're slippery with blood as well. She can hear Rani screaming and she wants to see her but she can't see anything but smoke and the hot tears pouring from her eyes.

"Rani! Rani!" Sabah shrieks. She hears noises, shouting. Someone is grabbing her arm, she thinks it's Hemant and tries to push him away. He doesn't let go, he grabs her tighter and pulls her from the room, pulls her into the hallway.

"Sabah," he coughs, and she tries to bite him and she slips and falls onto the floor, pulling him down with her. Sabah is kicking him and trying to get away and he's screaming

209

the same thing over and over. Suddenly she can hear, "We have to get you out of here." She looks at his face. He looks like Sanjay, but his face is black and covered with blood, it looks as though his cheeks are made of brown-and-black paper and it's tearing away in wet, red strips. Sabah closes her eyes.

"SABAH, SIT UP, behti, how will you be able to eat anything?"

Sabah wriggles back into the pillows, each movement shooting little jabs of pain into her legs. She gives herself a final push with her hands and instantly regrets it. She freezes, feeling the pain reverberate like sound waves through the thick bandages. "Araamseh, carefully, Sabah. Doctor said not to put pressure on your hands just in case there's still a little glass." Her grandmother puts the tray down on the bed, tucking the sheets into the metal railing. She sits down on the bed beside Sabah. "Here you are. Look at this wonderful food I've brought from the house. Here, have some pani, you must be thirsty."

Sabah nods and her grandmother lifts the glass of water to her lips. She gulps the water; she's so thirsty she barely notices the flat taste of long-boiled water and sharp smell of iodine tablets. She watches her grandmother's arms, she can see the blue veins under the apricot-colored skin. Even though her skin is loose, hanging like silk on her arms, the line of the muscle in her wrist is well defined. Her grandmother puts the glass down and picks up the fork, her fingers moving rapidly as she mixes the rice and dal and chicken curry. Strong woman, thinks Sabah. She's embarassed she hadn't reached her in Bombay. Sabah hadn't wanted to have a strict relative spoiling her holiday. "Thank you, Dadiamma," she says. "It looks delicious."

Her grandmother laughs, "Of course, it is. I'm famous for my cooking, didn't you know that? Wait until you taste this. You'll never be able to eat American food again."

She puts a forkful in Sabah's mouth. Sabah swallows almost without chewing. Her grandmother's right. She's a great cook and Sabah is ravenous. She hadn't realized how hungry she was. She practically bites through the tines of the fork with each mouthful. She wonders when she last ate. Her grandmother laughs, "You see? No wonder you've become so thin. Don't worry, I'll fatten you up so you can find a good husband. If you stay a little longer, you can come to my little Alia's wedding. That's the place to find boys. All the mothers and aunts and sisters are looking around for pretty brides. You just stay until November. That's when my darling is getting married," she nods, her dangling turquoise earrings swinging back and forth, hitting the folds of skin on her neck. "Jamal found a husband for her in London. Very, very good. Very rich," she nods. "Don't worry, I'll also find you one. And Yasmine. You tell your mother to let you stay with me for a little while. You and Alia will have so much fun together, like sisters. You'll love your little cousin."

211

She puts another fork of food into Sabah's mouth and slaps her leg as she chuckles. "Do you know," she waves a finger in Sabah's face, "this is the same hospital where Adam and Alia were born? When they brought you and your friend here they knew immediately who to call."

Sabah feels the blood draining from her cheeks. She chokes on the food as she tries to talk and starts coughing, waving a bandaged paw in front of her mouth.

Her grandmother pats her on the back. She becomes serious. "It's horrible." She shakes her head. "The poor girl. Some of those Hindu customs are so barbaric. Here, drink some water." She puts down the fork and strokes Sabah's hair as she drinks. "It's really terrible. The Hindus should have learned something from us. Her poor mother." Her grandmother's eyes grow hard and she purses her lips. Sabah stares at her. She's shocked at how much her grandmother's face looks like her father's. The same sad, sloping eyes, the lips that sink into the heavy cheeks, the bulbous nose, the wide neck. Despite her grandmother's soft, generous features, Sabah feels the strength in her, the power and control that rises through her center like a twisted rope of metal, an elevator cable. She lifts up the fork again.

"I can't," says Sabah. "I'm sorry, Dadiamma."

"A little bit more . . ."

"I can't."

"All right, behti," her grandmother sighs and picks up the tray. "Some boys have been wanting to see you," she says, disapprovingly. "Your friends. An Indian boy and an American. I told them you were getting better. Do you want to meet them?" Her eyes are sharp, cutting Sabah's face.

"Please, Dadiamma," says Sabah.

Her grandmother looks away. "You go to sleep, behti. I'm going to speak to your father again tomorrow. Your mother is so worried about you, they've been calling all day long. Do you want me to tell her anything?"

"Just that I miss her. And that Sanjay pulled me out of the fire."

"I'll ask your dada to telephone your friends just now. Perhaps they can come in the evening. Now you rest. All your medicine must be making you sleepy." Her grandmother seems to be right again. As she kisses her good-bye, everything is starting to look soft and fuzzy. Sabah feels like a sea otter sliding down into the pillows. She drifts into a dream almost before the light clicks off.

"SABAH? SABAH? Are you awake?" Sabah opens her eyes. She straightens up. The room is pitch black. Then the light flickers and she's blinking, half blinded, in the neon light. Sanjay and Brian hover in the doorway. "Can we come in? We didn't want to wake you up."

"If you didn't want to wake me up, why did you turn on the light?"

Sanjay giggles, "We weren't sure it was you in there. Who knows with all these rooms. And you know what nurses are like." He and Brian walk in, lugging an overflowing basket of fruit and bouquets of flowers. "Look, aren't these flowers fab? We found the best phoolwallah in Bombay. You won't believe the flowers he's got. And Brian insisted on these grapes."

Brian puts the fruit down on her bedside table. "Don't worry," he reassures her. "It's all safe. It's all washed with that red disinfectant. I had them do it at the consulate down here. You can eat anything you want."

"Thanks," says Sabah. For some reason she can't keep herself from crying, the tears keep pouring down her face. "I'm so glad you guys are here. Sanjay, can you scratch the top of my head? I can't wait until I get my fingers back."

"Of course, of course, why didn't you say something?" Sanjay sits on the edge of the bed. "Anything you need, you just ask."

"How are you feeling, Sanjay? My doctor said you were really lucky. No serious burns or anything."

"I'm fine. Apparently, the blood and all on me was from *your* hands and legs. How rude of you! Especially when I was trying to save your life!"

"The glass," says Sabah, "on the carpet. There was broken glass all over the carpet where I fell." She tries clumsily to wipe her eyes, waving a kleenex in front of her face.

"As soon as you're well, you can come back up to Delhi," says Sanjay. "If you can escape from your grandparents. Your grandmother's so happy to have you she might never let you leave."

"I have to go home," says Sabah. She looks at Sanjay. "I have to get out of here." She tries to focus on Brian, who's walked to the other side of the room. She squints. He's still blurred. Her eyes burn. Suddenly, her ears fill up like a wind tunnel, she can't hear anything. The whole room is gone.

213

She's in the dark. All she can hear is Rani screaming and screaming, her voice echoing and turning into Meera's wailing sobs, ringing back and forth through her ears like they did in the hallways of the hospital. "God, this is so awful," she says out loud. She tries not to cry again, but her eyes are already wet, tears sliding down her hot cheeks. She keeps seeing Rani's face, the twist of pain and then the flame blazing up in front of it. "I can't believe it." Sabah opens her eyes. She looks at Sanjay, his eyes are red, too.

He strokes her head gently. He says, "Hemant has no eyebrows or eyelashes left, the bastard. Right now he looks like the phantom of the opera. Just think how he'll explain that in London."

"What do you mean, in London? Aren't they going to charge him with anything?"

"Sabah, this kind of thing happens everyday. Hemant's father will pay the right people, and everyone will say it was suicide..." he chokes.

Brian stands by the window. "That asshole! That motherfucker!" He runs his fingers through his hair. "How can...how does...it's like an Indian movie, isn't it?" He shudders and leans against the glass.

"It must be very hard for Meera, poor thing," says Sanjay. "Rani was—God, I'm saying *was,*" his voice cracks. He clears his throat. "Rani was her whole life. I mean, she doesn't have a husband or anything. Just her mother and Rani. Poor woman." He gets up and straightens his jacket. He pulls an ironed handkerchief from his pocket and wipes his eyes. "Look, do you want some real food? You must be dying—oh God, that's not funny—I'll bring you something from the hotel. In the meantime, you just ask Brian for anything you want. OK?"

"Don't worry, Sabah," says Brian, dropping into one of the plastic Eames Chairs as Sanjay shuts the door. "Just concentrate on getting well." He looks at the chair. "Look at these antiques, when do you think they got them? 1955?"

"Hey Brian," says Sabah. "What are we all going to do?" But she knows already. She knew as she lay on the metal table, staring up into the square light as the doctor's tweezers removed the shards of glass from her hands and legs. She decided as his cold fingers smoothed the cream over her aching face. When she heard Meera's sobs, still resonating through the doors of the theater, heard her grandmother's voice and felt her strong hands grip her body for the first time in fifteen years, felt the anesthetic start to take hold of her body like tiny nails pinning her down to the bed, she was already gone. As she floated out of the room, watching the doctor and Sanjay and her grandparents get smaller and smaller, their faces becoming candy drops, her high school photography teacher was saying, "No one's head should be smaller than a dime" and holding the silver coin up, but they were already smaller than ants, just tiny fleas, and all the smells were being vacuum cleaned out of her skin and her hair, and she could hear a Muzak version of "Let the Sunshine In" that started playing as soon as the electric doors swung open...

215

"...back to Boston or California and your friends," Brian is saying. "And the rest of us are going to have to deal with being in Delhi. It's going to be really hard for Sanjay and Mahinder, they were Rani's best friends. I mean, they grew up with her...I wonder how I'm going to make it through the last month of this post." He leans back and slaps a drum beat on the sides of the orange chair. "Do you mind if I turn on the tape deck?" He jumps up and puts a cassette in the machine. "Wait 'til you hear this. I just bought it on the street. You can get bootleg anything in Bombay, it's like New York. Ready for some hip-hop?" Brian bops around the room. His shoes click on the gray linoleum like a tap dancer's. Sabah feels the tears beginning to drip down her cheeks. She hopes Brian doesn't notice, but he looks at her and she watches the memory of the last twenty-four hours sweep over his face like a wash of gray water color. He stops dancing and looks at his shoes, "I'm a jerk. I'm sorry. I really came down here to make you feel better." He looks like a child who's been scolded.

"No," Sabah tries to reassure him. "I'm sorry. It's not your fault." She wipes a bandaged paw over her face. "This is really embarrassing."

"Hey, no. No, it's not," says Brian, coming over to the bed. "You should cry, I cried the whole plane flight down to Bombay."

"The stewardesses must have been impressed."

"Relax. Cry. It makes me feel good to know you're not impenetrable." Brian sits down on the bed. "I was beginning to wonder if you had emotions." He scratches Sabah's head. "Want your neck rubbed? I took a couple of massage classes in college." His fingers move down behind Sabah's head, kneading the muscles in her neck. "International relations can get a little boring. When I realized I was going to go to graduate school and spend two more years doing the same thing, I decided I better take anything else I could." His voice is soft, soothing. His hands move down to Sabah's shoulders. She can feel the muscles soften and relax. She starts crying again, she can't stop herself. "It's OK. It's good, it means I'm doing a good job. I also took studio art, dance. Dance, I'm not kidding, can you see me in a leotard? Actually, I don't look so bad." He's massaging her arms now, and they feel like melting wax. "That's right. And some of my paintings are pretty good, too. I did a couple here. I'll show them to you if you swear not to tell anyone. I mean, I'm no artist..."

"Mmm," says Sabah, her eyes closed.

"You're lucky, Sabah. I don't know if you realize how lucky you are..." He leans forward and kisses her, and Sabah realizes she'd expected it all along, his fingers stroking her collarbone and her neck, drawing the outline of her jawline and her ears. "And you're really beautiful..." He puts his head down on her chest. Sabah can feel her heartbeat thumping against his ear. His hands feel like feathers brushing over her stomach, making little circles around her nipples.

Sabah smiles, "This isn't the best place for a seduction. And I have a feeling I'm not looking especially radiant these days." But when he moves his head, she pulls him back. She kisses him hard, her teeth biting into his lips, her tongue digging into his mouth, her hips moving involuntarily. She's starved.

"Yes, you are," laughs Brian, pulling away slightly. "You're really beautiful. All right, it sounds corny—not just your face or your body—I'm talking about the way you are. About the way you're part of two different worlds. These two bizarre worlds and you belong in both of them, more than I do in one, and you're still real. Real, not fake." He kisses her neck. "This all sounds ridiculous, I know. But I've been wanting to touch you." He looks at Sabah's face.

"I know," Sabah smiles. She can no longer feel any pain, except for the aching buzz in her breasts and groin that Brian has provoked.

217

He kisses her again, a long, slow kiss that leaves her breathless and flopping like a seal when his lips pull away. He sits up and pulls off his shirt, his skin pink and damp with excitement. Then he stands up and unzips his jeans, hanging them on the table. He slides carefully into the hospital bed and reaches behind her, untying her gown. It slips off as his hands slide across her body. "Tell me if I hurt you."

"Wait, stop," laughs Sabah. She's always surprised at how easy seductions are, especially if she's not really interested. "I'm an American, remember? I can't do anything without a condom."

Brian blushes, a wiggly smile trembling on his lips, "I have some. I bought them from a paanwallah, believe it or not." He holds a package with WET AND WILD in psychedelic lettering over the ample bosom of half-naked blonde woman. "Made in Japan."

Sabah rolls into him as he pulls her forward, rubbing herself against his smooth stomach and kissing his neck. She throws a bandaged leg over his hip.

"Now *you* wait," he gasps. "Not so fast. There's more to it than that." He starts to move his head down below the sheet.

Sabah reaches down, takes his head in her hands and presses his eyelashes between her lips. Then she lets him go, tilts his head up for a second to survey his face. One look and she knows he's serious, his face is open: earnest and vulnerable. "Brian..." she begins to explain, but she stops herself. She's not ready to give this up, yet. She wants him too much. She feels like a liar looking into his blue eyes, honest and clear as blue glass marbles. "I had this friend who really reminds me of you," she says.

218

"NO," SAYS SABAH, holding the phone receiver between her head and her shoulder. "I'm not going back to Delhi before I leave. I can't, Dad." She plays with the peacock-feather fan she'd bought in Delhi, the purple-blue eyes changing colors in the fading light.

"Sabah!" her grandmother shouts from the next room, "give my love to your mother! Tell me when you're finished."

She flips through her diary with her other hand. "I'm leaving tomorrow, which means I'll be in New York tomorrow, right? Does the time go forward or back, Dad? I'll spend two days in New York and then I'll come to Boston. All my friends from Delhi came down to say good-bye and bring all my stuff." She separates the wispy ends of the feathers, brushes the faint layer of dust off the wooden table. "No," she says again. "No. Dad, I know I promised, but I don't want to meet him. Please tell Dadiamma. She's already decided for me. She won't leave me alone. I don't want to think about getting married. Maybe I never will. I don't know." Sabah looks out of the window at the Bombay skyline, the lights beginning to come on in the buildings. She imagines the little boats bobbing through the flotsam toward India Gate and the light from the Taj Hotel. "Are you guys all right? How's Yasmine? OK, here's Dadiamma. Khuda-hafiz! Bye!" Sabah can hear her grandmother shouting into the telephone in her bedroom.

She opens the diary and takes out the photographs Sanjay had developed for her as a birthday present. She lays them out like a game of solitaire on the coffee table. She and Rani with shopping bags. Sanjay wearing the jacket she gave him, over a white T-shirt and blue jeans, his hair slicked back with hair gel—too hip, always hip. Who else could find gel in Delhi?—his arm around Rani. Sanjay in his disco gear. Pierre and Mahinder in smoking jackets at a cocktail party, toasting the photographer with crystal goblets of champagne. Brian in blue jeans with his bare feet up on the sofa, a cigarette hanging from his mouth like Humphrey Bogart—like a sweet, surprised Humphrey Bogart—his wide eyes red from the flash. Sabah looks closer at the picture and realizes that the fuzzy figure in the background is Rani, in a flamingo-pink sari. She can make out the laughing magenta-lipsticked mouth and the flash of white teeth, the reflection of the light on the glass in her hand.

219

Last night, she and Sanjay and Brian had sat on the roof of Café Naz, watching the sun set over the hanging gardens and melt down into the lights of Bombay. A sad twenty-second birthday party. The humid air drenched their clothes, made the tables sticky, so that the waiter had to shove the plates of fried rice across to each person. The grease glistened on their lips and left cloudy rims on their glasses of soda water. Sabah had refused a birthday cake. Refused to celebrate. "I'll just skip this year," she said. Brian and Sanjay had insisted on a dinner anyway.

A table of Arabs, in flowing robes and kuffiyehs, sat beside them, laughing and toasting each other and eating cashews from the huge bowls of spiced nuts they had brought with them. They asked Brian if he'd take a picture of all of them with their camera. He laughed and tried out the few words of Arabic he knew. They were thrilled.

"Sabah," moaned Sanjay, "I'll die if you leave."

"No, you won't," laughed Sabah. "Anyway, it's not 'if,' it's 'when.' I have to, because if I stay, my grandmother is going to force me to marry some guy. In any case, it's out of character for you to be so serious. It's disturbing. Stop it immediately!"

Brian stood at one end of the table while all of them, including the two women and the little boys, crowded on the other side, smiling and holding up their glasses as the flash exploded like a shooting star.

"It's just because you never take me seriously, you mean girl. But I am serious. There's no one else who understands me now that Rani . . . Why don't you stay? Why don't you come back to Delhi and . . ."

Then they all shuffled and joked to the other side of the table as Brian snapped the shutter and detonated the flash again, catching their faces, damp and brilliant, against the lights of Bombay. If this were a ship, thought Sabah, that side would be underwater. All the tables and chairs and people eating would whoosh across the deck, glasses spilling and plates crashing.

She smiled at Sanjay. He was wearing a Japanese designer shirt, a flaxen linen drape that became more beautiful as it wrinkled in the humidity. His hair had grown longer in the past few weeks, now it curled around his face like a baby doll's. He looked like a long-necked boy from an Orientalist painting. His brown eyes appeared and disappeared beneath the thick lashes—from her eyes to her mouth to her hands—trying to read something. How could she explain it to someone she felt so close to? "Oh, Sanjay. What would I do? How could I? Anyway, I can't. Brian's been try-ing to convince me too. I just have to leave. I just know it's time for me to go now." She reached across the table and squeezed his hand. "But I'll miss you. A lot."

"You could..." Sanjay's voice trailed off as Brian came back to the table. He licked his lip. Sabah knew he was melting, falling in love. She wondered why it didn't please her. Brian traced a line with his finger between Sabah's shoul-der blades as he passed, and she responded with her usual rash of goose bumps. She felt like grabbing him as he walked by, wanted to grip his arm or leg and feel how alive he was, the blood pumping beneath the skin, muscles twitching and tightening against her palm.

"No," said Sabah, as Sanjay pulled his hand away. "I wish I could. I have to go back home."

221

"BEHTI," SAYS an old woman in the immigration line at the airport. "Can you help me?" She holds up her departure card with one hand while she draws the dupatta tighter around her head with the other. Then she tucks the white cloth behind her ears, to hold it in place like paperclips.

"Of course, Auntie," says Sabah, as the old woman shuffles over to her. She's almost sorry for being so helpful because filling in the card ends up being a painfully slow process. The old woman is not sure about the answers. She's not even absolutely sure where she's going. All she knows is that she's going to see her daughter and her son-in-law and their new baby. Sabah shakes her head, but the old woman is tenacious. She opens her handbag and takes out a collection of tattered scraps of paper and a battered black diary and hands them to Sabah. Sabah checks all her tickets and reads the tiny faded handwriting in the book. She goes carefully through the woman's passport. "There you are, Auntie," she says, handing it back to her twenty minutes later, pointing out the right queue to get into, and wondering if this is going to make her miss her own flight.

"May God protect you, behti," says the old woman, blowing in her face as she leaves.

On the plane ride, every time Sabah starts to fall asleep, she thinks she hears a voice she knows, thinks she recognizes a profile that passes in her dreamy blur, and she jolts awake, ready to say, "Hi, Mahinder," or whoever. There's no one she knows on the flight, or at least not in economy class. But all the people around her look familar. The laborers who remind her of her aunt's servants, old women who make her think of her grandmother. The rich kids, with cans of Coke and music magazines in their hands, joking about the latest movies, heading back to universities or stockbroker jobs, seem like younger versions of Mahinder and Sanjay. Sabah closes her eyes again. She starts to doze when she hears someone laughing. A woman passes by Sabah's seat so close she can smell her lipstick and perfume. Her sari brushes Sabah's arm. "You idiot," the woman is laughing, "did you really think I was gone?" Sabah can almost see the face in front of her, the wide mouth and the dancing eyes. She closes her eyes tighter. She tries to force herself to fall back asleep. To sleep without dreaming. "Look at what I've done for you, you silly," says the woman. Sabah opens her eyes. A doll-faced young woman with candy-pink lips leans over the seat behind her, her round breasts almost rolling out of her sari blouse like cantalopes.

"How should I know?" the man teases. "I thought you'd gone to sit alone in first class."

"Even better," says the woman. "I've asked the steward to upgrade you and he agreed. So come on, we'll both move up."

"Well done, Cheeni," says the man, getting out of his seat and rummaging through the overhead compartment. "I'm lucky I'm marrying such a clever girl."

Sabah looks up at the woman as she collects her things. Her pretty features widen into a smile, her long black eyelashes flutter. She winks at Sabah before she walks up the aisle. Sabah's eyes sting. She bites her lip to keep it from trembling, but a tear escapes and drips into the corner of her mouth. She wipes her mouth with a napkin, and she can taste the salt seeping through her lips.

The movie is something about a boxer or a wrestler— no music, no cabaret numbers—just violence and patriotism. There are some Marines sitting in the front row, they shout and cheer the hero on.

Sabah remembers she still has some painkillers left from the accident. This is the time for them, she thinks, and swallows two with her mineral water. Her throat is tight, and even with the mineral water, the capsules stick in her esophagus. She orders an orange juice and gulps it down, but it feels like the pills drag down her throat, digging tunnels in the soft flesh.

She pushes the armrests up on the three seats beside her and stuffs the seat belts into the seats. She gets two pillows and a blanket from a passing stewardess just as the wallpaper is beginning to melt. Then she stretches out and falls into a deep sleep. She doesn't wake up until the plane lands in New York.

ALIA KEEPS DREAMING she is Adam. She's sweating under soft, blue flannel sheets, her face against a musky-smelling pillow. The air is hot and still. The sun is shining a rectangle on the sheet from a window above the bed.

Adam sits up. He kicks some grit out from under his legs. They'd told him that was the problem with having a mattress on the ground, there's always dirt in the sheets. He gets up and looks out the window. He stands there for a while, looking at the skyline, the long, crooked lines of buildings that surround him like a forest. He looks down at the ground, the sidewalks stained with black urine stripes that run down to the gutters. He wipes the sweat off his face with his T-shirt. From here he can smell the garbage rotting on the street. There is a pile of green plastic bags heaped against the side of the building, newspapers piled up beside them. The smell and the humidity make him think of Bombay. He smiles. In Bombay, he looked out from behind a thick plate of glass to keep the air conditioning and the scent of freshly cut flowers in the house.

"Adam, do you want some coffee?" The man says his name the English way, the *d* hard, and the second syllable quick and sharp so that it sounds like it's being shot out of a gun. Adam shakes a cigarette out from the package. He lights it and inhales, letting the smoke float around him in a little cloud. "You're not smoking up there, are you? I hate the smell of cigarette smoke in the bedroom."

Alia shivers. She opens her eyes. The bedroom is cold and damp. "Get up, darling," says Zenab. "It's so sad, it's raining today."

In the bathroom, Alia stands under the hot spray of the shower for a long time, trying to remember her dream, trying to wash off the soot she felt like was clinging to her skin.

ALIA DREAMS she is Adam walking through the Museum of Modern Art in New York. The rooms are square and cavernous. Even the biggest paintings are dwarfed to normal size by the walls.

A black boy enters the exhibition a half step ahead of him. His hair is long and hangs down in sausage-shaped clumps. He stops at a drawing and Adam walks in front of him, catching his wide brown eyes. The boy looks away, crossing his arms in front of his sweatshirt. Adam stops at the next one, a lithograph. He waits until the boy comes up behind him, and then he stands there, looking at the boy's reflection in the glass. His face is sweet and open. Adam smiles timidly, his lips barely curling up on the sides. The boy doesn't seem to notice. He walks on to the next piece. Adam can feel the cold air from the air conditioner drying the sweat on his forehead.

Adam steps back and actually looks at the lithograph. It is a graphic piece, sharp and formal. Adam stares at it and it becomes huge, filling the room. He trembles. For a second, his whole body seems to be shaking, and he holds his arms to try to keep them still. Then, just as suddenly, he stops shaking.

He looks around the room to see whether anyone else has noticed. Everyone else seems to be engrossed in the art or their own conversations. They walk through the exhibition in small groups. Most of them are wearing black, or black and white, or black and gray. They're well dressed and fashionable, in the museum light, and against the white walls they look like art pieces themselves.

A group of people stop near Adam to discuss the lithograph. They seem to know the artist well, and they argue about his career and personal life. They barely look at the work, standing far enough away that Adam wonders whether they can see anything more than the glare of the light on the glass and the reflections of their own faces. They walk on.

Adam follows them, a little behind so he doesn't look too obvious, listening in on their conversation. They don't seem to notice him at all. He's freezing now, his skin feels cold and tight, the air conditioner sucking all the heat and humidity from his body. He thinks of speaking to them, but he doesn't know what he would say. He looks down at the carpet. It is a lush green, the color of the golf course in Bombay, when the lawn is spongy and just watered. He looks at his shoes. They are brown and they look scuffed and schoolboyish on the clean carpet. He tries to shine them a

225

little by rubbing them against the back of his leg. He looks at them again. He stares at the worn brown leather as the voices of the group fade.

ALIA OPENS HER eyes. She sees the luminous green dial of the alarm clock. Two-fifteen. She looks at the bedside table. Her eyes close involuntarily and she drifts off to sleep. In her dream, she's dialing a telephone.

ADAM IS SITTING in a telephone booth in a bar, six quarters beside his address book on the wooden counter. He puts the receiver down and a coin clanks into the phone. He picks up the book and flips through it, holding the ragged pages to keep them from falling out. He holds the book up to the light coming through the glass window. Then he puts another quarter in the telephone and dials again. "Hello? Could I please speak to Marc? Oh. Yes, thank you. Just say that Adam called. Yes, that's right. Good-bye," he hangs up. They're playing a loud rock 'n' roll song, and he can barely hear the dial tone as he tries the next number. He's not sure whether what he hears is the phone ringing or the clink of glasses and laughter from the bar. "Hello? Hello? Sorry, I can't hear too well. Could I please speak to Marc? Is he coming back? Yes, I called this afternoon. Thank you. Thank you." Adam hangs up. He closes the address book and puts it into his jacket pocket. He blinks as he walks back into the light of the restaurant.

He slides onto the red vinyl barstool. The two men sitting beside him are deep in conversation. One of them glances at him absentmindedly as he sits down and then turns his attention back to his friend. "What can I get you?" asks the bartender.

"Oh, uh, a beer," says Adam. "Oh, no. Oh, could I have a Coke instead? Thanks." He takes a small brown paper bag out of his pocket and lays the three postcards on the counter side by side. One is of the Manhattan skyline at night, black buildings against an orange sky. Underneath it says, NEW YORK, NEW YORK in red letters. The second one is the Statue of Liberty looking out over a blue harbor on a sunny day. The third is the same Manhattan skyline in the day, with a bold LOVE FROM THE BIG APPLE! scrawled across it.

"Here you go," says the bartender, putting a wet glass down in front of him. "That'll be a dollar-fifty. Typical, but nice," he says, looking at the postcards. "You a tourist?"

"Mmm," says Adam, staring at the postcards. "Yes. I am." He looks up at the bartender's smiling face. "I'm trying to decide which one to send to . . . home."

"Home? Where's home? Wait, don't tell me," he looks at Adam. "I'm pretty good at accents. OK, OK," he taps the counter. "You're not Italian, I know that. Close, though, right?"

"No."

"I'd say Yugoslavian, I mean, I know some Yugoslavians who look exactly like you. Brian," he asks the sandy-haired man sitting next to Adam, "Brian, you know those Yugoslavian guys who come in here? Don't they look like they could be his brothers?" The bartender gives Brian a push. Brian looks appraisingly at Adam, his blue eyes sweeping across his face. He nods, and turns back to his conversation.

"No, I'm not Yugoslavian," Adam smiles. "You have one more guess." He puts two dollars on the counter.

"Brian, help me out here. Brian used to be in the foreign service. And before that he was a bartender here. The only reason he comes in here is because he gets his drinks on the house. Within limits, though, right Bri? A sort of diplomat, weren't you? Look, if a diplomat can't guess where you're from—just a second, I'll just get this guy his drink."

Adam looks at his postcards. He turns them over and reads the descriptions of the scenes. He takes out a pen.

227

"You're Middle Eastern? Israeli?" The bartender plunks two quarters beside the glass.

"No, I'm Indian. From India. But I've been living in France for a long time."

"Indian? No way. You don't look Indian. I never would have guessed Indian. Are you half Indian?"

"No."

"Brian used to live in India. India's pretty rough, Brian told me all about it, bride burnings and shit. He even knew someone, this girl, who got burned. It's like, so you don't like your wife—set her on fire and get another one. I can't believe it."

"I think it does happen."

"Brian, dammit, turn around. Brian, does he look Indian to you?"

Brian turns around and looks at Adam. "Sure, he could be Indian. Where in India are you from?"

"Bombay," says Adam.

"Great city," says Brian, "but weird—like New York. I used to live in Delhi. For two and a half years. That was the worst mistake of my life. Bombay is where the action is. But anyway, I don't have wonderful memories of the place." His face tenses, he tilts his stool onto its back legs, keeping himself upright by gripping the bar, the muscles in his chest and arms almost bursting through his polo shirt. "The last time I was there was when a good friend of mine was, well—hey, listen, are you going back any time soon? I have some friends I've lost contact with, if I give you an address, could you bring something for me?" He stands up to get his wallet out of his pocket and Adam thinks how tall he is. Americans are huge. "Goddamnit, I didn't bring my book." He looks at Adam strangely, "You look a lot like someone I used to know..."

"I don't know when I'm going back, actually," says Adam.

"Hey, do you know this restaurant there where you can sit on the roof and see the sun set over the city? In the hanging gardens. It's amazing. Called Café Naz."

"I think I know which one you mean. But I haven't been there in a long time. I live in Paris."

"Oh," Brian's face falls. He climbs back on his stool. "Well, have a good time in New York. Bob, remember I told you about this Indian movie star I met?"

More and more people are coming in through the swinging doors. The bartender is moving quickly between orders. The conversation and the music are becoming louder and louder. Adam looks back down at his postcards. He writes an address. Then he puts the postcards back in the bag. The noise seems almost deafening. He gulps his Coke. There are gleaming bottles of every possible shape and variety lined up behind the bar. Adam sees something move behind the bottles, and he realizes it's his own reflection in the mirror. He looks at himself. He looks pale and thin. Marc used to say that when he was tired his eyes looked opaque. Like pieces of colored paper. He thinks about Marc's baby-blue eyes. They looked like the eyes of an angel. He imagines Marc as an angel floating naked into the clouds.

229

In the mirror, Adam can see people walking in and standing around the bar. He wonders if he'll be able to move from his seat. Someone seems to be leaning against him. The noise is greater, swelling with the people. Adam can't hear anything but a roar. Almost like the ocean, he thinks. All those different sounds and voices become one loud roar like a wave crashing onto the shore. It seems like people are crowding into the bar in hordes. Adam takes a breath. His breath feels shallow, it doesn't fill his lungs. It feels like all the air is getting used up by the swarms of people in the bar. More people keep coming in. He is sweating now. Sweat is dripping down his forehead. "Hey," says the bartender. "Are you OK?

It can't be hotter in here than it is in India." Adam looks at him and he looks far, far away. Like he's looking through the wrong end of a telescope. Adam can barely hear him.

He gets up off his stool. He has to get out of here. He pushes through some people. He can hear the bartender's faint voice. He thinks the bartender says, "Man, those Indians are lousy tippers." The people stare at him. He's trying to get out and everyone is looking at him. They are trying to stop him from getting out and they are laughing. Their faces look big and far away. They are talking about him. He thinks he hears, "Indian." He pushes forward suddenly, and then he's at the door. He stops for a second and looks at the wooden door, he can see more people moving against the frosted glass. He throws himself against the door and it flies open. He bangs into someone, "Sorry." "Hey, watch where you're going." He trips down the stairs.

He stands alone in the street, listening to the cars driving down the street. The wheels hiss against the pavement. A car honks. Another screeches past. He realizes that it's hotter outside than it was in the bar. He takes off his jacket and puts it over his arm. He crosses the street and sits on the chain across the entrance to a parking lot. He imagines Marc. He sees him floating up to the sky and waving. Adam lifts his hand to wave.

"ALIA," SAYS ZENAB. "Perhaps you're sleeping with too many blankets. Here, drink some water. You're looking so hot. You were talking in your sleep. Abba and I could hear you from our room." She puts a cold glass of water in Alia's hand. "You don't have a fever, do you?"

Alia sits up, trying not to spill the water. She blinks in the morning light. She feels weak and trembly, as if she'd been shaken for hours.

"Here, behta. Take off some of these bed things." Zenab folds up the blanket. "It's almost nine o'clock, so everyone's getting up. Do you want to sleep a little more? I'll just close the door, all right?" Alia can hear Zenab's footsteps going down the stairs. She lies back down. She feels damp air blowing in from the window. The heat is fading away. She sinks into the pillow, the cotton cool and fresh against her cheek.

"I HEARD YOU walked all the way to the Indian takeaway this morning, Bhaijan," says Amna at lunch, her huge blue eyes flashing and her lips twitching with laughter.

"What? *Who* told you that?" Jimmy glares at the servant. "I had a walk around the neighborhood."

"It's lucky we have such good weather for being outside," says Zenab. "Alia and I spent the morning in the garden. I gave myself a pedicure." She takes a glass from the servant's vibrating tray. "Thank you."

"It's not her fault, Bhaijan. The poor girl's already terrified of you," Amna grins. She kicks off her high heels and curls her legs underneath her on the chair, sighing and tucking in her sari. "God, it's good to be home from work." She winks at Alia.

"Amna, even suspecting me is very rude of you," says Jimmy, pretending to be irritated. He gets up and heaps rice onto his plate. His appetite should be an alibi. "Here I am, your older brother. Coming to England, you've forgotten all about respect."

"Respect has nothing to do with it. I'm worried about your health, Bhaijan. And," Amna starts laughing, "one of my friends owns that shop. So I know exactly how many rasmalai you ate."

"The best rasmalai I've had in months," says Jimmy, his eyes twinkling with pleasure. "But if I knew the kind of sneaky people they were, I never would have gone there."

"Oh, no, they're very nice. The boys who work there are all from good families, you know," Amna looks at Alia.

"There is one that I'd mentioned to you. It's his older brother who's working for the bank here. Very nice boy. And Majjo is a saint," Amna takes Jimmy's plate away from him and puts it on the buffet. "That's enough for you. I'm amazed that you're still hungry."

Jimmy smiles, "Actually, they asked for my autograph. I autographed a few napkins. They gave me the tea and rasmalai on the house, I had to eat them. Listen," he adds, "I promised I would send an autographed copy of the last record. You must take it there."

Alia can't speak. She's been feeling strange all day. Like a princess in a fairy story. As if she'd been enchanted, taken over by something else. She spent the morning trying to write postcards to her friends in India. She lay on her stomach in the grass, the postcards spread out around her. She held the pen in her hand for two hours, watching the shadow move across the blank cards like a sundial, but she was barely able to write anything at all. She felt so self-conscious. Her fingers felt like they didn't belong to her. So instead, she'd painted, tried to paint the pictures that flitted through her mind like mirages. But somehow, they disappeared every time she reached them.

"Shall we all go and see a film tonight?"

"That sounds like fun, don't you think, janoo?"

"Why should we go out when we can see a video right here?"

"Really, Bhaijan. I wonder what kind of an actor you are."

IN THE DARK theater, Alia thinks about Adam. The film just seems like colored lights to her. She can see that her aunt and her parents are completely engrossed. She squirms in her seat. Anxiety is crawling up her spine and gnawing in the back of her mind like a rat. "Alia, what are you doing?" barks Jimmy. "Nobody can watch with you wiggling around."

"Go and buy some sweets, if you can't sit still," whispers Zenab. "Here, take my handbag."

Alia gets up and goes to the concession. She buys a chocolate bar. She takes a bite, but it's too sweet and thick, like a lump of paste in her mouth. She has to have a drink to choke it down.

She walks back into the theater. She stands blinded in the darkness for a few seconds. Then she sits down near the door. The film continues, but Alia has no idea what's happening. She tries to watch for a while. She sees a girl's face she recognizes, but she can't follow the story. She gets up again and leaves the theater. She paces the lobby. Something is happening, she knows. Adam has to come back. She closes her eyes, the colored shapes of the film projected against her eyelids slowly fading away. She sees an Indian restaurant, little red plastic tables with yellow tumeric stains on them, Styrofoam bowls of dal and chicken curry, slippery with orange oil.

233

ADAM'S FINGERS tear a chapati and dip it into the dal. He gulps it down, the smoothness of the dal mixing with the wheaty taste of the chapati. He eats some chicken, carefully licking all the masala from his fingers, almost tasting each spice alone, the sweet cinnamon and cardamom, the bitter cumin and coriander, the sting of the chilies. The smell makes him so homesick his eyes start watering. He thinks of his grandmother's chicken curry.

"Food all right, sir? Not too spicy?"

Adam swallows. The chicken is so sweet. He looks up at the waiter. "It's perfect," he says.

The waiter looks worried. "You want some yogurt, sir? To make it less spicy. Some raita. That is yogurt with cucumber in it. You know, cucumber."

"No, thank you," says Adam, smiling. "I know what raita is."

"Oh, yes, a lot of Europeans eat Indian food now. It's very popular in England as well. Yes, I can see you know how to eat like an Indian," he's leaning on the table now, he hangs the wet cloth over the back of the chair. "Me, I like American food. I never eat here. I eat at McDonald's or Kentucky Chicken. It's so funny, isn't it? Indians like American food and Americans like Indian food."

Adam laughs, "What's even funnier is that I'm an Indian."

The waiter's face is incredulous. "You're Indian? How can it be? You look English." He scratches the baby hairs sprouting on his chin. "You are from where in India?"

"From Bombay."

"Even I have my uncle who is living there. Very very exciting, like New York. Me, I come from Julunder. Do you know where that is? It's Punjab."

"No," says Adam, taking a bite. "No," he says through the dal, "I've never been there." He swallows and stuffs more chicken into his mouth. "Actually, I've been away from India for some time," he wipes the grease from his lips and gulps his Coke.

The waiter sits down in the chair. "Good food," he nods approvingly. "I also like chicken. What is your name, please?"

"Adam." He doesn't want to look up again from his food. The waiter smells of old sweat. His face is brown and spotted with red pimples. He pushes his stained sleeves up to his elbows and taps his dirty fingernails on the laminate.

"I am Talvinder—but everyone calls me Tom. You can call me Tom. It's easier to say for Americans." He holds out his hand for Adam to shake.

"Mmm," protests Adam, trying to keep as much of the food in his mouth as he can, "my hands are dirty. I don't want to get chicken curry all over you. But it's nice to meet you. As soon as I finish I'll wash my hands."

"No, no problem," laughs Talvinder. "You are eating. Eat. You want some tea also?"

"Yes, thanks, I'd love some. It's the perfect way to end this. The food, I mean."

"Yes, first you finish your food," Talvinder nods. "Where do you stay in New York? You have some relatives here?"

"No, I'm staying with a friend in the East Village. I have an uncle in America and his daughter, my cousin, comes to New York quite often, but I don't know where she is."

"Is she Indian? Then she must come to Jackson Heights. But why are you staying in Greenwich Village? It's very dangerous. There are all the strange people walking around there and taking drugs and things." Talvinder looks concerned, then his face widens into a grin. "But you're there for the girls, aren't you? That's a good place for girls. They're all over there, the fast ones, wearing short frocks and all."

"It's actually the other side of Greenwich Village. There are all these Indian restaurants near there. On East Sixth Street."

"What? Those? Those restaurants are all owned by Bengalis. That food is terrible. Horrible. They should stay at home and eat the fish heads their wives make for them. You should only eat here in Jackson Heights. Only here. You just bring those girls with you. That's the way to catch them. This is the best Indian restaurant in New York. Really. Just read that newspaper there, the *New York Times*, that is an article all about this restaurant, just written last year."

"I'll read it before I go," says Adam, taking the last bites of his food. "Could I have some tea?"

"Tea? Of course." Talvinder looks around the restaurant to make sure no one is in earshot. He leans forward. "Listen," he whispers, "you know a lot of American girls? I know some here, in Queens. They're not like our girls, yaar. They're completely crazy—puglee—you know. You come out with me and you'll meet some wild girls. Really wild. And they'll love you. I promise you. Masala chai." He gives Adam a quick pat on the shoulder and gets up to bring the tea.

Adam sighs and piles all the little Styrofoam cups into a little tower. He swings and slaps it with his hand. It topples down, orange oil spattering all over the tray, globs of yellow dal flying out, dripping down the sides of the cups and soaking into the paper napkins.

Talvinder plops a cup of thick milky tea on the tray. "Thank you," Adam says, lifting the cup slowly to his mouth, inhaling the smell of cardamom. "Ow!" he jerks the cup back, splashing tea on his shirt and jeans, and squirming in his chair as the boiling liquid burns his skin. The tea is searing. His tongue is numb.

"Too hot, yaar," laughs Talvinder. "Microwave. Don't worry, I'll give you a shirt to wear tonight. I'm finished with work at seven o'clock. Then you come to my house. It's just here. OK? No problem." He winks at Adam and picks up his tray.

"No, I'm trying to find someone. Thank you," says Adam. But Talvinder isn't listening to any excuses. He's already walking away. Adam, his eyes watering and his tongue still smarting, watches Talvinder's lanky body disapppear into the kitchen. Adam touches his tongue with his fingers. It feels like it's covered with little stinging sores. He sticks his tongue out farther, like an eel curling out of his mouth. He thinks about his tongue tracing the ridges of Marc's ears or moving around the corners of Marc's pink lips like a paintbrush on a piece of porcelain. His tongue burns.

236

ALIA LOOKS AT the cinnamon specks floating around in her tea like little waterbugs. "It's too hot," she sighs. She feels exhausted. She can barely lift the spoon to stir her tea.

"All the sugar makes it heat up faster," says Amna. "Here, pour it into your saucer so it will cool down."

"Alia," says Zenab. "You must not be sleeping properly. Falling asleep in the theater like that. My poor baby. You must be worrying too much. Don't worry." She strokes Alia's cheek.

"You see?" says Jimmy. "What a waste. Now, if we'd gotten a video, Alia could have watched it again." He's watching the television. Two women with slow American accents are glaring at each other across a room. Because of a man, he's sure. Why else do beautiful women fight with each other?

"Good night, Abba," says Alia, kissing him on the cheek. She doesn't leave, though, she stands there, staring at her father, thinking how much Adam looks like him. She sees a flash of concern wrinkle his face, making him older, and it hurts her. She feels sorry for him. They're just little boys, really, she thinks. They're little boys. She's shocked at the realization. She wonders how he—or Adam—would ever survive without Zenab to take care of them.

As Alia's soft lips leave his cheek, Jimmy smells the toothpaste and the rose soap she uses to wash her face. She's looking more jawa'an every day. Zenab is wrong in thinking she should finish her B.A. before she gets married. The truth is, like all females, she just can't stand to have her children leave her. Jimmy takes a sip of the tea Zenab's just poured into his cup. He rolls the sweet, milky liquid around his mouth. Yes, he thinks, it's better to have her safely married than out spoiling her reputation. Perhaps she shouldn't have come to Europe until she had been married for a few years. In her flowered nightgown, her dark hair open around her shoulders, she looks like a picture of Snow White from a children's book. Her face is pink and slightly wet. "Go to sleep, Alia," he says. He pats her arm. "Go on, behti."

Alia nods, but she doesn't want to leave the room. She knows she won't sleep, she'll just toss in her bed, sweating and getting tangled in the warm sheets. The humming tension while she's awake is not that bad. What she dreads is closing her eyes and the nightmares coming back.

A Nice Arrangement

"ALIA!" SHOUTS Jimmy. "Come downstairs." He settles back into the sofa, pulling the lapels of his blazer straight. Actually, he's lost quite a lot of weight since the heart attack. He feels very trim. He smiles at the two men across the room. Both of them could do with a little exercise, he thinks. "Have some tea," he encourages them. Poor things, they must be very nervous. It's not every day that they propose to the daughter of one of Bombay's biggest stars. The boy had probably never been in the same room with a film star before.

"Thank you," says the father, holding out his cup for the servant. The boy looks expectantly at the door. He's well dressed, thinks Jimmy, and not bad looking. Mature, too. Twenty-eight or twenty-nine is the perfect age to settle down. He thinks back over the boy's curriculum vitae—good university, good family, and an impressive salary—he can't remember what kind of car the boy has, a BMW or a Mercedes? He hopes it's a Mercedes. BMWs start depreciating the minute the tires touch the road. "So, my boy," he says, "what sports do you play?" He laughs to himself. He's already done so much research on the boy that asking him anything is a joke, really, a formality.

"Tennis," says the boy, "and a ..."

What an accent, thinks Jimmy. He sounds like an Angrez. That's the drawback of bringing children up here.

"...little football, and cricket, in school, of course—" the boy stops short. He and his father are staring at the door.

Alia stumbles in, holding a tray of cakes for the tea. She trips on the carpet and almost falls, all the cakes squishing together as they slide to one side of the tray. She stops short of collapsing in a heap in the middle of the room. Jimmy breathes a sigh of relief. She's wearing a yellow salwar kameez. She looks like a flower, thinks Jimmy. Thank God, Zenab had managed to get her out of her jeans. She puts the tray down on the table and starts to leave, just as Zenab walks in the door and pushes her back into the room. "Come on, Alia, you can finish your painting later. Come and meet Abba's friends," she says, looking appraisingly at the boy and his father. Zenab floats over to the sofa, her gold necklaces and bangles—she'd put on quite a few, she doesn't want them to think Alia isn't used to good jewelry—jingling as she moves. "Offer the cakes, behti."

Alia picks up the tray of mangled cakes and carries them over to the older man. The smell of sugar and chocolate rises from the plates. Her stomach seizes. She feels her skin become cold and wet. She has to close her eyes for a second to catch her breath. She sees the inside of a car, a cracked old dashboard, piled with empty chocolate wrappers, fuses, key chains. She feels like she's sitting on the torn upholstery, a spring pushing up through the foam and pinching her leg. The car smells of old curry. Alia squeezes her eyes tighter. Not now, she thinks. Not here. She tries to clear her mind. A key turns in the ignition, there's someone laughing and the radio starts playing. Stop, thinks Alia. Stop. She's been feeling so sick lately. She's never sure if she's awake or dreaming. She pulls herself back into her aunt's living room, forcing her mind to stay still. She trembles with the effort. In the back of her mind, she can hear the faint song on the radio, a sputtering engine. She focuses on her father's voice. Her hands shake, and when the man lifts a cake off the tray, the whole thing tips to the other side like a seesaw.

Jimmy wonders whether Alia is nervous. He hopes Zenab wasn't so silly as to tell her why these people had come. Especially right now, when she'd been so worried about Adam and having nightmares and fevers and all. As for Adam, well, if he wasn't going to amount to anything, at least Alia could. Jimmy had always wanted a son in the bank. And a son-in-law was practically a son. Jimmy hopes Alia doesn't upset things right at the beginning, now that he's found such a perfect boy. He watches Alia give him a small plate of cakes. The boy catches her eye and smiles at her. Alia stiffens and looks at the tray. Jimmy is pleased. That's how a decent girl should behave. He thinks she should have blushed a little, though. She's looking so pale.

240

"Sit down, Alia," says Zenab. "It's so funny, Imran has such a lot in common with us. Our Adam is also a banker. You must meet him when he comes back," she says to the boy. He's handsome. Not as handsome as Adam, of course, but he's a very bright boy. He seems to be a little sullen looking, but that's not bad for a boy. The man needs to be in control in a marriage. She puts her arm around her daughter. "Alia and Adam are very close," she says.

Alia curls into her mother's soft body. She looks up and realizes that Imran is staring at her. She feels uncomfortable. She doesn't like the way he smiles at her. He's not like the boys in Paris or the handsome black boy in the disco. She doesn't know why. He looks like he owns her. He smiles again, his round cheeks widening and his tongue gliding across his lips, leaving them wet and shiny. He winks at Alia. Alia's stomach flip-flops. The car roars and she's thrown back against the torn upholstery. Her lunch jerks up to her throat, the sour taste of curry, mixed with the sickly sweet taste of

Coca-Cola. She swallows hard. Alia looks at her mother, but Zenab is listening to the boy's opinions on British politics. Even her father looks impressed. Alia gets up and runs to the bathroom.

She shuts the door and sits on the toilet seat in the dark. She breathes slowly, trying to stop the tempest in her stomach. She closes her eyes and the vision flares up in her mind again, a radio blasts screaming rock songs she's never heard before. She sucks in the cold air in the bathroom, inhales, swallows, exhales deeply. She hears a deep sigh, almost a moan, and realizes it came from her own throat, from deep inside her body. I must be ill, she thinks. When she opens her eyes, she sees Imran's face, his tongue darting like a lizard's between his red lips, projected in front of her like a movie.

She bends over, puts her head between her knees, smells the sweet laundry soap and her own skin through her salwar. She inhales again.

When she walks out of the bathroom, Imran is standing there in the narrow hallway. Alia hadn't realized how tall he was. Now, one hand on the bannister and the other on the printed wallpaper on the other side, he seems like a towering ogre. "Hi," he smiles, his nostrils flaring and his thick lips parting around his white teeth. "I didn't think I'd get to talk to you in there." He opens his mouth in anticipation, little strings of saliva stretching up to his sharp front teeth.

Alia is paralyzed. Where is her mother, why doesn't she call her? Tell her to come back and serve the tea? She shouts but no sound comes out. Her voice gets caught in her throat. She wants to turn and run into the kitchen, but she can't move. Her feet feel like they're encased in cement.

"You're quite pretty, you know," he says. "Much prettier than I expected." He steps forward and touches her face. "Beautiful skin, too," he says, coming even closer, so close she can smell his breath. It smells musty, like a room that's been

241

locked up during the monsoon. "And beautiful eyes." He throws his arm around her waist and pulls her to him, his soft body pressing against her as he kisses her. Alia starts to scream, but his tongue blocks the noise. She hates him. All she wants is for him to let go. He smells old and rotten. She gasps for breath, and she breathes in the air exhaled through his nostrils. She feels it spreading into her like smoke and dust.

Finally, he releases her with a pleased smile. "I don't suppose anyone's kissed you like that before." He squeezes her hand. "I really think you'd be a wonderful wife," he says. He steps past her toward the bathroom and gives her a little push. "Go on now, they're waiting for you in the living room. And don't you dare tell them about our secret." He winks and shuts the bathroom door behind him.

Alia sits on the edge of the armchair, waiting for her mother to ask her where she's been.

"Well," Jimmy is saying, "Alia is still very young. We don't want to rush her marriage." He notices that Alia has walked in and he changes his tone. "As I was saying, it seems we're all agreeing about almost everything." He looks over at Zenab and smiles. He's done his job well, he thinks. What father could do better for his daughter? Zenab nods and smiles back. "So we'll start it all moving," he smiles again. "But, thank God, from here on out, it's the ladies' job," he winks at Zenab. "Our work is finished," he laughs and gets up and shakes hands with the old man.

"Oh, Alia," says Zenab when they've left, giving her daughter a little squeeze, "aren't you excited? You're going to get married!"

Alia slides her feet in and out of her chappals, "But Ummi…"

"We'll start shopping tomorrow. How lucky that we found out while we're in London. We'll buy all sorts of lovely things for the wedding. And for your jehez. I'm so happy, behti!" Zenab giggles and puts a jeweled hand over her mouth like a schoolgirl.

"Don't go spending all my money," says Jimmy gruffly as he climbs the stairs. He smiles to himself, his daughter will never have to learn to count pennies. The boy is very well off, Jimmy had made sure of that.

Zenab gives Alia a big kiss. "Come, behti, let's go and telephone your dadiamma, shall we?" Alia follows her mother into the kitchen, her orange-and-purple sari swirling around her. "She'll be thrilled. Except I wish he lived in India. I'm going to lose my little baby." She sits down at the table with the telephone on her lap. "Alia...come quickly! I've reached them right away!"

Alia opens the sliding-glass door, and sunlight and the scent of grass and flowers flood the room. She takes off her chappals and walks barefoot into the soft grass, digging her toes into the earth like a baby.

"Yes, he's very handsome!" Zenab shouts into the receiver. "And so nice...*In Bombay! In the fall!* She's *thrilled!*"

Alia lies down on her stomach and pulls up a clod of dirt and grass. She shakes the grass and the dirt crumbles, tiny bugs leap back down into the gap in the lawn, like people jumping from a burning building. All the time, in the back of her mind, the music keeps playing. One faint rock song after another whines through her brain, making her head and neck ache. Everything is getting worse and worse. She has to get Adam back here. If she told him the story, he'd help her. He is the only one who can help her.

"Alia, what are you doing?" says Zenab. "You must stop behaving like a little girl. Don't you want to write some letters to your friends? You're so lucky, my baby." Zenab walks out and sits on one of the garden chairs. Alia looks at her and Zenab sees how forlorn she is. "Come here, darling," she says. "Come here and sit with me." She pulls Alia to her lap. "Don't worry, London is not so far away from Bombay.

We'll see you all the time. Now your Abba will have to send me to visit you. And we'll have a lovely time, just the two of us!" Alia wiggles into her soft lap, puts her head on her breast. Zenab kisses her, "See, you silly, you'll come home with us first. So you can see all your friends. And we'll have a beautiful mehndi for all the young girls."

"Ummi," says Alia, "he's horrible. Do you know what he did?" She is crying now, her tears dripping into her ear and soaking her mother's orange blouse.

"Who, behti? Who did something to you?"

"That boy. He...Imran...he kissed me. There was nothing I could do. He forced me to. He's disgusting and I don't want to marry him..." Alia blurts out and then collapses into sobs.

"How naughty he is," smiles Zenab. "Oh, my poor Alia. How would you know what to do, my little bird?" She pats Alia's head and stares off across the garden. "But it's so romantic, isn't it? Almost like a Mills and Boons. Aren't you lucky."

Things That Go Bump in the Night

"NEW YORK IS great, yaar, really great," laughs Talvinder. "Here I am working in restaurant and I meet the son of a movie star! It's great. You like this music? The best radio station in New York—hey, hold on—red light!" The car screeches to a stop, Adam flies forward, the seat belt slapping his chest, and then falls back, hard, into the seat, the springs creaking and poking into his legs. "Sorry, Adam, sorry. There're too many policemen in New York, you know?" Talvinder rolls down his window and turns up the radio. He puts his arm out the window and thumps the side of the car in time to the music. "Great, really great," he laughs and steps on the gas. "Don't worry, Adam. My house is just here. Everyone will love to meet you." He pulls into the driveway of a split-level brick house. "Come on!" he jumps out of the car and runs up the cement steps three at a time.

A young girl opens the front door, she looks hopefully at them. "Hi, Talvinder bhai, will you take me to a movie tonight?" She's wearing a pair of skin-tight stretch jeans and a T-shirt, a long black braid hanging down her thin back. Adam compares her pointy face to Alia's soft one.

"Sorry, Chotu, I have my friend Adam here. Adam, this is Chotu, my niece. She's a real American. Aren't you, Chotu? Chotu, who is Jimmy Al-Hussain?"

"I don't care," snaps the girl, crossing her scrawny brown arms over her chest, "some Indian nobody." She flounces up the stairs.

"Hey," Talvinder shouts after her. "Get me something to drink."

Adam follows Talvinder down the green carpeted stairs. He can hear the sound of a Hindi film. It's a dance number, a girl is giggling and a man is singing "Que Sera, Sera" in Hindi. Suddenly, Adam hears a whole chorus of off-key voices, "Jubh meh choti larkhi thee . . . when I was just a lit-tle girl . . ." Talvinder walks into the darkness.

The television flashes colored lights around the room, Adam can make out people sitting on sofas along both walls, their faces alternately red, green, and orange. "Sit, sit," says Talvinder, handing Adam the glass of brown liquid his niece brought and pointing at the crowded sofa. Adam takes a step into the room, tripping over something and half falling onto a body on the floor. "Watch out! Behave yourself," says Talvinder as the small body lunges for Adam's leg, teeth flashing. Talvinder gives the head a cuff, sending the child rolling into the others, who begin shouting, "Stop it! Leave me!" Adam realizes that there are three or four children on the floor.

"Chup! Quiet!" warns a woman from one of the sofas. Adam leans against the door frame. "Vilayet-ke-bac-che!" she growls. "Go and do your homework!" The children are instantly silent.

"I'll be right back," reassures Talvinder. "This is my family."

"Oh," says Adam. "They're very nice." He holds the glass in his hand, trying to guess what it is. He thinks it's Coke. The whole room smells of cold rice and dal and cumin and harsh drug-store perfume. With the curtains drawn and the door shut, the battling scents make Adam's eyes water. He leans against the door frame, trying to get fresh air from the hallway. He thinks of Marc's parents and their clean, drafty house in Paris. He wonders if he should run out the door. If he went fast enough, he'd be out in the cool air on the street before anyone noticed.

"Talvinder!" shouts the woman, as Talvinder leaves. "Oh, Talvinder! You don't even see your mother anymore? Come here! Where are you going?" She sighs and the person beside her pats her shoulder. "What a son I have." She notices Adam hovering in the doorway. "Come here, behta. You are Talvinder's friend? Come, come," she gestures for Adam to approach. "What a nice boy," she reaches out and grabs Adam's face as he steps over a child, squeezing his cheeks as he loses his balance. "Good boy. You are American?"

"No," mumbles Adam through his mangled mouth, "Fren...Indian."

"Indian?" She is incredulous.

"Indian?" says the woman sitting next to her. "No, never."

"What is your good name?" asks Talvinder's mother. "Where are your parents?"

"He looks ek-dum foreign," says a man on the sofa, putting his running shoes up on the table and crossing his legs. "Are you Kashmiri?"

"Adam," says Adam. "I just met Talvinder tonight, at the restaurant. I'm from Bombay, but I live in Paris, I haven't..."

"Oh-ho," laughs the man, "Bumbai-wallah! Are you a film star?"

"He's so white, he must be an actor..." says another voice. Adam can make out three Indian men in salwar kameezes and sweatshirts lolling on another sofa. "Hey, Sandy!" he laughs.

"I haven't been in Bombay in a long time."

"Oh, you live in New York?"

"What is your family name?"

"Al-Hussain. No, I live in France."

"You are a Muslim?"

"Yes."

"We also have some Muslim friends," says Talvinder's mother. "They live just here," she waves her hand off into the darkness, "they're from U.P., their name is Bothelwallah. Do you know them?"

"No. Sorry. But I haven't been here very long."

"Muslims make the best halwah," she says. "Do you like halwah?"

"Yes, yes," adds the other woman, "remember they sent some halwah last month? It was so lovely. They're very nice. It must have been Eid. Was it Eid?"

"Muslim? Muslim?" says a quavering voice. Adam makes out a withered old woman on the edge of the sofa. As the idea sinks in, she starts coughing violently, her tiny body shaking beneath the swaths of white cloth. "Do you know what the Muslims did to us during partition?" she shrieks. "Get out! Get out!"

"Shh, shh, Barima," soothes Talvinder's mother. "That was not all Muslims...this is Talvinder's friend. He's very nice."

"You know, not all Muslims are dirty, like in India,"

reassures one of the men. "In America, they are very good. Just like us. At Quaker Oats, at the factory, I work with lot of Muslims. I am forklift operator."

"They burned down our house in Lahore! Burned it down, everything was burned! I had nothing when I got in the train. Nothing! Get out!"

"But in Punjab, the Muslims are so bad," explains another man, shaking his head. "So dirty, and they are stealing and doing all bad things, not like in America. In America, Sikh, Hindu, Muslim, we're all the same. My job also, I make pizza, and we are all bhai-bhai." He leans over and slaps Adam's arm.

"You stole everything! Everything my mother gave me! Get out!" shrieks the old woman. "Go!"

Talvinder walks back in and grabs Adam's arm, he starts shouting in Punjabi, "You don't have any izzat? This is my friend! His father is Jimmy! And look at how you treat him! Come on, Adam," he says, in English. He takes the glass of Coke and puts it in the young girl's hand. "Let's go."

"Jimmy? The film star?"

"Get out!"

Adam hears the glass smash as he walks up the stairs.

"They are very rude," apologizes Talvinder as he jerks the car out of the driveway. Adam snaps his seat belt on. "They think they're still in the village." He laughs and winks at Adam, "Not us! We're in America!" He blasts the radio, "Let's go! Debbie and Paula are waiting for us. They are crazy girls, really crazy!"

THE SHATTERING GLASS RINGS in Alia's ears. She looks at the floor. In her sleep, she must have knocked her glass off the bedside table, a large brown Coca-Cola stain is spreading into the pink carpet. She climbs out the other side of the bed and runs to get a wet towel from the bathroom.

She picks up the pieces of glass and rubs the carpet with the towel, trying to soak it up. She pours some water from the vase of flowers onto the stain and rubs again. She rubs harder and harder, but the Coke doesn't go away. Finally, she gives up and leans against the bed, crying in exhaustion.

Amna walks into the room in her dressing gown, swishing her long black hair over her shoulder. "Alia, what's wrong, darling?" She looks at the carpet and then at the towel in Alia's hand. "Never mind. There's some carpet cleaner in the kitchen. We'll do it tomorrow." She takes Alia's arm and pulls her to her feet. "Back to bed. It's one in the morning."

Alia leans against her aunt, crying more violently. "I can't," she gasps. "I can't."

"Of course you can. Do you want some chamomile tea? It's very relaxing." Alia shakes her head. Amna wipes her eyes with a tissue and helps her into bed. "Are you feeling sick? Shall I wake up your mother?"

"No," Alia whimpers. "I have nightmares. I can't sleep." 249

Amna sits down on the bed. "Nightmares? What sort of nightmares?"

Alia shakes her head. "Nightmares about Adam. About Adam being in New York. And about Imran. I dream he's cutting me up with a knife and fork, but then, the knife isn't strong enough to cut through and he gets angrier and angrier—and then he just bites me—he bites me and tears me up! I hate him. I can't marry him. If I bring Adam here, he'll stop them. I wish I'd gone with him."

"No, of course you don't," says Amna. She helps Alia back into bed. "Oh, dear," she sighs, "there's no reason you should do anything you don't want to do. But then, so many arranged marriages start like this and end up very happy." Amna looks down the hall at Alia's parents' room. "And what do I know about marriage?" She twists her hair, tying it into a loose knot that quickly slips back into a sheet of shiny hair. "Don't think about it anymore." Amna gets up with a small sigh and walks slowly out of the room, her slippers padding over the carpet. She stops at the door for a last glance at Alia's face. Then she tosses her black hair again and turns off the light. "Sleep well, darling."

Alia lies on the bed, looking at the little lines of light around the edge of the curtains. She thinks about marrying Imran, lying beside him on a bed in an airless room, his smell a cloud around his body, soaking into the sheets and pillows, surrounding her. She imagines his hands and his wet lips on her body. The thought makes her shudder with revulsion. Adam will come back and fix everything. She knows he will.

ALIA OPENS THE refrigerator door and pours herself a glass of water. A bell rings behind her and she freezes before she realizes it's the kitchen clock. One, two, three, four. Four chimes, four in the morning. Adam, she pleads, when are you coming? Suddenly, rock music roars in Alia's head so loud, she feels like it's pouring out her ears like loud-speakers. A jagged rip of high-pitched laughter cuts through the music and the animal sound of the engine. The slap of the hand across the polyethylene upholstery seems to hit her own head. The kitchen floor flies up toward her, Alia feels her body hit the linoleum and the chairs and table grow huge like mushroom clouds filling the sky.

"WHAT BAR ARE we going to, Tom?" asks Debbie, putting a finger in his ear as he drives. She's sitting sideways in the passenger seat. She looks back at Paula and Adam, and she and Paula burst into hysterical giggles.

"Stop it, crazy girl," Talvinder laughs and slaps her hand away.

"Tom, your friend is really cute," says Debbie. "Paula, you lucked out tonight, honey!"

"Yeah," laughs Paula, running a polished fingernail from Adam's forehead to his chin. "Usually when they say 'blind date' it means you should be blind to the guy! I mean, if a guy says 'I got a friend,' it's like, his friend is a loser, right?"

"You sure are cute," agrees Debbie. "But are you really Indian? You don't look Indian at all. Come on, baby, light my fire," she sings along with the radio and gives Talvinder a peck on the cheek.

"Uh-huh," says Paula. "Talvinder looks like a real Indian. You look like, I don't know, like you're American or something. Most Indians are darker, aren't they?"

"I know! I know!" says Debbie. "We'll go to that place in the East Village. Remember, Paula? You'll love it, Adam. You want to go there, Tom? There are all these artists there, I think. I mean all these people who look like artists."

"That's for sure," says Paula. "I mean, you couldn't go to work looking like any of them. They have purple hair and tattoos and even the boys wear makeup. They must be artists, they sure look weird enough."

"Yeah, it's really fun, Adam. It's like a circus or something, you know? Like there's always something funny to look at. So you never get bored. But don't worry," Debbie giggles and bats her eyelashes, "you won't get bored with Paula and I! Right, Tom?"

"He sure won't get bored with you guys, that's for sure," laughs Talvinder.

"Guys?" teases Paula. "Tommy, you're calling Paula and I guys? Adam, do we look like guys to you?"

"No," says Adam. Paula takes his hand and puts it on her stockinged thigh. She moves closer to him. Adam takes his hand back. He wonders where Marc is, if he's left for France already.

251

"Talvinder, listen, I—thank you, it sounds nice, but I'd like to go home."

"Hey, don't worry, yaar! No East Village crap bullshit," says Talvinder. He winks at Adam. "Adam and I have to go there another time. This time we'll go to Jackson Heights."

"Anything you say, Tom," laughs Debbie. "You're the boss. As long as they have frozen piña coladas. I love those."

"You know what I love," purrs Paula.

"No," protests Adam, squirming in his seat. "No, really, my mother might try to call..."

"Mother, whuther!" Talvinder laughs. "They love worrying!"

"Strawberry daiquiris, Paula," Debbie giggles. "That's what you love! Pink ones! Look, here we are! I love this place."

There are a series of small explosions as they get out of the car, and Adam jumps. Gunfire! "Scared you, huh?" laughs Paula. "Those are just firecrackers! You know, tomorrow's the Fourth of July! You can be a red-white-and-blue all-American Indian like Tom."

UMMI AND ABBA are standing over the sofa looking down at her, their round faces falling forward like cushions. "Alia, behti," says Zenab. "Are you feeling better, baby?" The bright morning sunlight deepens the lines of concern furrowing her forehead and cheeks.

"I'm sorry, Ummi," says Alia, rolling her head back on the red sofa. From this angle, the intricate paisley pattern looks huge and clumsily printed. "I'm fine." She sees Abba's face, it's as gray as the jacket of his flannel suit, almost as pale as when he first came home from the hospital.

"Of course, you are," says Jimmy. He looks relieved. "Gallavanting around is not good for young girls." He pats her on the head. "You should sit quietly in the house sometimes."

"Yes, Abba," says Alia. She closes her eyes. She feels water soaking through her sleeves. Her arms are on the counter of a bar. A pair of sticky lips press against her burning cheek.

"WHAT DO YOU want?" says Talvinder, leaning across the bar as the bartender approaches. "Anything for the star's son! It's on me!" He slaps the bar and grins at Adam, "I can't believe it, I come to America and I meet Jimmy's son at the Jackson Heights Diner! It's true, anything can happen in New York City. Crazy!" Adam squirms uncomfortably on his barstool. He wonders if Marc has tried to call him.

"I want a piña colada!" says Debbie. "Frozen, with cherries in it. Can I have extra cherries?" she asks the bartender. "And I know what Paula wants."

253

"I'll have a strawberry daiquiri. And Adam will have one too. Don't you want to try one? They're so good. They put fresh strawberries and ice and sugar and lots of rum in the blender..." She pushes her stool closer to his.

"Sure," says Adam, trying to attract as little attention as possible. If he waits until they're drunk enough, he can slip away and try to reach Marc again. He leans on the bar and looks at Paula's round stomach pushing through her Lycra miniskirt. Her stockings are so sheer he can see the blue veins and the white skin on her thighs.

She notices him looking at her legs and smiles, "Like these? I just bought these pantyhose. They're French." She hooks the heels of her pumps over Adam's leg rest. She leans her head on her arm, her long curly hair falling down like a curtain around them. "So how do you like New York?" As she speaks, the shiny layer of lipstick on her mouth folds and crinkles like icing on a birthday cake.

"It's very nice," says Adam. All he wants right now is to be alone in the barsati on the roof of his parents' house in Bombay. Sitting on one of the wicker chairs and smoking a cigarette, listening to the sound of the bells on the servants' bicycles as they ride back down the road from the market, and the noise of the vultures flapping their wings and stumbling around the branches of the trees. In the spring and summer, he used to like leaving the air-conditioned house and feeling the hot, wet air paint his face with sweat and grit as he smoked.

Paula taps his arm with her red fingernails. "I wasn't kidding before. I think you're great. Like, I never knew any Indians before Debbie went out with Tommy."

"Oh," says Adam. He can almost hear his mother's voice calling him, telling him to come downstairs. Through the dust, he can feel the hum of the air conditioner in his bare feet. He can hear the gardener mowing the lawn, and the sweet smell of cut grass, like watermelon, fills his nostrils . As it gets darker, the fireflies come out and dance around him like hundreds of cigarette ends held by invisible smokers. He hears Alia's chappals slapping up the marble stairs.

"Hey," says Paula. "What are Indian girls like? Are they like us? I mean, we see them in Jackson Heights sometimes, but I don't really know any, you know? They're kind of shy, aren't they?"

"Yes," says Adam, sweat dripping down from his hair into his ears. He thinks about his little sister. He can almost see Alia's face, sweet and twisted with worry, on Paula's body. It's strange, he knows his sister's worried about him, he can feel her anxiety like a burning wave of radiation all the way from London. "They're not like American girls." He feels very hot. He unbuttons the top two buttons of his shirt. "Excuse me," he apologizes to Paula, the way Marc used to when he took off his tie or jacket in public.

The bartender puts their drinks down on the bar. Talvinder's obviously lost interest in his previous offer. Adam puts a twenty on the only spot that's not wet. The bartender picks it up and winks at him. "Lucky guy," he says.

"Thanks," smiles Paula and takes her gum out of her mouth. "I love these." She looks up at Adam while sipping sexily from the straw.

Adam holds the wet glass to his burning cheek. Then he gulps it down in three swallows.

"Good, huh?" says Paula. "Want another one? Bartender!"

Adam drinks two more and orders a third. They're delicious. They taste like the fresh fruit drinks he used to buy at Crawford market in Bombay.

"You're pretty thirsty," giggles Paula. She's still sipping her second one slowly through the straw. "I can't keep up with you. I'm going to the ladies' room," she says, sliding off her stool. "I'll be right back." She looks over at Talvinder and Debbie. They're engaged in an amorous clasp, their mouths pressed together and their limbs writhing. She looks back at Adam and winks. "God, those two," she says, as she struts toward the bathroom in her stilettos, her round bottom rolling with her hips from left to right and back again with each step. Adam gulps his drink and watches her walk away. A huge firecracker goes off outside, making the all glasses on the bar start shaking. "Happy Fourth!" bellows the bartender.

"ALIA," SAYS AMNA, "Wake up, baby."

"Where am I?" croaks Alia. She opens her eyes and shuts them again, stung by the light.

"You're having a nightmare, baby," says her aunt. "But you're awake now." She strokes Alia's forehead. "You're in London."

Alia stands up, her head spinning. People swim around her, appearing and disappearing, like schools of bright tropical fish on a television screen. Alia walks out of the room like a skin diver. Her arms and legs float around her, slow and heavy.

After the effort of opening the door, Alia sags against the wall, her stomach heaving with liquid. The house seems to be shaking, the movement making the liquid swish from right to left and back again like waves in an aquarium. She staggers down the hallway toward the bathroom, swaying from side to side.

"Are you all right?" asks Amna, trying to steady her.

"I feel sick," chokes Alia. She runs into the bathroom and starts vomiting into the sink, a steaming stream of red liquid gushing out of her mouth and flooding the white basin. She gasps for air. She tries to stop. She cries. But the red juice takes control, bubbling up again, pouring out of her, pulpy and seedy, lumps of fruit clogging the drain. Her stomach is lurching and swinging against her muscles as if she had drunk all of New York City. She looks into the mirror, at the foggy reflection of her aunt holding her hair, patting her back. The mirror looks like it's coated with steam. Alia twists her neck to look back at Amna, but everything is wet and hazy, Amna's blue eyes semiconcealed by gray clouds as though she's standing in a mist.

"HEY, ADAM," says Paula, patting him on the back. "Adam, are you all right?" Adam has his head on the bar, his face pressed against the cool wet wood. His arms are wrapped around his head, to block out the light that burns his eyes, to block out the music that blasts through his brain. "Adam," she slurs. "Adam, don't be sick, OK? 'Cause I really like you. I mean it. I know I look like I have tons of boyfriends, but I don't. I swear on my grandmother's grave. I hardly ever go out with anyone. I never meet anyone I like, you know?" She bends her head down to look at him. "Hey? Hey, Adam, you listening? I'm not dicking around with you." She lifts up one of his arms and looks at his face. "Adam, you look bad. Maybe you better get some fresh air. Hey, Tom, your friend's…" She turns around to ask him what to do, but Talvinder and Debbie have disappeared. "Oh, shit, they're off humping in the car again," she complains. "Come on, Adam. We're gonna go outside. OK. You'll feel better outside." She pulls Adam up, steadies him to his wobbling legs.

The bartender looks suspiciously at them. "Hey, don't have him tossing his cookies in here," he warns Paula. "Get him outside or something."

"Real nice guy," Paula shakes her head.

"There you go." They stumble out onto the side-walk. She tries to prop him up against a PED X-ING sign, gripping his shoulders through his shirt. He slips forward, and she loses his shoulder and finds herself holding only his collar. "Whoa," she says, as he topples and falls to his knees, the shirt ripping, leaving her clutching a scrap of white fabric. He hangs over the edge of the sidewalk, wretching into the gutter. Paula kneels beside him and pats his back, "That happens to me, too, sometimes. You gotta be careful with those things. They go down like ice cream but they sure pack a punch." She pulls his hair out of his face as his stomach seizes again.

"Excuse me," he coughs. Then he thinks he must be back in Bombay. His ayah, the one who's been patting him on the back since he was born, has come to take care of him. He feels better now that she's there. She's patting his back, with the same rhythmical slap she used to make him sleep at night. "Nin-ni baba, nin-ni. Nin-ni baba, nin-ni," he sings after her.

"You must be really sick. You're probably not used to drinking like this. I bet they don't go to bars a lot in India. Are there bars in India?" She looks up at the sky. "You know, I used to want to go to India or Africa or some place far away—you know, someplace where they ride elephants—did you ride elephants? I guess that was just in the old days, huh?"

257

A car slows in the intersection, its radio blaring dance music. A man leans out the window. "Your boyfriend's dead, baby! You want a live one instead?" he screams, throwing a hissing firecracker out of the window. It bangs and showers the sidewalk with bits of burned paper. The man and his friend laugh hysterically.

"You see, Adam?" she looks out across the road. "Hey, look," she says, "look, that's that Indian thing—like the Taj Mahal or something." She stares at the long, low building in the middle of a huge parking lot. It has three white domes like sugar-cake decorations on its flat roof. Its three wide doors are separated by intricate white columns. "It's beautiful, isn't it?" she breathes, "like a fairy castle..."

Adam sighs and puts his head in the ayah's lap. He closes his eyes and waits for her rough hands to comb his hair, the way she always did. He waits for the cool washcloth to wipe the sweat and vomit from his face. "Pani," he mumbles. "Glass pani." But she doesn't seem to hear him, because she's pulling him up, trying to make him stand. His mother must be calling him. He can't stand, though. His legs don't work, they've become soft, like rubber. He thinks he must be a baby. He's too small to walk. He has to crawl. The ayah is standing up, walking away, and Adam crawls after her. "Ayah! Ayah!" he shouts, his baby voice making the word sound long and silly. He giggles and says, "Don't leave me," in Hindi. But she just keeps walking.

She's crossing the road and Adam is crawling after her and giggling so hard he starts to hiccup. His legs hurt from the road and he shouts for her to come back and pick him up. He wants her to carry him now, he's tired. He thinks she must be angry at him, because she doesn't turn around.

A horn blasts through Adam's ears. It's loud, wailing like an air-raid siren. He looks up. Suddenly, there are beams of light bearing down on him, so fast they seem like shooting stars, exploding when they reach him, the mud-spattered

chrome bumper, huge and silver and glinting in the light, flying into his eyes before he can gasp. The screech of the tires
on the pavement mixes with laughter turning into screams
and Adam feels the crushing weight of the tires against his
stomach, hears his hip bone crunch and crush, his arm slide
into the space where his ribs were. Then footsteps, a voice
growling, "He's drunk, get the fuck back in the car. Let's get
the hell outta here. Come *on!*"

A woman is screaming, "Oh, God! Dear God!..."
her voice fading away with the hiss of the tires.

Adam's trying to get up, trying to pull himself along.
He can move. He can crawl, but it hurts so much he can't
speak, he can't make a sound. He holds his arm to his ribs,
keeps his shoulder pressed into his armpit so it stays together.
He can see her ahead, she's pulling open the heavy doors. A
man walks up behind them and holds the door open for her. But
he drops it as Adam crawls through and it hits him hard on
the back. Adam falls into a pile of shoes. He gasps and coughs
into the shoes, spitting up hot salty liquid. He screams for the
ayah. This time, she comes back. She says something to him,
but he doesn't understand. She tries to help him stand up. He
falls again and drags himself into the room. He giggles, there
are dolls all over the place, the pain is fading away, he's in a
dream. There are beautiful dolls in saris and dhotis with garlands of flowers around their necks. He pulls himself toward
the doll, the prettiest doll, the elephant doll with the blue face.
He wants that one. He grabs the box that the doll is on with
his other arm. He tries to pull himself up, he touches the edge
of the elephant's beautiful dress and it starts to come toward
him. It slides forward into his hand, when someone kicks him,
someone hits him, hard, in the back. Someone shouts, "No!"

Adam's chest hits the ground and he chokes. He loses
consciousness.

259

"ADAM!" SCREAMS ALIA. Her eyes burn and water, she feels like she's looking through a cloud of smoke. There's smoke pouring in the window over her bed. She coughs and slams the window shut. Out the window she sees a white building, a three-domed castle, the smoke billowing out of it. In a gust of wind, the castle fades as if it's made out of smoke itself. She closes her eyes.

"Alia," says Zenab, snapping on the light. "You must stop this now, you're not a little girl anymore. You're going to be married soon, and Abba is very worried about you." She helps Alia sit up and pops one of her father's tranquilizers in her mouth. She holds the glass while Alia drinks. "Now you go to sleep."

Alia drops back into bed. "Adam will come," she whispers. "Adam will save me..."

Zenab clicks the switch off.

It's black.

The Rainbow Sign

SABAH WALKS OUT the doors into a rush of cold air, her chappals slapping the shiny floors. Everything seems to glisten, the chrome guardrails, the bright plastic signs telling the way to the bathrooms and taxis, the fresh clothes of the chunky pink-faced people waiting. It's not just the painkillers; walking out into the clear light, Sabah suddenly feels relaxed, comfortable. She's home.

Rob is standing in a group of chauffeurs holding signs for hotel guests and businessmen. Sabah barely recognizes him, he's wearing a suit and a T-shirt, and his curly hair is cut so short it looks straight. He's chatting with a man in a uniform holding a sign that has MR. SINGH written in black Magic Marker on the white cardboard. He waves at Sabah.

"Hey!" he yells. "Welcome to New York City!" She wheels her trolley of suitcases over to him. "You look great," Rob says, kissing her politely on the cheek. "This is Darrell. He's been here for like two hours or something, right, man? He keeps getting the wrong guy. Good luck," he says as they walk away. Rob looks at Sabah's salwar kameez. "Cool clothes, Sabah. They made you give up those sexy dresses out there, huh?"

"Thanks," says Sabah, dragging her folding trolley. She stops and switches her bag to the other shoulder. Rob is loping a few steps ahead of her, looking at the parking ticket and trying to remember where his car is. She struggles toward him. "So much for chivalry," she says. "The least you could do is offer to carry some of my stuff."

"Sorry, I keep forgetting you're not liberated." Rob takes the trolley handle and swings the bag over one arm. "My—Pia would never let me carry anything for her. You have to meet her, Sabah, she's really great."

"Pia? Oh, your girlfriend," says Sabah. "Isn't she someone I knew from San Francisco?"

"I'll tell you about that at dinner, OK?" He puts a hand on Sabah's shoulder. "Do you think this ticket says level four, section three, or level three, section four? Hey, I have a great place to show you now that you've had your *Roots* experience."

Sabah's whole body aches from lifting the suitcases on and off luggage carousels and trolleys. The rows of shiny American cars gleaming in the dim light of the parking garage seem endless. She trudges over the speed bumps and the shiny black oil spots on the gray concrete. She wishes she had her aunt's chauffeur. "Rob, how long have you been in New York now?" She knows she's whining; she realizes it as she says it, but it's too late to stop herself before the rest of the words come out.

"Sabah, it's good to see you're the same spoiled princess who left," laughs Rob. "I've been here since graduation.

261

And you won't believe how together I am. I'm working at Chase Manhattan, I have a great apartment, credit cards, and a car phone in my Rabbit. Are you impressed yet?" He gives her a wide, natural smile that irritates her. Ignorance is bliss, she thinks.

"Totally. You're a real yuppie. You probably listen to Vivaldi in the car during rush hour." She looks at Rob's Armani suit and tries to imagine him with his long hair again, high on acid and making up blues songs on his guitar.

"This Indian guy at work told me about the best Indian restaurant in New York. And I'm starving. Aren't you hungry? Hey, all right! There's my car! And nothing's stolen either!" He unlocks the door of a fluorescent green convertible. As he does, his jacket falls open and Sabah realizes he's wearing the ice blue silk kurta underneath. The one that stared at her from the shop window because it looked like it was made out of the same cloth as his eyes.

262

"Oh, God, not Indian food. Anything but Indian food."

"TELL ME THIS isn't a great place," says Rob, putting the tray down on the red laminate. "It's a classic American diner, the Jackson Heights Diner—American Indian, the real thing," he grins. "Like you."

"Rob, I just got out of the Third World. I was looking forward to McDonald's . . . or Le Cirque." Sabah looks at the tray, shiny with streaks of grease and dotted with the dal and curry that splashed from the Styrofoam cups as he was carrying it.

"You get all this food for ten dollars. Can you believe it?" He pulls out the chair and wipes it with a napkin before he sits down. Sabah smiles. "Dry cleaning is not cheap," he defends himself. He hands her a napkin. "Sit down, sit down. OK, so did you find a husband and a new identity in India or what?"

"Or what," answers Sabah. "I gave the old one a coat of fresh paint. And it's already beginning to peel. Stop! I'm a foot shorter than you and I'd like to stay sixty pounds lighter..." Rob is emptying cups of rice and dal and chicken curry onto her paper plate. "So where'd you learn to eat this stuff?"

"Hey, I'm cosmopolitan now," he says, through a mouthful of food. "How's your love life?"

"Dead," says Sabah. "How about yours?"

"Cheerful tonight, eh?"

"Of course not. I go to India and my best friend dies, I come back to America and my cousin Adam, who I have never met, is lost somewhere in New York City and my boyfriend is a yuppie and madly in love with someone else."

"Mmm," says Rob. "I'm sorry about your friend and, don't worry, your cousin will turn up..." He had carefully rolled up his sleeves before he started eating. He pretends to be checking them to make sure there are no spots, trying to sound offhand. "Well, do you remember this girl from UCLA, Pia?—Piedad, actually, she's half French and half Spanish, blonde hair, about three inches shorter than I am—oh, you know what's funny? Her brother Marc works for some Indian bank that you've probably heard of, and he's a count or something. Isn't that bizarre? Marc's in New York right now, with some Indian guy—his boyfriend, I think—the son of some hugely famous Indian movie star."

"Not Piedad Cosnard de Closets!" says Sabah, dropping her fork. "You've been going out with that pseudosurfer girl with the French accent? She's in New York?"

"Actually, we're married. I mean—"

"You're married? In two months?"

"Part of the reason was that Pia needed a visa to stay in America. But the wedding was really small, anyway. Just her parents and Marc and my mother and Alan and Mike and a couple of other people—"

"Her parents flew out from Paris?"

Rob is blushing. Sabah remembers that blush, like the first time he told her he was in love with her, starting at the back of his neck and spreading out from behind his big ears all the way to the tip of his nose. He has a crooked smile, like in a Charlie Brown cartoon. "Sabah, you left, remember?"

"Congratulations," Sabah says incredulously. In the same tone of voice she would have murmured, "You are the biggest jerk..."

"Anyway, she's sort of nervous about meeting you. So be nice to her, OK?" Rob looks at her hopefully.

"She's nervous about meeting *me*?" Sabah puts her plate back on the tray. "Why should I meet her anyway? I don't want to be part of your harem."

"Sabah, you broke up with me. You were the one who said you couldn't deal with commitments."

"And that's obviously all you wanted."

"You'll really like her, I promise," he smiles reassuringly. "She's really nice—and good. I mean, she's the only person I know who is really good, straight through. Like, if heaven exists, Pia is on her way."

"Sounds like a fun girl."

"She's nice, Sabah." Satisfied, he pushes his plate back. "Am I allowed to burp loudly in Indian culture? Or is that in Japan?"

"Indians are actually very repressed," says Sabah, making sculptural mounds with the cold rice and thick dal paste. "Want some chai?"

"Pretty good. Pia's got you more sophisticated than I ever did."

"I learned that myself. I'm a regular here. Pia's pretty busy at night, she's working on her master's. I haven't had a chance to take her around to my haunts. I used to come here and imagine what it was like for you in India."

He blushes again and clears his throat. "But this is nothing. Wait 'til you see where we're going next."

"Where?"

"You want me to wreck the surprise?"

"That's enough surprises for one night."

"It's this supermarket that's been turned into a temple by this Hindu priest. Seriously. He put red carpets down at the A&P. Crystal chandeliers on the ceiling, big wooden elephants. This façade of fake white columns in the front and three sugar-white domes on the top. The final cultural synthesis. And you're the first person I've ever taken there. I found it myself."

"Very cool," says Sabah. "Let's skip the tea and go."

"Tuesday nights are really great. It's packed. All these Indians in—like what you're wearing—and saris and sneakers and blue jeans. That's when they do the thing to the monkey god. They even give you bananas afterward."

"Hanuman." 265

SABAH STUMBLES as she steps inside, holding the heavy door open with her shoulder. She looks down. There are shoes scattered all over the entrance way. Mostly they're running shoes or canvas sneakers, but there are a few rubber chappals and worn slippers. A few pairs near the door seemed to have been splashed with brown paint. Sabah leaves her own chappals out of the way next to the metal garbage can. Rob has already slipped off his alligator loafers and put them on a shelf. They walk gingerly into the huge room full of Indians, feeling conspicuous and artificial. Her bare feet sink into the red carpet. The smell of garlic and dirty socks is harsh and penetrating. "Look," says Rob, pointing at the statue of Hanuman, the people lined up in front of it, bowing and kissing the railing in front of it and touching their foreheads to the ground. But Sabah is looking in the other direction.

She stares at a group of men standing together, one of them holding a platter of lighted candles, waving it like a birthday cake in a circle above something on the ground that hypnotizes the rest of them. Young mothers rush forward and grab their children, kicking and screaming, away. Fathers pull their sons back to the railing by the ears. A trail of black splotches lead off across the carpet toward the men.

Suddenly, a blonde girl in a black leather jacket and miniskirt hurtles toward her like a hallucination, banging the wind out of Sabah as she hits her. "He's dead!" she screams, jumping back to her feet. "He's dead!" She bolts out to the street in her stocking feet, the door thudding shut behind her. Sabah hears a hiss, a flash of flames, red and black and blinding like lightning, seven of them rise up like a mountain in front of her, crackling and burning up to the ceiling.

Then she sees the boy.

His face is chalk white. So white against his black hair and the blood red carpet, it looks like milk. In the noise—the babies crying, the conversations in Hindi and Punjabi, the Sanskrit prayers, the temple bell ringing—Sabah can hear the boy's voice, as clearly as if he were speaking to her in the hollow silence of an unused room, the nursery, after all the children have grown up and gone away. He's telling her about sounds, sounds she didn't know she remembered. The heavy sound of her father's breath as he walked up the stairs, the staccato sobs of her baby sister's crying, the sound of her mother's feet on the wooden floor as she danced alone all night in the dark living room, the music not stopping until the sun rose pale and lemony in the window. Behind it all, like a rhythmic background, Sabah hears the quavering voice of an aged ayah singing her charge to sleep. Then, clearer, even louder, she hears the sound of her father growing up, her grandmother's hand squeezing his sunburned arm and throwing the cricket bat to the ground, dragging him away from the servants' children, back into the cool shade of the veranda.

The boy is telling her about smells, the smell of rough, handwoven cloth, the smell of kheer, woody with kewra water and cardamom, the smell of melting chocolate-covered cookies as the lid is lifted from the tin, the sour smell of old sweat thick with oil and spices in an unwashed shirt, the smell of paan and betel nut and sweet, smoky perfume like incense.

Now, sharp and intense, she smells the smoke of burning hair and flesh, she smells caked, dried blood, hears the smash of breaking glass and the long howling scream of searing pain.

The story rushes through Sabah with the force of a rough gale of wind, carrying scraps of sounds and torn swatches of smell, broken chips of images flying up and brushing past her, pieces of tastes spinning around her mind. The story is like a tornado that's lifted up an entire town, torn it to shreds, and now flings the remains crazily around the countryside. And it calms. It's over by the time she touches him. She knows it by heart as she kneels beside him. She wipes his scorched face with the wet cloth, wiping away the red.

"Rob! Call an ambulance!" she shrieks, her voice so high-pitched it almost fades away. She holds her breath as she takes his wallet out of his pocket. She doesn't have to read the name on the credit card. Before she recognizes the handwriting on the scraps of paper, before the face smiles at her through the plastic on the identification card, she knows who he is. "This is Adam," she whispers.

"Pani," mumbles Adam, a muscle spasm rippling through his shoulders and stopping at the twisted arm, his contorted side. Sabah gets up and runs back through the people. They scatter, spreading out around her, small children falling down, dropping their plates of burfi, her feet smashing through the cardboard, grinding the crumbly sweets into the carpet.

"Water!" she shouts and somebody opens the door to the bathroom. She runs back and falls to the floor, trying

267

to pour water down the boy's throat while hundreds of tiny lights explode around her, shooting blinding sparks into her retina like little flashbulbs, and the boy is gulping, slurping the water and flailing greedily at the cup, spilling water all over Sabah and his stained shirt.

"Sabah!" someone shouts. Sabah looks back at the door. Policemen are storming into the building, swinging their billy clubs and forcing their way through the families of worshipers, their boots tracking mud across the carpet. Rob is running toward her, shouting, "Sabah!" thrusting confused policemen out of the way like a linebacker, as if he's the only one who knows what's going on, the only one in control.

Rob stops two feet away from them. He freezes like a statue. Sabah turns back to Adam, but she has to shade her forehead with her hand, squint at him through half-closed eyes, because he's glowing like a light bulb. "Adam," she says. The boy opens his eyes.

SABAH LOOKS AT Adam, she thinks she sees a waft of smoke rise from his chest. Then she hears a crack. His shirt catches and he's on fire, his whole body engulfed in dancing flames. "Not you!" Sabah throws herself on his body, trying to smother the flames. She beats his chest and legs with her hands, "No! Not you, too!" until a medic pulls her off and she sees that there's no fire this time.

Home

ROB LOOKS BACK in the rearview mirror. "Strange place for a family reunion," he says gently. He taps the steering wheel with his fingers.

Sabah nods. "Coming to America and never going back is one of the strangest things," she mumbles.

At the entrance to the hotel, Rob heaves Sabah's suitcases out of the trunk. "You're sure you don't want to stay with me and Pia?" he asks, the corners of his mouth sinking.

Sabah shakes her head. She's not sure she can speak again without losing it. "My dad," she explains slowly, "this hotel...is a welcome back...present."

"Will you call me?" He gets back in his car.

Sabah walks into the hotel. "Hey, Sabah," he yells. Sabah stops and turns around. "Sabah, if you talk to Piedad, don't talk about my playing guitar, OK? She wants me to take my banking seriously."

Sabah bites her lip and nods. She can't seem to lift her arm to wave as he drives away.

"WHAT HAVE YOU got in these bags?" complains Bibi as they load them into the car. Muzzafer is taking his bags out and putting them on top of hers, so they'll be easier to take out at the airport. He's going to London to see his sister and brother and spend some time with his family. Sabah, Yasmine, and her mother will drive back to Boston together.

"Just like old times, the way we all did when your father went on business trips," says Bibi, looking exhausted from the long drive down. "Except this time you both can drive a little, I hope. Then we'll have time to catch up on everything."

Yasmine kisses Sabah and admires her suntan and asks her what she bought for her. "So, how bad was it?" she asks. "Are you going to be sick if you see another fried, greasy thing? Aren't you glad to be back in civilization after four months in the bush?" She sparkles with excitement. "Guess what? I'm in the photography club and I just got picked to be cheerleader this year."

269

In the car, while the women wait for Muzzafer to pay the bill, Yasmine whispers to Sabah, "I can't believe they expect us to get all upset about it. I mean, Dad was there when he was born. I never even met him."

"Shut up, Yasmine," says Sabah.

Her mother says, "Don't speak like that to your sister, Sabah, she's so excited to see you. She's been talking about it all week." But Bibi gives Sabah a hug and says, "I think you understand us a little more now." Sabah smells the fresh citrus perfume she always wears, feels the surge of energy and endurance in her mother's arms underneath the silk shirt, the stamina underneath the music in her voice. "Meera said you are a wonderful girl. Poor thing. It's so sad when a young person dies. And now Adam."

"Have you been painting much?" Sabah doesn't think she can bear to talk about Rani right now. She knows that if she says her name, she'll disintegrate. She blinks hard and opens her eyes wide to keep from crying.

"Oh, Sabah, I just haven't had time," Bibi shakes her head. But then, she reaches for Sabah's hand and kisses it. "Perhaps I will now that you're here to help me."

"How's Rocky?" Sabah asks hesitantly. No more bad news, she wills, only good now. Please.

"Oh, that Rafique," sighs her mother. "He's much better. He's working at the garage again. I just wish he'd get his act together. He said to tell you he's now the bionic man. And he also said, 'Rod.' He said you would know what that meant."

Sabah smiles. She leans across the car seat and hugs her mother's shoulders, "I'm glad to see you." Tears well up in Bibi's eyes and Sabah knows her mother's as close to tumbling off the cliff of emotions as she is. Sabah hugs her harder and kisses her cheek.

"Here he comes," says Yasmine. "Honk the horn so he'll see us." Sabah moves closer to the door and pulls

Yasmine over to her, so that he'll be able to hang his blazer over the seat. "Stop it!" Yasmine pretends to be irritated, but she wiggles happily next to Sabah. Sabah looks out the window, watches the polished cars glide down the smooth street, the sidewalk dotted with people walking silently past each other in spotless gray suits or black coats, like a television with the sound and color turned off. "You're back," smiles Yasmine.

A man comes out of his shop, shouting and gesturing. Sabah sees that he's yelling at a beggar, the only incongruous element in the scene, an emaciated man leaning against the shop window, holding a tin cup, his clothes black and shiny with dirt. The man turns his face toward the shouting voice and Sabah realizes he's blind. From the car, she can't read the cardboard sign he's holding.

Bibi turns the key in the ignition, the engine revs. Sabah stares at the blind man. She wants to get out of the car and run down the sidewalk to the beggar, the car door slamming shut behind her. She would stop in front of him. She'd hold out her hand and help him up. He'd grasp her arm, pulling himself to his feet, his black fingernails digging into her sleeve. As he walks slowly beside her, the smell of sweat, urine, garbage, and feces rising from his coat, his face would crack into a smile beneath the matted hair. She walks him over to a bench while he talks about the way things used to be, and she crumples a five-dollar bill into his cup. She shakes his hand, saying, this is for a friend of mine, she would have done the same thing...

"We're very late," Muzzafer says sharply to Bibi, as she turns into the Lincoln Tunnel, the car darkening. "Do we have a map?" He switches on the light and fumbles around in the glove compartment. "Look, Sabah, here's that tape you kept making us hear all last winter. Now you'll really feel like you're back." He clicks the tape in and Pete Seeger asks, "Why don't you come with me, little girl, on a magic-carpet ride?" Sabah leans on the door, her cheek pressed against the glass, recognizing the feel of the upholstery, suddenly remembering how she learned to drive. The car smells of grape soda and McDonald's and banana peels: traveling smells. She looks down and pushes the debris on the floor with her feet, wondering if there's a box of Crackerjacks somewhere. There isn't. She gives up and tries to look out. All she can see in the window is her own reflection.

ADAM OPENS his eyes and Marc is standing in front of him, all pink and rosy in the Bombay sunlight, like an angel. He smiles and gets pinker and pinker until he's the color of a rose, the color of his shirt. Adam laughs at his joke because Marc's face is really a shirt, a pink T-shirt, and Alia is wearing it. Alia is saying, "Adam, Adam, Ummi's calling you." Her face is fresh and happy. She's laughing like an ad for Cadbury Biscuits, but then the ad ends and she becomes sad, her mouth twitches, and a tear drips down her nose. The tear catches a sparkle of sunlight, and when Adam tries to see Alia's whole face again, all he sees is dazzling light, brighter and brighter until he can't see anything, it's like looking at the sun. He squints because his eyes are burned from staring at the sun.

He's blazing hot and zooming up into the huge brilliant sun that is getting bigger and bigger as he slides toward it, as he's sucked up into the ray of light. The sun swallows him whole and he swallows it, like a gigantic egg yolk, the elastic membrane closing around him, encasing him like a bubble. He dives headfirst into the gleaming yellow center. He reaches out his arms, he stretches them out as far as they can go, and the tips of his bent fingers graze the edge. He uncurls his hand, his fingers pulling out of their sockets as they touch the bright, blinding spot.

He's Light.

UPSTAIRS, JIMMY is in a deep, drug-induced sleep. He tosses slightly under the blankets, his pajamas getting caught in his legs. The shock of this morning's news was too much for him. He took a few of those muscle relaxants with a big glass of water. He's dreaming he's walking with Adam on the beach in Bombay. Adam is five and he's wearing a little pair of bathing trunks. He's running back and forth into the sea, screaming and laughing, his scrawny legs poking out of his tennis shoes as he kicks the little waves. The cold water splashing on his tight stomach turns the muscles pink, and he flaps his arms to warm himself, his thin shoulder blades like little wings. Jimmy is holding a camera, and Adam is running toward him, his shoes getting stuck in the sand, yelling, "Photo! Photo!" and stopping every few feet and striking muscleman poses like Hindi film-poster heroes.

273

"Come on, Adam!" laughs Jimmy, snapping the camera shutter, "Let's see those muscles, Mr. India. Come on, show me!" Adam is laughing and laughing and laughing, so hard he almost starts to cry. "Oh, little boy," teases Jimmy, "do you know who Adam was? Do you know who you're named after?"

Adam runs back to the sea, chest thrust forward, fists in the air like he'd just won the Olympics, "I'm the first man!"

Jimmy laughs, "Well done! And who's the first woman?"

"Alia!" shouts Adam, as he runs into the waves.

Five-Star fiction titles from Serpent's Tail

'Undoubtedly the most exciting development coming in 1998. Puts the bite back into books' – Ian Brereton, Waterstone's

Mr Clive & Mr Page   Neil Bartlett

Gone Fishin'   Walter Mosley

Always Outnumbered, Always Outgunned   Walter Mosley

The Silent Cry   Kenzaburo Ōe

Altered State: The Story of Ecstasy Culture and Acid House   Matthew Collin

Bombay Talkie   Ameena Meer

If He Hollers Let Him Go   Chester Himes